MW01531716

Georgia Boys

A Father's Legacy

By

Joanne Carani

ISBN: 1-4107-2340-2 (e-book)
ISBN: 1-4107-2351-8 (Paperback)
ISBN: 1-4107-2352-6 (Dust Jacket)

Library of Congress Control Number: 2003093572

This book is printed on acid free paper.

Printed in the United States of America
Bloomington, IN

1stBooks – rev. 05/12/03

This Book is in Memory of:

Frank Carani
Deceased

And Dedicated to:

Brett and Stephanie Carani
T. J. Carani

Brad and Angie Carani
Whitney Carani
Savannah Carani

Special Thanks to:
My Mother, Ruby Haynes
My Sister, Nita Brown and her husband,
Terry

Prologue

The Edwards family lived by principles and values that was passed down through the family for generations. Their honesty, compassion and willingness to help other people won them a prominent place as a law enforcement family in Littleton, Georgia. Their name has been well known in the law enforcement circles around the area for years.

The Edwards family consist of the parents: Thomas and Claire, and the children, in order: Cody, Steven and Traci. Thomas, the father, age 53, was a Captain in charge of the Investigation Section in the Little County Sheriff's Office. He was a strong, good-looking man with dark brown hair and dark brown teasing but serious eyes. He was very strong-willed, but a compassionate man and was very proud of his family. He was killed in the line of duty about six months ago.

Claire or 'Mama E', as she was called by friends of her children, age 51, the mother, is a wonderful homemaker and a loving and generous parent. She has light brown hair and hazel-blue serious, but smiling eyes. She enjoyed raising her family and seeing that they live a happy and full life.

Cody, age 25, is a Sergeant in the Investigation Section. He was just assigned to this section about two months ago. Before that, he was in the Uniform Section as a Corporal. He has a strong muscular build with an authoritative voice and has medium brown hair and deep blue serious, but smiling eyes. Cody is more serious-minded of the Edwards, but his sense of humor takes an edge off his seriousness with his friends.

Steven, age 23, is in the Uniform Section as a Corporal. He was just promoted to Corporal a month ago. He is of medium build, muscular body, with light shades of blonde to medium blonde hair and dark blue-green expressive eyes. He has a great sense of humor and is full of life which makes him a favorite among friends and, especially the females.

Traci, age 20, is employed with the Juvenile Section of the Little County Sheriff's Office. She has been employed for about a year. As soon as she becomes twenty-one years old, her plans are to go through the Police Academy. She is tall and slim with dark brown shoulder length curly hair and big brown expressive eyes with golden specks in them. She is somewhat reserved, but friendly. She has a lot of friends, but she chooses her close friends with care because of the family's involvement in law enforcement.

The Edwards live on the Edwards estate which consist of about three hundred and seventy-eight acres of farming and grazing land. With the help of Jake and Sara Carter and some extra workers now and then, they take care of approximately two hundred head of red and black angus cows and growing hay and garden vegetables.

The farm is located on the outskirts of Littleton, Georgia, about fifteen miles outside the city limits. It is the largest city in Central Georgia. The farm house is a large two-story wood house which has been remodeled and almond colored vinyl siding and medium blue-green trim was put on the outside. It has a large balcony on the front of the house along with a porch stretching across the front. The inside was remodeled to have four bedrooms upstairs with two bathrooms: one large bathroom between Cody and Steven's bedrooms and one large bathroom between Traci's bedroom and the guest room. Two bedrooms are downstairs at the back of the house with a large bathroom between them. Also, there is a half bath down the hall past the kitchen. When you enter the foyer from the front door, straight ahead and toward the right is the great room. From the foyer and to the left is the kitchen and dining room. The kitchen is large enough that there is a breakfast room with a large table and chairs adjoining it. The family always gather there most of the time for their meals and snacks when they are not having their meals outside under the trees in the back yard.

It is a beautiful plantation style home with a large yard where swings, hammocks and tables and chairs have been set up among the magnolia, red maple and dogwood trees with pine trees in the background.   Shrubs placed around the yard are honeysuckle, forsythia and gardenia bushes and other colorful bushes and plants. The whole family for several generations have worked over the years to bring the estate to what it is today. Now they are enjoying rewards of their labor. Their only regret is that the husband and father is not there to enjoy it with them. He left them too soon and it is hard to try to get on with their lives. They do entertain some, but they are not much on entertaining large crowds, only their closest friends. They are a very close-knit family.

Chapter 1
April 1990

"Good morning, Mom." Traci said as she walked into the kitchen this Saturday morning. She noticed that her mother did not turn around to face her as usual, so she walked over to her mother and put her arms around her shoulders and turned her to face her. Noticing her mother's red, swollen eyes, Traci pulled her closer and hugged her. "Having a rough morning, huh, Mom." Traci held her for a moment without saying anything. Then she pulled apart and smiled. "Why don't you take the pills that Dr. Smith left here for you to take when you get upset. They helped you a lot right after Dad died." Traci then walked over to the cabinet and reached up into the cabinet where some medicines were kept. There were some of the pills left, so she poured a glass of water and placed a couple of the pills in her mother's hand. "Here, Mom, take these and go back to bed. I'll prepare breakfast and do what is necessary around here. .....Have you eaten anything this morning?"

"No, just some coffee. I was waiting for you all to come downstairs and eat with me. ..I'm sorry, Honey. Tom has been gone for six months, but sometimes I get into a depression. I miss him so."

"I know you do, Mom. We all miss him and it will take a long time to be contented enough to go on with our lives as usual. We will always remember him and he will always stay in our hearts. ..You go lay down and I will bring you a tray to your room. Steve is working and Cody got in late last night from working a case, so Cody won't be down for awhile." Then Traci put her arm around her mother's shoulders and led her to her bedroom which was down the hall and to the left of the house. After putting her mother to bed, Traci started back to the kitchen. As she was walking back to the kitchen, Traci was whispering to herself. *Oh, Dad, why did you have to leave us so soon. We all miss you terribly, especially Mom. She is having a hard time of it. You and she were so close. We, kids, are trying very hard to cope with it, too. We all miss you.*

She fixed her mother a couple of scrambled eggs, bacon, toast and a glass of milk. She wanted her to eat something before the pills made her drowsy and put her to sleep. She timed it just right. As she entered her mother's bedroom, her mother was just coming out of the bathroom.

"Oh, Honey, my stomach seems to be upset. I guess it is my nerves this morning,"

"Here, Mom, eat this before you get back into bed and get comfortable. Then you will feel better. You didn't eat much last night. By the time you finish eating, the pills will relax you and you will be able to get some sleep. Your stomach will feel better, too."

So she sat on the side of the bed while Traci fixed the table in front of her and placed the tray on it. *My daughter. What would I do without her. She is so good to me, as well as my sons. I hope and pray that they will always be as they are.*

Mama E smiled as she looked at her daughter, "Your father made this table for me before you were born. Dr. Smith put me to bed several weeks before you were born. He knew how much I hated to eat in bed, so he made this table so I could be comfortable while eating. He wanted a girl so much. Because of the problems that I had while carrying you, he said, 'I hope this one is a girl because I am not going to put you through this again.' And he kept his word, although I told him that the next one would probably be as easy as the first two. He would not take that chance."

"Daddy was very stubborn and strict in the things that he believed in, but he was a teddy bear most of the time to his family. Most of the times, he would give in to us with whatever it was we wanted."

Her mother smiled and then there was silence for a while. Traci sat there with her while she ate. She wanted to make sure that she ate all of the food before she stopped. Once in a while one or the other would make a comment. By the time Mama E finished her breakfast, she was beginning to feel drowsy and was ready to sleep for awhile. So Traci covered her up and closed the drapes. Then she took the tray back to the kitchen and then started fixing her own breakfast when Cody came into the kitchen.

Traci, with a surprise look on her face, said, "Oh, good morning, Sleepyhead. I didn't expect you to be up this early. It was rather late when you got in last night or early this morning, I should say. ...And by the frown on your face, you should go back to bed."

"Uh, good morning, Sis. I woke up early and couldn't go back to sleep. So here I am. I'll just have some toast and coffee. I'll fix it. You finish with yours."

"O.K., Bro, I'll take you up on that. I just put Mom back to bed. She didn't sleep much last night. She had another one of her bad nights. Their anniversary is coming up in a few days. That might have set her off. Anyway, she ate a good breakfast and took a couple of sleeping pills and is now laying down. She was getting very drowsy a few minutes ago. I told her that I would do whatever needed to be done. ...So, Bro, what kind of case are you working on that takes half the night?"

"Nick had a lead on one of the old murder cases and he wanted me to go with him. His partner had other commitments. They both were on their off time, but Nick wanted to get this information while he had the chance. It was the type of information that he did not want to be alone when he received it. Other than that, I would prefer not to talk about it." *What Cody did not want to discuss was the fact that this information could have been about corruption within the Sheriff's Office or even higher up. As it turned out, the information was that there may be a witness to a drug deal involving officials. This informant did not have all the information, but he knew the person that did have that information. The person was his girlfriend and he did not want to talk about her on the phone. She was not in Georgia, and he did not want to say where she was in case she had changed her mind about talking to the police. He would find out if she still wanted to talk about it and let Nick or Cody know.*

3

"Sure, Bro, I understand."

While they were eating, Cody looked at his sister and wondered if he should say anything to her about seeing Rich with someone else last night. Finally, he decided that she should know, and then he asked, quizzically, "Trac, has anything happened between you and Rich? You haven't gone out this week and you usually went out at least one night during the week."

She looked at Cody curiously and wondered what he really wanted to say to her, but she answered his question. "Rich and I had a talk or a discussion, whichever you want to call it, last weekend. He invited me to have dinner with his parents last Saturday night. When I got there, I saw the writing on the wall immediately. So, I apologized to Mr. and Mrs. Samuels before we sat down to dinner, I asked the butler to get me a cab and I came home. That is the end of Richard and I."

"I'm sorry, Sis. I know you had a crush on him before he asked you for a date. And then, when he did, you were ecstatic. I thought everything was fine. You have been dating him about five weeks now and all the phone calls. ..Then he added, grinning, "I thought you had met your true love."

She laughed. "Well, to put it bluntly, his parents doesn't think I am good enough for their son. From the time that Rich and I walked into that house, the remarks that were made about my family being a cop family and then when Crissy walked in alone, I knew where that was going. So, like the Edwards that I am, I took the lead and ended it before they had the pleasure, and then I excused myself and walked out. Rich followed me out the door. He was really stunned. I think he really care about me and wanted to continue the relationship, but I said 'no can do.' I am not about to fight his parents."

Cody was amazed and very proud of his sister. "You stood up to the Samuels. ....I can't believe it. What did you say?" And then he began to laugh and then she joined him. They both laughed, heartily, looking at each other.

Then Traci started demonstrating what she said and did. "When we stood up to go to the dining room, Mrs. Samuels said in a low voice to me, 'Traci, if you have a problem with which fork to use, just watch Crissy. She will be sitting across from you. I don't want you to feel embarrassed.' I don't know what happened to me, but I saw red. That was a slam on my parents. So I said very loud and clear. 'Mr. and Mrs. Samuels, I appreciate very much for the invitation to have dinner with you, but you see, I must excuse myself. I am sure that my family upbringing of what is really important in life is quite different from yours. You see, my parents did a very good job in raising my brothers and I and that is why my association with you is a mistake. I am sorry if I have inconvenienced you, but I will not stay in this house and be insulted and looked down upon anymore. By my standards, I really feel sorry for you. Goodbye.' I walked into the hall and the butler called a cab for me and said as I walked out the door. 'Ms. Edwards, I am sorry this had to happen, I think they could learn something from you. Have a good night.' I looked at him and said, 'Thank you.' We both looked at each other and smiled. That made me feel real good about myself."

Cody said as he smiled at her, "I can't believe you said that to Mr. and Mrs. Samuels and in their house. But I am proud of you, Sis, real proud. Dad would be, too. ...What did Rich say?"

"He followed me out to wait for the cab and tried to apologize to me for his parents. I told him that it wouldn't work and that I am not in the mood to talk about it now. Then the cab came and I got into it as fast as I could and he walked slowly back into the house."

Cody was smiling a very proud smile while looking at her. He looked at her a long moment to see if she was affected by the breakup, but he did not see that she was upset about it. In fact, she seemed happy about it. So, he said, "I noticed that Rich was out last night with Crissy. Nick and I stopped at Antonio's Italian restaurant to get a bite to eat after our meeting. They were there with another couple. I don't know who they were. This was about eleven o'clock or so. I must add that Rich didn't look like he was enjoying himself."

"He has called me several times here and at work, but I told him that it would not be wise to continue the relationship. However, if he wanted to be friends, I would like that. He is rather nice and he cannot help how his parents think and act." She smiled and started to say something, but changed her mind.

Cody smiled at her and said, "Come on, now. Don't start to say something and then stop. You have my curiosity stirred up now." They both looked at each other and laughed out loud. Then Traci put her finger to her mouth and told Cody to shish. "We may wake Mom."

"Oh, I forgot. But I want to hear this."

She looked at him blushingly and said, "It is personal, you know, but I will tell you since you are my brother and confidant and won't say anything about it. Like I said, I think he cared about me some, anyway, but I was not sure that I wanted to get serious with him. At first, I wanted to date him, but after I really got to know him I just wanted to be friends. No more than that. The feeling that I wanted to have just didn't materialize. ...Don't laugh at me now. Promise." Cody promised by shaking his head up and down. Then she continued. "He was trying very hard to get me in bed with him, but I just didn't feel that I wanted him to be my first." He started to laugh. "Now, you promised not to laugh at me. Most of my girlfriends have already had sex, but I am the odd ball here. I just can't, unless I am with someone that can turn me on and I haven't found him yet. Am I making sense?"

"Sure, Sis. In a way, I am surprised, but in another way, I am not. After all, you are our sister. I am glad that you are waiting. Girls are too quick to jump into bed with any male nowadays. I think that is why relationships do not last very long anymore."

"You and Corrie have been seeing each other for a long time. Did she give you a hard time at first? Is that why your relationship has lasted almost two years?" She smiled teasingly at him, not really expecting him to answer her. Her brothers were always looking out for her, but they were very secretive about their personal lives, especially with females.

"Are you kidding? She was all over me the first night we dated. I haven't been able to keep her away from me. And all these other girls that are running after me. I must have charisma, or is it sex appeal?" Then he burst out laughing.

Traci just sat there half-way smiling and half-way laughing at him. "Are you trying to change the subject, Brother? I can't answer for the other girls, but I do know that before you started going steady with Corrie, girls were always asking me about you. You may not want to tell me, but I know that you had your share of girl friends."

"Yes, Sis, I guess I did, but when I really got to know Corrie, I knew that I wanted to spend as much time as possible with her. And, now, to answer your question seriously, yes, it took both of us awhile to be sure that we really wanted each other. We both talked about it and am now very happy that we took our time in getting into a serious relationship. One day we plan to get married. It seems that everytime we start to set a date, something happens or it is not the right time. We were going to announce a date, but Dad was killed before we said anything about it. So, now we are just waiting for the right time again."

"You know, Bro, you have really settled down since you and Corrie became an item. I remember when you were quite wild. Dad had to calm you down a few times."

"Yes, at one time I thought I knew everything, but Dad was right. I still had a lot to learn. Now, Steven is going through that wild stage. He is the one that has all the females following him. Only thing is that Dad is not here to calm him now, but a lot of what Dad has said is instilled in our minds, and, evidently, yours, too. He is handling himself alright. And, so are you, Sis." Cody reached across and put his hand on hers and squeezed it.

"Yes, Steven will be alright. Let him have his fun. He's twenty-three now and you are twenty-five and look at you. He'll be alright."

About that time, the phone started to ring and Cody answered it. "Hello, Edwards residents."

"Good morning, Cody. Nick, here. I have some information from our meeting last night. Could you come over for a cup of coffee or something? I don't think this should wait until Monday."

"Sure Nick. That sure was fast. See you in about thirty-five minutes." Cody hung up the phone and turned around facing Traci. He had a puzzled look on his face.

Traci, with a frightened look on her face, asked, "Cody, what is it? What did Nick say? Is something wrong?"

Cody changed his expression and looked at Traci and said, as he tried to smile, "No, just that Nick has some more info reference the meeting last night. I'll be at his place if you need anything. I'll call you later if this is going to take some time."

"O.K. Bro. I'll be here with Mom. What she needs is rest right now. See you later. Be careful."

Cody nodded as he turned to go toward the upstairs to get his gun and badge, along with a light jacket and then he went out the door. Traci sat there for a few moments just thinking about the conversation that they had earlier. *I am so lucky to have the family that I have. I only wish that Dad was still with us. I feel that this case that Cody is working on with Nick may be very involving. It must be dangerous because of the look on Cody's face earlier, but I know he can take care of himself. Nick is a good backup man for Cody. They have been good friends since high school. They work good together. Besides, Nick is Corrie's brother. That means a lot.*

Traci looked up and her mother was standing in the doorway. "Feeling better, Mom? You didn't sleep very long, though. We didn't wake you, did we?"

"Yes, Honey. I needed that sleep. No, you didn't wake me, but I thought I heard the phone ring."

"You did, it was for Cody. Nick called and wanted him to come over to his place. It was about some case they are working on together. He will be back a little later. How about a cup of coffee now?"

"Yes, I do want some coffee."

Traci got up and fixed her mother a cup of coffee and then sat down with her while she was drinking it. Mama E was not in a talking mood. The pills still had her a little drowsy and not completely awake. So Traci got up and put the dishes in the dishwasher and started cleaning the kitchen.

After her mother had finished her cup of coffee, she said, "Trac, I think I am going to go back and lay down for awhile. I still feel sleepy and groggy. I thought the coffee would clear my head, but it didn't."

"You go back to bed, Mom. I am not going anywhere today. I'll be here. Don't you worry about a thing. Maybe later when those pills wear off, we can do some shopping or whatever you feel up to doing."

Her mother looked at her and answered slowly and in a low tone, "Sure. That will be fine."

Traci knew that by the way her mother answered her that she did not want to go out anywhere today.

After her mother left the kitchen, Traci finished cleaning the kitchen. Then she went into her bedroom and started cleaning it. Each person was responsible for cleaning their own bedroom and bathroom and picking up after themselves. Sara, a long-time companion of her mother's, usually did all the vacuuming and dusting of the rest of the house every Friday.

Traci's cellular phone rang and she fumbled around until she found it and answered it.

"Hello"

9

"Hi, Traci. This is Rich. Please don't hang up on me. I miss you. Can't we just meet and talk about this for awhile. I know my mother's jabs about your family being a cop family wasn't right and I don't blame you for getting upset about it. If it will help matters any, I really let her and father know how disappointed I was in them. My mother would not say what she said to you to set you off. My father was angry with her, too."

"The truth is, Rich, that your father looks down his nose at my family, too. He may not have made any comments, but he agrees with your mother that they do not want you and I to have a serious relationship. I know that, so it would not be in our interest to start this relationship again. I have nothing against you, because I feel that you do not share the same snobbishness, self-centered and narrow-mindedness that your parents do. .....I understand that you were out with Crissy last night and that is fine with me. I know that makes your parents happy."

"Trac, I don't want to be with Crissy, but you are leaving me no choice. I want to be with you. Please meet with me."

"No, Rich, let it go. If I met you, we would only be prolonging what needs to be done. And that would mean that I would have to break it off again. So, let it go, Rich. We can be distant friends, if you want that. O.K. See you around, Rich."

"See you, Trac," Rich said as he slowly put the receiver back on the phone. He sat there a few moments with his head in his hands feeling sad and lonely before he got up and went downstairs to meet Crissy for a game of tennis.

Traci felt bad for Rich, but she knew that she was right. She did not want to go through last Saturday night again. She was proud of her family and would not listen to anyone try to belittle them.

After a couple of hours, she heard Cody coming up the stairs and go into his room and close the door. She knew that he had something important on his mind and did not want to be disturbed so she stayed in her room and did not go to him. He would tell her when he wanted to talk. She and Cody had a good rapport. He was her confidant, a person that she could talk to and feel good about it. She and Steven had a good rapport, too, but it just wasn't the same as talking to Cody. She knew that Cody and Steven shared secrets between them, but when she would ask, they would tell her that it was a male thing so she didn't push them into telling her.

Cody came out of his room after making a couple of phone calls and walked to Traci's door. He knocked and then said, "May I come in?" Traci looked up and smiled, "Sure, Bro, I am just catching up on some of my reports so I won't have so much to do Monday. You look like you have a big, big problem." *Oh, my big handsome, brown-haired, blue-eyed, brother. You sure do our family proud. I am so proud to be able to call you my brother.*

"I am not sure what I have right now. Nick and I are going to Houston for a day or two. I just talked to Tex and he is expecting us and will help us run down a lead. I am telling you this, but no one else should know why we are making this trip, not even Mom. As for Mom, I'll tell her that we are going to visit Tex. O.K. Sis."

"Sure, Cody. It must be something very important. Is it dangerous?"

"Sis, all our work is dangerous, but we can take care of ourselves, right?"

"Right, Bro," Traci said with a half-grin and half-frightened look on her face.

"If you will make plane reservations for Nick and I on the earliest flight, I will go by and talk to Steven. Would you do that for me?" he asked, as he put his arm around her shoulders and kissed her on the cheek.

"You know I will," she said more relaxed now and smiling, as she squeezed his hand that was around her shoulder.

"Sis, I wish I could tell you more, but right now we are not sure where this investigation is going yet. We hope to find out what direction to take when we get to Houston."

"I understand, Cody. I have been around law enforcement all my life. Remember."

"Trac, thanks. See you later." He then squeezed her hand and then turned and walked out her door and down the stairs.

Traci picked up her phone and made the reservations for seven o'clock that evening. Then she called Steven. When Steven answered, "Little County Sheriff's Office, Corporal Edwards speaking," she was so proud of him.

"Hi, Steven. This is Trac. Cody is coming by to see you. Tell him that the plane reservation is for seven o'clock tonight. He will know what you are talking about. I don't want to say anymore. He will tell you when he stops by your office. We will probably eat a little earlier tonight so Cody can eat before he has to catch the plane. What time will you be home?"

"I'll be home the regular time, about 4:30. See you then. O.K."

"Sure, see you then."

After she hung up the phone, Traci went downstairs to check on her mother. She sure was sleeping long. When Traci walked to the door, her mother raised up and said, "I am really taking advantage of you today. I can't seem to wake up."

"That means that you needed the rest, but it would probably be a good idea for you to get up and walk around and get some exercise. It will be time to go back to bed before long. It is almost three o'clock now. I am going to start dinner earlier because Cody came in and said that he and Nick are going to visit Tex for a couple of days. Their plane will leave at seven o'clock tonight."

"Cody hasn't said anything about going to see Tex. Why ....."

Before Mama E could finish, Traci cut her off and stated, "Cody talked to him on the phone and then decided to go see him. They are very close, you know, and it has been a long time since they have seen each other. Also, Nick wanted to go to Houston, so they decided to go this weekend. I am sure Cody will tell you about it when he comes home."

"Yes, I am sure he will. ....Trac, Sara partially cooked a big roast yesterday. It will only need about an hour to finish cooking it and to make sure it is completely heated through. If you will peel some potatoes and carrots, I'll be back to help you in a minute. I need to wash my face so I can wake up completely."

Traci had the potatoes and carrots peeled by the time Mama E came into the kitchen.

"I'm sorry, it took me longer than I had planned. I decided to take a shower and I am glad I did. I really feel alive now. Now, what do you want me to do?"

"If you will put the roast, potatoes and carrots in the oven, I will fix a fruit plate. I think that will go good for tonight instead of having a dessert. We all need to cut down on the sweets."

Her mother, laughingly, said, "Speak for yourself, Dear. I have a big blackberry cobbler that Sara made yesterday. Sara is my angel. She is so good to me. .. ..She knows that blackberry cobbler is my favorite."

"My, you are feeling better. Maybe, you shouldn't take anymore of those pills. ..Just kidding. I am glad you are feeling good. We didn't get to go shopping, but we can do that another time."

By the time that dinner was ready to be put on the table, Steven, Cody and Nick had made their entrance. Cody had invited Nick to come over and have dinner with them so they could go directly to the airport.

Cody had told Steven everything that he and Nick knew about their case. So between the three of them and Traci, they kept the conversation on everything except the trip to Houston. They did not give their mother a chance to ask questions. It was a lively dinner ...with dessert.

After dinner, Steven drove Cody and Nick to the airport and then drove over to Dee's. They had a date to go to a special movie that Dee wanted to see. He did not want to stay out late because he had to be at work early the next morning and then he would have four days off.

After they had cleaned the kitchen, Mama E settled down and started watching television. Mama E had her special programs that she liked to watch. Traci went to her room first, not knowing what she wanted to do. It had been a long time since she had been home on Saturday night. Finally, she decided to keep her mother company and watch television together.

After a few minutes the phone rang. Traci got up to answer the phone. She answered with, "Hello, this is the Edwards residence."

"Traci, don't hang up on me. I want to talk to you."

"Rich, we have nothing to talk about. We have discussed this several times. Why aren't you out with Crissy?"

"I don't want to be with Crissy, I want to be with you."

"Rich, I am going to hang up the phone. You have been drinking and I don't want to talk to you when you are like this. We will talk some other time. O.K."

"Trac, don't hang up."

Then she heard a voice in the background calling, "Rich, it's time to go." Then the phone went dead. So she hung up the phone. She felt sorry for Rich, but she just could not start a relationship with him again.

Mama E knew what had happened last Saturday night, but would not say anything about. She felt Traci did the right thing. From the first time Traci started dating Rich, she was not happy about their relationship because she knew how the parents felt, but she did not say anything. She knew that Traci would do what she felt was right and she did.

Chapter 2
Houston, Texas

As Cody stepped off the plane, he spotted Tex with his big hat standing over to the side waving at him. After Cody introduced Nick and Tex, they all got into Tex's Ford Explorer and headed for his home. On the way, Tex asked, "How is your Mom and Traci?"

"Mom is doing good most of the time. She has good days and some bad days. As for Traci, she is Traci. She is working with the Juvenile Section of the Sheriff's Office now, just waiting until she turns twenty-one so she can go to the Police Academy. Then we all will be in law enforcement."

"How about Steven? Is he still enjoying the thrill of being a law enforcement officer?"

"Oh, yes, he is being us two years ago." They all laughed.

"I know what you mean. ...I am off for three days now and I can drive you around and help you find where you want to go. We are in luck. My sister is out of town this weekend. Only my father is there, and he won't interfere or ask a lot of questions. Since he was in law enforcement, too, he understands what my work is about. He can be of help if we need him. What is the situation here in Houston?"

Cody looked at Nick as he took a deep breath as if to get his approval, and then said, "I told you a little on the phone. I didn't want to discuss too much then. But, in other words, the summary of the story is this: Nick has an informant that says that his girlfriend saw a murder in Little County, Georgia, and is now living in a small town outside of Houston. She got scared when a friend of hers told her that someone was looking for her. She did not know who was looking for her so she skipped town. She did not want to wait and see who was looking for her. This informant came forward because he trust Nick and doesn't want his girlfriend to get hurt. He is afraid that if he follows her to Texas, he might lead them to her. That is why he is giving us what information he knows. He gave Nick her address this morning, and says that she will be willing to cooperate and tell us everything if we can keep her safe. She has never been in any trouble with the law. She was just in the wrong place at the wrong time."

Then Nick spoke up, "She is living in a small town called Bristol with a cousin. I have the address in my brief case along with a picture of her, but it is about two years old. She is expecting us in the morning at about 10 o'clock at the Bristol Diner where she is working. I was thinking that we will go there for breakfast and get friendly with her while we are eating and let her get to know us before we get serious. That way she will be a little more relaxed."

"Sounds good to me, but can you trust her enough to believe what she says?" asked Tex.

Nick said a little agitatedly, "I would not be here if I didn't have faith in my informant. Chip has been a good informant for me for over a year and everything he has said before was true. I have no reason not to believe him. Cody and I plan to investigate any information that we can get from her. We have had a couple of murders that has not been solved. That is why we are taking this very seriously."

"I'm sorry, Man. I didn't mean anything about my question. I just asked the normal question without thinking who I was talking to. I had a full day today at work. I'm sorry, Nick. ....It is too late tonight to go into a small town to look around, anyway. They close down the town by nine o'clock. Have you two had anything to eat?"

Cody answered, "We had dinner at my Mom's and a snack on the plane with a few drinks." They laughed.

They stopped at a bar that Tex use for relaxation and had a couple of drinks and just shooting the bull, so to speak. Tex introduced them to some of his deputy buddies as friends visiting for the weekend. They all exchanged war stories that they had experienced or knew someone who had. It was very interesting and relaxing interacting with another law enforcement group.

After about an hour, they headed for Tex's place. His father was already in bed. Tex showed them to their bedrooms and showed Nick where the bathroom was. Cody had been there several times before. They were tired and ready for bed. Tomorrow would be a big day, or it could turn out to be nothing. *Cody had not said anything to Nick or anyone else, but in the back of his mind, his father's death was a puzzle to him. He had no evidence at all that his father's death was intentional, but there had been a question in his mind all along. He had planned to look at the cases that his father had been working on, but ever since he had come into Investigations Section, he had not had a chance. Cody felt that Nick had the same thoughts and that was why Nick asked him to be involved in this investigation.* Cody had mixed emotions about this investigation, but once he finally put it out of his mind, it did not take him long before he was sound asleep.

Meanwhile, Nick was having the same thoughts, but had not said anything to Cody about it. He wanted to have some evidence before he told Cody his thoughts.

The Tyler house was a big, comfortable two-story house similar to the Edwards with the upstairs for extra bedrooms and baths, but no balcony or porch. The outside was brick trimmed in white wood. The yard was small, not much room for entertaining except for a patio for grilling and relaxing there. A small flower garden was surrounding the patio and some of the spring flowers were beginning to bloom now.

Cody awoke early the next morning, so he dressed and went downstairs and into the kitchen. No one else was up yet, so he made some coffee and then walked to the patio door, staring out at the spring flowers that was starting to bloom, remembering the good times that he and Tex had when they were in college. He had to smile at himself. When the coffee had finished brewing, he poured himself a cup and walked out on the patio and sat down. It was a beautiful morning with the sun just coming up and the morning dew on the colorful blooms and rich green leaves making them sparkle. Before very long, he heard the door open and out walked Mr. Tyler. "Good morning, Son. Tex told me you and a friend of yours were coming for a visit." He walked over and put his arm around Cody's shoulders as Cody was getting up from the chair. They hugged each other and then they both sat down. "It's good to see you again. You know, you seem like our family. It's always good to have you visit."

"Thank you, Mr. Tyler. It's good to be back here again. I never thought I would like Texas, but I do, or maybe it is the people that I know that live here."

They both smiled at each other. Then Cody continued, "I was very fortunate to meet Tex in college. We hit it off right away. He is like a brother to me and I believe he feels the same about me."

"Yes, he does. He always wanted a brother and he found one in you. I must say that you two make me very proud, not only being in law enforcement, but the way you two turned out. You're O.K. in my book."

They both had a smile on their face as they nodded to each other. "You know, when we were in college, we talked about being a lawyer but our hearts weren't in it. ...We called them legal liars and then would laugh about it. We would always end up talking about law enforcement. 'That is where the action is' Tex would say."

"Oh, yes, he was always looking for action. Thank the Good Lord, he has settled down some. I had always thought he would take over my oil business, although he never seemed to be interested in it. But when he came home from college and said he was going into law enforcement, I will never forget the look on his face. I knew then that he would never be interested in my oil business. ...Don't get me wrong, I am very proud of Tex and what he is doing. I was in law enforcement up until two years ago. Even when the oil well that I was dabbling with, struck oil, I found that I could not give up my work. So, I hired my best friend, Tom Kelly, to look after it for me. He knew more about the oil business than I did, anyway. He has done good by me and is still working there part-time now teaching Kristen

19

the oil business. She is more interested in it than Tex ever was. She's good at it, too. One day, she will take it over."

Cody laughed and said, "Law enforcement just seems to get in your blood and once it is there, it is very hard to get it out. Maybe, one day I may be a lawyer, but right now, no way. But at least we both have something to fall back on in the future."

"Yes, that's good. ....By the way, you make very good coffee. How is your Mom doing? I was so sorry to hear about your father's death."

"She has her good days and she has her bad days. Tomorrow would have been their twenty-seventh anniversary. She was a little depressed, but by the time I left, Traci had gotten her in a good mood."

Mr. Tyler stood up and stretched. "I hear some noise in the kitchen. We better go and put our name in the pot." So they walked back into the kitchen and found Tex cooking some bacon and eggs. Nick was setting the table.

Mr. Tyler winked at Cody as he said, "Cody, we should have stayed on the patio a little longer."

Tex said, aggressively, as he was putting the scrambled eggs in a bowl. "Oh, no you don't. If you want something to eat, you better get in and help prepare it."

So, they all pitched in and helped with breakfast and while they were eating, Tex said, "I know we said that we were going to eat breakfast out, but we all are up earlier than we had planned. We will eat breakfast here and then we will take off and I'll show you around the sites. Nick has never been to Houston."

Cody said, "That will be fine with me. I'll see how you all work around here." He winked at Nick and continued with, "Maybe we can teach old Tex here a few things."

"Oh, yeah, you Georgia boys are tough, aren't you? I'd like to see you in action. Bet we can walk circles around you," goaded Tex.

Mr. Tyler interjected, "Alright, you guys. No competition here. I would not want to run into either one of you in a dark alley......I have an appointment so I will leave you three to fight it out for yourselves. Will you all be here for dinner tonight?"

"No, Dad, we are going out for dinner tonight. Why don't you come with us? We won't be out late."

"Yes, I am sure you won't. You are always saying that you won't be late and you come in just before dawn. No, you guys enjoy yourself. I have a poker game tonight down the street so if I don't see you later today, I will see you in the morning, but in any event, take care of yourselves and 'NO COMPETITION'."

"Sure, Mr. Tyler. You have a good time." Nick and Cody said almost simultaneously.

After his Dad left, Tex said, "I didn't mention anything to Dad about why you all are here. I told him that you were just coming for a visit, but I think he knows something is up."

Cody, looking at his watch, said, "We better get the kitchen cleaned up so we can get going. It is nine fifteen now."

"Oh, you put the dishes in the dishwasher and I will wipe the table and counters. Hattie is coming to clean the house tomorrow. She will take care of the rest. Let's get going."

So they all piled into Tex's Ford Explorer and took off toward Bristol. Nick had given Tex the address of the diner. As they came into town, Cody spotted the sign which read, 'Bristol's Diner, 2 1/2 Miles on your left'. Tex pulled into the parking lot at 9:57 a.m. They walked into the diner and sat down at an empty booth about middle of the diner across from the counter. There were about six other people in the diner. Most of the breakfast eaters had already left. Casey came over and said nervously, "Good morning, I am Casey and I will

21

be your waitress." She started to put the menus on the table, but Tex said, "Good morning, Casey. Just coffee for us, please."

So Casey went back behind the counter and brought out three cups of coffee and set a pot of coffee on a mat on the table. She knew who they were right away. Then she went in the back room to her cousin John's office. She said frantically, "John, those men are out front. They didn't say, but I know who they are. They look like policemen. I can't go through with this. I can't, I can't", she cried.

John got up from his desk and came over to her and put his arm around her shoulder and let her cry for a moment. "Casey, you have been so strong and said this is what you wanted to do. It is the right thing to do, you know. If you don't do this now, you will be scared and running all your life. They will protect you."

"I know, Mama always told me to trust the police, but John, it was a policeman that was involved with the murder. How do I know that I can trust them?" She cried some more while John was silent. She had a point, but this was something that she should do. They had to take a chance and trust Chip's judgment.

Then John asked, "Didn't Chip tell you that the victim was the father of one of the men that is here to talk to you?"

"Yes, he did, but why are there three of them?"

"I don't know, Casey, but I will talk to them first and if I think it is safe for you, I will let you talk to them and I will be with you all the way. Will that make you feel better?"

"Yes, I want you with me at all times."

"I will be. I will be right beside you all the time. You go into the ladies lounge and wash your face and make yourself presentable while I talk to them. I will come get you when I need you. O.K."

"O.K."

So, Casey went into the ladies lounge and John went out front and walked over to the three men. By then, all except one couple had left the diner and they were almost finished. Jamie, the other waitress was behind the counter.

"Good morning, I am John Branson. You three must be passing through. I haven't seen you here before."

"Good morning, Mr. Branson. I am Tex and I live in Houston. These are my good friends, Cody and Nick from Georgia. They are visiting me for the weekend and we are doing some riding around. Cody and I have been friends for several years. This is Nick's first time to Texas."

So John pulled up a chair and sat down and said, "I am glad to meet you. Gentlemen, since this is the first time in my diner, the coffee is on me."

Cody spoke up, "Thank you, Mr. Branson, but we prefer to pay. Our policy says, 'No Gratuities'. But thank you, anyway."

John looked a little surprised, but yet, he felt good about it. *That was one point that meant that they were straight up. He only hoped that he was right. He had some law enforcement officers that came in and would take anything that he was willing to give. It was good to find some that didn't.* He said, "You are welcome and you are welcome in my diner anytime."

By that time, the couple was at the cash register paying their bill and talking to Jamie. Finally, they left.

As he got up from his chair, John said, "Gentlemen, come back to my office. I would like to talk with you."

Tex said, "Sure," as he put some money on the table to pay for the coffee and tip.

John looked at Jamie and said, "Jamie, we will be in my office. How about bringing in a pot of coffee? Would you gentlemen like anything to eat?"

They said 'No' and then followed John back to his office. After they were seated, Tex said, "Casey, the girl that waited on us, is she still around?"

John looked at Tex a moment and then said, "Yes, she is, but I want to talk to you first."

Then Jamie came in with a tray of pastries and coffee. She said, "I know you said just coffee, Mr. Branson, but Casey said you always want pastries, too when you have a meeting." She smiled at John.

John smiled at her and said, "Thank you, Jamie. I see that Casey trained you well. We do not want to be disturbed. Casey isn't feeling well. She is in the lounge so if you will take care of the front, I would appreciate it."

"Sure, Mr. Branson." Then she left and closed the door behind her.

Nick said, "Nice place you have here, Mr. Branson."

"Thank you. I try to keep it that way. Just call me, John. I am not too much on this formal stuff, but because of what is involved here, I would like to know your full names before we start talking."

Cody said, "Sure, I am Cody Edwards, this Nick Carillo. We are with the Little County Sheriff's Office in Littleton, Georgia, and this is Tex Tyler, who is with the Harris County Sheriff's Office in Houston."

"I am glad to meet all of you. I must tell you that Casey was upset when she realized who you were. She had a little stage fright. She said she could not go through with it, but I talked to her and she knows what she must do. She trust me so she wanted me to talk to you first. You have to realize, she is only eighteen years old and is scared. She doesn't know who to trust because one of the persons she saw at the murder scene was wearing a shirt with 'POLICE' written across the back of it.

They all looked at each other with a stunned look on their faces. Cody said, surprisingly, "You mean the police are the ones that did the shooting."

"The only thing I know is that Casey told me that one of the men had a shirt on with the word 'POLICE' on the back of it. That is why she is so scared."

Nick said, "I can understand that. If that is the case, she and Chip, both, have a right to be scared."

Cody could not wait any longer. He had to find out if the murder was that of his father's. So he asked, "John, do you know the exact date that this murder took place that Casey saw? We have had two murders that have not been solved."

"This particular one happened on the night before Thanksgiving Day of last year." John was looking at Cody and was startled just as Nick got up and stood behind Cody and put his hands on his shoulders. Nick knew then that Cody knew, too, that it was his father that John was talking about because of the strained and horrible look that Cody had on his face.

Tex was puzzled and said, frantically, "Cody, what is wrong?" But Cody could not say anything. Then Tex said, "That is about the time your father was killed. Do you think it was murder?"

Nick shook his head as a 'yes' at Tex. Then Nick said, "I think Cody and I both were thinking that all along, but neither one of us would say anything. That is why we were pushing this trip once Chip told us about Casey." Then Nick looked at John and said, "John, Chip is really worried about Casey. That is why he gave us this information. He trust me completely and I believe in him. He has not led me wrong yet. We have worked together for over a year. He is a nice kid. I want you to know that. He loves Casey very much and is frightened for her."

John said, "I am glad to hear that. Casey speaks of him daily. I have never met him. She says that he is planning to go to Georgia Tech this September."

"Yes, that is what his plans are. He is working toward that goal."

Tex, keeping his eye on Cody, said, "Don't worry, Cody. If your father was murdered, we will find the bastards that did it. I will come to Georgia and help on my own time."

Cody looked at Tex with a calm look about him now and said, "I have always felt that something was not right about the information that was given to my mother as how my father died."

John, while watching Cody's reaction, said, "Let's don't jump to conclusions now. Wait until you hear what Casey has to say. She spoke to me some about it, but she didn't tell me everything. .. ... Before she talks to you, I have to have your solemn word that you will do everything in your power to keep her safe. It seems that it would be her word against anyone else involved. I assure you that she is not making this story up. She is truly frightened. When she first came here, she was so frightened that she would not leave the house. She will only work here because I am with her. Will she be allowed to stay here with me until she is needed in Georgia, if she is needed there? Do I get that promise?"

Tex spoke up, "John, I promise that we will keep her safe. We will have someone here that I trust to watch out for her while she is here. But we need to get that information and see how to handle it."

They all shook hands and John went to the ladies lounge to get Casey. When they came back to the office, the three stood up and shook hands with Casey when John introduced them. Then John said, "Casey, I believe that you will be in good hands with these three. You will be able to stay here with me and you will have protection here until you are needed in Georgia. I want you to understand that before you say anything. I will not let anyone come near you that I don't trust."

Cody said, "Casey, please don't be afraid of us. We will not hurt you or put you in a more dangerous situation than you are in now. You are in a dangerous situation now because of what you saw. Do you understand that?"

"Yes sir, I do. That is why I am so scared. Chip wanted me to come forward before, but I just couldn't. I don't know who to trust."

Nick said, as he looked her straight in the eyes, "Yes, we can understand that. Do you trust Chip, Casey?"

"Yes, I do. I love him and he loves me. We want to be together, but he won't come here because he is afraid he will lead whoever is looking for me to me."

"That's right, Casey. Chip is worried about you. Chip and I have been friends for about a year. Has he ever mentioned my name to you?"

"Yes, a few times he told me that he was going to meet you on other cases."

"Casey, I am asking you to trust me. And I assure you that you can trust these two. Cody and I have been the best of friends since high school. Cody and Tex have been friends since they started college. We want to know what happened and to do whatever we have to in order to solve these murders. We are all in this together. O K."

"I am ready now." She smiled and looked a little more relaxed.

"Good. Do you mind if we tape this conversation? It is necessary in our line of work to be precise about what information we collect."

She looked at John and John nodded that it was O.K.

So, she said, "Yes, it's O.K, but do I have to mention Chip's name in this?"

"No, Chip is my informant. We do not use their names. That is why we call them Informants. He does not have to be mentioned in this conversation. If at anytime, you want to say something off the record, give me a signal and I will stop the tape. O.K."

"O.K. I'm ready."

They all moved to a table which was located at one side of the office. They could all set around together and hear each other as they spoke. After being seated, Nick took out his recorder and spoke into the microphone. "This is an interview with a witness on this date, April 24, 1990, in Bristol, Texas. The witness is Miss Casey Branson, who is here with her cousin, John Branson, and the deputies are: Sergeant Cody Edwards and Corporal Nick Carillo, both from the Little County Sheriff's Office in Littleton, Georgia, and also, attending is Sergeant Jared "Tex" Tyler of the Harris County Sheriff's Office in Houston, Texas. ...Alright, Casey, why don't you start from the beginning and tell us what you saw."

"Well, I worked at Six Flags Over Georgia in one of the pizza places on site. My friend came to pick me up outside the gate at about 10:00 o'clock at night. I got into his car and we took off. He was going to take me home, but before we got there he said that he had to meet someone and asked if I had time to go with him. He said that it would not take long and it was on the way to my place. I told him that I could." Then she began to cry. "Oh, God, I wish I had not gone with him."

Nick placed his hand on hers, which was clasped together on the table, and said in a low calm voice, "It's alright, Casey. You are doing good. Take your time." ...Seeing that she had relaxed some, he asked, "What day was this?"

"I don't know the calendar date, but it was the night before Thanksgiving Day of last year. We went to Thirty-Third Street to a garage and parked the car. My friend had talked to the owner before about a part-time job there. The owner would be there until about 11:00 p.m. because he was working on a race car that he was entering into a race the following week. My friend loves to work on cars and he thought this would be something that he enjoyed doing and could get extra money to help his mother pay for his college. He is planning to start at Georgia Tech this coming September. As he got out of the car, he said that he should not be long. The owner was expecting him. He went just inside the door while I stayed in the car. I could see them talking, but the owner kept working while he talked to my friend. So he was gone for quite a while. I got tired of just sitting in the car, so I got out of the car and walked around the area. My friend still had not come, so then I walked up the street to the end of the block. There were some street lights so it wasn't real dark. As I was nearing the corner where I was going to turn around, I began to hear some voices. I did not want to be out of sight of my friend if he came back to the car before I got back. I thought it was just someone walking on the sidewalk. When I started to turn around to go back, I saw the back of one of the men who had a shirt on that had 'POLICE' across the back. I felt safer then, but was about to start back to the car when I heard a shot. ...No, two shots. One right after the other. I stepped back beside the building so they couldn't see me. I didn't know whether to run or not. I wasn't sure if they had seen me. I was afraid they may hear me running on the pavement. So I stayed where I was for a minute."

Casey took a deep breath and then said, "I heard someone say, 'you killed him. He didn't know anything.' Then the other guy said, 'He was getting too close, that's why I disguised my voice when I called him and told him that I had some information for him.' Then, the other guy said, 'That's Edwards, you Son Of A Bitch. Do you think you can get away with that? The department will be all over you.' Then the other man said, 'All we have to do now is get his files and destroy the ones that point to us. He was getting too close. A friend of his told me that Edwards knew that higher ups were involved in drug deals, but he wasn't exactly sure who.' Then they both got into the cars and left. When I heard the cars leave, I was afraid that they may come that way and see me, so I ducked into a doorway down from the corner. It was dark there. When I thought they had enough time to be far away, I ran down to the garage and my friend was standing by the car worried about where I might be."

Cody asked in a shaky voice, "How many men were there and did you recognize any of the men?"

"No, I didn't recognize any of them. There were three men. One in the police shirt with his back to me standing near a light away from the other two. The voice of the shooter was very strong and distinct from the other one. I don't think the one with the shirt on said anything. If he did, I didn't hear him. He was the closest to me. The other two that were talking were up from the corner. I really did not get a good look at the other two."

"How far away were they from the corner? Just give me an approximate number of feet," said Nick.

"I would say it was about thirty-five or forty feet up from the corner. The guy in the shirt was about ten or fifteen feet from them, closer to the corner."

Cody was trying his best to stay calm. He was fighting different emotions now. He asked, sharply, "Are you sure that he said Edwards?"

"Yes, it was very clear. The other guy was very upset that he had shot him. Oh, yes, he told the guy that did the shooting, 'you said that there would be no killing in this business.' That is when the shooter said 'we have to do what is necessary to safeguard our business. Besides, we have friends in the right places. They will take care of us." The other guy said, "they had better come through or we are in deep shit. That is when they got in the car and left."

Tex asked, "Casey, are you sure he said friends in the right places? These are important facts in your statement and I am just pointing them out."

"Yes. What that means, I don't know unless it means in the police department."

"Casey, I am not doubting your word. I just want it understood on the tape."

Then Nick asked, "Is there anything at all that you have left out. Maybe forgotten or anything else you want to say?"

"No, I don't remember anything else."

Tex said, "I will give you my card and I will also keep in touch with you. So, if you think of anything else, no matter how small it may seem, would you let me know?"

"Yes, I will."

Nick, looking around the table, asked, "While we are on the record, do either of you have anymore questions for Casey? If not, I have one."

Cody said, "No. Not at this time. I may have some later after I digest this and think about it."

Then Tex said, "No. Same as Cody. Maybe later."

"Well, if that will be all I will shut off the recorder. But first, Casey, you were afraid someone was after you, can you tell me why you felt that way."

"A friend told me that she overheard two girls saying that I was in trouble. She was concerned about me is the reason she told me. She asked me, 'What kind of trouble?' I told her, 'No, I was not in trouble.' The shooting was the only reason that I knew of that anyone would be looking for me. That was why I left town suddenly. I didn't stay to find out what they were talking about. I have not told anyone about that night except Chip and Mom. And, of course, John and Elaine."

"Thank you, Casey Branson. Let me ask you another question while we are on record. Before you gave your statement, were you promised anything, except protection for your statement? Were you coerced or forced in any way by Sergeant Edwards, Sergeant Tyler or Corporal Carillo to make this statement?"

"No, Corporal Carillo. I am giving this statement of my own free will."

"Thank you, Casey Branson." And then Nick turned off the recorder.

Cody said, "I am having trouble trying to absorb what I have heard. I am flabbergasted. I thought this but it just didn't seem real until now."

Nick looked at Cody with a concerned look on his face and said, "Cody, we had the same feelings about your father's death. Like you, it just didn't seem real until now. We have something to work on now and we will do everything possible to bring these men to justice. No matter how long or how many or how high they are, we will get them. ...We will get them."

Tex said, "I can't believe it. Cody, you don't know how sorry I am. I was devastated when I heard of his death, but now, it is like hearing it all over again. He was like a second dad to me." He put his arms around Cody's shoulders and repeated what he had said before. "We will catch the bastards."

Cody said, "All along I felt that my father was murdered, but I had no evidence whatsoever. All I can say is, Casey, I am so proud of you for coming forward. I have something to work on now. We will have to be very careful because of not knowing who to trust in our department, but we will find them and see that justice is done. Casey, I don't know how to thank you."

Casey answered with tears in her eyes, "I'm sorry it was your father, Sergeant Edwards. I was just too scared to come forward earlier."

John put his arms around Casey and hugged her. "I know that you are doing the right thing. Remember, I am proud of you, too. I will walk with you every step of the way."

Tex asked, "Casey, do you feel safe here. Do you have any reason to think that anyone might come here?"

"No, only Chip and my mother know where I am as far as I know. My mother lives by herself. I worry about her. She and I have not talked to each other since I left. John's wife, Elaine, corresponds with her where she works. My father and John's father are brothers."

Then John spoke up, "For right now, I think she is safe, but as the investigation progress, we may have to change things."

Tex said, "Cody, I am going to take some vacation time or get a leave of absence from my job and go to Georgia to help in this investigation. You are like a brother to me and your family is like my second family. I am not taking no for an answer. Casey, like I said, I am going to give you a card and John one and you can contact me at any time while I am in Houston. I, also, will be checking on you when I am here. In the meantime, when I leave to go to Georgia, I will let you know. My father is a retired law enforcement officer and he will be my contact while I am in Georgia and you may contact him. His number is on the back of these cards." He wrote the number on the back and handed one to Casey and one to John. "Please call me or him day or night for anything."

Then John got three cards from his desk and wrote his home phone number and address on the back and gave one each to the men.

Cody and Nick also handed them a card each and told them to keep them where they could get to them easily. Then Nick asked Casey to write down her mother's home address and office address and phone numbers. He and Cody made a promise to her that they would check on her mother often, but do it discreetly so as not to draw attention to it.

When Nick was putting the recorder back into his pocket, he realized that he had a letter in his pocket. "Casey, I'm sorry, I forgot that Chip gave me a letter to give to you. He said it was very important." He pulled the letter out of his pocket and handed it to her.

Her eyes lit up and she smiled at Nick, "Thank you. I will go in the lounge and read it, and then, I should go out front and help Jamie. The lunch crowd is probably coming in now."

"Casey, I told Jamie that you were not feeling well before. Do you feel up to working now? If not, I can call Elaine and she will come in."

"John, I will be alright. I feel like a load has been lifted from my shoulders. I'm fine." And then she turned to the three standing there and said, "I hope you catch the killer."

Cody said, "Oh, Casey, before you go, one last question. Do you think you would know the voices if you heard them again?"

"Possibly the shooter because it was so strong and distinct. The other one, I might. I am not sure."

"Thank you." Cody said as he shook her hand.

Then she shook hands with the other two and left.

The three stayed to make sure that John had everything in control and that she would be alright. They shook hands and John showed them the back door so they would not have to go out front since it was probably full of patrons for lunch.

The three of them got into Tex's Ford Explorer and headed for home. They had a lot of talking to do and plans to make.

They didn't feel too much like riding around or doing anything except to go home and start making plans. They all were very angry and geared up to do something toward getting the killer. Cody and Nick wanted to go back to Georgia and start making plans, but Tex talked them into staying until Monday morning.

When they got to Tex's place, Cody phoned the airlines and made reservations for eleven o'clock Monday morning. That was the next flight out of Houston to Georgia. That was settled.

Tex said, "I think we all could use a drink. I seldom drink during the day, but this is one day, we could all use one." He went to the bar and made three drinks.

They were setting around the table when Mr. Tyler came in. "Tex, when did you or Cody start to drink during the day? Do you want to tell me about it? Can I be of any help?"

Tex looked at Cody and then said, "Dad, you sure are full of questions, Aren't you?"

"Yes, I am, Tex. I know that this trip from Cody and Nick is not a social visit. I know that something very disturbing is in the air. I know that whatever it is, it is something very important to all three of you. And whatever is important to you three is very important to me."

Cody said, "Sir, while Tex is telling you why we are here, I will fix you a drink."

"That will be fine with me, Cody, if you think I will need one."

Cody was going over the information in his head. He did not want to hear it again right now. So Cody got up and went to the bar and started fixing Mr. Tyler a drink. And Tex started telling his Dad what they had found out.

"Dad, Nick's informant gave him some information about a murder which led Cody and Nick here." And Tex proceeded to tell him everything that had been done and said up until now.

When Tex had finished, Mr. Tyler shook his head and said very angrily, "I can't believe this. They are the lowest animals that there are. I hope that you catch them and string them up like the animals that they are. The greedy Son-Of-Bitches."

35

Then Tex said, "Dad, I am going to take some vacation or get a leave of absence and go to Georgia for awhile and help Cody and Nick on this investigation. Since the corruption is in the department and higher up, they don't know who to trust. So the three of us will be working on this for a while.

Cody spoke up and said, "Tex, I know you want to do what you can, but ...."

Before Cody could finish, Tex said, "I will not take no for an answer. I am going to Georgia as soon as I can get approval of some time off."

Mr. Tyler spoke up, "I think Tex is right. He can find some place there and work under cover. He may be able to find out some things that you can't. Everyone there know you two."

Mr. Tyler called and cancelled his poker game for that night. He made dinner from leftovers while the others talked, putting in his two cents every once in a while. They all talked until late in the night.

After discussing the situation thoroughly, they decided that Mr. Tyler and Tex would take a ride into Bristol and Tex would introduce him to John and Casey Branson. They wanted Casey to feel completely safe and at ease. He would be looking out for them and passing on any information as to what was happening in Texas. Cody and Nick would take the plane at 11:00 o'clock the next morning back to Georgia and work as though nothing had happened, but in the meantime, try to find out about the files and look for whatever evidence they could find without causing anyone to become suspicious of what they were doing. Hoping that they could find someone that they could trust to work with them.

In the meantime, Tex was going to put in for his vacation time using the excuse that he had to go out of town on business for awhile. He felt sure that he could get it, but he felt that would be better than the leave of absence right now. Later, he could extend his vacation or ask for a leave of absence depending on the situation at the time. He would start his vacation the following week. That would give him time to clear his desk of anything that had to be done the following week and delegate the other. After all, he had two good reasons to go to Georgia, but he wasn't ready to tell Cody the other reason yet.

They felt that they had everything figured out for now. So they got ready for bed and fell sound asleep with the help of the alcohol. They all were pretty well leaning to the drunken stage with it by then.

When the alarm went off the next morning around seven o'clock, it was hard for them to get up. They laid in bed for a while before getting up and facing the day. Finally, when they all went downstairs, Mr. Tyler was up and had breakfast prepared.

"Good morning, you drunken sots. I knew you would not be able to get up right away, so I set the alarm for seven o'clock to give you enough time to really wake up and drag yourselves out of bed. I was right. Thanks to me, you now have time to eat your breakfast and plenty of time to catch the plane." He looked at his watch and saw that it was now 8:30 a.m. "It only took you an hour and a half to get out of bed."

"Yeah, Dad. You think of everything. That makes me think that you have had your binges and that is why you know what to do now."

Mr. Tyler laughed. "You'll never know, Son." They all laughed.

They were feeling better after eating their breakfast and drinking their coffee. By the time that they had finished, they were in a jovial mood and was raring to go to work.

Cody said, "Tex, Mr. Tyler, despite the reason we came here, it has been good seeing you again. We accomplished a lot this weekend as far as information is concerned. It has given us a new outlook as to what we have to do. Me, personally, am looking forward to looking into the background of these high and mighty people who think they can rule the world. I don't know how I am going to keep this information from Mom and Traci. They should know, but I think it is best that they don't know at this point."

Nick spoke up, "Not only you, Cody. I am looking forward to it, too. You're right about your mom and Traci. Your mom is still having a hard time with your father's death." Then to liven it up a little, he continued, "I would like to propose that the day these guys are convicted, we all and I mean, we all will celebrate.

Tex said, "I get your meaning, Nick. And I'll drink to that. We all, including Casey and Chip will celebrate. No matter how long it takes, we will reach our goal. We will get the bastards and that is a promise."

They all laughed, nodding their heads.

After saying goodbye to Mr. Tyler, Tex drove Cody and Nick to the airport. As they were saying their goodbyes, they put their arms around each other and made a promise that they would come out on top. Tex made a promise to see them the following weekend. They went to catch their plane, while Tex made his way back to his Ford Explorer and drove back home.

When Tex got home, he and his father made a trip to Bristol's Diner.

Chapter 3
Littleton, Georgia

Steven was there to meet Cody and Nick when the plane landed. He was very anxious to see them as he had been on pins and needles ever since Cody had told him the reason for this trip. They had carryon bags so they did not have to wait for their luggage. They came off the plane and straight to the farm's Ford Explorer. It was used most of the time for business or farm use. Today, Steven figured it would have more room in it for the three of them. On the way home, Cody explained to Steven that it would be best for him to wait and hear the tape. That would be better than him explaining it to him now. They went home since Nick's car was there, and, as they pulled up in the yard, Cody said, "Mom's car is gone. Do you know where she is, Steven?"

"She and Sara went shopping to buy groceries for the week. Their weekly trip."

"Good, Bro, we will go upstairs and I'll play this tape for you and we will explain what we know."

Cody could see the anxiety on Steven's face, so when they got out of the car, Cody put his arm around Steven's shoulders and said, "Steven, do you remember when we were told that Dad had been killed. The first thing that you said was, 'no way. Dad can take care of himself. He was murdered. I don't believe what you said.' Well, you were right." Steven looked up at Cody with tears in his eyes and said, "Was Dad murdered? Is that what you are saying? ...I don't know why I said what I did, but I always thought Dad could do anything and that nothing would happen to him." They both were feeling very emotional at this moment.

"Yes, Brother, we have a witness to his murder." They both hugged each other while tears rolled down their face. Nick stood by watching the two brothers grieving all over again with their emotions running high. He was feeling so sad, yet so angry at what had happened to his best friend's family.

Steven was very anxious to hear the tape, so after a few moments, they went into the house looking to make sure Mom wasn't home, then the three of them went upstairs to Cody's room. Nick took out the recorder and gave it to Cody. He said, "Cody, I don't have a safe place to put this. You have a safe here and I think it should be locked up. No one knows that we have this except the three of us. Let's keep it that way."

They all agreed. Cody plugged it in and started to play it for Steven. They all listened closely so as not to miss anything on the tape. When the tape finished, Steven put his head in his hands and cried softly. He said sadly, "She said higher ups and have people in the right places. That means higher ups in our department, judges and/or district attorneys are corrupt. ...I just can't believe this. Cody, what are we going to do?"

"Steven, Nick and I are going to look into this since we are in the Investigation Section. We will keep you informed as we go. We will need your help some of the time. We..."

Steven was very adamant and would not let him finish, as he said in a very determined voice. "I am going to be a part of this investigation. Don't tell me NO, Bro."

"Steven, we have to be very careful because we do not know who we can trust. Cody and I can move around without arousing suspicion. It will be very difficult for you on some of the issues. Believe me, you will be in on the investigation, but we all have to look at this for the best way to handle it and abide by it."

Steven looked at them for a moment, "I'm sorry. .. I understand. I am just frustrated as a son and not as a police officer. I just don't know how I feel at this moment."

"That's alright, Bro. I can understand that. I went through those same feelings when I heard her saying these things. Regardless of what happens, no one else will know about this tape and what we are doing. Is that understood?"

Nick and Steven both nodded as they said, "Yes."

Cody took the tape and sealed it in a small box and they all three put their initials on it. This way they can identify the box without opening it. The three of them then went downstairs to their father's office and put the tape into the safe. Cody changed the code and gave it to Steven and Nick as he said, "No one else will have this code for the time being. Steven, if Mom or Traci want to go into the safe, they will have to go through us. They are not to know about the tape or what we found out this weekend. They think it was a social visit. We will tell them when the time comes. O.K."

"I understand. They don't use this safe, anyway. Traci has a safety deposit box at the bank that she uses for her and Mom. So, this will work fine."

Nick was concerned about Steven's emotions as a son interfering with the investigation, so he said, "Steven, this investigation can become very dangerous if we hit the right buttons. The less people know about this, the better. The best thing for you to do is to just act naturally. O.K."

"Sure, Nick. I know. I have some experience, too. I have been on the department for two and a half years now."

"Sorry, Steven, I just want to stress the importance of this investigation, and it being about your father is going to make it double hard for you and Cody to deal with some of the incidents. No matter how much you want to crack someone's head, you won't be able to react to your emotions."

Cody, feeling frustrated, said, "I am going to go make some coffee. Do I have anyone else interested? Also, I am getting a little hungry. Let's see what is in the kitchen. I think we, or at least Nick and I, need a break from this conversation for awhile. My head is beginning to feel all jumbled up."

They all went into the kitchen. Cody was making some coffee when Sara came in with a load of groceries. Nick and Steven went out to the car and brought in the rest of the groceries.

When Mama E came in, she hugged Cody and said, "How was your trip? It was a short one. ....Maybe you two should have stayed a while longer so you could have really enjoyed yourselves. I bet Tex was glad to see you all."

"Yes, he was. It was great, Mom. Nick had never been to Texas. He couldn't believe the oil wells and the big wide open spaces."

"You enjoyed it, eh, Nick. You didn't stay long enough. You'll have to go back when you can stay longer than a day or two. How was Tex and Charles? And Tex's sister? I can never think of her name."

"Yes, Ma'am. I enjoyed it very much. Tex and his father are doing fine. They sure are two likeable people. I didn't get to meet the sister. I believe her name is Kristen. If she is anything like her brother and father, I would like to go back and meet her. She was out of town this weekend."

They all laughed. Then Cody spoke, "Nick, she is a very pretty gal and gutsy, too. Mr. Tyler said that he is teaching her the oil business, since Tex doesn't seem to be interested in it. According to him, she is doing great, too."

Sara spoke up, "Alright, you guys, take your coffee and go. Claire and I have to get dinner going here."

So the guys took their coffee cups and some cookies and went outside into the yard and sat under the trees trying to relax after the rough weekend. It was beautiful outside. The spring flowers were just beginning to bloom. It was so peaceful with a light breeze blowing.

42

After several minutes of just relaxing in the shade, Nick got up and said, "I hate to break this up, but I have to get back to my place. I'll see you at work tomorrow morning, Cody, and take care, Steven."

"Alright, Nick," answered Cody and Steven about the same time. Then Nick turned and walked to his car and drove off.

He had a cottage closer to town down about three blocks from his mother's house. Corrie still lived at home with her mother. Nick and his family were very close, but he did not feel like talking to anyone now. He just wanted to go to his place and be very quiet. He stopped and picked up a pizza and brought it home and sat down and ate some of it. Then he took a shower and relaxed in his favorite chair and listened to some slow music that was soothing to his ears. Before long, he was sound asleep.

In the meantime, Cody and Steven stayed out under the trees and finished their coffee and cookies. They were bringing up memories of when they were younger and laughing about some of them when Traci walked up.

"Hello, you guys, what are you talking about? Can a girl listen in on it?"

Steven spoke up, "Sure, Sis. Mom and Dad's anniversary being today made us think about when we were all together. We were just talking about when we were growing up. You were always tagging along wanting to go with us everytime we left the house. We couldn't do anything without you tagging along."

They all laughed. She said laughingly, "Yes, and you wouldn't let me play ball with you all and you ran off and left me. But I made it to the ball field and some of the other guys let me hit the ball. I showed you that I could play ball, too."

They all laughed again. Then Traci asked, "Bro, how was Tex and his family?"

"They are doing great. Kristen was away for the weekend. We didn't see her, but she is fine. She is learning the oil business and Mr. Tyler is very proud of that. Tex doesn't have an interest in it."

"You know that I have had a crush on Tex ever since he was here last. Gosh, he is such a hunk. Sure would like to see him."

"You may get your wish. He is thinking about coming here next weekend."

Traci's expression changed to a very excited look, "Bro, are you sure? Oh, that would be great."

Steven spoke up, "I am not so sure he should come. Our sister may put her clutches into him."

They all laughed.

"It is not definite yet, but he will let me know. So, Sis, don't say anything about it now. You know how Mom is about Tex." Cody did not want to discuss anymore about his trip to Houston right now.

"Sure, Bro."

Then they were called in to get ready for dinner. The three of them went into the house laughing. Dinner was enjoyable and the conversation was kept in a happy mode. The kids did not want to give their mother time to remember that it was their anniversary. If she did remember it, she did not let on that she did. Traci talked of her work that day and the progress report that her boss had given her. It was a very good report. A few questions about Cody's trip that he answered smoothly. Soon it was over and he could excuse himself and go upstairs so he could take a shower and get ready for bed. He was tired. His Mom had said that it was a short weekend, but he felt different about that. It had been a long and tiring weekend for him. He also felt guilty about not telling his mother and sister what he knew about their father's death, but he just couldn't for now.

The next morning as soon as Cody got to work, Lieutenant Harlen Moss called him into his office. They worked good together and got along good, friendly, but mostly businesslike. Cody was puzzled and didn't know what to think of it. He wanted to talk to him, but had not decided what he was going to say to the Lieutenant.

As Cody walked into Lieutenant Moss' office, he greeted him with a smile as he said, "Good morning, Lieutenant."

"Good morning, Sergeant. ..Did you enjoy your day off yesterday?"

"Yes Sir, I did." Cody did not want to say anymore than he had to as to what he did.

The Lieutenant took a deep breath and then said, "Well, good, because we found another dead body last night only a couple of blocks from where we found the last one. We now have three murders to solve. ...I say three because, somehow, I feel that all three may be connected. I feel sure they involve drugs because of the victims past."

Cody saw his opportunity and took it. "Lieutenant, I assume that you are going to give me this case. And, if you are, with your permission I will get the other two cases and study them as we go along with this one. Compare the information between the three murders. Does that meet your approval?" Cody was very anxious, but yet could not believe what was happening.

"Yes, Sergeant. I was about to suggest that. The other two led to nowhere. Maybe with the three of them together, we'll come up with some new information. Keep me informed of what you find out. I picked you because you are my most thorough investigator. I mean that very much. You may not know this, but I requested you to come into this group. I worked under your father and if you are anything like him, you will go places in this section. I don't say it very often, but for the past two months since you have been here, you have not disappointed me. That is why I am going to let you pick someone to

45

work with you on this. You know who you can count on when you need help."

Cody tried very hard not to show how excited he was at this moment. "Thank you, Lieutenant. If it will meet with your approval, I would like for Corporal Nick Carillo to work with me as my backup on these investigations. He and I work good together."

"You have my approval. Carillo is a good investigator. He will go places, as well as you, Edwards. I might add, you work the hours that fit with the investigation. Keep track of the hours for you both. I will give you the folder with the police reports and autopsy reports as soon as I receive them. ....That will be all, Sergeant."

"Thank you, Sir. As soon as Carillo comes in, we will get right on it. Exactly where is the crime scene, Sir?"

Then Lieutenant Moss handed him a form that had some of the information on it to start an investigation.

Then Cody turned and walked out the door back to his desk not really believing what he had just heard. Then he started to doubt his good luck. *This was handed to him on a silver platter, or was it? How much did Lieutenant Moss know. He worked under my father for a year or more. I wonder if we can trust him, or if he is testing us to see how much we know. Or maybe he want to keep us close to him. We'll have to wait and see.*

Cody was straightening up his desk so that he could get organized. He was going through his mail when all of a sudden, he realized that someone was standing at his desk. He looked up and saw Lieutenant Moss standing there, smiling. "Oh, Sergeant, I forgot to tell you when you were in my office, but the office down the hall is vacant. You and Corporal Carillo can move into that office so that you will have more privacy. I want these cases solved. Here are the two older files." He handed the two files to Sergeant Edwards.

"Yes Sir, Lieutenant. We will get started right away."

The Lieutenant turned and walked back into his office. *He knew that Sergeant Edwards was the image of his father and that he would be a good investigator. He could count on him. If an Edwards told you something, you could stand by it.*

By that time, Nick had come in. Cody went over to Nick's desk and said, "Come with me, Corporal." Nick looked at Cody with a puzzled look on his face. He did not know what to expect.

The two of them walked down the hall to the office and saw that it was empty except for a couple of chairs and a table. He said as he grinned, "Corporal, this will be our office for awhile. The Lieutenant has just given us three murder cases to solve. He thinks we should be here so we can have some privacy."

Nick started grinning. Then he said excitedly, "He gave us the murder cases." Cody started grinning with him. "Yes, Nick, I think we should move this table out front and bring our own desk in this office for better working conditions, what do you think?"

"I can't believe this." Before Nick could say anymore, Cody put his fingers to his lips and pointed to his ears.

Nick shook his head that he understood.

They searched the table and chairs for a bug and then moved them out into the hall. Then they proceeded to move their desk into the office. Most of the investigators had gone out, but there were a few at their desk in the front office. They looked up but did not pay much attention to what Nick and Cody were doing. Someone was always moving around.

As Nick and Cody moved their desk into the office, they inspected them for bugs in case someone had put one there someplace. You can't be too careful. They moved the big table to the front office where their desks had been. They found a smaller one in the storage room and put it in their office. After everything was in place in their new office, they sat down and started talking about what they could add to their office to make it more workable. Then Cody looked at the report of the latest murder to see where the crime scene was.

Just as they were about to go to the crime scene, Lieutenant Moss came by and handed Cody two keys for the office. Then he said, "Good morning Carillo. Cody will fill you in on the cases that you and he will be working on. Good luck to both of you."

"Thank you, Lieutenant. Edwards and I will do our best, Sir."

"I know that you will, Carillo. That is why you two have the cases." Then he turned and walked back to his office.

They locked their door and went out to the crime scene, talked to the officers there and made their own notes. The officers promised to give them personally a copy of their reports. Then they went to the Medical Examiners Office. There, they were promised a report within the day.

Then they went back to the office and looked over the other two files and went through them comparing whatever they could. Then they decided to go next door for lunch.

On the walk to the diner next door, Nick said, "I can't believe our luck. The Lieutenant just called you in and placed this in your hands?"

"Yes, I was as shocked as you seem to be. He said he wanted his two best investigators on these murders." *Cody didn't tell Nick that he was the one to pick him, but the Lieutenant had agreed with him. That was the same thing.* "At first I felt great about it and I believe he was sincere, but we have to ask ourselves these questions: Can he be trusted? Did he know we went out of town this weekend and where. He shouldn't, because we didn't tell anyone but my family and Corrie, and they did not know why we were going out of town. Did he give these to us for the reason he said, or did he want to keep us close to him so he could follow the investigation? Also, how much does he know? He worked for my father for about a year. We have to keep these questions in mind until we are satisfied that he can be trusted."

"I see what you mean." Then he added with enthusiasm, "But this is what we wanted. I can't believe it was so easy."

Cody said, "The next thing we have to do is inspect our cars, make sure there is not a bug or tracker in them. I know that they were at our homes over the weekend, but you never know. The Lieutenant could have told someone else that he was going to give us the cases."

"I agree with you. We have to be very careful."

By then they were at the diner and they went in and had their lunch discussing some of the cases lightly. A few of the other investigators were in there and spoke to them. One came over and said, "I hear that you two are going to work the murder that happened last night. Good luck with it. The Lieutenant told us that you two were on special assignment and that we had to carry the rest of the work load. If I can be of any help, let me know."

Cody and Nick both said, "Thanks. We may be calling on you."

After finishing their lunch, the murder scenes were their next stop. There were not much to see on the old ones, but they wanted to see the layout exactly where the murders had occurred and to make their own notes as they went over the scenes. Also, they rode by where Captain Edwards was killed and looked at the corner where Casey had been. By the time they had finished at the scenes, it was getting late. So they went back to the office and picked up the files and headed for Nick's place. After going over both cars checking for any bugs or trackers, there wasn't anything found to make them suspicious.

After Cody and Nick carried their work inside, Cody went to a chinese place and ordered some food to go so they could work without being disturbed.

By the time that Cody got back with the food, Nick had spread each case and their notes out on the table. Nick said, "Put the food on the counter and we will fix a plate." He got the plates down and they prepared their plates and set them on the table. Then Nick went to the refrigerator and got out two beers.

Cody laughed and said, "You are getting prepared to work, aren't you?"

"Yep, we have a lot to do. Might as well enjoy it while we can."

Cody picked up the phone and called Traci to let her know that he was at Nick's if they needed anything and would probably be late. Then he settled down to the table with Nick and they read reports and made notes as they ate. Nick took one of the old cases and Cody took the other one. Cody said after looking through the file, "Evidently, there are a lot of reports missing out of this file. There is very little to go on."

"There are some reports missing from here, too. Some words blackened from what is here. There is hardly anything to go on except where the murder occurred. Do you think the Lieutenant know about this?"

"I don't know if he does or not, but he will in the morning, I assure you."

They looked at each other realizing what lay ahead of them. *Where are the missing pages and who took them.* Then they made notes of the important details that they could figure out from the files. Anything that they could compare with the last murder and also his father's murder whenever he could get a file on it. When they finally closed the two files, Cody said, "These first two murders occurred within a block of each other and they were young kids. Let's compare what we have written down on these two before we go to the other one."

"O.K., they occurred within a block of each other. It looks like the same gun killed them both." Nick was reading from both sets of notes while Cody was making new notes of what was the same. "The gun was a 9 MM. Victim #1 was shot in the shoulder and chest.

Victim #2 was shot in the chest area and then in the back. They lived within five blocks of each other. Victim #1 was seventeen years of age and lived on Thirty-First Street and Twenty-Sixth Avenue. Victim #2 was sixteen years of age and lived at Twenty-Seventh Street and Twenty-Sixth Avenue. In that neighborhood, most of the kids know each other and most of them is either on drugs or sale drugs. The number of dropouts in school is very high."

Cody said, "Yes, that is a problem neighborhood. The more we worked that area, it seems the worst it got. Only a few ever get out of there and make it good. As fast as we arrested someone, they were out of jail and back on the streets again in a few days."

Nick stared at Cody, "That's what we have to look at now. How did they get out of jail so fast? One had been arrested two times and the other three."

"It looks as if they had the same probation officer and the same attorney representing them. The judge was different. We are short of probation officers so that could be on the level. We will have to look at other drug cases in order to follow this line of investigative work. According to Casey, there is corruption possibly in the department and other government offices. I wonder just high up this corruption really is. We will have to take all of this into consideration. So, knowing who the judge, attorney, probation officer or whatever is important."

Then Cody added, "Also, there were no witnesses in either murder case.

As Nick looked over the files again, he started to read out loud, "Victim #1 was killed around nine o'clock at night and Victim #2 was killed around eleven o'clock at night. ...Wait a minute, Cody. There was one witness to Murder #2."

"Nick, do you have the name of the witness in the case of Murder #2?"

Nick looked puzzled. Then he said, "That's odd. In this report it says that there was a witness and the information is on the attachment, but nowhere in this file is an attachment to this report."

Cody said, "Unless, someone took it out of the file and did not notice that the witness was mentioned in this report."

"These files are kept in our office vault and no one other than the persons working on these cases in our Section is suppose to have access to them. Anyone other than the investigators on the case have to go through the Lieutenant to have access to it. Do you suppose someone in our Section is involved in these murders?"

Cody said very slowly, "I...don't know. I...don't ....know..... I think we should call it a night for now. We don't want to continue this conversation any more until we have some more evidence. The next thing you know, we will be trying to figure out who in our Section would do something like this and we don't want to start suspecting anyone we work with until we know for sure. ...The last few days have been rough for me. ....We'll start again in the morning." Then Cody got up and started helping Nick clean up his kitchen.

Nick was ready for bed, too. It had been rough for him, too, but he knew that it was double that on Cody. So, he walked Cody to his car and opened the car door for him and said, "You're right, Cody. There is no need to discuss that until we compare notes on the other file and have more evidence. We'll see you in the morning. Goodnight."

As Cody drove away from the curb, Nick walked back into his house. It was a nice house, more like a little cottage. He had it fixed for his taste in the shades of brown, beige, green and blue-green. He loved to have greenery around the living area with a few yellow and salmon colored roses here and there. Roses were his favorite flower. It was very masculine looking and very comfortable. He came into the front room and sat down in his comfortable recliner chair and laid his head back for a few minutes. *No matter what Cody had said, and I know that Cody is right, but the thought of someone in our Section being dirty was very disturbing. If I had to pick one now, I honestly do not know who I would pick. Tomorrow morning, first thing, I will write down the name of all investigators listed on the cases. We need to check that area, too.* That was the last thing that he remembered before falling asleep.

He awoke with a startled feeling. He thought he heard a noise and that was what made him wake up so quickly, but it was very quiet now. He looked at his watch and saw that it was three o'clock in the morning. He got up and looked around and everything seemed fine, so he went into his bedroom and started taking off his clothes. After taking a shower, he went to bed but could not go back to sleep. Finally, a little before five o'clock, he got up and got dressed and went to the station.

As he walked in, there were three other investigators in the office. They all said their 'good morning' and Nick said 'good morning' to them and continued to walk down the hall to his new office. Investigators were coming and going at all hours, so it wasn't anything out of place for him to be coming in early.

About half an hour later, Cody walked into the office. He looked at Nick and laughed. "You couldn't sleep either, huh?"

Nick laughed, "No, but my problem was that I fell asleep in my recliner and woke up about three o'clock. Then I took a shower and went to bed. I stayed in bed as long as I could, and, finally, I got up and dressed and got here about 5:30. How about you? What was your problem?"

Cody said as he put the files on the table and then came around to his desk, "The last part of the conversation we had last night weighed heavy on my mind. I did get some sleep, but I kept waking up during the night. So here I am."

Then Cody started pulling out a coffee pot, coffee and sugar. He said, "Since we are a distance from the big coffee pot, I thought we could use this one in our office. It will be easier for us to have it here, don't you think? Plus, we will probably be working a lot of nights, too."

"Yes, that's a great idea. Hey, I remember seeing a small table in the storage room. I'll go down and see if it is still there. It will make a terrific coffee and doughnut table."

Cody laughed, "If there is a refrigerator or anything else you think we could use, bring it."

They both laughed.

While Nick was gone, Lieutenant Moss came into the office. "Gee, you two are settling in good. I just came in to see if you two came up with anything last night."

Cody said, reluctantly, "Not really. We studied the two older murders and compared them. This morning we are going to study the new one. We will let you know when we find something to go on."

"Good. I would like to be kept up to date."

Cody looked Lieutenant Moss in the eyes and said, "Lieutenant, my father was killed within the area of these murders. We feel sure that these were drug related because of the victims, but my father was in that area that night for a reason. If we could see the information in his file that may help us with our investigation."

"Cody, you do realize that your father was killed in a shootout and was under different circumstances, don't you?"

"Yes, Sir. I do realize that, but I feel that it may be related. My father was in that area for a good reason. I would like to take a look at it. If it does not shed any light on these cases, I'll give it back to you."

"I'm sorry, Sergeant, I wasn't trying to be difficult. I understand how you must feel. I don't want to stand in the way of your investigation. Of course, you may have the file and keep it as long as necessary. Come with me."

In the meantime, Nick had come in the door and had heard some of the conversation, but did not say anything to disturb the conversation. When the Lieutenant turned around, he saw Nick, and said, "Good morning, Corporal." And then he and Cody walked out of the office. They went to the Section File Room and the Lieutenant signed the file out and gave it to Cody. The Lieutenant had to sign for any of the files that were to be taken from the file room. Cody was wondering how he was going to ask for other files, but decided that it was too soon. It would be best to wait for later. They had enough work to do for now. He did not want to push his luck with the Lieutenant. But he took his chance to ask about the keys to their office. He said, "Lieutenant, does the key that we have for our office fit all the offices in this section?"

"No, they are not suppose to. The keys that I gave you should only fit your office. Try them and let me know if they fit any other offices. Each office should have it's own key."

"Yes, Sir, I will. I would rather not lug these files home with me every night. If we have these files out, we should keep them locked up when we are not with them? That is the way I work, Lieutenant." And Cody sought of halfway smiled at the Lieutenant.

The Lieutenant smiled with a half-laugh and said, "You are a good investigator, Sergeant, and I like the way you work."

By the time Cody got back to the office, Nick had made a pot of coffee and had the notes spread out on the table. They could both set down at the table so that is where they worked together. That way they had room to spread out and not have to rearrange things on their desks. "Did the Lieutenant give you a hard time about the file?"

"No, Nick, he didn't, but it was like he started to, but backed down. I know that he is strict on who gets these files. I was told that the Lieutenant before him was very lenient with the files. Anyone could go in and get one without signing them out, although they were suppose to sign for them. I remember Dad talking about that. He called the Lieutenant on the carpet several times about that. In fact, Dad is the one that made that rule when he came here, but the

Lieutenant didn't abide by it. So, finally, Dad put a lock on the door and no one could go in unless they went through him. He kept the key in his office in a locked drawer. Several of the files came up with reports and papers missing from the files and, of course, Dad was to blame for that because he was in charge. So he made it hard for them to get a file."

Nick looked at Cody smiling, "I don't blame him. These files are confidential and not everyone, even in this Section, should see them unless they have a need-to-know basis."

"Another thing, the Lieutenant has a lot on his shoulders. They never replaced Dad here, so Lieutenant Moss is acting Captain and has been for about six months or more. I pushed my luck with the Lieutenant in getting Dad's file. Then I was afraid to push any more and get more files. That will have to wait for later. He did give me a few reports that just came in on Victim #3." He grinned at Nick.

Then they laughed. They were feeling better about the investigation.

Nick said, "We better get to work or the Lieutenant might change his mind about us investigating these cases and we sure don't want that."

"You're right. Things are going our way and we sure don't want to mess that up." By that time the coffee was ready and they poured themselves a cup.

As they sat down to the table, Cody said, "Let's compare Victim #3 to the other two victims. You read from the file and I'll make notes."

"O.K., let's see. This victim is forty years old. He has never been arrested according to the reports here, but he does live in the area of the other two victims. In fact, he lives at the same address as Victim #2. He could be the stepfather or maybe the mother's boyfriend."

Cody continued to make his notes as Nick read the reports. "The gun was a .38 Caliber and he was shot twice in the chest. There doesn't seem to be anything like the other two murders, except Victim #2 and Victim #3 lived at the same address. That leads me to believe that they are connected."

"Yeah, me too."

Then Cody picked up his father's file and opened it. There were only two reports in the file. He said, "The police report states that he was shot with a 9 MM in the chest twice. No one else was injured in the shootout. The autopsy report says that he died instantly of gunshot wounds to the heart. It is not like Dad not to wear his vest." Then he added angrily as he slammed the file down, "An officer dies in a shootout and this is all that is in his file." Cody got up and walked around the room to the one window in the office and stared out the window.

Nick picked up the file and looked. Then he just shook his head. Then he walked over to Cody and said, "Let's get out of this office. Let's go talk to Victim #2's mother. That will be a good start."

Cody walked back to the table and put the files in his case. Then he said, "That's a good idea." He then picked up his attache case and started toward the door.

Nick picked up his attache case and followed him in the hall. They locked the door and left. Nick said, "I'll drive." Then he got behind the wheel. Usually, Cody liked to drive, but he got into the passenger seat and they took off to try to find some answers. They pulled up in front of Kevin Koster's home and sat there for a moment just looking around. The area was dirty and rundown and the paint was faded from the houses. It was very discouraging just looking around the neighborhood. They got out of the car and went up to the door trying to miss some old broken toys on the walkway.

Cody knocked on the door and there was no answer. He knocked again a little harder than before and they waited. A few moments later, a little girl peeped her head around the side of the house. Nick walked over and said, "I'm Corporal Carillo. What is your name?"

She stared at him and then said, "Mama told me not to talk to strangers."

Nick said, "That's good. Your Mama's right. You shouldn't talk to strangers, but I told you my name and I am a police officer. Do you live here?"

"Yes."

Cody did not want to scare her so he stayed where he was and let Nick talk to her.

Nick smiled and said, "Is your mother home?"

The little girl turned around and ran to the back yard. So Nick and Cody followed her to the back yard. There was a small woman in her late thirties or early forties hanging clothes on the line. They walked over and stood about three or four feet from her and Cody said, "Good morning, Ma'am. I am Sergeant Edwards and this is Corporal Carillo from Little County Sheriff's Office. Could we talk to you for a few minutes?"

"What is this about?" she asked.

Cody said, "We are investigating your son's murder. We are hoping that you can give us a new lead in this case. It has sat for too long because there are no answers to a lot of questions that we have."

Then Nick spoke up and said, "Mr. Harris, the man that was killed a couple of nights ago lived at this address. Was he Kevin's stepfather?"

By then, the little girl had gone and stood by her mother and put her arm around her mother's leg. Mrs. Harris looked at them a moment and then said, "Yes, he was my second husband. He was a good husband and father to Kevin and Kathy. I gave a statement to the officer that came here right after my son's death. And now my

58

husband has been killed. Is that what it takes in order to investigate a murder?"

Cody spoke up, "Mrs. Harris, I am sorry about your son and your husband. No, it doesn't take two murders in order to investigate one. Like I said before, we have just run out of leads. These three murder cases have just been assigned to us. We feel that they are connected somehow. That is why we are here. Trying to get what information we can to give us some leads. If this is a bad time, we will come back later. I know that you have arrangements to make and things to do, but if you could spare just a few minutes. Again, I am very sorry for your lost. A mother and wife should not have to endure losing a son and then her husband, especially so close together."

By then she was through with the clothes. So she said, "Come into the house. You came at a good time. Friends and neighbors have been here off and on. They were wanting to do things for me, but I feel better by doing the usual myself. My husband won't be buried until day after tomorrow because of an autopsy being performed."

Cody asked questionably as they walked into the house, "Mrs. Harris, thank you for seeing us now. I know that it is a bad time, but the earlier we can start investigating the better. You said you made a statement to the police at the time of your son's death."

She looked at him puzzled, "Yes, I did. The officer asked me questions about my son's activities and if I knew of anyone that would kill him."

Nick looked at Cody and said, "Mrs. Harris, do you remember the officer that asked you these questions?"

"Well, let me see. I think his name was Edwards, no, the first officer was Roberts and the second one was Edwards. I remember Edwards because he was puzzled when I said that Sergeant Roberts had already taken my statement a week before that. Then he said that evidently Roberts misplaced it, so he would like to take it again. He sat right at this table with John and I and we told him everything that we could think of at the time. He was a nice man. Sergeant Roberts was very rude. He didn't ask many questions and when I asked him if he wanted to write my statement down, he said 'no' that he could remember it. John was not here at the time, but I thought that odd that he didn't want to write it down."

Nick said, "So, Mrs. Harris, you are certain that Sergeant Roberts did not make any notes when he was here, but you said that Captain Edwards did."

"Yes, but, Edwards did. He wrote down everything that we said. He said 'you never know what is important until you start investigating.'"

Cody said, "Mrs. Harris, Captain Edwards was my father. He was killed about six months ago. We have been assigned your son's and your husband's cases. I am very sorry that things have happened like they did on your son's case, but I assure you that Corporal Carillo and I will do everything possible to find the killer or killers. Now, if you will sit down with us and give us a statement, we would appreciate it."

They all sat down at the table. Cody and Nick both had noticed how clean the house looked on the inside. It looked so different from the outside. They both were thinking of what a shame she had to live in this neighborhood. She didn't fit here.

She agreed to record her statement and she signed a statement to that effect. When they left, they assured her again that they would find the killer or killers and they gave her a card to call if she thought of anything else.

After they got in the car, Nick said, "There is a lot of sloppy police work going on, don't you think?"

Cody shook his head and said, "I can understand the frustration that my father had a couple of months before he died. He tried not to show it, but he was frustrated before he died. Now, I can understand what he was going through."

They stopped by where Darrel Douglas had lived and talked to his Mom. His Dad had split years ago. She could not add any more information to what they already had in his file. She knew that her son was into selling drugs and thought his death was a result of being involved with the drug dealers. She didn't know the names of anyone that her son associated with, except a girlfriend, Angel, that lived down the street. Her son was seldom home. She stopped looking after him when he was arrested the last time. When he got out of jail, he did not come home.

At least they got a name from her that they did not have 'Angel'. They thanked her for her time and then left. They went to the address that Mrs. Douglas had given them, but Angel was not there. She had not been home since right after Darrel was killed. She left home and her mother had not heard from her. She had no idea where she could have gone, but if she heard from her, she would call them.

She was not very friendly to Cody and Nick. They knew that they would not hear from her. It would be up to them to contact her the next time.

So, Cody and Nick headed back to the station, but stopped a short distance from the station and ate lunch. While eating, Nick said, "You know, Cody, we need to talk to Angel. I don't remember seeing anything in Darrel's file about her. She might be able to give us some information and that is why she hasn't been home. She may be afraid to stay around here. And that might be why her statement is not in the file."

Cody looked Nick in the eyes and said, "Are you thinking what I am thinking?"

"I think we both have the same type of workings of the mind."

Cody laughed as he said, "I hope you don't know what I am thinking most of the time."

Nick, laughingly, said, "No, I can't read your mind and I wouldn't, especially, if it pertains to my sister, but our minds do work in the same direction on certain things."

After finishing their lunch, they were anxious to get back to their office. As they walked through the front office, Roberts was there and said, "Hey, Cody, I hear that you are working on the murder cases."

"Yes, we are."

"Have you had any luck on them?"

Cody stopped and stared at him. He did not want to give away what they had found out so he said, "We are working on them." Then he and Nick walked straight to their office. After getting a cup of coffee, they took the files out and started writing down the main details of what Mrs. Harris had said.

After a couple of minutes, Cody looked up, "Nick, what we need is a typist to type this information. I don't know who to trust here. We haven't been here long enough to know. I'll take this home and get Traci to type it tonight and we will have it in the morning."

Nick looked puzzled at Cody, "Do you really want to get Traci involved in this. Why don't we get Corrie to type it. In fact, she will be home early today and I am sure she wouldn't mind. That would be better, don't you think?"

"Yes, sure. That would be great. What time will she be home?"

"Probably by the time that we got there. I'll call her to make sure that she can do it this afternoon."

So Nick called Corrie at work, but she had already left. He said, "We can run by there and drop this off and then go find Chip. Maybe he has heard something."

In between sips of coffee and comments, they put their files in their attache case. Just as they started to go out the door, Roberts came in. "Oh, you all are leaving, huh?"

Cody said angrily, "Yes, we are in a hurry. What do you want?"

Roberts looked at Cody and said, "Hey, you are very uptight today. I am interested in these cases because I was the first to investigate them, but I was taken off the case. I wish you all good luck with them."

Then Nick said, "Thank you, Roberts. We will need a lot of good luck because we have nothing to go on."

Cody said sarcastically, "Yes, Roberts, where are your reports if you investigated these cases. They are not in the files."

He looked at both of them for a moment and his expression changed to a sincere look as he said, "Honestly, I don't know. ....Cody, I was suspended for several days by your father because my reports were not in the files. He never believed me when I told him that I wrote them up and put them in the files so he went out and interviewed the same people. So his reports should be there. One of the interviews that your father asked me about was Mrs. Harris'. I admitted then and I admit now that when I interviewed Mrs. Harris, I didn't write anything down then. She was upset and didn't really tell me much, but when I came back to the office I wrote down what she said. The others I made notes there when I interviewed them. I swear, I don't know what happened to them. I knew your father did not believe me at the time and I started thinking that maybe your father took them out of the file and blamed it on me."

Cody grabbed him by the collar and got very red in the face with anger. Nick grabbed Cody and said, "Easy, man."

Then Roberts said very quickly, "Cody, you didn't give me a chance to finish. You have to put yourself in my place. I never said anything to anybody what was between me and Captain Edwards because everyone admired him and respected him highly. A couple of days before he was killed, he called me into his office and apologized to me. He was always formal in the office and believed in using your title at all times. He said, 'Sergeant Roberts, I am very sorry for the disagreements that we have had. I find now that you were telling the truth. I should have believed you, but you must understand my position. I know what happened to the reports and that person or persons will be punished.' Then I said, 'Captain Edwards, I am so glad that you have found out. I didn't know how I could persuade you to believe me. I respect you highly and I wanted your respect as well. Thank you, Sir, for telling me. He said, 'My pleasure, Sergeant Roberts. That will be all.' That was the last conversation that I had with him. It has puzzled me since his death as to what he was investigating and what he had found out. I have heard no one say anything, not even rumors as to what he found out. I assumed his reports were in the files."

Cody looked at Nick, "Nick, I know you want to catch Corrie when she gets home, you go ahead. I'll catch up with you later. I would like to talk to Sergeant Roberts a little more."

"Sure, Cody. See you later." And Nick went out the door and closed it behind him.

Cody sat down behind his desk and motioned for Roberts to sit in the chair in front of his desk. Then he said, "Sergeant Roberts, do you have any information that my father may have told you about these cases or what you know about these cases?"

"No, to your first question about your father. He did not say anything to anyone about his investigation of these cases that I know of. He only mentioned that about the files to me because it was my reports. Like I said before, Mrs. Harris told me very little. She said that I would have to talk to her husband. That was why I did not write it down then. Her husband was not at home at the time. I planned to go back and get his statement later, but before I could get back with them, Captain Edwards called me in and asked me where the reports were. Then he took me off the cases and handled them himself. His reports should be in the files."

Cody said disgustedly, "There are no reports in the files." He did not want to say too much at this point.

Roberts looked stunned. "Not even Captain Edwards' reports. They should be there. .....Something strange is going on here. What has happened here, Edwards? Are you telling me the truth?"

Cody studied him intensely and was beginning to believe that he really didn't know that the reports were missing. Then Cody said, "No, not even Captain Edwards. The only reports that are in the files tells us nothing but the basic. ....And yes, I am telling you the truth. I would appreciate it very much if you would not mention that to anyone else."

Cody handed Roberts a pad and pen and said, "Would you mind writing down all the people that you interviewed on these two cases?"

"Sure, be glad to. And, Cody, I'm sorry for any inconvenience on my part reference the cases. What is said in this room stays here as far as I am concerned." He wrote down several names and made notes as to the best of his knowledge what they said, but it was very little. Also, he put down approximately where they lived. He then handed the pad and pen back to Cody and said, "Sergeant Edwards, of all the names I gave you, you should interview Angel, and, if I can be of any help to you, let me know. I hope you can nail the bastards that did the killing, and, also, the ones that took information out of the files."

Cody looked at him and smiled for the first time, "Thank you. We will get them. I promise you that."

They shook hands and left. Roberts went back to his desk and Cody went to meet Nick at his mother's house. He found Nick and Corrie in the room that they used for an office. It had a desk with a computer and file cabinets in it. He stood in the doorway looking at Corrie. She was so beautiful with her long dark brown hair pulled back in a ponytail with a yellow ribbon and her dark brown smiling eyes when she looked up and saw him. "We'll let you come in." He walked around the desk and bent down and kissed her on the cheek.

"Hi," he said. "Thanks for helping us out. Do you mind if we stay here while you type this?"

"No, you don't make me nervous. I like you being here." She smiled, and then continued, "Besides, I may have to ask you some questions. Nick explained a little of it to me."

Nick said, "I'll go get us something to drink." So he left the room and Cody sat down in a chair across the desk. He took out the information from Roberts and was reading it when Nick came back with two cans of beer and a glass of tea.

"I figured that we weren't going out to interview anyone else today, so a brew would taste good especially after your talk with Roberts."

"On the contrary, he was very informative and sincere, I think. In fact here is some information that he wrote down for me." He handed it to Nick. "Anyway, the more I talked to him, the more I believed that he was on the level. Don't get me wrong, I am not trusting anyone until they have proven 100% that they can be trusted. He told me about the interview with Mrs. Harris and what he told me made sense. ....He said we need to talk to Angel. She can be a big help to us. I didn't tell him that she had skipped town. In fact, I didn't tell him anything. So, tomorrow, we will go back to the area and try to find out where Angel might be living. There are a couple of other names on that list that we need to find and talk to, although he said they knew very little at the time."

"Yes, I see what you mean. If he was involved in anything, I don't think he would have given you this much information unless it was to mislead us."

"I don't think so, Nick. He actually looked stunned when he asked about my father's reports and I told him that they were missing, too. I wish you could have seen his face. Don't get me wrong. He is still on my bad list."

They talked for a while, and finally, Corrie said, "You guys look at this and see if I need to change anything?"

Nick grinned at her and said, "We don't want you to change anything. We just want typed what you heard on the recorder."

She said, "Bro, I didn't change anything. It is as I heard it."

Cody walked over to her and kissed her and said, "Thanks, Sweetheart. This will help us immensely. We really appreciate it. You feel tied down when you can't trust anyone."

"Glad to do it. If you need anything else let me know. Now, I have to go and help Mom prepare dinner."

"Thanks, Sis. Cody and I are going for a ride. I'll be back in time for dinner."

"Sure, see you two whenever. I know that you two will be working a lot of hours, so I understand about not going out much. See you whenever." And she walked over to Cody and squeezed his hand as she walked out of the room and into the kitchen where her mother had already started preparing dinner.

Cody watched her walk away and he thought how lucky he was to have found her. She meant everything to him. Nick looked at him without saying a word as though he knew what Cody was thinking. Nick was also thinking of how glad he was that his sister and Cody had hit it off.

After a moment, Nick and Cody went out to Cody's car and drove off to try to find Chip. Nick wanted to speak to him. They finally found him as he was walking home from the garage where he was working now.

Nick hollered, "Chip, how are you?" And Cody pulled over to the curb. Chip got into the car and they drove around. Nick asked, "Chip, do you know a girl, named Angel, of about fifteen or sixteen that live in the neighborhood of Thirty-First Street and Twenty-Sixth Avenue? Somewhere close to that area."

"No, I don't remember anyone by that name. I'll see what I can find out. Do you know her last name or if Angel is her street name?"

Nick said, "No, Angel is all we know. She was the girlfriend of Darrel Douglas before he was killed."

"I'll see what I can find out. The rumor around here is that nobody's talking. Everyone seem to be afraid of someone or something."

"Appreciate it, Chip. You doing alright now?" asked Nick.

"Yes Sir. Casey's mother got a call from Mrs. Branson and she said that Casey was fine. Your friend, Tex, had been to see her to make sure. We all appreciate it. I just hope one day she can come back here."

Cody said, "We hope so too, Chip. We promise that we will do everything we can."

"Thanks." By then they were near Chip's home so they put him out and then went back to Angel's mother's place. Her mother still had not heard from her or would not talk to them. So they went riding around the neighborhood. Then Nick saw a girl he thought he had talked to before on another case. She was standing in a yard with two boys talking to them. Nick called out, "Jeanne, could we talk to you a minute?"

The two boys stood there and watched as Jeanne walked over to the car. Nick said, "Jeanne, you live in this area, don't you?"

"Yes, this is where I live."

"Do you remember me? I am Corporal Carillo and this is Sergeant Edwards."

"I may have talked to you before, but I don't remember."

"We would like to talk to a girl named Angel. Do you know where we can find her?"

She looked a little upset, but she said, "No, I haven't seen her."

Cody could tell that she was lying, so he said in his authoritative voice, "That is not what we asked you. Do you know where we can find her. We need to talk to her about Darrel. We understand that she was his girlfriend when he was killed. We are investigating his death. She may have some information that will help us solve this murder. It has been too long already. We are on the same side here, Jeanne."

"How do I know that I can trust you? The law around here hasn't helped us much before now. Angel told me that Darrel went to the law and that is what got him killed."

"What do you mean by that, Jeanne?" asked Cody.

"I have said too much already. I have to go."

Nick was trying another approach. He smiled and said, "Jeanne, we are on your side. We are trying to find Darrel's killer. We need your help. Is there anything else that you can tell us?"

"No, that is all Angel said to me. She told me that the day she left. She wouldn't tell me anymore because she didn't want me to get involved. She was afraid and that was why she skipped town."

"Do you know where she is?"

"I'll find out and let you know tomorrow about this time." They gave her a card and told her to call day or night and that they would be back tomorrow at the same time.

They went back to Nick's mother's place. He got out of the car and told Cody that he would see him later after dinner. Then Cody drove home. Dinner was almost ready.

Traci said as Cody walked into the kitchen, "Tex called a few minutes ago. He said he would call you back later. ...And dinner is almost ready."

"O.K., Sis. Is everything alright here?"

Mama E said, "Yes, we're fine. How was your day?"

"The usual. Will be down in a minute."

Cody went upstairs and laid down on his bed for a moment trying to get his head straight. Everything seemed to be jumbled up together. Then he said to himself, "I'll think about that later." Then he got up, washed up and then went down for dinner. By that time Steven had come home. They all sat down and had started eating when the phone rang.

Cody said, "I'll get it. That is probably Tex." He answered the phone, "Hi, Tex." And then he said, "Yes, how are things there?" He listened for a moment and then said, "Yes, that will be fine. Are you sure you can put up with us Georgia boys?" And then he laughed. "Yes, be glad to have you. we'll see you then." And then he hung up the phone and came back to the table.

Mama E said, "Sounded like he may be coming here for a visit. Is that right?"

Cody laughed and said as he was looking at Steven, "Yes, he want to see what Georgia will be like for awhile. It will be alright if he stays here, won't it, Mom?"

"Son, you know we would love to have him. When is he coming?"

"This weekend. He is taking some long awaited vacation time and want to spend it here." Then he looked at Traci and grinned, "Sis, you don't mind him staying here, do you? You will control yourself while he is here, won't you? You remember you did have a crush on him before."

Traci's face turned pink and she said, "Yes, Bro, I will control myself. I will not make eyes at him. Besides, he probably has several girlfriends in Texas and won't even notice me."

Mama E spoke up, "Now, you two. Stop that. Tex is a friend and don't either of you forget that."

They all laughed.

Steven said, "Is he flying in or will he be driving into our lovely state?"

"He will be driving. He will leave late Friday evening and will probably arrive late Saturday evening. He want to have his own transportation when he gets here. I guess Nick and I convinced him that living in Georgia was a lot better than Texas. He couldn't take it, so he is coming here to see for himself." He winked at Steven.

Steven said, "It will be nice to have another male in the house. I like him very much. Besides, when he was here before, he kept Mom laughing all the time. She could use a few laughs now."

Mama E smiled at Steven and said, "Yes, he is a joy to be around. I liked him very much when he was here before. I look forward to seeing him again."

By then, they were through with dinner. Cody and Steven got up and started taking the plates off the table and Traci started putting the food up. She said, "Mom, you go do what you want to do. We will clean the kitchen. You cooked, so scoot." So, Mama E went to the family part of the great room where her favorite chair was and picked up her knitting basket and started knitting. She was smiling as she thought, *I am so lucky to have my family here with me. I lost a husband and they lost a father, but we are here close to each other. Tex lost his mother, but he has a sister and his father at home together. We are also fortunate for Cody to have met Tex because what my children have lost in a father, they have gained through Tex's father. What Tex lost in a mother, he has gained through Cody.*

71

It is the next best thing when you have two families come together such as we have. I will see to that.'

Cody and Steven came out of the kitchen and went upstairs, while Traci went over to where her mother was and sat down and started watching television. She said, "Mom, I will move my things in the other room downstairs so that the males can have the whole upstairs."

"Honey, that will be good. Are you sure you don't mind? I really enjoyed knowing that you were across the hall from me when you stayed there a couple of months ago after Thomas died."

"No, I don't mind. It will work out for both of us. They will probably be coming in all hours of the night, anyway."

A few minutes later, Cody and Steven came down and said they were going out. Cody said, "I have my cellular phone with me if you need either of us."

"You boys be careful."

"We will, Mom," they both said.

After they got to Nick's and had settled down with a beer and the papers scattered over the table, Cody said, "I brought Steven with me, I want to keep him up to date on what we have in case he hears or sees anything that will help our case. He is out on the streets most of the day and know a lot of the punks out there. Also, Tex called me tonight. He will be here late Saturday evening. He is driving his own vehicle."

"That will be great. We need all the help we can get. Between the four of us, we should be able to raise some stink around here. This is a mess, Steven, and we are starting from scratch. It looks like so far, someone has gone through these files and have taken information out of them."

After they told Steven everything that they had learned and about the conversation with Roberts, Steven said, "Cody, I remember how frustrated Dad was the last couple of months before he was killed. I understand why now. But you know Dad, he always had a backup on anything that was important."

"I know that, but I have looked everywhere in his office at home. I haven't found anything pertaining to these cases. The only thing that was in our safe at home was personal things for the family. Now the tape of Casey's interview."

"He amd Mom also have a safety deposit box at the bank. Do you think he may have another one in his name that he used especially for his work?"

"I haven't thought about that. We will check that out tomorrow. It would be a big help if we could find the missing reports. We know of very few people that we can talk to that may know something about these murders."

Nick was holding the transcribed interview that Corrie had typed. He started reading over the report out loud.

"Mrs. Harris said that Kevin got his drugs from someone in the sheriff's office, but he would not tell them who it was. He said that if he did they would kill him. That was all that she knew about the drugs. John had found out some information, but would not get her involved in it. They both tried to get Kevin to stop, but he kept saying he couldn't. The night that Kevin was killed, he had mentioned a big drug deal to John before he left the house. The reason she knew this was that she had overheard some of the conversation because John raised his voice to Kevin and said, 'You are not going. You've got to stop. You are worrying your mother to death.' They thought that I was in the back yard, but I had come into the kitchen while they were talking. Kevin started crying and said, 'John, I can't, I can't. I wish I could. I have been threatened by the Big man.'"

Cody said, "The Big man. God, we've got to find him, Nick."

Nick stared at Cody, "We will, Cody, We will."

"Yes, we will. We will have to start thinking of someone higher up that could possibly be involved in this."

Then Steven said, "First thing to look for is the car that they are driving and where they live and how they are spending money compared to what their income could be. Another thing is to look up the date of Kevin's death. Then you will know when the drugs come in, that is, if they come in the same day each week."

Cody laughed, "Little Brother, you will make a good investigator some day."

Steven grinned and said, "Someday, huh. I can out investigate half the department now. We have some lazy-ass people in the department. All they want to do is get their pay check."

They all laughed.

Cody said winking at Nick, "Let's don't get over confident, Little Brother."

Steven looked up grinning, "Big Brother, you know it's the truth, but you can't say it because you are up there in the high ranks where you can't express your opinions and feelings."

Nick said, "I agree with you, Steven. We have the best investigators on the department in this room. I can say it because I am still low on the totum pole."

They all laughed again, feeling more relaxed now and ready to hear more of the interview.

Then Nick continued. "The night that Kevin was killed. He rushed out of the house and said, 'I've got to go.' After about ten minutes, I walked into the living room and John was sitting there with his head in his hands. When I walked in, he said, 'You didn't hear our conversation, did you?' I said, 'Yes, enough of it.' He got up and hugged me and said, 'I'm going looking for him.' I begged him not to go, but he said, 'I'm sorry, but I've got to do something.' Then he left the house. The next thing that I knew, which was about three hours or more later, he came back very upset and didn't know how to tell me, but he finally came over and took me in his arms and said, 'Honey, Kevin is dead. I saw the officer and the man that was talking to Kevin. I don't know their names, but I will find out. I have their tag number and I heard their voices. He shot Kevin twice and then ran. Then the officer left. When I saw that they were gone, I went over and Kevin was dead. I went to a phone and called 911 and went to the hospital with him. While I was there, an officer came and I told him what I had seen. He took me down to the station and they questioned me, but they finally let me go. He was not the one at the scene. I think they think that I did it. I then went back to the hospital and made arrangements for Kevin's release and called the funeral home. They will take care of the rest.' I don't remember much that happened the next few days.

"After the funeral, when John and I were alone, he said, 'Honey, I am going to find out who killed Kevin. I know one of them was a police officer and they won't investigate their own. But I promise you that I will find out and kill him myself if I have to.' I said, 'No, John, let the law handle it.' Then when Captain Edwards came and talked to both of us, I told John that he would take care of it. So we waited and waited, and then we heard the news that he was killed. We felt that our last hope was gone. John went out looking for the car that the killer was in that night. He got part of the tag number that night. All he remembered of the tag number was 396. It was an unmarked dark car. Maybe dark blue, dark green, dark brown or black. He had a badge at his waist and a shoulder holster for his gun. ....I hope you will find Kevin's killer and bring him to justice."

When Nick had finished, Cody said, "At least we know who the witness was. That is probably why he was killed. Tomorrow, we will get a list of the unmarked, dark vehicles and who they are assigned to, and narrow the list down with the tag numbers of 396. And, also, check the bank for another deposit box. I don't want to arouse suspicion by asking my mother anything about it. She probably would not know anyway. Dad kept a lot of things from her because she would worry too much."

Steven inquired, "Are there anything that I can do other than keep my eyes and ears open?"

Cody said, "No, we don't want to arouse suspicion within the department yet. We have to investigate outside the department now and then we will start talking to suspicous characters after we have some evidence against them."

Just then Nick's phone rang. When he answered it, Jeanne was on the line.

Nick said, looking at Cody, "Yes, Jeanne, have you gotten in touch with Angel yet?" Then he was silent for a minute and then he said, "What is the address? Well, then, where can we meet her? This is very important to us, Jeanne. The sooner we catch these rats, the sooner Angel will be safe." Then Nick wrote down an address and said, "Thanks, Jeanne, we appreciate it. Remember, we are on your side. If you have anymore information, please call. O.K." Then, he said, "Thanks, again," and hung up the phone.

"Jeanne came through for us. Angel will meet us at this address in Glenville. That is South Georgia, about one hundred and thirty miles from here."

"What time will she meet with us?"

"She will stay at this address all morning. She will have to leave for work at 1:00 p.m. The address is a friend of hers, not where she is staying," said Nick.

"Cody, while you and Nick go to Glenville in the morning, I will go to the bank and check on the safety deposit box and I will talk to Susan about the list of vehicles. She and I have a good relationship. I can trust her. I will think of a good reason for the list."

Cody said, grinning, "That's right, you dated Susan a few times. I hope your breakup was on good terms."

Steven, grinning, spoke up, "Who said we broke up. We still see each other once in a while. Neither one of us want to get serious now so we keep it on a friendly basis."

Nick said, excitingly, "That will be great. That will help us a great deal, Steven."

"Yes, it will, Bro. We will meet back here after dinner tomorrow night and go over what we find out. Is that a date?"

They all agreed. ...Then Cody said to Nick, "I'll pick you up about six o'clock and we'll stop somewhere and get breakfast and try to be in Glenville around nine-thirty or ten. We don't want to spend too much time down there than we have to and we don't want anyone to know where we are going."

"Sure thing."

After about another thirty minutes of general conversation, Cody picked up the files and put them in his attache case and he and Steven left for the evening.

After they got into the car and started for home, Steven said, "Cody, please don't leave me out of this investigation. I can take care of myself even though you think of me as your ...Little Brother. This investigation means everything to me. I don't think I have to explain that."

"No, Steven, you don't. It means everything to both of us. I have no intention of leaving you out of the investigation. After all, who else can we trust now. I don't even trust my superior right now. I am going to have to make a report to him and I don't know how much I should put in the report. Hopefully, I won't hear from him until we get back from Glenville tomorrow and I can better define what we have found out."

Steven looked at Cody as he said, "Mama and Traci are wondering why you are working at night this week. I told them that you and Nick are working on three murder cases and that is going to take a lot of time to get new leads, especially on the two old ones. That you all would be working all kinds of hours, meeting witnesses, etc." Then he grinned and said, "I, also, told them that I would be working with you because I wanted to become an investigator. That worked. So now we do not have to worry about answering questions from them."

"Thanks, Little Brother."

Steven looked at Cody and with a stern voice said, "You're welcome, Cody." *Cody knew that Steven did not like being called 'Little Brother' around the department so he refrained from doing that, but outside the department, he would always be his Little Brother.*

Cody just looked at him and grinned. *Steven knew that he got the message.*

Then Steven noticed that they were going toward the station where Cody worked. "Where are we going now?"

"I thought while we were out, we would ride around the parking lot at the station and see who is working tonight, especially with dark cars with 396 on their tag. In your travels and around the downtown office, you will be checking during the day tomorrow."

"That's cool, man. Glad to."

"You know, Cody, I am looking forward to seeing Tex again. I like him very much. He seems like one of us. Not at all like I pictured Texans to be like." Then he laughed. "Remember when he was here before, he picked Mom up and started dancing with her outside. Dad did not know what to think, but everyone was caught up in it and started dancing, too. We all had a good time."

"Yes, he is fun to be around. That was the best thing that could have happened to me outside of my own family was to meet him. It was like we were destined to be good friends. I have never felt about anyone else like I do him. ...Other than our family and Corrie, of course."

"How long do you think he will stay?"

"I don't know, but he said he was going to help with this investigation until it was solved. And I am sure that he meant it even if he will have to quit his job in Houston. So, you see, Bro, we mean as much to him as he means to us. I would do the same thing if the situation were reversed. See what I mean."

Steven smiled, "Yes, I do."

They were quiet for a while as they rode around the parking lot slow and then went into the garage, but did not see anything worth checking out. Then they headed for home. Mama E and Traci were already in bed, so they went upstairs softly and into their bedrooms.

Chapter 4
Glenville, Georgia

The next morning Steven went to work and Cody went to pick up Nick and they headed for Glenville. They stopped about half-way there at a town called Sandy Hill and ate breakfast at a restaurent that was located in the middle of town. Most of your small South Georgia towns are similar with just a couple of red lights. Most of the stores are feed and seed, drugstore, family dollar, hardware, a couple of clothing stores, Hardee's, Huddle House and a family-owned restaurant. The citizens of Sandy Hill were very friendly and spoke to them as they got out of the car and went into the restaurant. When they had finished their breakfast, they continued their journey to Glenville with a few comments about the case and their work. They were a little early so they decided to go into a cafe there and get a cup of coffee. They received a friendly welcome from the patrons and workers there. When they had finished their coffee and paid their bill, they drove around town looking for the address that was given them.

They drove up to the address and Angel came out of the house. As she got near the car, she said, "Could we go somewhere else to talk. I don't want my neighbors seeing this car in my friend's yard."

Nick said, "It is an unmarked car, but if that is what you prefer, we'll do it."

She said, "You can still tell that it is a police car. Let's go around the corner. There is an abandoned store and very few people go down that street. We'll just stay in the car if you don't mind."

Cody could see that Angel was frightened, but he was unsure as to how her mind was working and what her plans were. He wanted to make sure that he and Nick were protected from any accusations. So before he answered her, he asked, "Is your friend in the house?"

"Yes, she and her mother are inside."

Then Cody said, "I think it would be best if you and I go into the house and Nick will park the car up the street. How is that?"

"That will be fine. I just don't want my friend to get in trouble."

Nick said, "She won't get in any trouble." Then he smiled and said, "Angel, we don't always bring trouble. We do good sometimes, too." He wanted to get her to relax more and she did.

So Cody got out of the car and walked up to the door behind Angel. He could see the mother and daughter just inside the doorway. So, he walked inside the house with Angel while Nick drove the car down the street and turned around and came back and parked down from the address and across the street at a vacant lot.

When he came in, Cody introduced him, 'This is Angel's friend, Jamie and her mother, Mrs. Thomas. And this is Corporal Carillo. We are working on Darrel's case together."

Mrs. Thomas led them to the table and she went into the kitchen to make some coffee. Angel sat down across from them and Jamie sat with her putting her hand on top of Angel's on the table.

Cody said, "Angel, please don't be afraid of us. We are here to solve Darrel's murder. ...To find the person or persons that killed him. We are on your side. ....You don't mind if we record your interview, do you? We like to make sure that what information we have is accurate."

"No, but will I have to testify in court when that time comes?"

Nick said, "That depends on what you have to tell us. You may or you may not. If we can convict this killer without your testimony, we will. But we want you to understand that there is a good possibility that you will have to testify in court. We do not want to mislead you. Do you understand that?"

"Yes, I do."

As Nick was taking out the recorder, he said, "Alright, I am going to switch on the recorder and at anytime you want to stop it and say something that you do not want recorded, give me a signal. O.K."

She smiled. "O.K."

So Nick turned the recorder on, "Angel, this is Sergeant Cody Edwards and I am Corporal Nick Carillo with the Little County Sheriff's Office. Today is April 29, 1990, and we are here to interview you in reference to Darrel Douglas' murder, but first I would like to ask you a question. Are you being coerced or forced to give this statement? Also, have you been promised anything in order to give it?"

"No, I am giving this statement of my own free will and, no, I have not been promised anything."

Then Nick said, "First, say your full name and in your own words, tell us what you know about the murder of Darrel Douglas. I understand that you were his girlfriend, is that right?"

She frowned as though it was still hard for her to talk about him and then a calm came over her and she said, "Yes. My name is Angeline Stevens and I have known Darrel Douglas most of our lives. We had been neighbors and had gone to school together as well. He and I have been going together steady for two and a half or three years."

Then Cody asked, "Angel, when did Darrel get into the drug scene?"

Angel looked at him for a moment and then said, "When we were in the eighth grade, a senior approached Darrel and asked if he wanted to make some money. I begged him not to and at first, Darrel said, 'No'. But my birthday was coming up in a couple of months and he decided to sell some pills a couple of times and then he would not sell anymore. He did not tell me he was doing that. And when my birthday came and he gave me a birthstone ring. I asked him where he got the money because I knew that he did not have a job and his mother did not have that much money that she would give him to buy me a present. It was expensive. I gave the ring back to him and asked him to take it back to the store and get his money back. It wasn't that I didn't want the ring, I did. It was beautiful, but I knew how he had bought it. He said he wanted me to have it. I told him that I would keep it, but I was not going to wear it until he quit selling drugs. He promised me he would stop, but he never did. Once you start, they won't let you stop. Then they made him sell stronger drugs: such as crack, cocaine and more pills."

She put her head down in her hands and cried. She said as she sobbed, "I have never had the ring on my finger." Nick switched off the recorder. He wanted to say something to her that would console her, but he didn't know what to say. Finally, he said, "I know that it is hard for you to talk about it, but you are doing real good. Take your time." By then, Mrs. Thomas had brought out the coffee and some pastries that she had made early that morning. She poured the coffee for them. They made small talk for several minutes. Then Angel said that she was ready to start again. So Nick switched the recorder on again.

She said in an angry voice, "I begged and begged him to stop, but he kept saying, 'I can't. The Big Man won't let me stop. They are watching me all the time.' I asked him who was watching him and he said, 'Wilson, his probation officer. He is the one that reports us if we don't do what we are told.' He is the one that gives them the drugs to sell. I don't know who else is involved. He would not give me names because he did not want me to get involved. I was with him one time when he received a phone call from his probation officer. He told me that he had to leave. I asked him where he was going. He said, 'I have to take some pills up on the hill.' He would not let me go with him. They call the section near the Country Club 'The Hill'. ...He hated every minute of it. Once you start, you can't stop. .. ....That is about all I know. He did tell me he was going to the police, but I don't know if he did or not. It wasn't but a day or two after that conversation that he was killed."

Cody asked, "Do you know any of the other kids that are selling for the Big Man?"

"No, Darrel wouldn't give me any names, but I assume they would probably be the ones that are under Darrel's probation officer."

Then Cody asked again, "Can you think of anything else that you could tell us. Anything at all. Sometimes, the smallest and simplest things are important."

"No. I can't think of anything else right now. I don't know if I have been of any help, but I sure hope you can catch whoever killed him."

Nick said, "Angel, we are going to do our best. You have been a big help to us." Then he switched off the recorder. He then handed her a card with his home phone number and Cody did the same. Then Nick continued, "If at anytime you remember anything, please call either one of us day or night. Would you do that?"

"Yes, I will."

Then Cody asked, "Do you feel safe here?"

"Yes. It's been ten months. If they were going to come after me, they probably would have by now."

Cody smiled at her and put his hand on her shoulder and said, "You are very brave. You keep in touch with us. O.K."

She smiled, "Sure."

They thanked her and said they would contact her.

They thanked Mrs. Thomas for the coffee and for her time because she sat right there prodding Angel along.

After they got in the car, Nick said, 'Well, we got another lead, the probation officer. Also, the Big Man lives on the hill near the Country Club."

Cody said, grinning, "Yes, I think we should go by the Probation Office and shake up our Probation Officer Wilson. What do you think?"

Nick said, laughingly, "That's a good idea. We're getting there now, huh?"

"Cody, looking at Nick grinning, said, "Yep, we're getting there. ..You know, after we talk with him, the Big Man is gonna know that we are investigating these murders. We need some more information before we talk to him. When I talk to him, I want to bring him to the station. We'll go to the station and while I am writing a report to give to Moss, you go to Juvenile Division and get a list of all the teenagers that are on probation. If you run into Traci, don't give her anymore information than you have to. O.K. I'll tell her in my own time about this investigation." He looked at Nick and Nick nodded.

When they got to the office, their door was open and Lieutenant Moss was sitting at Cody's desk. Cody was very angry and it was all he could do to control his anger. He did not like anyone sitting at his desk and going through his desk.

"May I ask why you are sitting at my desk, Lieutenant?"

"Yes, I wanted to know how the investigation is going."

"All you had to do was ask, Lieutenant. I was just going to write a report for you when I got here."

Cody walked over and closed the door softly and said, "Sir, I don't appreciate anyone sitting at my desk and going through my things unless I invite them to do so. I don't think you would like it, either. ...Sir."

"I'm sorry, Sergeant. You're right. I should not have set behind your desk. I haven't gone through your things. In fact, I just walked in. I found a key and wanted to see if it fit, and it does. And while we are here, I would like to discuss the cases." Then he got up from the chair and walked around to the opposite chair in front of the desk and sat down.

In the meantime, Nick had sat down at his desk. He felt that he should be quiet and let Cody do the talking unless he was asked. He could tell Cody was really angry and trying to hold his temper. He also wanted to calm his partner down if he had to, but Cody was doing a good job of it for now.

Cody, still feeling some anger, said, "Sir, the information that we have up to now indicate that drugs are involved in these murders and that they could very well be connected. We are having to start from scratch on this investigation. I am not sure if you are aware that there are a lot of statements, reports and information missing from these files. Are you, Sir?"

"Yes, Sergeant, I was aware of it. I looked at the files when I took over this office and, also, before I assigned these cases to you. It was decided a week ago that these cases would be assigned to you because your father had worked on them. Like I said before, I can trust you and Corporal Carillo to do a good job. I put my two best investigators on these cases....And I might add, I know that this is a big and dangerous job for you to do. I will stand behind you every step of the way." *He was letting them know that he knew what was ahead of them. He wanted them to know that they could trust him.*

Cody smiled but he was still cautious, "Thank you, Sir. The information that we have is that John Harris was evidently the witness to Koster's' murder. We think that was why he was killed."

"How did you know there was a witness?"

"Whoever took the papers out of the file failed to remove this page." And Cody handed him the page that mentioned a witness.

"Good, I missed that when I looked over the file, but I just glanced through it to see what was left of the file."

Then Cody put the bait in to make sure that the Lieutenant was on the level. He said, "Today, we found out that a probation officer is involved in the drug deals. We plan to talk to him later. Hopefully, by tomorrow."

"Good, I knew I could count on you two. Sergeant, I don't need a written report on these cases. It would be best if you keep everything that is involved with these cases at a minimum and with you. If we start making copies and giving it out to even me, we are taking a chance that whoever is involved in these cases will be looking for anything we have on these cases.... They have already started searching my office. And, Cody, that is why, when I found this key, I wanted to know if it fit this office. I do not want any keys laying around that fit this office and mine. I have a locksmith coming in later, when most everyone has gone, to change the locks on this office and mine. You two and I will be the only ones to have a key. And I assure you that I will not come into this office again unless one of you are here and I expect you two to do the same for me. The key you have will also fit my office. I want it that way in case of emergency that you have to go in there. .....O.K., enough for now. Carry on. Keep up the good work and with your time."

Then the Lieutenant or Acting Captain went out the door and they looked at each other and were a little puzzled at some of the things that he had said. Even though he was Acting Captain, he still wanted to be called Lieutenant. If and when he made Captain, then he would be called Captain. That was the way that he wanted it.

Nick got out the debugger and swept the office. It was clean as well as they could tell. Nick, looking at Cody, could tell that Cody was still burning, but he was sure that it was not so much at the Lieutenant as it was of the overall problems with the cases. Wanting to give Cody a few minutes to be alone, he said, "I'll go get the list. See you later."

Cody nodded. He was still thinking about Moss. *He must be on the level. We will know by tomorrow when we go to see the probation officer.*

By the time Nick came back, Cody had written down all the advantages of their investigation. He liked to work this way because he would have all the important details all together and could look at everything at a moment's notice. This is kept separate from the files. He had his own folder. So when Nick walked in, Cody handed him what he had written down and Nick handed Cody the list.

After a moment of reading, Nick said, "Good, looks like we are getting somewhere. ....I noticed that on the list I gave you, there are six out of fifteen that have been arrested for selling drugs while on probation. These are all Wilson's boys. While there, I got the other list that is in your hands for the boys of the other probation officers. There are five probation officers in this district. They have fifteen or sixteen boys each under their supervision. Of the sixty-two boys of the four other probation officers, there have been eleven arrests while on probation. Six of these arrests were for burglary and five were for selling drugs. These eleven are distributed between the four other probation officers. You expect some to fall back into their old life, but six out of fifteen under the same probation officer. These six were put back on probation under Wilson. Of the eleven arrests of the other groups, only three were placed back on probation. the other eight are in Juvenile Detention now. That is something to check out."

Cody was looking at Nick with a stunned look on his face. Then he said, "Yes, it is. I was thinking about going to talk to these boys, but if we do, it would spook Wilson before we talked to him. I think we should talk to him first thing in the morning. Bring him in here and put pressure on him. Then talk to the boys later. We will have to earn their trust first. Then they will talk."

Nick said as he was smiling at Cody, "Yes, I want to see his face when we confront him. ....Are you about ready for something to eat. You know, we didn't have lunch. After eating that pastry that Mrs. Thomas served us, I haven't thought about food until now. I'll stop by Mom's and get a sandwich to eat. That will last until dinner."

"Yeah, it's too late for lunch now and too early for dinner. I'll get a sandwich at home. ....There is not much we can do here now. See you after dinner. I hope you don't mind us meeting at your place.

We could meet at our place, but you know the problem we would have there with Traci and Mom."

"Oh, no. I don't want to be put on the spot with your Mom, trying to answer her questions. My place is fine."

Then Cody grinned and said, "We will probably be meeting every night this week. I know this will put a damper on your going out.....

Before Cody could finish, Nick said, "No, this is important. I am not answering to anyone except myself so don't worry about that. There will be plenty of time to go out and celebrate when we catch these bastards." He was really getting into this investigation.

Cody laughed. "That's the spirit. I'm glad Corrie thinks like her brother and understands our job and responsibilities. I am going to ride around the parking lot before going home. See you later."

They both left at the same time.

That night at dinner, Traci announced that Rich had called her and invited her to dinner for Friday night. So, she finally accepted to try again.

Steven asked, "What made you change your mind? You were so angry at the way his mother talked down to you and the things she said to you. I am just curious, that is all, Sis. By the way, I like Rich."

"Thank you Steven, he said that his Dad had really belittled her and told her she had to apologize. His Dad can be very arrogant and rude when he wants to be. So I decided I would go this time and see what happens. Everyone deserves a second chance. I guess I feel sorry for Rich, but I still can not see anything coming out of this relationship. I have tried to get that through Rich's head, but he won't take 'no' for an answer."

Cody said, "I agree with you, Trac, on the second chance, but don't take no crap from them or anyone."

"You know me, Bro. I am an Edwards, too."

They all laughed.

Mama E said, "I am glad you are going out. She is driving me crazy staying home every night. She gets bored very easily, and I like my peace and quiet at night. .....By the way, Cody, you are working hard on these cases. I know what Steven told me but you are working all day and half the night. Take care of yourself. Don't run yourself down. Are you trying to catch up so that when Tex comes in, you'll have some time off. If you are, that would be great for you all to spend some time together without working."

"No, Mom, we have two old murders and one new one that Nick and I are working on. We have some new leads and we are checking them out. Also, Steven is helping us out. That's all. When we were in Houston last weekend, Nick, Tex, Mr. Tyler and I were seeing who could tell the tallest tale, I guess. We had fun in doing so, anyway. Tex is coming for a visit and also going to work with us on these cases. He volunteered to come. He want to see what Georgia is like living here. I think he has another motive, but he wouldn't commit himself." Cody laughed, looking at Traci. *He was also trying to direct the conversation in another direction. Although Tex had not given him any indication that he was interested in Traci, Cody felt that what he said was true.*

Traci looked at her brother with a growl on her face and said, "Oh, no, you don't, not again. I did have a crush on him when he was here before, but I have grown up a little more now. Besides, he didn't give me the time of day, except as a friend and that is fine with me."

Steven spoke up, "Sis, you don't understand males. You may think he didn't give you the time of day, but when you weren't looking, believe me, he was watching you. It's a male thing. You stay low and watch while the other males make their play for a girl, then before you know it, the one watching you is making a different play. He doesn't want to appear like the average joe, if you know what I mean."

They all laughed and then Cody said, "Watch out, Little Brother. Don't give away our secrets, but I noticed that, too. And, Sis, Tex is not serious about anyone in Texas. If he was, he would not be coming here to stay awhile."

Mama E, smiling, "You, kids. I don't know what I would do without you. You keep me going. When I get depressed, I think of how lucky I am that I have you three with me. I am so proud of all three of you. Your father would be too."

Steven said, "I'm glad, Mom, because you are going to have a hard time getting rid of us, or me especially."

Cody said, "Well, I hate to break this up, but Steven, we better get started if we are going to get any work done. Mom, we are working mostly at Nick's place or the office. You can reach us at either place if you need either of us."

So they got up from the table and got their things and took off to Nick's place. They were silent on the drive there. Finally, Steven said, "I didn't have any luck checking the cars in the parking lot. I did see several dark cars, but none of them had a tag with the numbers 396 on them. I'll keep looking for it up town. I talked with Susan. She said that she was real busy, but she would try to get the list in the morning, if possible."

"Good. I looked around the station a couple of times today, too, but I haven't seen it either. It is bound to turn up sooner or later."

"I, also, went to the bank, but Dad did not have an extra box there. Knowing Dad, he kept an extra copy of everything important to protect himself, especially, in something like this."

By this time, they were at Nick's place. Also, Corrie's car was there.

As they walked in, Nick said, "I asked Corrie to come over. I thought you might want her to type up your report. She brought her typewriter over. We will set it up on this table. That way she won't be running back and forth. This will be better suited for what we want her to do."

"Yes, that will be great. It is a lot better trying to read something typed rather than my hand writing. Thanks, Corrie." He leaned over and gave her a quick kiss on the lips and squeezed her shoulders.

They settled down at the table while Nick got out three beers and set them on the table. "We can't work unless we have these. Corrie, would you like something to drink?"

"No, thank you."

Steven said, "Nick, I didn't have any luck reference the safety deposit box, nor looking for a certain car. I will have the list of vehicles in the morning, though."

"Great, that list should help us locate the car. Do either of you have any idea as to where your father's hiding place might be? ....Cody, you said that he was famous for keeping his own information to protect himself."

"I have looked everywhere at home that I think he would have hid it and I haven't come up with anything."

Steven looked at Cody with a puzzled look on his face, "Bro, you know there are filing cabinets in the office at the barn. But Jake would have said something at the time of his death if there were anything important there."

"I have already asked Jake and he said there was not anything, nor a hiding place there that he knew of, but we were welcome to look."

Nick said, "I am changing the subject, but Cody, what did you think of the Lieutenant's remarks today?"

Cody shook his head, "I want to believe him and he gave me the impression that he was telling the truth, but I mentioned the probation officer intentionally. So, we will see tomorrow morning when we go to get the probation officer. I want to believe him. He knew that information was missing from the file, but he didn't tell us in the beginning. I don't know. We will have to wait and see. But don't say too much in front of him for now."

"I won't. You are the lead investigator and I am not going to say anything unless he ask me. Then it will be as little as possible. In one way, he gives me the impression that he is trustworthy, and in another, he puts a doubt in my mind."

They grinned at each other. Cody had the same feeling and knew exactly what Nick was saying. They did work good together.

After Corrie typed up Angel's interview, Cody gave it to Steven to read. She typed up Cody's report, talked with them for a few minutes and then she left. Nick and Cody did not want her involved no more than necessary.

After Steven finished reading Angel's interview, he said, "The Big Man living on the hill near the Country Club. That is where Rich lives."

"Yes, that's right, Little Brother, and our sister is going out with Rich tomorrow night. Do you think that could be a coincident?"

Steven thought for a moment and said, "You know, it does seem strange that the father would jump all over the mother and force her to apologize to Traci for what she said. Then, again, he could be sincere. I think he likes Traci or he was always nice to her. We're know after tomorrow night, won't we, ...Big Brother."

Cody looked at Nick and grinned. Nick knew that Steven didn't like being called Little Brother and that Cody did it just for spite. Cody is very proud of his younger brother.

Cody, looking at Nick said, "Tomorrow morning we will pick up Wilson and bring him to the station and question him. That should start something rolling because whoever in our office is involved will make sure the Big Man knows. It has to be someone in our office who destroyed information from these files. Also, I plan to talk to

Lieutenant Moss. We need to know for sure if he will back us up or not. I think the best thing to do is lay it on the table."

Nick said, "Maybe, we should have him in on the questioning of Wilson. That way we can see if he shows any sign of wanting to get some answers."

"Maybe, we will. At least, we will know where we stand. If he is with us, he will approve some warrants to check bank accounts of some of the people on the hill. But we have got to come up with a good reason with names in order to do that. Angel did not know the exact address."

Steven said, "The hill is in my territory. I can go by and talk to Jan at the Court House. If she is in a good mood, she may help me look up some of the names." *Steven was also thinking about asking Lana for a date. She lived there on the hill. He saw her at a party the other night and she was making eyes at him. He felt that she was out of his league, but he knew a flirt when he saw one. It wouldn't hurt to try. I am not going to say anything to Cody or Nick about it now. I don't like to use people, but this is important. Besides, she is asking me for a date by flirting with me.*

Nick laughed. "Steven, you really do get around, don't you? Oh, to be young again."

Steven said, laughingly, "You never get serious about someone until you are ready to settle down. It pays to play the field."

They all laughed. As they drank a couple more beers, they discussed the Lieutenant and Probation Officer Wilson as to what they needed to know from them.

After about an hour, Cody said, "I have a feeling that tomorrow will be a busy and long day. We better get some sleep tonight. I have a gut feeling that we are going to have a new perspective on things by then."

So Cody and Steven left and drove home in silence. When they got home, they found Traci sitting in front of the television. She said, "I'm glad to see you two. I set up so I could ask you something. When I mentioned about going out with Rich tomorrow night, you both had a surprised look on your face. Do you think I should go out with Rich?"

Cody looked at Steven and said, "Sure, if you want to. Like you said, everybody deserves a second chance. You are the one to make that decision. Are you having second thoughts about this for some reason?"

"No, I just got the impression that you didn't want me to go."

"No, Sis, if there was a reason that we didn't want you to do something, we would tell you and then demand that you didn't do it."

Steven put his arm around her shoulder and said, "Sis, don't worry, we will always be here for you and we will look out for what is best for you. If there is anything, we will let you know. Remember that."

She turned around and kissed him on the cheek and said, "I know that you will, you two. Goodnight. I feel better." Then she went upstairs to her room and closed the door. *She didn't understand the feeling that she had about that date. She wanted to go, but yet, she didn't and she didn't know why.*

Steven and Cody looked at one another, but said nothing. They went upstairs and into their bedrooms and closed the door.

The next morning at the office, Cody got there before Nick did and found that their key did not fit the door. Then Cody remembered that the Lieutenant said he was going to have the locks changed. So Cody went to the Lieutenant's office. He was there. So Cody went in and closed the door behind him. They said their good mornings and Cody sat down across from his desk.

"Lieutenant, evidently, the locks were changed, my key doesn't fit now."

"Yes, they were. Here is your key and one for Nick. I have one, also. This key will fit your office as well as mine. We are the only ones that have a key for either office." Then Moss stopped a moment and then said, "I understand that you are going to question a probation officer this morning. Is that correct or did I hear wrong?"

Cody said, "Yes Sir, that is correct. We have a witness saying that he is involved in selling drugs. We plan to bring him here and question him. Would you like to be in on the questioning?"

Moss, not liking the undertone in Cody's voice, said, "Sergeant, maybe I started off wrong by not telling you all that I know about these cases. It seems to me that we are playing cat and mouse here. You don't know whether you can trust me or not and I can understand your feelings. I should have told you about the missing reports in the files, but I wanted you to get the feel of what this is about without me telling you. I wanted you to come to me with your information, but I can see where I was wrong. It only made you feel that you could not trust anyone here, and especially me. To set your mind at ease, I know what this involves and you are right about trusting people."

Then there was a knock on the door. Moss motioned for Nick to come in as he said, "Come in." Nick came into the room, "I'm sorry, Sir, but I couldn't get in our office."

"That's alright, Corporal. Come around and set down. Sergeant Edwards and I were just getting ready to discuss these cases. I am glad that you are here. Cody can fill you in on what has been said before. I was just going to tell him what I know of these cases. I knew that selling drugs are involved in these cases and that there is corruption in our local government. I don't know if it goes to the state level or even federal level, but I want my best two investigators to find out. I know that I did not give you much to go on and I still haven't because I don't know who is involved. ....The reason that I know this is because Captain Edwards told me before he was killed. The last week before he was killed, he called me in and told me that much. He wanted me to know in case something happened to him. I knew he was getting close to something, but he wouldn't give me any names. He was my superior so I accepted what he said. I certainly wasn't expecting him to go so soon."

Cody said in a more friendly voice, "Sir, my father always had a backup of anything that was important or to protect himself. Did he say anything to you about it?"

"No, he didn't say anything to me, but you are welcome to look if you feel he hid it in here. Since I have been in here, I have looked for anything that might give me a clue as to why he was at the place where he was killed, but I haven't found anything."

Cody, feeling better about the Lieutenant, said, "Sir, I may take you up on looking in here, but I want you to be here when I do."

"You may look now if you like." So the three of them looked all around, pulling drawers out and looking on the bottom and all in the desk in the file cabinets and everywhere they could think of but nothing turned up anywhere.

After a few minutes, Cody said, "Nick, I think we need to go and pick up Wilson." Then he looked at Moss. "Sir, we will take him to our office since it is away from the other offices around here. You may join us there, if you like."

"I will, Sergeant. Let me know when you get back."

Cody said smilingly, "Thank you, Sir. I am glad we had this talk. I have a better perspective on things."

"Me, too. Like I said, I should have told you before what it involved, but I wanted to see what you could find out and see if it confirms what little I know and I see that it does. See you later."

They left and went to their office and put their things away. Cody gave Nick his key and then they left to go pick up Wilson. They both were feeling good about Lieutenant Moss. Maybe he could be trusted and would do what he could to help them investigate these cases.

Chapter 5

When Nick and Cody got to the Probation Office, Wilson was in his office by himself with his feet propped up on his desk. He looked at them with a frown on his face, "Who the hell are you?"

Cody said as he looked him in the eye, "We came to to be of service to you. In fact, we came to give you a free ride to the station so you can answer a few questions for us. So, we are asking you to come down to the station with us." Cody was trying to be as nice as he could be for now.

"For what. I'm not going anywhere with you until you tell me what this is about."

Nick spoke up, sternly, "O.K. You don't want to cooperate with us. We can pick up six of your kids and they will talk, but we would rather hear it from you."

Wilson frowned, then answered, "Alright, I'll go with you voluntarily." *He was anxious to find out what they had and he did not want them to talk to the boys. They know something because they said six kids.*

Cody was looking around as they walked to the car to see if anyone was there, but he did not see anyone around. He had noticed the log on the table when they went in that the other probation officers were signed out. They rode in silence on the way to the station. Nick and Cody did not want to say anything. They wanted Wilson to squirm a little before being questioned.

When they got to the station, Cody walked with Wilson to his office while Nick went to let Lieutenant Moss know they were back.

After they all got settled in the office. Cody said, "Wilson, we know that you are involved with selling drugs and have six of your kids and possibly more selling it for you. Would you like to tell us about it?"

Wilson tried to put a blank expression on his face, but they could tell that he was worried. "I don't know what you are talking about."

"Yes, you do. We want to know what you know about the drugs. You give us what information you have or you take the fall. This is your only chance."

"You don't have anything on me. You either arrest me or let me go."

Nick looked at Cody and said, "Would you want to arrest him now or let it be known that Wilson came in voluntarily and talked?" Cody knew that just bringing him to the station had shook him up, and, just maybe, it would get something started.

Then Lieutenant Moss had the same idea and spoke up, "I think I would let the others take care of him. Let him go. He's too dumb to know that we are offering him a deal here. Besides, you have the kids. I would rather give them a chance to do the right thing."

Wilson looked from one and then the other with a worried look on his face. They let it sink in as to what they were going to do. Then Cody said, "Nick, take Wilson back. We don't need him, anyway. I have someone else that will talk."

Nick said, "O.K. Wilson, let's go. We'll let the others take care of you."

Wilson was looking more worried now. He said, "Who else are you going to talk to?"

Cody said, "Don't let it bother you. You had your chance. Take him, Nick. Oh, by the way, go through the front office."

Wilson was really beginning to look worried wondering what Cody had in mind. As Nick led Wilson out, Cody followed him to the front office. Cody wanted to see who was in the office and who Wilson would look at when he walked through. Cody looked around and saw Moss standing behind him. Then Wilson had a change of expression on his face as he looked toward Garcia. And Garcia looked up and straight at Wilson with a surprise look on his face. Then he looked down.

As they went out the door, Cody looked back at the Lieutenant and said, "Sir, did you see what I saw?"

Moss smiled and said, "Brilliant, Edwards, brilliant. We now know who destroyed information out of the files."

"Yes, we do. Now we have to find out some things about Garcia."

"Go for it, Sergeant."

They walked back to Cody's office. Moss sat down and said, "Cody, I assigned you and Nick because you are my two most trustworthy investigators, but I also knew by instinct that you never thought your father's death was an accident and neither do I. I want you to know that. I will back you one hundred percent. Don't you ever forget that."

Cody smiled. "Thank you, Sir. This has been a day to remember for me and I am grateful for it."

"I'll go and let you get to work. Keep me informed. I don't need a written report. The less information laying around, the better."

"Yes Sir."

After he left, Cody got on the computer and started looking up information on Garcia and making a list of his closest friends that he knew about. Of course, he could only get the basic information that was on the computer for all the law enforcement officers. Then, he checked his social security number, driver's license number, what organizations he belonged and any information he could think of. He printed out what information he could find that they would want to check, but it wasn't very much. They could check his address as to what his salary is. He was living alone, or at least he was divorced and had listed no one living with him. Also, find out what type of car he was driving or owned.

By the time Nick got back, Cody had marked the information to check out on Garcia. He told him about Garcia and what the Lieutenant had said. Then he showed him what he had printed out.

Nick said laughing, "Looks like we need to watch Garcia and see who his friends are. ....You know, this address is not on the hill but it is in an area where you need to have money to keep up with the neighbors."

"Yes, that is what I thought. ....Nothing to do here now. Let's get out and take a ride and see Steven and then go to the hill section and look around. By the way, did Wilson have anything to say on the way back to the Probation Office?"

"Yeah, he wanted to know if he could think about it and talk to us later. I told him that he had his chance and now it was too late. He was quiet the rest of the way, but he was thinking a mile a minute."

"Good. At least he knows that we know he is involved with drugs. We need to watch him for awhile, too. We didn't think to ask Angel if she knew what day Darrel was given the drugs to sell. She probably didn't know, but we should have asked her. It would make it easier on us to watch him. He probably thinks we are watching him now."

After a moment, Cody said, "Steven mentioned that we should look up the night that Kevin was killed. That will give us an approximate time the drugs come in." As Cody was talking, he was opening Kevin's file. "He was killed on a Thursday night. Tex will be in tomorrow night. We can put Tex on his tail since he doesn't know Tex."

Nick said as he was laughing. "That will be a good idea. I am sure Tex will appreciate that. And I know he will have a comment about that."

Cody joined in laughing. "We want to start him off easy to see if he can do the job."

They put their files away and locked the door and took off in Nick's car. They went into town at the main office and went by Steven's desk, but he wasn't in the office. As they were leaving the parking lot, Steven drove in and saw them and parked his car and came over to see them.

Steven grinned and said, "Hi, Big Brother and Nick. What brings you two to this part of town?"

Cody said, "We brought Wilson in this morning, but he wouldn't tell us anything. We didn't really expect him to, but on the way out his expression changed when he saw Garcia looking at him."

"Oh, Hmm, he gave you more than he thought he did, didn't he?"

"Yep, Little Brother." They laughed.

Steven said, "I knew you were going to get it in somewhere." They laughed again.

"Nick and I are going by the telephone company to get a list of calls from his phone for the past year. That will give us some more information. Did Susan come through for us?"

"Yes, she did, ...Big Brother." He opened his book and took out a list of the vehicles and a list of the people that lived near the Country Club and gave both lists to him. "I think you will find this helpful. It seems that either the Major or Internal Affairs may have some problems. They both drive dark cars with tag numbers starting with 3. The Major live on the Hill."

Cody looking at both lists, said, "Yes, it will be very helpful. We are going to take a ride on the Hill and look around. This will be helpful."

Steven said, "Don't count on me tonight. I have a date."

They laughed as they were shaking their heads.

Cody said, "We will probably take tonight off, too, unless something comes up. There isn't anything pending for tonight. I need to take Corrie out. She has been great. ..We are going to take your advice and give Tex the chore of following Wilson to see when the drugs come in."

Nick asked grinning at Steven, "Steven, who is your date tonight, Jan or Susan?"

He said sarcastically, "I'll keep you guessing, but they gave me this information voluntarily, but I will probably take them out to dinner one night." He laughed and then continued, "separately."

They all laughed.

They drove off and Steven went into the building.

Nick said, "Now there goes a happy fellow. Oh, to be even two years younger."

"Yeah, you are an old man. I don't know why you are saying that. You are not serious or attached to anyone. You are thinking about us two years ago. That is the way we were."

"Yeah, until you got interested in my sister and now you act like an old man."

Cody looked at him and said, "You wish."

Then Nick had a serious expression on his face, "No, Cody, I am glad you and my sister hit it off. I will be the first to welcome you into our family."

"That's mighty nice of you." They both grinned.

Cody said, "Well, here we are at the telephone company. I hope Katie will be as accommodating to me as Susan and Jan were to Steven."

Nick laughed, "That's right. You were dating Katie until you and Corrie got together."

Cody looked at him and grinned.

As they walked up to Katie's desk, she looked up and a smile came over her face. "Well, what brings you two here? Good news, I hope."

Cody said, "Hi Katie, you are looking good as ever. How have you been doing?"

"Thanks, and I have been fine, and it is good to see you again. How may I help you?"

"We need a printout of all the phone calls on this number. It is a county number. And, if I am not pushing my luck, we could use the same on this number. It is a residential number." Cody said as he looked sheepishly at Katie.

She smiled and said, "Cody, you always did know how to get what you wanted with that smile. I might add, also, that you were always, well, maybe not always, a gentleman. I will be right back."

They went over to a couple of chairs and sat down and grinned at each other feeling very proud of themselves. One girl that they didn't know came over and offered them a cup of coffee, but they refused.

After about fifteen minutes, Katie came back and handed Cody the papers in an envelope, "Cody, here is a printout of your bill. Hope it will help you. It is good to see you again."

They stood up and Cody said, "Thanks, Katie. Same to you. You don't know how much this means to us."

She knew that it was probably for a case he was working on. "Glad to help any way that I can. See you." And then she turned and walked back behind her desk and smiled as they turned to walk out the door.

After they got into the car, Cody noticed that she had given him the printout that had the names by the phone numbers that called that number. Of course, that meant the name that the phone number was assigned to, not the name of the caller. Evidently, this was something new because the list that he had gotten before, it only gave the phone numbers. Cody started laughing.

Nick looked around at him wondering what had come over Cody, "What the hell is wrong with you? Did Katie write you a note or something?"

Cody looked over the list quickly and said, "No, to both questions. I'll be dammed. He sure made a lot of calls to someone in the main office because of the prefix and vice versa. Their's is not the same as ours. There is an exchange of phone calls to someone in our office, also. These could be legit, but we will need to check them out. But there are a lot of calls on here to and from the phone number of Tanner and, also, several to Samuels house. Samuels, Rich's house. Why would he have contact with the Samuels. They do not have any juveniles living there. According to this, Tanner lives across the street from the Samuels. You know, we better keep this low because I don't know if Katie was suppose to give me all this information. I sure as hell don't want to get her in trouble. We will use this as information for us only unless we find out different. O.K."

"Sure. I am not going to tell anyone where we got that and I am sure you are not. It sure pays to have friends in high places." He laughed as he pulled the car over to the side of the street and stopped.

Cody gave him the printout and let him look at it. Nick whistled, "This is great. There are several numbers that we need to check out. Remind me to thank Katie personally. You don't mind, do you?" Nick really liked what he saw when he looked at Katie, especially her smile.

"Of course not, Katie is a great gal. We are still friends, but I think she is dating someone steady but it doesn't hurt to ask."

"Think I will. Think I will."

Nick started the car up again as he said, "Let's take a ride down that street and look at the houses just for the sake of it. Tanner and Samuels live on this street. Any other names on this street that we should look at while we are here?"

"Sure. That is why we are here. I don't see any other numbers, but we can look around while we are here. The numbers within our department, we will have to look up, naturally. There are some other numbers on this list, but they are probably friends or relatives, or maybe some of his clients. We can check these against the list of boys he has as his clients."

They were silent for a few minutes as they rode by the two houses on the street. They were both looking for anything at all that looked suspicious. Finally, as they were nearing Samuels house, Nick said, "This is where Traci is going tonight, isn't it?"

"Yes, she is. I don't want to alarm her now. I don't think she will be in any danger now as long as she doesn't know anything. She is pretty outspoken and will tell them what she thinks when she feels she has too. In fact, she did a couple of weeks ago. Her words are, 'she is giving Rich's mother a second chance.' And believe me, that is all she will get. There is no third chance with Traci." Cody was feeling very proud of his sister as he pictured her when she was telling him about the night that she ditched Rich at his house.

Nick laughed. "Just like her brothers."

Cody said, "Looks like our probation officer is good friends with the two richest men on the hill or they have business. What do you think?"

"I think they are in business together. Now we have to prove it. Let's go back to the office and check these other numbers with our department numbers."

Nick drove straight back to the office and started checking the numbers. They were getting anxious now to find out who else could be involved. Most of the calls were to Eduardo Garcia in the Investigators Section, a few to Randall Johnson in the Uniform Section and quite a few to Domenic Santino in Internal Affairs.

Cody said, "What would a probation officer have in common with Internal Affairs. Who wants to be friends with anyone in Internal Affairs. Johnson may be legit and Garcia may be legit, but after seeing Wilson and Garcia this morning, I don't think so, unless they are very close friends. We should have gotten a list from Garcia's phone. I didn't think about it. Hand me that list of Wilson's boys."

Nick handed him the list. "I'll be glad to go back and get a copy from Katie." Nick said as he grinned at Cody. *He had been thinking about Katie ever since they left her. She sure made a big impression on me. I have never felt this strong toward a female before, but Cody thinks she is going steady. I like Angie very much and I know she likes me, but we both know that friends is all we can be. We both have accepted that.*

Cody laughed and then Nick joined him. Then Cody started looking at the list of boys that Nick had gotten from the Juvenile Section. Then he went to the base computer in another office and started looking up the information on all of Wilson's boys; the arrest, who arrested them, who handled their cases in court, who the judge was on the cases, etc.

In the meantime Nick was looking over the phone list and checking the vehicle list.

By the time Cody came back to the office, it was getting late so they both left and each went to their home for dinner and to change clothes. They had decided that they would meet for an hour or so at Nick's to bring things up-to-date on Cody's file before going out.

Cody did not get to speak to Steven alone because Steven was in his room getting ready to go out for dinner and he did not want to disturb him. Cody was also taking a shower and getting ready to go out after dinner. Cody decided he would wait until later and let Steven read his report. After having dinner at home, Cody left and went by to pick up Corrie and then they went to Nick's place. While there, they started bringing the report up-to-date.

Corrie started typing what Cody and Nick were telling her. Nick said, "So far, we have Angel linking Probation Officer Robert Wilson to selling drugs, possibly linking Wilson to Eduardo Garcia and Officer Randall Johnson in Uniform and, also, Domenic Santino in Internal Affairs. Outside the department, possibly linking Wilson to Richard Q. Samuels, Sr. and Robert Tanner on the hill. We are drawing a line from one to the other, but we have got to find a way to get evidence to prove all of this."

Cody said, "The tag number 396 on a dark unmarked car did not show up on the vehicle list for this year. Santino has a dark unmarked car assigned to him, but the tag number is 332. O.K., now for the list of boys that are now under Wilson's supervision. The six that have been arrested for selling drugs and went to court had the same attorney each time and the attorney paid their bail. They all got light sentences, doing community service and probation, but no jail time. They went before the same judge, except for two times. But they got light sentences with the other judge, too."

Nick said, "There have been talk about Judge Turner being shady, but nothing has ever been proven. I have not heard any officer say they liked to go before Judge Turner. Most of them complain about him. He and Judge Mason are close friends. That is another suspicious point that need to be checked."

Cody, looking at Corrie and thinking *how beautiful she was, was beginning to get other ideas. He could feel himself losing control. It had been longer than he thought since they had been together and really had good sex. It had been awhile, and now, he was so wrapped up in finding out who had murdered his father that time was slipping away from him.* Losing interest in the work, he said, "Yes, it is, Nick.

That's enough work tonight. Sweetheart, where would you like to go tonight?" Hoping that she would say somewhere that they could be alone.

Corrie, knowing that this was not a good time to be alone with him for her, said smiling up at him, "I feel like dancing. How about you all?"

Nick said, "I think Angie would like that, too. I'll give her a call and we will meet you at Johnnie Lee's. They have a good band on Friday nights."

Corrie said, looking at Cody, "That's fine with me." She could tell that he was disappointed, but she was too. She hoped he would understand. She would explain it to him later.

Just as they were going out the door, Cody was saying, 'We'll go and get a good table for us. It starts to get crowded by nine o'clock. It is only a little after eight now."

Nick had gone out the door and was holding it for Corrie, when all of a sudden, a dark car drove by and a shot rang out. Cody leaned toward Corrie shielding her and shouted, "Get Down." Another shot rang out, but Nick had gotten down on the walkway and saw the car as it speeded off up the street. He came back to them a little shaken and asked, "Are you two alright?" They said they were. But they all were shaken by this and surprised. They had not expected anything like that at this time, anyway.

Then Nick said puzzled, "Cody, the tag number was 396 and it was an unmarked car. In fact, it looked like Santino's or the one that is assigned to him."

"But we checked and it had a different tag number."

They went back into the house looking to see where the bullets hit. One had broken the window so it would be inside. The other was probably in the wall outside.

Nick said, "This calls for a drink." He went over to the bar and poured each a drink and came back. They sat there in silence sipping their drink for a minute. Then Corrie asked in a shaken voice, "What are we going to do now?"

Cody, with his arms still around her, he could feel her shaking. He smiled at her wanting to help calm her, said, "We planned to go dancing and that is where we are going. What about you, Nick?"

"I think we should do just that. This was a warning. They did not intend to hit us. We'll get the bullets in the morning."

So they finished their drink and Cody and Corrie left for Johnnie Lee's and Nick went to pick up Angie. When Cody and Corrie got to the club, it wasn't very crowded. They could get a good table that was sort of in a corner, but yet near the dance floor. They went over and sat down and ordered a drink while they waited for Nick and Angie.

Cody looked at Corrie with concern and asked, "Are you alright? You are quiet tonight, but very beautiful."

"Thank you. I am fine, just a little shook up because I wasn't expected to be shot at tonight."

"I'm sorry, Sweetheart. Nick and I will make them pay, believe me. I know Nick and his temper."

"So do I. I have lived with him all my life. No one does anything bad to Nick or his family and get away with it. I will be fine as soon as this drink take effect." She laughed. And so did he, because he knew that she did not drink very much, but, tonight, this was her second drink.

A couple of minutes later, Nick and Angie came in and sat down at the table and ordered a couple of drinks for them and another round for Cody and Corrie.

Cody and Corrie looked at each other and laughed. Cody knew Corrie was going beyond what she had before. They didn't mention the shooting. Angie wasn't around law enforcement much, except for being with Nick. They dated once in a while, but Nick was not going to be tied down right now. They didn't want to discuss the cases either. They talked about the usual things. Then Nick ordered another round of drinks, but Corrie said, "Hey, Brother, just ginger ale for me. I have had too many as it is." Then she looked at Cody. "I want to remember everything that happens tonight."

Nick said, "That's alright. You could use another one tonight."

By the time the drinks came, the band was beginning to start up. They got up and danced the first dance, then the second, switching dancing partners. Then they sat the third dance out just to relax. They had seen some people that they knew and spoke to them. They were relaxing and getting rid of the tension that had built up over the week and the surprise shots that was fired toward them tonight.

A few minutes later, Nick nodded to Cody to look to his left. He did and he saw Santino at a table about three tables down from them. They could tell that he was watching them, but they acted as though they did not know he was there. But Nick and Cody were also keeping an eye on him.

Angie and Corrie went to the restroom. While they were gone, Steven and Susan came in and immediately saw them and came over to their table. They pulled another table together so they could set together. As they were setting down, Cody winked at Nick, "Susan, I want to thank you for the list of vehicles and tag numbers and their assignments."

Nick said, "Me, too. The information will help us a great deal."

"You're very welcome, but Steven is thanking me by taking me out tonight. We had a wonderful dinner at Michael's Steak House and now he is going to dance with me." She grinned at Steven as she said it. "I got the better end of the deal. All the girls want to go out with Steven so I feel flattered that he asked me even though I bribed him." She was still grinning as he reached over and kissed her on the cheek.

They all laughed.

Then Susan said, "Always glad to help the good guys. I hope that you found what you were looking for."

Steven knew that he could trust her, so he said, "As a matter of fact, it did help a great deal, except for one thing. We were looking for a certain tag number but it wasn't on the list. The list is good for information and checking out other things."

"That is a complete list of all the vehicles that the department has. What number are you looking for?"

Cody said, "This is all confidential, Susan. We are working on murder cases. You understand that, don't you?"

"Yes, of course. I don't discuss my work with anyone outside the department and only a very few within the department."

Cody saw Steven nod and then he said, "Good for you. Because the tag number we are looking for is on a dark unmarked car. The number is 396. That is all the information that we have."

Susan looked as though she was in deep thought for a second, then she said, "The numbers starting with 3 belong to Internal Affairs Section. There is something about that number that bugs me, though. Let me think about it for awhile."

Cody said, "Sure, Anything that you can tell us about it would be of great help. Here comes the girls. End of discussion. We came to enjoy ourselves. Work can wait until Monday."

They all said, "Amen to that."

The girls were back and they ordered another round of drinks and danced the night away. It was around one o'clock when they decided to leave. They all went out to the parking lot together. The others left, but Cody and Corrie sat in their car for a few minutes. He told her that he wanted to see which car belonged to Santino as his personal car. Then he added, "Besides, it will give you some extra time to sober up before going home. Also, what I really want to do is cuddle up with you. That is my main motive."

She laughed and kissed him very passionately. Of course, Cody was very pleased. She was feeling the results of too much alcohol. He knew that and that is why he tried to control himself. Besides, the parking lot was not the place for what he had in mind.

It wasn't long before Santino came out by himself.

As they watched him, he got into a brand new Jaguar. Cody said, "I didn't know anyone on the department made that kind of money. Do you mind if we follow him home?"

She said, "No, I want to be involved and help you as much as I can to solve these cases."

He looked down at her and kissed her on the lips and smiled at her. He wanted her so much, but he knew that it would have to wait. He straightened himself up and tried to think about Santino.

As they followed him, he went straight home. He lived in one of the most expensive condos in the city of Littleton. Cody said grinning, "Remind me to call here and find out the prices of these condos. We might want to live here."

Corrie smiled and said, "Sure, It looks fine to me. It would be nice to look out the window and see the park and the lake. Good view. Huh."

He pulled her close as they stared at the building and kissed her a long time and just held her. Then he said, "Don't get too use to the view. A policeman's salary alone would never be able to afford this."

"I could never get use to living in this, anyway. I wouldn't know how to act."

"Neither would I."

He turned the car around and they headed for home. When they got to Corrie's house, he told her that Tex was coming in tomorrow evening. I don't know the exact time. He is driving by himself so I'll call you when I find out anything."

"Sure, talk to you then."

He kissed her very passionately and then they said their goodbyes. He drove home thinking *about Corrie and how much he loved her. As soon as this investigation is over, we will set a date and fast, too.* Everybody else was in bed except Steven. Cody was thinking as he got ready for bed. *I wonder how Traci's night went. She is in bed already. Hope it was O.K. I know that she does not have the type of feelings for Rich that it takes to make a good relationship. She should just break it off now. Or maybe Tex will when he gets here. I know he cares for Traci more than he is willing to admit.* That was the last thing he remembered before falling asleep.

The next morning when they all were at the breakfast table, Traci announced that she had a great time at Rich's for dinner. They were very nice, but they did ask a lot of questions about her job and her brothers, especially Rich's father. The mother didn't say too much, but she was nice. Rich had asked her out tonight, but she had declined because of Tex coming in and she wanted to be here.

Cody said, "Good, Sis. I'm glad you had a better ending last night than before. I'm, also, glad that you will be here tonight when Tex comes. I know he will be glad to see you.........I'm going over to Nick's for a while. We have some unfinished business that we have to take care of. Steven, would you like to come along?"

"Sure. Just give me a minute."

So, on the way over to Nick's, Cody explained that someone had shot two shots into Nick's place last night as they were leaving. They wanted to dig the bullets out and have them checked.

Steven said, "Evidently, no one was hurt since you all were at the dance last night. Did they aim at you all or was it to scare you?"

"I think just to scare us, but the ironic thing is that Nick saw the car and it was a dark unmarked car with the tag number 396. ..Get that, 396. That number is not on this year's list of tag numbers," Cody said, a little frustrated.

Steven said, "Susan and I talked about that on the way home last night. Maybe, it is an old one, but we do turn the old ones in when we get a new one. Susan was puzzled about that number last night, but then she forgot about it. She did say that she was going to check on it. I'll go see her Monday morning and ask her if she had found out anymore information."

Cody, looking at Steven, started grinning. Then said, "I wonder why she forgot about it."

Steven laughed, "You'll never hear it from me, Big Brother."

"Just kidding. But, Steven, thanks, we appreciate everything you are doing to help us."

"Hey, man, I have a stake in this, too. I would be furious with you and Nick if you left me out of this. What I really want is to have Casey come back and identify the voice of the man that shot Dad."

"Me, too. Steven. And we will soon. We want to get a little more information as to who all is involved before we do that. Also, we don't want to expose her as a witness too soon. She is our ace in the hole."

"I understand. I am just so frustrated and anxious to get to the end of the investigation without going through the beginning and middle of the other murders."

"I know, I am, too. But there are a lot of other people involved in these cases other than our family."

When they pulled up to Nick's place, he was digging in the wall of his porch. They got out of the car and walked up on the porch. Steven asked, "Have you found anything yet?"

"Yeah, I got the slug out of the living room and now I have this one. It looks like a .38. We'll turn these in Monday morning." As he held them out for Cody to see, he said, "You all come on in and have something to eat with me."

Cody said, "Hey, Man. You haven't eaten yet. You go ahead and fix your breakfast. I'll get some coffee for Steven and me."

"Sure. Here is a couple of cups and the sugar is on the table," Nick said, as he handed the cups to Cody.

As they sat down to the table, Nick asked grinning, "How was Traci's night last night with the Samuels? Did she get a chance to show her Edwards' temper again or did it go alright?"

Cody and Steven laughed. Then Cody said, "She said she enjoyed it. Mrs. Samuels didn't have too much to say, but she was nice. Mr. Samuels talked to her asking about being in a police family. I accept it as he was being nice, but I also have to accept that he may be just trying to get some information out of her along the lines of our work. I am assuming that the next time, he will probably go a little deeper with his police conversations. I feel that he is playing with her right now and that she isn't in any danger. So the less she knows now, the better. ......Don't worry, she won't give him any information. ...Right now he doesn't know how much we know or what Dad may have left behind. We have the upper hand now....And, also, all we have on him is the few telephone calls Wilson made to him."

Steven said, "That's right, but, Bro, when do we tell Traci. She does have a right to know."

"Yes, Steven, she does, but not now. The less she knows, the better right now until we find out if and how deep Mr. Samuels is in this corruption."

117

Nick said, "I agree with you, Cody. You all just have to watch her closely and listen to what she says."

About that time Nick's telephone rang. Nick answered, "Hello, this is Nick." Then he waited a minute and said, "Is he in his office now?" Then Nick waited a minute longer and then said, "Thanks, Chip. You are doing good. The more information that we can gather, the sooner you two can be together. Thanks again, Buddy." Then Nick hung up the phone.

"As you know that was Chip. He heard from Casey and she is fine. She has not heard anything from anyone. Tex has been checking on her. Also, he said that the word on the street is that Wilson was beaten up because of him talking to us. He has been threatened and he, in turn, threatened the boys in his care that if they talked, they would end up like the other two, meaning Douglas and Koster."

Cody said, "Does that mean what I think it could mean? Maybe, Douglas and Koster talked to Dad or some other officer and that was why they were killed. Could be that it wasn't a drug deal gone bad. That sheds a new light on things."

"Could be. I think we need to pay another visit to Wilson. He is in his office this morning and today is Saturday. What do you think?"

Steven said, "Sounds good to me. I would like to go with you two."

Cody grinned and said, "Let's go."

They got into Nick's county car and took off to the Probation Office. As they walked in the door, they could hear Wilson in his office on the phone. No one else was around. As they turned into Wilson's door, he looked up and said, "I'll call you back." And then he put the phone down.

Cody said, "Good morning, Wilson. We are glad to see you, too. Looks like someone worked you over since we last saw you. What you got there? Looks like a broken arm and a few cuts and bruises."

"What do you want, Edwards? I don't have time for any of you."

Nick said, "We just came by to see what damage was done after we let it be known that you talked to us. You may not have time for us now, Wilson, but you will the next time we come for you because it will be for good."

Steven just stood back and watched with a grin on his face. He was enjoying seeing all the different expressions on Wilson's face and seeing him squirm.

Cody said, "I understand that you call up on the hill quite a lot. What is Samuels to you?"

His expression changed because he knew that they had talked to someone. "Samuels don't mean nothing to me. He lives across from my uncle."

"Alright, what does Tanner mean to you, then?"

"Tanner is my uncle. I talk to him whenever I feel like it. It is none of your business."

Nick said, "Oh, you mean Tanner is your uncle and he associates with the likes of you."

"Yes, he is my uncle. He is my mother's brother. He made it good, but he never forgot where he came from. He still treats us like family."

"Well, that may explain calls to Tanner, but it doesn't explain calls to Samuels. What is Samuels to you?"

"He is Uncle Robert's neighbor. I may have called over there when I couldn't reach my uncle. I don't remember every call I make."

Then Cody said, "Alright, Wilson, since you don't want to play it straight with us, Garcia will. He has already shown interest in talking to us, but we have put him off. We wanted to see what you had to say. You may not be this lucky next time because we are going to let it be known that we talked to you again."

"What do you mean Garcia will talk."

"Like I said, he is interested in talking to us. We just wanted to give you another chance, but since you don't want it. Good Luck."

And then as they turned and started to walk out the door, Wilson was frantically calling to them, but his phone started to ring and he knew that he had to answer it because he was waiting for an important call.

Cody said as they were getting into the car, "Looks like he is not afraid of dying. Looks like our next move is to talk to Garcia. If Tanner is really Wilson's uncle, we are back to who on the Hill is involved. We need to find the car with the tag number 396 on it."

Nick said, "Want to go by the station and see who is working today. Garcia may be there or we could talk to anyone in the office and try to find out what they know about these cases."

Steven said, "Sounds like a good idea to me. I don't have anything to do, do you all?"

"No, Bro, I am just waiting around for Tex. He is due in sometime this afternoon or evening."

Nick said, "Let's go for a ride."

They went to the main office looking to see what cars were there, but did not see what they were looking for. So they drove back to the station. When they went into the building, they saw Roberts and a couple of others that were just leaving. They went over to where Roberts was standing and asked him if he would come back to their office with them. He said he would be glad to.

After they got settled in the office. Cody asked, "Roberts, you said you would help us any way you could reference the murders. Is there anything else that you haven't already told us."

"I don't know much. Your Dad didn't talk about the investigation to anyone that I know of. The only thing I know is that I have heard a couple of the guys say that they were confused and feel as though what they do is useless. They arrest these drug dealers and somehow they get out with a very light sentence and are back to selling drugs again. I only talked to Mrs. Harris and Angel before I was taken off the case. Angel was the only one that had any information. I never got to go back to talk to Mr. Harris and a couple of the others on the list that I gave you really didn't know anything about the murder. Have you talked to Angel yet?"

"Yes, she is a big help. We know that Wilson at the Probation Office has some of his kids selling drugs. Do you have any information as to when the drugs come in and how?"

"No......Wait a minute. The rumor was that it came in on Thursday afternoon and sometimes on Friday afternoon. I was following Wilson to find out, when your father took me off the case. I'm sorry, I didn't think of that when I was talking to you before."

"That's alright, Roberts. Another thing, Robert Tanner that lives on the Hill. Is he Wilson's uncle?"

"Yes, he is. I did check that out and that is true, but it does not mean he is not involved."

Nick said, "True. How about Richard Samuels that live across from Tanner?"

"I don't know anything about him."

Cody said, "Roberts, I am sorry if it seems as though we are interrogating you, but we need to confirm some answers that we have been given. You are helping us a lot and we are grateful."

"Edwards, that's alright. I know how frustrating that these particular cases are. It seems that you can't get straight answers around here. I'm glad that I can help. Anything that I can do, I will be glad to."

Cody said, "Thanks, Roberts. We appreciate that. One last question. What do you know about Sergeant Garcia?"

"Hey, now wait a minute. I am not going to rat on my fellow officers. Besides, I don't know very much about him. He sort of keeps to himself."

"Roberts, I am not asking you to rat on him. I just want to know who he hangs around with or who his friends are."

"Well, I don't socialize with him, but he seems nice enough. I don't know anything on him or who his friends are. I have seen him lunching sometimes with some guy in Internal Affairs. I don't know who. Some of the guys won't hang around with him because of that."

"Cody said, "Thanks, Roberts, you have been a big help. We may call on you again sometimes. By the way, who was my father's best friend here in the office?"

"Anytime, I'll be around." Then he said, "Edwards, I don't know. He was friendly to the Lieutenant more than anyone else. He was very businesslike most of the time."

They both said, "Thanks, Roberts. We really appreciate it."

After Roberts had left the office. Steven looked at Cody and saw a frustrated look on his face and asked, "Why did you ask that question?" Up until this moment, Steven had sat in the corner and said nothing, but that question puzzled him.

"Because Casey said she heard the killer say that a friend to Edwards told the killer that Edwards knew that higher ups were involved in the drug operation but did not know who. Nick, is the Lieutenant playing us for a fool?"

Nick said angrily as he hit the wall with his fist, "Damn, Damn. Just when we were beginning to trust him."

Steven sat there and looked from one to the other with a concerned look on his face. He knew that something was very disturbing to his brother and friend. He did not know what to think. He knew that at first they did not know whether to trust their Lieutenant or not. Then he asked, "Cody, what is it?"

Cody said angrily, "Let's go home. We will explain on the way home. The whole week has taken a toll on me, mentally. Now this. I was beginning to trust him. I am going home and take a nap. That is what I will do. We will take the files home so we can go over them with Tex over the weekend."

He put the files in his attache case and Nick put the rest in his and all three walked out the door and started home. As they neared Nick's place, Nick said, "I'll be home, probably taking a nap, too. If anything come up or when Tex gets in, call me."

"Sure thing. See you later." And Cody and Steven went home feeling very low.

As they came into the house through the back door, Mama E and Traci were in the kitchen. Mama E said, "Tex called a few minutes ago. He said he would probably be here around 7 o'clock. Trac and I were just talking about waiting to prepare dinner so that it would be ready by then. Is that alright with you?"

"Sure, Mom. That will be fine. I want to lay down, anyway. I'll be up in my room if you need me."

Steven said, "I'll be upstairs, too."

Then they headed upstairs to their room.

Mama E and Traci looked at one another. They knew that something was wrong, but they had learned a long time ago not to ask questions. Something about the cases that they were working on was worrying them. When they got ready to tell them, they would.

Just as Cody finished taking his clothes off and putting on his comfortable lounging pants, his phone rang. He almost didn't answer it, but decided that it might be important.

"Hello, this is Cody."

"Oh, Cody, Nick here. I hate to bother you now, but I thought you would want to know as soon as I heard anything."

"Yes, Nick, I do. I wasn't in bed yet. Just ready to lay down. What is it?"

"Chip just called me and said that he had some information for us. He will come over tomorrow morning and talk with all of us. He didn't want to talk on the phone."

"Good. We'll come over about 10 o'clock. Will that be too early?"

"No, that will be fine. Chip said he would be here around 10:30 a.m. Well, I just wanted to keep you informed and let you know before you went to sleep. We'll see you later."

"Sure, Thanks."

Cody then hung up the phone and laid down on the bed. His last thoughts before he fell asleep were that things would look a lot better this time next weekend. His thoughts were of things beginning to come together on these cases and then all scrambled together.

Chapter 6

Cody opened his eyes when he heard a knock on his bedroom door. He was accustomed to waking up with the slightest sound or anything that was out of the ordinary. He said, "Yes."

Traci said, "Bro, Tex just came in and dinner is almost ready."

"O.K. Sis, I'll be there in a few minutes."

"Bro, may I come in?"

"Sure, come on in. I'm decent."

She came in and sat on the side of the bed where he was laying. She leaned over and kissed him on the forehead. Then she said, "These cases are getting you down, aren't they?"

"No, Trac. I can handle it. I have to admit that trying to investigate all three cases is very trying. When you think you are making headway, something comes up and set you back a little. I will be alright. This week has been mostly mental work. Next week will be easier."

"Would it help to talk about them? I am a good listener, you know."

He smiled and kissed her on the cheek. "Yes, you are, but I would rather not talk about it now. Maybe, later when we are more into the investigation. Things are still up in the air. We are now confirming some things that we have found out. O.K."

"Sure, Bro, I understand. Get dressed now." Then she got real excited, and continued, "Tex is downstairs and he sure looks great. In fact, as for me he is a HUNK. I may have to go back on my word about him." She grinned. Then she said blushing, "Cody, when he put his arms around me and kissed me to say hello, I had the strangest feeling in the pit of my stomach. ....I know who I want to be my first."

Then they laughed.

She said, "Promise me you won't say anything to him about what I just told you. I don't know what happened, but I had a strange feeling that I have not had before. Promise."

"Sure, Trac. That makes me very happy, but also sad." He also knew that Tex was interested in her although he had not said anything.

"Why, sad?"

"Because you are and will always be my little sister. But, I won't say anything to anyone and I wish you the best. Tex is a great guy."

"Thanks. See you in a few minutes." Then she got up and walked out of the room with a big smile on her face.

He was smiling at his sister as she walked out the door. He was real proud of her.

Just as he was putting his shirt on, the door swung open and Tex walked in and grabbed Cody and hugged him. He said, "I have been waiting for this day all week. It seemed as if the days were turning into weeks. I guess I don't have to tell you that I am ready for action."

"No, you don't. You will probably be getting your wish this coming week. We are suppose to go over to Nick's in the morning around 10:00 o'clock. We will fill you in then, plus Nick has some new information for us. Mom and Traci do not know anything except that I am working on some old murder cases and that Steven is helping out some getting experience. So, we should keep a tight lip here for now. O.K."

"Sure. Let's go down and eat. Mama E and Traci has prepared a dinner that I can't miss. I haven't eaten anything since this morning. I didn't want to stop once I got started this morning."

Tex had brought some of his things upstairs and had set them down in the hall. When Cody saw them, he said, "Let's put these in your old room. Traci decided that she didn't want to be outnumbered by three up here, so she is going to use the bedroom downstairs. Also, Mom needs some company now and then. Plus the fact that we will probably be in and out late at night."

As they came into the kitchen, the others were just sitting down to the table. Tex and Cody sat in their places. Everyone was in a good mood and happy to have Tex with them.

Steven said, "Tex, Old Buddy, you want to see how the Georgia Boys work, huh?"

Tex laughed, "Sure, we'll see who learns what from whom. We play by the rules in Texas."

Steven laughingly said, "Yeah, just like we do."

Then Tex said, "Mama E, you're still the best cook in Georgia and Texas. This was worth the trip already."

Mama E laughed, "Eat up you all or you will be eating this for breakfast in the morning. Tex, you haven't changed a bit, not that I would want you to change. We love you just the way you are."

Cody said as he winked at Tex, "Yes, all she has talked about this week was that she would be glad when Tex came because she would be appreciated then."

Mama E said embarrassed, "Cody, you know that's not true, although I am glad to see him. Maybe one day your father and sister can come to Georgia."

They all laughed.

127

Traci said, "Mom thinks there is no place anywhere like Georgia. Everyone should come to Georgia at least once."

Tex said as he winked at Traci, "That's true. This is my second home by choice."

Steven asked Cody and Tex, "What are your plans for tonight. I know Tex is probably tired, I thought I may go back to Johnnie Lee's for a little while just to unwind. Would you two like to go and even you can go this time, Sis?"

Cody said, "That's up to Tex. I slept a couple of hours this afternoon."

Tex said, "Yeah, that sounds good for an hour or so." Then he looked at Traci and said, "Trac, how about you. Why don't you come with us?"

She looked at her Mom and Mama E said, "Don't stay here on my account. You go with them if you want. You need some relaxation."

"If you all are not going to stay long and I won't cramp your style, yes, I'll go with you."

Then Steven spoke up, "Cody, you go by and pick up Corrie and I'll take Trac and Tex with me. We will meet at Johnnie Lee's. Or call Nick and have him and Corrie meet us there."

"Maybe we should go down to Dixie's Place. That will be closer and not as crowded. I'll pick Corrie and Nick up and meet you there."

"Sure." He then realized that Cody did not want to be at a popular place for some reason. He would ask him later. Maybe he was expecting trouble and did not want Trac with them. Then Steven got up and started cleaning the table off. He said, "I'll help Mom in the kitchen. You two go and get dressed."

Tex said, "Yes, I would like to take a shower after being on the road all day." So, after putting his plate and glass near the dishwasher, he then went upstairs and started unpacking his clothes. Then he went into the shower thinking. *Traci sure has grown into a beautiful woman. I wonder if she is serious about anyone now. If she doesn't have a date on Saturday night, she must not have a steady beau. I sure hope she is not serious about anyone because she really does something to me when I look at her beautiful brown eyes with her long dark brown curly hair. I had a strange feeling when I hugged her and kissed her. Wow, she felt great in my arms. I really wanted to pull her closer to me and kiss her deeper. Gosh, I believe she felt it, too. I'm glad that she is sleeping downstairs. That will help matters some. I certainly don't want to do anything foolish in Mama E's house. I feel good being here.*

When he had finished dressing in his jeans, light green shirt and cowboy boots, he went downstairs and talked to Steven for a few minutes. Then he looked up and Traci was standing in the doorway with her curly long brown hair down to her shoulders, dressed in jeans and a pale yellow shirt. She sure did fill them jeans out. She also had on cowboy boots. *WOW, she sure look beautiful.*

She said, "You two ready to go dancing. I am."

Steven said, "We sure are, Trac. You are gonna knock'em dead tonight."

Traci was looking at Tex and thinking how goodlooking he was. *He was so handsome with his brown curly hair and dark brown smiling eyes. The light green shirt looked so good on him.*

Then Tex said with a frown on his face, "Not if I can help it. May I have every dance with you?"

She looked surprised, but said, "You sure can, except for my brothers." Then she looked at Steven with his light blonde hair and blue-green laughing eyes. He was so handsome, so full of life. He always looked so fresh, as though he just stepped out of a shower. His blue shirt brought out the blue in his eyes and his jeans fit just perfect. He sure was sexy. No wonder all the girls wanted to date him. She was so proud that he was her brother.

He said, "That's acceptable."

Steven winked at Traci to remind her of their conversation before. She did remember and smiled.

They left in the Family Ford Explorer so that they would have more room. And as they pulled into Dixie's Place, Traci said, "I don't know why Cody said to come here. They have a better band and more room at Johnnie Lee's."

Steven said, "Cody has his reasons, Sis. Besides, we are not going to be out late. The three of us are suppose to be at Nick's place at 10:00 o'clock in the morning. Nick has some new information on the cases that they are working on. Plus, since Tex is going to be working with them, they want to bring him up-to-date on everything."

"I understand, Bro. Cody is usually right. He knows what is best. We look to him since Dad is not here any longer."

Steven said, "O.K. Enough about work. We are going to enjoy ourselves for an hour or so. I think what we all need most is a couple of drinks and just relax and then a good nights sleep. I know Tex will be ready for bed early tonight."

Tex said, "Cody's plans suit me just fine. We will have plenty of time to hit the hot spots later. But, I still want to dance with you, Trac."

She laughed and said, "We will."

So, they went in Dixie's Place and found Cody, Nick and Corrie sitting at a table in a corner but near the dance floor. It was dimmer than the usual place, but Cody thought that would be good. They had already had one drink and they all ordered another when the others had gotten there. Tex was introduced to Corrie and the mood was good for all of them. The place was moving slower than Johnnie Lee's, but it felt good to just sit and sip on a drink.

The band started up and Tex and Traci got up to dance.

Cody said as he was looking at Tex and Traci, "Bro, do you see what I see?"

Steven smiled and said, "Yep, I think I do."

They all laughed.

Then Cody said to Steven, "Steven, the plan I have for Tex is to work some undercover since he is not known here. I don't want us to be seen in public around here with him for the following week. I'll explain tomorrow morning when we meet at Nick's. Our friends from the department do not come here very much, especially on Saturday night."

"I understand, Bro. This is fine."

They all danced three or four dances and ordered a couple more drinks. They were really feeling relaxed. Then about an hour and a half later, Tex said, "I am bushed. I don't want to break this up, but I am about to go to sleep on my feet. If you all want to stay, I will find my way home."

Cody said, "Oh, no, you don't. We all will leave. We didn't plan to stay long, anyway. We will have time to go out and celebrate later."

So they paid their bill and left. Cody, Corrie and Nick went their way and Steven, Tex and Traci went home. Cody had already explained to Nick and Corrie why they were going to Dixie's Place instead of Johnnie Lee's on the way to the club.

On the way home, Traci said, "I enjoyed tonight, but the atmosphere would have been so much better at Johnnie Lee's. It doesn't sound like Cody to switch all of a sudden. He always wanted to go to Johnnie Lee's before. Now, all of a sudden, he changed his mind and wanted to go to Dixie's Place."

Steven said, "First of all, Tex is tired and we just needed somewhere quiet to have a drink and relax. Sis, Cody still likes

Johnny Lee's, but tonight he had his reasons for going to Dixie's Place."

Tex spoke up, "I am sure Cody was thinking about me and I appreciate it. Dixie's Place was the right place to relax tonight, not too many people and it wasn't real loud. This was a good choice. Traci, we will have time to go out later and have a rip-rowing good time."

They laughed.

Traci said, "Well, if you enjoyed it, that is fine. I was just thinking about your impression of Georgia on your first night here. You're right. Tonight was not a good night to really enjoy ourselves."

By this time they were driving into the back yard. They got out of the car and walked into the house. Mama E was still watching television. She said, "My, you all did not stay out long. I hope you enjoyed yourselves."

Tex said, "We did. I am afraid that I was the one that broke up the party. I am very tired after driving all day today, and tomorrow will be a full day, so we wanted to get to bed early."

So Tex and Steven said their goodnights and went upstairs to bed. Traci stayed and watched television with her mother for awhile. But it wasn't long before they were ready for bed, too. In fact, they were already in bed when Cody came in later.

The next morning everyone was up around 7:30 and in the kitchen preparing breakfast. They had a wonderful breakfast. It was a new day and everyone was rested and ready to start the day, especially Cody. He wanted to hear what information Chip had for them. After a lot of conversation and eating a big breakfast, they helped Mama E clean up the kitchen. Then Cody, Steven and Tex left for Nick's place. They were a little early, but it was alright. Nick would not mind.

When they arrived, Nick had finished breakfast and was cleaning up his kitchen. Cody made a pot of coffee while Nick finished.

As Tex was looking around Nick's place he was wishing he had something like this that he could call his own. Then he said, "Nick, you have a nice, comfortable place here. I like it very much. I am impressed with your taste." And they laughed.

"Thank you, Tex. It doesn't look like your place in Texas, but this is mine and just like I want it."

"My place in Texas is my parents. I don't own a place of my own. I thought about moving out, but everytime I mentioned it, Dad would say something like 'this house is too big for just me. If you and your sister move, I will sell it.' So, that ends any conversation of moving out. That is his way of telling us that he doesn't want to live alone and ...I don't want him to."

Cody said, "That is about how we feel. Our place is plenty big for us and we don't want to leave Mom. The whole Edwards family has lived there for several generations."

Steven said, "Besides, where could we move and have the conveniences and companionship that we have now."

They all agreed with Steven.

By that time, the coffee was ready. So they sat down to the table and spread the files on the table. They explained everything up to date to Tex, even about Lieutenant Moss.

Then Tex asked, "Do you all know where Wilson gets the drugs that he distribute to his boys?"

Cody said, "No, we were saving that for you." He and Nick laughed. Then he said, "Wilson knows us, but he doesn't know you. We want you to follow him around or work with Marci and Kato, two of our undercover cops with the Georgia Bureau of Invesigations. We need to talk to them before we do anything. I have worked cases with them before. We don't want to interfere with any of their investigations. We want to work with them if they are working on these cases. In fact, I will call them now. We don't know for sure, but we understand that the drugs come in on Thursday and/or Friday morning or afternoon."

As he picked up the phone, there was a knock on the door. He put the phone back down. Nick went to the door and there stood Chip and a boy a little smaller than Chip. "Good morning, Chip, come on in. We don't want to stand out here too long."

They came inside and Chip said, "Nick, this is Tim Carson. He is one of Wilson's boys. He is scared and doesn't know what to do, so I told him to talk to you."

"Well, Tim, you came to the right place. Come on into the kitchen." As they walked into the kitchen, Nick said, "this is Tex, Cody, and Steven. You all, this is Chip and Tim."

Cody said, "Chip, glad to see you again. What do you have for us?"

Chip said, "Tim is one of Wilson's boys and he wants out, but Wilson has threatened him. Tim, you tell what you know. They will help you."

Cody said as he pulled out two stools, "Yes, Tim, you are better off here than anywhere else. Do you mind if we record your statement? We want to be accurate on witness testimony."

Tim looked at Chip and Chip said, "Tim, it's O.K. This is the best you will ever get. You may end up like Darrel and Kevin, remember."

Tim said with a frightened look on his face, "Yes, I remember. Wilson keep reminding us of how we will end up if we say anything. ...I'll take my chance with you all. I trust Chip, but I don't trust cops."

Nick said, "Tim, all cops are not bad. We know that some cops are mixed up in this drug business. We are trying to find out who they are and put them behind bars. You may be able to help us."

"I'll do what I can. I can't go on any longer. If it means death, then it will have to be."

Nick said, as he walked behind Tim and then put his hands on Tim's shoulders to give him courage, "Tim, please listen to me. You are doing the right thing. We will do our best to keep Wilson away from you. O.K."

"O.K. I'll do whatever you want me to do."

Nick got out his recorder and turned it on and made his usual introductions in the microphone.

Then he said, "Tim, have you been promised anything or coerced into making this statement other than being promised protection?"

"No. I am doing this because I can no longer go on like I am. I don't know where to turn."

Nick said, "Tim, tell us in your own words what you know about the drugs that are coming into Little County. Start at the beginning."

Tim took a deep breath. "I was arrested when I was fourteen for Breaking and Entering. It was my first time. I was angry with my father and I went out and met these guys. I didn't realize what they were into until it actually happened. I am not blaming them for what I did that night, but I am just telling it like it was. I went before Judge Turner and he put me on probation because it was my first time, or at least that is what he said. I found out later that even though the others had been arrested before, they were put on probation, too."

He paused for a moment and then he continued. "The first time I went into Wilson's office we were alone. He told me that I had to do whatever he asked me to do. That was what being on probation was all about. If I did not, I would go to jail. He would see to that. I told him that I did not want to go to jail. He said 'good, because I don't want to put you there. Be here next Thursday afternoon at 1:00 o'clock sharp.' I asked him why and he told me that I was never to ask why."

"When Thursday came around, I was there before one because I was frightened and did not want to go to jail. About thirty minutes later, Wilson came in with several containers of different pills and some crack cocaine. He gave me some of the pills and the other pills and the cocaine to the other guys. Since it was my first time, he started me off only with the pills and only a few. We had to sell it and bring the money back to his office no later than eleven o'clock on Thursday night. If we had not sold all of it, we had to sell the rest by Friday night and be at his office at eleven o'clock. I was to go with one of the guys to learn the ropes. We went into certain neighborhoods and sold most of the drugs. We would switch neighborhoods every week so that the same sellers would not be in the same neighborhood two weeks in a row. After three weeks, I was on my own and had to sell where he told me to go."

Cody asked, "How many boys under Wilson is selling drugs?"

"All his boys are selling drugs. Some of them have not been caught the second time. They have learned how to do it in a sneaky way so that you don't notice them."

Cody said, "I am going to read the names that I have. Will you tell me if all these are selling drugs? This is just for the record."

"Yes Sir."

Then Cody read the list of names. All eleven of them.

Tim was nodding his head 'yes' as Cody called the names. When Cody had finished, Tim said, "Yes, all of them are selling drugs. Some of them have been arrested since I have been there, but they got probation and came back to doing the same thing. Some of them just laugh about it, but some are scared and want out of it, but they are afraid not to do what Wilson tells them to do."

Cody asked, "Do you know where the drugs are coming from and how they get here?"

"They come into Savannah on a boat. Two men bring them here to a warehouse. Wilson gets the drugs there and brings them to us. The only names that I have heard for the two men are 'Zooly and Cooty'.

Then Steven asked, "What do you know about Judge Turner or Judge Mason?"

"I don't know anything other than Wilson said that if we got caught, we would go before Judge Turner and he would put us back on probation."

Tex asked, "Do you know where the warehouse here is located and who owns it?"

"I know that it is on the block of Thirty-Sixth Street and Twenty-Eighth Avenue. I don't know who owns it, but someone on the Hill has been mentioned, but no name."

Chip spoke up and said, "That is only a couple of blocks from the garage where I work. It is around the corner from the garage. That is where Mr. Edwards was killed."

They all looked at each other. Then Nick asked, "Tim, is there anything else that you can tell us no matter how small it seems?"

"No. I can't think of anything now, except what do I do now?"

Nick said, "We'll talk about that later. Do either of you have any more questions for Tim?"

Steven asked, "You say, some of the boys expressed something about wanting to get out of this mess?"

"A couple have mentioned that they would like to, but are too afraid to do anything about it."

Steven said, "Would you like to point them out for us for our information?"

"They are Doug Ward, Johnny Lowe and Tommy Downey. They won't get in trouble because of me, will they?"

"No, they won't. When this goes down and they help us, we will try to help them."

He said, "Good. They are good guys."

Nick said, "Well, if there are no more questions, I will shut off the recorder." And he did.

Nick asked, "Tim, would you feel safe going back and continue to do what you have been doing? Does anyone else know that you came here today?"

"No, not that I know of, but Darrel and Kevin did not know that anyone saw them go to the police, either, and they are dead."

Nick said, "They may have gone to the wrong ones when they went to the police. And then, too, they may have been followed. Tim, if you would feel better, you and Chip could stay here for a couple of days until we can figure things out."

Tim said, "I sure would appreciate it. And Chip, some of the guys saw you talking to me. If I don't show up on Thursday, they may come looking for you. I don't want that to happen, and I don't want to face Wilson again unless he is behind bars."

Cody said, "If it is O.K. with Nick, you two stay here until we can get things together. But, promise me that neither of you will go out of this house unless we know about it."

They both promised.

Nick said, "You will need to get your clothes and personal items. We will take care of your probation with the right people. Don't worry about that."

Steven said, "If you will call your mother and have her get your things together, I'll pick them up."

Cody said, "O.K. Steven, you take care of getting their clothes and I will contact Marci or Kato."

After each of the boys had talked to their mother, Steven and the boys left to pick up their clothes. Tex, Cody and Nick left to go to Kato's place. Cody had the address of where Kato lived and the address of the work house. Kato stayed at the work house most of the time. He did not want anyone to know where his own place was, but he trusted Cody because they had worked together in the past.

Tim and Chip did not live very far from one another so Tim asked his mother to bring some of his things over to Chip's house and she said she would. Chip told his mother that Mrs. Carson was coming over with some things for Tim and that they would explain when they got there.

When they arrived at Chip's house, they all went inside. Chip introduced Steven to Mrs. Roberts and Mrs. Carson. Then Steven explained as to what was happening and then said, "I don't suppose I have to tell you that your boys are great guys and I assure you that they are doing the right thing. We will do everything in our power to protect them. I am asking that you do not try to contact them. We will let them contact you when we feel it is safe. They will be staying at Nick's place a day or two. The less you know about where they are, the better for you. Hopefully, Wilson will not know that Tim is missing until Thursday. I can't guarantee that, but let's hope that it is true. That will give us time to work things out."

While Mrs. Roberts and Steven were talking, Chip and Tim were explaining to Mrs. Carson some of what Tim had been forced to do.

Mrs. Roberts said, "Corporal Edwards, you don't know how much I appreciate what you, Nick and all are doing. I know that it is dangerous and that this is the right thing to do. Nick has guided Chip for a year and he has not led him wrong. I trust you."

Steven said, "Thank you, Mrs. Roberts. Just call me Steven. The less police work come into our conversations, the better."

"I understand."

Mrs. Carson said, "I didn't realize what was going on until now, but if Mrs. Roberts feels good about this, so will I. I only want what is best for Tim."

Steven said, "Mrs. Carson, I don't want to scare you, but this will be dangerous for you and your son when Wilson finds out that Tim is missing. They will start watching your house and where you go. That is why I am instructing you not to try to contact Tim. You and Mrs. Roberts may call each other, but it would be best if you did not visit each other. If you see anyone that does not belong in this neighborhood hanging around either of your houses, please contact one of us. And if you need to contact anyone, please call this number and he handed her a card and also one for Mrs. Roberts. He had put Cody's and Nick's numbers on there, also. Put this where no one else can see it and you can get it if you need to call. We will keep in contact with you, but we will not let you know where they are for your own safety, and, expecially for theirs. After early Thursday morning, we will start riding by your house to check things out. Now, I want both of you to promise me that if anyone comes around looking for Tim or Chip or you see any strangers hanging around, please call that number day or night."

They promised. Then Steven said, "I am taking the bags out to the car and will wait for you guys there. You say your goodbyes, but be fast about it. We need to move out of here now."

So Steven said goodbye and thanked them and walked to the car carrying the bags. As he was going to the car, he was looking all around but did not see anyone around.

Meanwhile, Tex, Cody and Nick had arrived at Kato's place. Kato was alone, but he invited them in because he knew Cody. He had seen Nick, but did not know him.

Cody introduced them, "Kato, this is Corporal Nick Carillo and this is my friend, Sergeant Tex Tyler from Houston, Texas. He is visiting with me and is going to help me on some murder cases."

Tex and Nick liked him right away. He looked just as they expected an undercover cop to look, long hair, beard, halfway neat clothes this morning. He had a nice smile, though. Also, he had a soft, teddy bear look about him, but he could be tough if he had to.

"Yes, ...Cody, how have you been getting along? I haven't seen you in awhile. Come on in the kitchen. I just made a pot of coffee."

"I'm fine. I know that you are probably busy, but we would like to talk to you about these cases we are working on."

"Sure. If I can be of help, I'll be glad to do what I can."

Cody said, "The cases that we are working on are murder cases, but drugs are involved. That is why we wanted to talk to you. Since no one around here knows Tex, He was going to do some undercover work for us, but we do not want to interfere with your work."

Kato said, "So, tell me what you know about these cases and I'll tell you if we know anything and what."

"O.K. Kato. I'll play by your rules only because I have known you for some time and have learned to trust you. We are working on the murder cases of Darrel Douglas, Kevin Koster and John Harris and they are connected to drugs."

Then Kato laughed, and then he said, "Cody, I know about the cases you are working on. I think we can be of help to each other. In fact, I was thinking about contacting you. You are right about the drugs. We have just started working in the Savannah area and into this area. We do know that drugs are coming into Savannah on a boat called 'My Fantasy'. It is owned by someone on the Hill. We haven't found that out yet. I have one man going to Savannah in the next couple of days to start checking when the boat comes in and how often."

141

Tex spoke up. "From what I understand, the boat comes in on Thursday mornings and/or Friday mornings. What do you think about me going with him and we work together? We can decide whether to work together or separately down there depending on what is to be done."

"Sounds good to me. I'll give him a call and have him come over now." He got up and went to the telephone. A few minutes later, he came back and said that Tony was not there and would not be back until Wednesday. He had to go home on an emergency leave. Marci works with us. She will be right over. You don't have an objection to working with a woman, do you, Tex?"

"No, if she can handle herself and don't expect me to have to look after both of us."

"I would rather have her as my backup than some of the men I have worked with over the years. You can talk to her and make up your own mind."

"If you feel that way about her, then I'll take your word for it."

Then Kato said, "Like I said, we are just beginning to work on these two areas. If you have any information that will help us, we would appreciate it. It would be great to work together again, Cody."

Cody smiled and said, "Yes, it would. ..We know that Probation Officer Robert Wilson receives the drugs here and distributes it to his boy's, all of them. They have to be at Wilson's office on Thursday or Friday at 1:00 o'clock to pick up the drugs, whichever day the drugs comes in. Then they have to report back by 11:00 that night to bring the cash. We just found that out about an hour ago."

Kato started shaking his head. "It is disgusting what some people will do for money."

Cody said, "We also think that this goes high up in our department and possibly other county officials. One of the judges may be involved."

"Do you have evidence of this, Cody?"

"Not evidence, but information that makes it a good possibility. I know that the files of the three murder victims have been tampered with. Most of the investigative reports and interviews that were worthwhile have been taken out of the files. A man who had on a shirt that had 'POLICE' across the back was at the scene of two of the murders. A lot of things that make us want to treat it as such that we don't know who to trust."

Kato shook his head. "Sounds like you may be onto something. Yes, I think we should work together and very quietly. Who else knows what you have found out?"

"Only my brother, Steven, and Nick's sister know a little of it. She has typed some of our reports for us at home. We didn't know who to trust so she has been typing for us."

"That's good. Let's keep it that way."

Cody said, hesitantly, "Also, Kato, we have found out that my father was murdered, not shot in crossfire. He was investigating the first two murders and was close to something when he was killed. Almost all of his paper work is missing from the files. So you see why we think that there is corruption in our department."

Kato said, very angrily, "You guys, when I hear something like that, I want to go to work right then and there. Let's get those bastards. Every last one of them. We won't stop until we do."

They all were getting riled up now and ready to go to work.

Nick and Tex had stayed in the background watching and listening to Cody and by the information that Cody was giving to Kato, they knew that Cody trusted Kato but did not want to divulge the witnesses.

Then Nick asked Kato, "Do you know Eduardo Garcia in our section or Domenic Santino in Internal Affairs?"

Kato thought for a moment and said, "No, I don't really know them, but I have heard that Santino is living above his salary at the department. Of course, he may have legit money from family estate or other investments. We have not had occasion to check him out. I have seen Garcia, but do not know anything about him. Why?"

"Wilson has called both quite often from home and at work. We brought Wilson into our office to see what we could get out of him. Of course he didn't say anything, but when I led him out, he and Garcia exchanged glances and their expression changed. We found out that a couple of days later, Wilson had been beaten up. Also, Garcia has been seen having lunch with Santino a few times." Nick laughed, "Now who do you know that will eat lunch in full view of anyone in the department with someone in Internal Affairs? They are really asking for trouble."

They all laughed as Cody got up and refilled their cups with coffee.

Kato said, "It's worth checking out."

Then there was a knock on the door. As Kato got up to answer it, he said, "That is probably Marci."

A moment later, Kato and Marci walked into the kitchen. Kato introduced her to the others. Then he said, "Marci, Tex is from out of town and is working on the murder cases with Cody and Nick. We have decided to join forces since the murder cases are connected to the drugs that are coming into this area. They already have information that could help us."

She looked at each one of them as though she was looking them over, "Sounds good to me. The more help we have, the better." Marci is an attractive tall, muscular girl with short blonde hair and blue eyes. She also had the look that she could handle herself. The others were looking at her and sizing her up, too, especially Tex.

Cody said, "We know that drugs come into Savannah on a boat early on Thursday and/or Friday morning. Kato says it is called 'My

Fantasy'. The drugs are brought here to a warehouse on Thirty-Sixth Street and Twenty-Eighth Avenue. We need to find out who owns the warehouse."

Marci said, "Well, you know more than we do. It will be a pleasure working with you all."

Kato said, "Yes, Marci, we were thinking that Tex will work with us as undercover since he is from out of town and no one knows him around here."

Marci smiled at Tex and said, "I'll vote for that."

They all laughed.

Tex said, "There is no reason for us to go to Savannah until Wednesday unless you two have some more information. We could look around the area and see if anything comes up looking suspicious while we are waiting for the boat to come in. ...And Cody, you mentioned someone on the Hill is involved by the name of Samuels and Tanner."

Then Kato spoke, "Hey, they have been suspected in some of our cases, but we couldn't prove anything. What made you suspect that they may be involved?"

Cody said, "One of Wilson's boys that were killed mentioned to his girlfriend that he had to deliver some drugs up on the Hill. And on Wilson's telephone list, he made a lot of calls to Tanner and some to Samuels. They live across the street from one another. But, according to Wilson, Tanner is his uncle. We haven't had time to really check that out."

Then Cody added, "My sister, Traci, is dating Rich Samuels once in a while. She knows nothing about this. I feel that as long as she doesn't know anything, she is not in any danger if Samuels is involved. We are watching everything she says. Don't worry, she does not say anything about our work to anyone. She grew up in a law enforcement family and if she hears anything, she comes to me with it. She only knows that we are working on the murder cases."

Kato said as he was nodding his head, "Good. I'm glad you told me just in case I come across this guy Samuels I'll know how to handle it."

Then Cody continued, "Traci had dinner there Friday night and Mr. Samuels talked to her at length about her law enforcement family. He didn't say anything out of the way. He could have been just making conversation. That is what Tracie said. To let you know how she is. The story is that Traci went for dinner there two weeks ago and Mrs. Samuels put her down in front of Crissy, Rich and Mr. Samuels because she was part of a law enforcement family. Traci got up and told Mrs. Samuels off and left before dinner. Rich has called her almost every night begging Traci to go out with him, but she wouldn't go. Rich is real nice and I think he likes Traci a lot. Supposedly, Mr. Samuels chewed out his wife and had Rich invite Traci back so that his wife could apologize to her. She did, but did not say very much more than that to Traci during the visit. Traci had refused to go out with Rich from that time until Friday night. Her words were that everyone deserves a second chance and she would do that, but she knows that nothing can become of their relationship."

Marci laughingly said, "Good for her. I would like to meet her."

Kato said, "I certainly would, too, but for different reasons."

Tex spoke very sternly and said, "Oh, no, she is already taken. She just doesn't know it yet."

"O.K., O.K. I get the picture."

Nick and Cody were looking at each other and wondering what was going on with Tex. But they did not say anything because Tex had that 'I am not kidding look, don't mess with me'.

Kato said, "Why don't we all meet here tomorrow morning around nine o'clock. We'll check out that warehouse to find out who owns that. You're right, Tex, there is no need to go to Savannah before Tuesday evening or Wednesday morning. That will give you and Marci enough time to check out when the boat is due in, and also, go to the courthouse and check on any property in the Savannah area under Tanner, Samuels or any other suspect's name. Marci, you know how to get in touch with Pepper. He is an informant in Savannah that we use occasionally. See if he knows anything."

"Yes, we'll do that."

Then Kato continued, "Cody, I sure am glad you called. I was going to call you, but hadn't got around to it."

"Yeah, I'm glad, too. We had better go. Steven has two of Wilson's boys that we have got to find a safe place for them to stay. One of them is not one of Wilson's boys, but he is associated with the other so we decided to keep both of them out of sight because of what happened to Darrel and Kevin. I forgot to tell you but what we have heard is that they were killed because they talked to someone in the police department. Also, Wilson is scaring the boys by telling them that."

Kato shook his head, "The more information you tell me, Cody, the more it seems that you may be right about corruption in the department."

Marci looked surprised, "Huh. What is this?"

Kato said, "I'll bring you up to date before in the morning on what was discussed before you came."

"Sure."

They all got up to leave and agreed to meet back there Monday morning at 9:00 o'clock.

On the way back to Nick's place, Nick said, "I had forgotten Steven was going to bring those boys back to my place. I locked the door. He is probably cussing me out. I sure hope he is not riding around with them in his car."

"I am sure he thought of something. At least we will find out in a few minutes."

As they were driving into Nick's driveway, "Well, they are not here. Cody, tell Steven, I am sorry. I just wasn't thinking."

"That's alright. He'll manage. You know Steven."

"Yes, I do. To be young again. I'm sure that he thought of something."

"I'll let you know where the boys are when I find out."

"O.K. Tell him that I will be home the rest of the night in case he want to bring the boys back here."

They laughed as Nick was getting out of the car. Cody said, "We'll pick you up in the morning. We don't need to have so many cars over at Kato's place at one time."

"O.K. I'll see you then. Like I said, I plan to stay home tonight if you need me."

"O.K. See you."

As they drove home, they were discussing and wondering where Steven was and what he did with Chip and Tim. When they pulled into the back yard, they saw his car. When they entered the kitchen door, he was sitting at the table with Traci playing checkers.

"Hey, you two, where have you been for so long?"

Cody said, "We were wondering where you were."

"Well, I found two guys that wanted some work for a while. So, I brought them here and talked to Jake and he said he could use a couple of extra hands for the next few weeks. We fixed a place in the barn for them to sleep and Sara said she would see that they got plenty to eat. So, there, Big Brother, how is that for your ....Little Brother."

They laughed while Traci just stared at them.

"I am proud of you, ...Little Brother. I am sure Jake was happy, too. He could use some help."

Tex said, "Who's winning here?"

"I am because Steven did not have his mind on it. He was just trying to pacify me. He did not want to leave me alone, but he didn't really want to play checkers, either. Mom is laying down. She's O.K. She just didn't get much sleep last night."

Then Cody asked, "What's for dinner?"

"Mom and I have already fixed it. We just have to put the finishing touches to it and you all are going to grill the steaks."

Tex said, "That sounds good. I don't mind cooking like that. I can't cook in the kitchen, but I can cook on a grill. That way, you can set down with a cold beer and just watch it on the grill. In the kitchen you make a mess and don't have time for a beer."

They all laughed.

Then Traci asked, "Are you all planning to go out tonight? I am asking so that we will know what will be the best time to eat."

Cody looked at Tex and he shook his head. So, Cody said, "No, we'll stay in tonight. Maybe, we all can play some ball or something after dinner."

Steven said, "Sounds good to me. I'm not planning to go anywhere. Sunday is for families, so I don't make any plans for just myself."

Traci said, "I am going to lay down for a while. I know you three have other things to do. So, I'll see you later." And with that, she walked to the back of the house to her now bedroom and closed the door.

The three of them went out in the yard and laid in the hammocks under the trees. It was a beautiful day and it felt good to lay in the hammocks and let the cool breeze blow over you. Very relaxing.

Cody said, very genuinely, "Steven, I am very proud of you. It will be better for the boys to be here with Jake. Nick would feel bad about leaving them alone at his place, but we didn't know where else to take them for now."

Steven smiling, "I told Jake that these two boys were working with us on some cases and needed a place to stay for awhile. Someone may be looking for them after this coming Thursday. I, also, told him and the boys that they were not to leave the place unless one of us gave them permission. They know and they are scared so I think they will stay put. Jake and I cleaned out the extra room. Mom had a couple of twin beds and a dresser in the attic of the barn. We got them down and between the four of us, we made it look nice. And they have the bathroom, towels, soap and all the comforts of home for themselves. Only Jake knows that they are working with us. The others only know that they are here to work for a while to help out."

Cody said, "I better call Nick and let him know. He really felt bad about locking the door, but this is better anyway." So Cody pulled out his phone and called Nick and told him what Steven had done. He laughed. After Cody hung up the phone, he said, "Steven, Nick said that we should draft you over to our section. You have some good ideas."

"I told you that I was good. One day someone will listen to me."

They laughed.

Then Tex and Cody told Steven what had transpired at Kato's place. Also, about working together and that Tex and Marci would be working together in Savannah and possibly follow the two men back here, I think they go by the name of Zooly and Cooty."

Then Cody winked at his brother and said, "Hey, Little Brother, did you know that our little sister is already spoken for? I heard that today."

Steven said seriously still looking at Cody trying to get a signal from him, but didn't. "No, I haven't. I sure hope it isn't Rich. Are you sure about this? She hasn't said anything to me about it."

Cody said smilingly, "She hasn't said anything to me about it, either. In fact, I think the words were, 'She's already taken, but she doesn't know it yet.'

Then Steven realized that Tex had said that. He and Cody just stared at each other waiting for Tex to say something.

Finally, Tex said with a straight serious look on his face looking from one to the other, "You boys laugh if you want to, but like I told Kato, 'She's taken. I trust him as for working with him because you trust him, but I do not trust him with females, and especially one that will belong to me after this mess is cleared up."

"Big Brother, looks like we might have a brother-in-law. What do you think?"

Cody said seriously and with a straight face, "He's got to prove himself to me first that he would make a good husband. Besides, Rich is still in the race. Traci is not one to accept anything. He has got to convince her first that he is a better man than Rich." He winked at Steven again.

"Go on and have your fun. One day you two are going to wake up and have another legal brother."

Cody and Steven laughed out loud. Tex joined in with them. He knew that they were teasing him.

151

After a few moments, Tex asked seriously, "Do you think she really cares about this Rich?"

Cody said, "Tex, no, she doesn't. She is only seeing him because he won't quit calling. Other than him, she is very selective about who she goes out with."

"I am glad to hear that. But, you guys better not say a word to her about this conversation. I will say something when the time comes."

Cody said seriously, "Tex, I thought you were getting serious about some girl in Houston you were going out with. What happened to her?"

"Nothing. I went out with several, but haven't found anyone that I wanted to get serious with. For some unexplained reason, I always kept thinking of Trac. Wondering how she was now that she was older, trying to picture her. She was always beautiful as best I could remember. And when I saw her when I came Saturday and hugged and kissed her, I knew why she has been on my mind. She was everything that I had pictured. So, you see, you did not have to ask me to come and help you with this case. I was planning to make a trip here, anyway."

Cody laughed and said, "Tex, I don't remember asking you to come. You volunteered right away. But I am glad as hell you did."

They both got up and went over and hugged him. No words were needed.

Just then Traci came out with the steaks and saw them. She asked quizzically, "What's going on here?"

Steven said, laughing, "We were just welcoming Tex into our family."

"He has been in our family for a couple of years, what is so special now?"

Cody said, "Sis, you always did ask a lot of questions. Is dinner about ready?"

"Yes, it is, Cody. Time to fire up the grill. You always cut me off when you don't want to discuss anything. I guess this is a male thing."

Cody said, "Yes, it is. Let's go boys and get the steaks cooked." And they went over to the grill and Traci turned and went back into the kitchen to finish dinner.

A while later, the boys walked into the kitchen with the steaks. About the time that they sat down to the table, the phone began to ring. Traci said, "I'll answer it. You all go ahead and start eating while it is hot." She got up from the table and lifted the phone receiver off the hook.

"Hello, this is the Edwards residence." Then she said, "No, I cannot go out tonight. I have other plans for tonight and the rest of this week." She waited a moment and then said, "Rich, you know that this is a waste of your time and mine. Your mother does not like me and will never like me. I was brought up on the wrong side of the track, remember." A few moments went by, and then, she said, "Rich, I don't know. Call me closer to the weekend. We are in the middle of dinner right now. O.K." Then she said, "Bye." and hung up the phone. She came back to the table and sat down with a very disgusted look on her face. Cody and Steven both noticed that Tex was very concerned, but he did not say anything.

Cody said, "Rich trying to get you to go out with him again."

"Yes, ...he knows it won't work. There is no need in pretending that it will. I only wish he would see that. His mother wants him to date Crissy. I don't know why he won't. She is a very pretty girl and in his class."

Tex said, "Pretty isn't always the best thing. It helps, of course, but it isn't everything. You have to have other things to go along with

153

it. This guy, Rich, knows something exquisite and wonderful when he sees it. He is afraid of losing it."

Cody and Steven were looking at each other and then glancing at Tex in amazement. They did not know what to say nor what Tex would say next. He sure was full of surprises.

Mama E said, "Honey, I believe that was the best compliment that any girl could ever get. Tex, do you have such a girl?"

Tex looked her square in the face and said, "Yes, Mama E., I do have a girlfriend that meets all those qualities and more." Then he looked at Traci right into her eyes, but did not say a word. He was at a loss for words. All he could do was stare at her.

Then the expression on Traci's face changed to a frown and it looked as though she was going to cry. She immediately got up from the table and went straight to her bedroom. She was devastated because her feelings for Tex was growing each time she was around him and he was always flirting with her. *If he had a girl back in Houston, why was he flirting with her. We are suppose to be his second family. Oh, Lord, I don't want to have bad feelings about him because of Cody. Maybe I took too much for granted. I feel so foolish now. How can I face him again.* The tears started to fall and she did not want to cry. She wiped her eyes and then just laid down across the bed facing the wall.

Then there was a knock on her door. She didn't say anything. There was a knock again. Thinking that it was her mom or Cody, she said, "Come in."

When the door opened, she did not even turn around to see who it was. She really didn't want to see anyone at this time. She lay there waiting for someone to say something, but no one did. Then she felt someone set on the side of the bed and put their hand on her arm and leaned over and kissed her on the cheek. She knew then that it was Tex.

"Go away. I don't want to see you."

"Traci, I'm sorry if I hurt you. I certainly did not mean to do that. You are the last person on earth that I would hurt intentionally. Please turn around and talk to me."

"No, I feel so foolish. I can't face you."

"Oh, yes, you can." He put his arm around her shoulder and pulled her over toward him. "Now, look at me. I want to say something to you." So, she opened her eyes and looked straight at him.

"Trac, first of all, I don't have a steady girl in Houston." She started to say something, but he put his fingers across her lips. "Listen to me. Don't interrupt until I finish, then you can ask me anything you want. O.K."

She shook her head to let him know that she would not interrupt.

He continued with, "I have not been able to get serious about anyone because I could never get you out of my mind. I am not shooting you a line, nor am I playing with you. I would not do that. The girl I was talking about to Mama E is you." She stared at him very confused. "I have been thinking about you since the last time I saw you, but I really did not know how I felt about you until I saw you this time. When I hugged and kissed you Saturday, I had a feeling about you that I have not had before. You did something to me and I feel that you responded as though you had the same feeling. Am I right about that?"

She didn't answer right away. Finally, she said, "I did have a strange feeling and it seems that whenever I am around you, I feel frustrated."

He laughed.

"Trac, I don't want to move too fast here, but when these cases are over, we will do some serious talking about us and our future. O.K."

She smiled. "Yes, ...sure."

155

Then he leaned down and kissed her on the lips lightly, and said, "Are you alright now?"

"Yes, thank you. I really do feel foolish now. Everything just caught me by surprise."

"No, you don't. You should not feel foolish. I didn't handle it right. I brought you a tray." He went over and brought the tray and put it on a table by her bed. "Eat up now. We'll see you later."

He leaned down and kissed her again on the lips a little stronger, but not passionate. And then he walked to the door and looked back at her and she smiled at him and he smiled back and then walked out the door.

After he left, she smiled and then began to eat. *He makes me very happy. I am so glad that Cody went to Houston last weekend. He is such a hunk. He is my Prince Charming. He is charming.*

After she finished her dinner, she waited until she heard them go out the door before she went back to the kitchen. Only her mom was there drinking a cup of coffee. She sat down with her and said, "Mom, Tex is wonderful, isn't he?"

"Yes, he is, Dear. He is crazy about you. I can see it everytime he looks at you."

"I like him very much, too."

They smiled at each other, finished their coffee and then went outside to watch them play tag football. Before long they had her in the group playing with tag football with them. Traci laughed to herself thinking about when she was little, they would not let her play. Now, she was grown up and they wanted her to be a part of their activities. It was an enjoyable evening for all, including Mama E.

Chapter 7

Monday morning came early for the household. After breakfast, Cody and Tex left to pick up Nick and meet at Kato's place and Steven and Traci left for their workplace. Mama E and Sara were at home having a quiet talk and drinking their coffee before cleaning the house and going to buy the week's groceries.

When Cody, Tex and Nick arrived at Kato's place, Marci was already there.

"Come in, you guys. Marci is already here. We are in the kitchen having our second cup of coffee."

As they walked into the kitchen, Marci said, "Good morning, you three. Are you all ready to go to work?"

Cody said, "Yes, I am. Did Kato bring you up to date on what information we have?"

"Yes, he did. You all have been busy. Looks like we have a lot of work to do in order to bring all this together. From what Kato tells me, we have three old murders, drugs coming in from Savannah by someone on the hill and being distributed here, plus corruption in the Sheriff's Department. Any idea of what other departments or higher officials may be involved?"

Cody did not want to correct her and say four murders. He wanted to leave his father's murder out of it for now. He had his witness and did not want to expose her. He did not want anyone else to know about her. Cody said, "No, other than possibly Judge Turner and Judge Mason. Wilson told one of his boys that if they got caught, they would go before Judge Turner and get probation. That suggest to me that someone in the Clerk's Office may be in on this mess, too, since they assign the cases to the judge. That is all the information that we have now."

Nick said, "They always have the same attorney who post their bail and get them out of jail. That poses another thought that the District Attorney's Office may be involved because they let this happen." He laughed. "That is just a thought."

Kato snickered as he said, "We won't know till we investigate, will we. ....Let's play with this idea a bit. ....Suppose Tex and Marci go ahead and arrest the boat crew and follow the two here with the drugs. When they are in the warehouse, we arrest them and Wilson."

As Cody started to interrupt, Kato continued, "If we do that, we are taking a chance as to whether they will talk. Most of the time in these big drug rings, the small punks do not know the big guys. What we want is to get the big guys that are involved in this and hopefully get all the bad guys. What do you think?"

Tex said, "I think we should follow all the way through this time. We know that they come here every week. By next week, we will know more about it. Plus we can arrest one of the boys that has the worst record and follow it through to Judge Turner. That will tie in the court system."

Cody said, "I agree with Tex. We don't want to act too quickly and do anything to mess this up. We want to get as many of them as we can at the beginning."

Nick nodding his head, said, "I agree. Another thing that we have forgotten to mention is about someone shot into my house last Friday night before we went out. I got a look at the tag number and it had a 396 on it. It looked exactly like Santino's car, but I could be mistaken. It was a black unmarked car. We have a lot of those, but the 396 suggest that it is an Internal Affairs car. We have checked, but cannot come up with that tag number. We have a list of all cars and assignment of each one and none of them have that number."

Marci spoke up, "It could be an old tag that is put on the car when it is involved in a crime. Have you guys checked with the Vehicle Section? We have found that to have been done in a couple of other investigations that we have worked."

Nick said, "You got something there, but we are suppose to turn our old tags in when we get a new one. Steven got the list from Susan last Friday and we have checked it. She does not know why we wanted the list. Steven bribed her with a date." They all laughed, and then Nick continued, "At the dance Friday night, she was with Steven and she asked if the list helped us and Steven told her that we were looking for a certain tag number. He asked her about that tag number. She said that she remembered something about that number, but couldn't think of it then. Of course, she had her mind on Steven."

They all laughed again.

Cody said, "I'll get Steven to remind her."

Kato said, "Is it all agreed that we do not arrest anyone now unless there is no other choice?"

"Agreed," they all said in unison.

Then Kato continued, "Tex, the reason I think you should go with Marci is because she and I have worked that area before. If they see us together, they may get suspicious. If they see her with someone else that does not look like a hippy, they probably won't recognize her. So, you two follow through with what we said and when you get back here, give one of us a call."

Marci said, "You've got it. Tex, What time do you want to leave to go to Savannah?"

"We should leave Wednesday morning. That will give us plenty of time to check the courthouse about property there, and spend some time around the boat yard, etc."

Then Kato said, "Today and tomorrow we need to find some answers to the suspicions in this area. Cody, do you have any suggestions as to what we should do? You know more about what is going on around here than I do."

"Tex could stake out Wilson and find out what his day consist of today and tomorrow. Steven's patrol area is on the Hill. He can keep an eye open there for anything suspicious. Also, he can keep after Susan to try to remember about that tag number 396."

Kato said, "That sounds good. That leaves the warehouse here to be checked out. What about Garcia and Santino?"

"Since Nick and I know Garcia and I am sure that he knows we are working the murder cases, you and Marci should handle him and see what you come up with. Don't get to Santino yet unless Garcia leads you to him. Also, check out Lieutenant Harlan Moss, our boss. Be discreet about that. It is only a precautionary measure. Nick and I will continue to try to track down the car with the 396. Somehow, I feel that Santino is mixed up with that and I want evidence. And check out the warehouse here and see where that will lead us. ....Nick, did you ever turn in the bullets to the Crime Lab?"

"No, I haven't. I thought we would go there when we leave here unless you have somewhere else to go."

"No, that will be fine." Then Cody continued, "Nick, you and I can show Tex where Wilson's office is located and then we can go to the Crime Lab and then to the warehouse."

Then Marci asked, "Should we meet back here at a specific time or somewhere else?"

Kato said, "We can meet here tonight around eight o'clock. Here is my card." And he handed each one a card and said, "In case you want to get in touch with me or need some help. We will use this as a headquarters."

Then Cody, Tex and Nick handed Kato a card. Tex wrote his cellular phone number on it. They had another cup of coffee and was making comments about themselves and each other, just getting to know one another and having a little fun.

During this time, Nick's phone rang and he answered it and then he said, "Calm down. Who came by there? I can't understand what you are saying unless you calm down." Then a moment later he said, "We'll see you in about twenty minutes. O.K." Then he hung up the phone.

"Cody, that was Jeanne. Someone came by there about an hour ago and started asking her some questions about Angel. She is upset. I think we should go by and see her."

"Sure, let's go. See you all tonight."

Nick said to Kato, "Jeanne is the one that led us to Angel, the girlfriend to Darrel who was murdered."

Then they got up from the table and cleared the dishes away and they each went in their own direction agreeing to meet back that night at eight o'clock.

Cody, Nick and Tex went toward where they had seen Jeanne before. When they got there, they did not see anyone. They went by Mrs. Stevens' house first. She remembered Cody and Nick from before. She opened the door and invited them inside.

Cody said, "I'm Sergeant Edwards, this is Corporal Carillo and this is a friend of ours, Sergeant Tyler.

Mrs. Stevens said, "I remember you two. I guess you are here because Jeanne called you. She called from here. She was very upset and afraid."

Nick asked, "Do you know where we might find her now? We want to talk with her and make sure that she is alright."

"She went home to get some clothes. She feels safe here and wants to stay here. She feels that they will not look for her here."

"Do you think that will be wise since they know you and that you are Angel's mother?"

"Yes, I think she will be safe here. Before when Probation Officer Wilson came to talk to me. I told him that I did not know any of Angel's friends and did not know where she was. She never brought anyone home, not even Darrel. When she left, we were not on good terms and that I have not heard from her. I also pointed out that I did not want to see her again."

Cody, studying her face, spoke up, "You were lying, weren't you. You do keep in contact with her, don't you? Do you feel that you convinced him and that he would not come by here again?"

"Yes, to all three questions." She smiled. "I love my daughter very much and she loves me. As long as I don't hear from her now, I know that she is alright. That is the way we decided to handle this. If she hears of anything or sees anyone from here, her friend, there, will contact me."

Nick said, "When we talked to Jeanne, she was in a yard down the street. If you will tell me where Jeanne lives, I'll go pick her up and escort her back here."

"She lives in the yard where you saw her before."

After Nick was gone, they sat down at the table and Mrs Stevens poured three cups of coffee. She was in a remembering mood. She said, "Angel was a very sweet child when she was growing up. Very active. She and I are very close. Her father left when she was two. We only had one another. Everything that I told that man was a lie and I call him that man with a lot of disgust. He should be in jail."

Cody was enjoying hearing her talk. Then he said, "Mrs. Stevens, that is what we are working on, but there are several others that should be there, too. That is why he is still walking around now, but hopefully, not for long. We are gathering as much evidence as we can to make sure that they stay there for a long time." He gave her his card and told her to call him day or night if anything at all happens.

Then Cody added, "We will be patrolling by here as often as we can. We will not stop unless it is necessary because we do not want to draw attention to this house. If, at anytime you or Jeanne do not feel safe here, call one of us. Do you understand what I have told you?"

"Yes, I do. And I assure you that I can act very mean and am very convincing when I want to be. That is why I feel that Jeanne will be safe here. My problem may be in trying to get her to stay in the house. She is very much afraid now, so, hopefully, that won't be a problem. If it is, I will let you know. Other than that, she is a good kid."

Up to this point, Tex had been quiet, but he spoke up, "Mrs. Stevens, you remind me very much of my mother. She was a good actress, too."

"You say was. Is she still living?"

"No, she died several years ago. I have one sister and my father at home. I live in Houston, Texas, but I am here with my friend, Cody, helping him with this investigation."

"I appreciate anything that you all can do to put these terrible people behind bars. This neighborhood is a little better than a couple of blocks over. That area is pretty bad. I had thought about moving when Angel was here, but it seems we just couldn't get enough money ahead. When she was in school, it took everything that I had extra to keep her there. I don't regret it. She and Darrel were good kids growing up. Darrel happen to get with the wrong crowd one time and was caught. He wasn't into stealing and burglary and did not know what to do, so the others left him to take the fall. That does not mean that he didn't do anything wrong. He did and he realized it as soon as it happened. That is the reason he cooperated with the police. Then after he got Wilson for a probation officer, he couldn't get out of it. He tried. Finally, he went to the police and that is what got him killed. So you see, if no one around here cooperate with you all, you know the reason why."

Cody said, "Mrs. Stevens, thank you for giving us this information. Believe me, we will get Wilson and the others. I have a personal interest in this investigation. I will not stop until I have put all of them involved in this behind bars. I am very thankful for Tex here and Nick helping me. They both are very good investigators. The only thing is that Tex is not familiar with this town, but he is learning. He is like a brother to me. I have one brother and a sister younger than me."

A few moments later, Nick and Jeanne came into the kitchen.

Cody said, "Hi, Jeanne. Are you feeling better now?"

"Yes, now that I know I have someone I can trust to help protect me. I am not afraid of Wilson anymore."

"Then why don't you sit down and tell us what Wilson said to you."

"I was in the yard talking to these guys; the same ones I was talking with before when you guys drove up. Wilson drove up and asked me if I was Jeanne, I said that I was. He came over and asked me where Angel was. I told him that I didn't know. I had not seen her for about six months and had not heard from her. I was not one of her friends."

"He caught me by the arm real tight with his good arm. The other one was in a cast." She pushed her sleeve up and there was a couple of bruises. "He demanded that I tell him. He said something like, 'Tell me where she is or you will wish you were dead.' I said, 'I told you I don't know where she is. I wasn't her friend. I saw her in the neighborhood a few times. That was all.' He started to slap me and when he drew back his hand, the other guys were there then and held him back. They told him that if he hit me, he would wish he hadn't. Then he jerked free and turned around and walked to the car. Then he turned around and faced me and said, "I'll be back and you better know where she is. Then he got in his car and drove off."

Nick said, "Jeanne, do you feel safe here with Mrs. Stevens. If not, we can put you in a safe house. We don't want to put you in any danger."

"Yes, I feel safe with Mrs. Stevens. He would never think of me being here."

Mrs. Stevens said, "Sergeant Edwards gave me a card and told me to call day or night and we will do that at the first sign of trouble. I have double bolts on the doors, and with all due respect to you three gentlemen, I have a .32 caliber pistol that I bought a few years ago. I haven't had to use it yet, but I will if I have an occasion to use it."

Cody said, halfway smiling, "Mrs. Stevens, I have not seen a gun so I do not have to ask you if you have a permit. And under the circumstances, I do think that we should forget what you said about it. ....You will be careful with it, won't you?"

They all laughed, and then she said, "Yes, I know how to use it, Sergeant Edwards, and I will only use it when it is necessary."

"That sounds good to me. You be sure to keep your doors locked and if anyone breaks in, well, you know what to do." They smiled at each other. Then Cody continued, "Jeanne, you listen to Mrs. Stevens and don't, and I repeat, don't go out of this house unless she approves it. I am telling you this for your own good. You hear me, Jeanne."

"Yes Sir, you won't have to worry about me."

Nick interjected, "We will be patrolling by here as much as we can. We will not stop by the house unless it is necessary. The less attention that is drawn to this house, the better."

Cody spoke up, "I have already explained that to Mrs. Stevens, but, you, Jeanne, should know that as well. We will not stop by here unless you call us or we think that it will be safe for you."

165

Cody and Nick looked at each other and decided that it was time that they left. So they said their goodbyes and left to take Tex by Wilson's office. Wilson's car was there. They pointed it out to Tex and he wrote down the tag number. Then they went to Cody's house and they decided to have a sandwich for lunch while there. Cody gave Tex a map of Little County so that he could study it while waiting. Then Tex got in his car and followed them back to Wilson's office. Wilson's car was still there. Then Cody and Nick left to find the warehouse.

The warehouse was where they had thought it would be. They tried to go in but it was locked. The windows were so high that they could not see inside. They decided to come back later tonight. After looking around a few more minutes, they decided to go up town and turn the bullets into the Crime Lab and then go by the station to bring Lieutenant Moss up to date on what they were doing. They were beginning to trust him, but after talking to Roberts again, they were not sure. Now, they were not sure how much to tell him but they had to tell him some of it.

When they got to the Crime Lab, a friend of theirs was there. Nick said, "Well, Hal, I sure am glad that you are here. We came at the right time."

"How's that, Nick. Hello, Cody. Good to see you two. Haven't seen you in a while."

"Well, some lowdown scum shot a couple of bullets into my house. Would like to keep this between us three because we think it may have been a department weapon. The car that drove away looked like an unmarked department vehicle."

"I see. I see. I'll check against what I have on those guys first. Glad you told me. Nick, Cody, we have been friends for a long time. I'll do what I can, and don't worry, it will be between us. I will be here by myself most of the day. Two of the others are in court and the other is on vacation. I'll do what I can today. Drop by tomorrow and I'll give you a copy of the report. My copy will be in my safe place with my other reports."

"Thank you, Hal. We'll see you tomorrow."

"Sure thing."

As they were leaving, Steven had seen them and was walking toward them. As he came near, he said, "Hello, you two. Are you goofing off again?"

Nick said, "Yes, we are." And a little lower, he said, "We brought those bullets here to the Crime Lab. Now, we are on our way to the station."

Cody said, "Little Brother, have you talked to Susan yet about that number?"

"No, I have been real busy this morning. I was called out and am just now coming in the office. I will make it a point to go by and talk to her before I go home today."

"Good, we all are meeting at Kato's place tonight at about eight o'clock. It would be a good idea for you to come with us and catch up on everything. I have been thinking about something that I will be bringing up tonight and it involves you. I am not sure yet. Kato and Marci are working with us."

"O.K. Big Brother, I'll see you tonight. Be good."

"You, too."

So Nick and Cody walked closer to the parking lot and there stood Kato and Marci up from where they were parked. They got into their car and headed for the station. They thought it wise not to acknowledge them other than speak to them, so they just threw up a hand and kept walking to their car.

After they got into the car, Nick asked, "What do you have in mind that involves Steven? You haven't mentioned it before."

"I have been thinking about how and when we could bring Casey here to see if she can identify the person or persons that was at the site

167

when Dad was killed. Traci mentioned the other night about a spring dance at the Country Club next week. She said that Rich wanted her to go. She wants to go but not with Rich. And now that Tex has claimed her, she doesn't know what to do."

"You mean that Tex has put in a claim for Traci. I know what he said at Kato's, but I thought he was just steering Kato away from her. Which I thought was a good idea, by the way. I can't see Traci with Kato. She can do a heck of a lot better than that."

"Yes, he did right in front of Mama E while we were having dinner the other night. Hey, are you trying to put a claim on her, too?"

"No, I love you guys and Traci a lot, especially since you and Corrie have gotten serious. Traci means a lot to me, but not in the way you are thinking. She and Corrie are cut from the same pattern, so to speak. I just want her to be happy and I don't think she should get involved with Kato. He is a good law enforcement officer, in fact, one of the best, but he is too set in his ways to have a girlfriend like Traci. That's all. Tex is more her style."

Cody laughed. "You know what. Katie is just right for you. Have you asked her for a date yet?"

"No, I haven't, but I plan to as soon as the worst of these cases are over."

"Good, because she is a great gal and I hope it works out for you. Anyway, what I started to say was that if Traci does not go with Rich, maybe Steven could go with Lana. She has been making eyes at Steven and she lives on the Hill. And I thought that we could have Casey brought here and get Tex to take her to the dance and let her listen to the voices at the dance. But what I really want is for Traci to go with Rich and invite Tex and Casey as friends to go with them. That way, we would be out of the picture. I am sure that Mr. Samuels and Mr. Tanner will be there. See what I mean."

"Yes, I do. That would be great. ....You do think that Mr. Samuels is the one that murdered your father, don't you?"

"Let's just say that I feel that it is someone on the Hill and right now he is a suspect. There was an officer and two other men there. One had a very, very distinct voice, authoritative. The other one was not as authoritative and distinct. If she can identify it,... good. If she can't, then we can look elsewhere."

"Sounds good to me, but that will mean that you will have to tell Traci what is going on, or some of it anyway. How will you suggest that she go with Rich without arousing suspicion."

"I have thought of that." He looked at Nick and grinned, and then said, "The hardest problem will be to get Tex to let Traci go with Rich. And even if he does agree, how will he act at the dance. He really shows his emotions right up front."

They both laughed.

By that time, they were at the station. As they pulled into the parking lot, they noticed that the Lieutenant's car was gone. Nick said, "Looks like Moss is not here. Maybe we won't have to give him any information today."

"That would make my day. I don't know how much to tell him. I don't plan to tell him about Kato and Marci working with us, at least not now."

"You do all the talking to the boss. I am your backup and I don't want to say anything that you feel he should not know."

As they walked through the front room, they noticed that Garcia was not there. In fact, only a few of the men were there.

They spoke as they went through the room toward their own office. Nick stopped by their mailbox to pick up their mail and then followed Cody to the office.

"Here is a note from the Lieutenant. He says that he will be on vacation today, but will be in the office tomorrow and he gives a number that he can be reached if we need him."

"Good, I won't have to give him a report today. I didn't know what to say to him, anyway." Cody looked around the office and then continued, "We checked in, now we can check out." He laughed.

"Pardner, why did we come by here?"

"I felt that we needed to check in with Lieutenant Moss since we didn't show up this morning. Even though he told us to work our own hours, I think we should at least check in with him once a day. He is the boss and he may have some comments or questions. Since he is not here, we can go to the courthouse and check on the owner of that warehouse."

So they left and headed for the courthouse.

As they walked into the courthouse, They saw Judge Mason in the hall going into the elevator. They spoke to him and he spoke back before the door closed. They proceeded on down the hall since the Tax Division was on the first floor. As they entered the door, Jan looked up and recognized them. Smiling, she said, "Good afternoon, you two. What are you up to this afternoon?"

They both spoke and then Cody said, "Jan, we are looking for the owners of a specific place."

She led them back to where the books were, and then said, "If I can be of any help, let me know. I'll be up front at my desk."

"Yes, thanks, Jan. We can handle it."

"I'm sure you can. How is Steven? He was suppose to come by today, but I haven't seen him."

Cody laughed, and said, "We just saw him coming in the parking lot of the main office. He said he was called out and had been busy. He will probably be by later."

"Yes, sure. He may be your brother, but he is my favorite....friend, and he is always welcome to stop by here."

They laughed. And she turned and walked up front to her desk.

Nick and Cody settled down in their chairs with some books. Nick was looking in the alphabetical books and Cody was looking at the maps of the streets and avenues. They were not in the best of moods. This was not their idea of police work. It was very boring.

After about thirty or thirty-five minutes, Nick looked up and said, "I have looked up Samuels and cannot find him owning a warehouse. He owns several pieces of property, but they are listed as houses in a residential section. He owns a large building downtown where his office is located and there are several other offices in it. And that gripes my butt that the reason that he owns these buildings may be because of drugs."

Cody just looked at Nick and after a few minutes, he said, "Nick, don't let it get to you. We have a long way to go yet. ....That's odd. I know that this is the warehouse, but it is listed as being owned by Little County. What about Tanner?"

"Under Robert Tanner, there is no warehouse listed. He owns a building downtown where he has his insurance business and another building next ot it that he is renting to other businesses for office space. They are medium-sized buildings compared to the one Samuels own."

They just looked at each other in dismay. In fact, they were very disappointed. They were so sure that they would find something to go on. Finally, Nick said, "What now?"

"Let's talk to Jan and find out how she has the warehouse listed. If it is owned by the county, they would not be paying taxes on it. But you know how things can get screwed up when you have crooked people trying to outsmart the law and what some people will do to keep from paying taxes."

171

Nick laughed. "Right, Pardner. Talking to Jan is better than looking at these books."

"Hey, where did you get this 'Pardner' thing? .... Hey, you taking an interest in girls, huh?"

They laughed. They were beginning to feel very angry, then silly and frustrated now.

"Oh, just something I picked up to make life interesting on the job. And what do you mean interested in girls? When was I not interested in girls?"

"Oh, you don't think I am interesting on the job, huh. And the answer to your other question is 'never'. You are always interested in girls."

They both laughed again.

When they got to the front, Jan wasn't there. The other girl at another desk said that she would be right back. She had to go look up something for someone.

Cody said, "We'll see her later."

As they were walking out to the car, Nick with a half grin on his face looked at Cody and asked, "Why can't we wait until she get back. It is not like we are in a hurry and this is not important. I guess you have something else in mind." And then he grinned more.

Cody said laughingly, "As a matter of fact, I do. Steven owes Jan a dinner, right. We will send him by here tomorrow to check with her and he will have to ask her out. That will pay her back for lying to us."

"How did Jan lie to us?"

"She told us that she would be up front if we needed her. When we needed her, she wasn't there. So, now she will have to pay by going to dinner with my brother."

"Your brother is going to realize one day how you manipulate his love life and he is going to pay you back and I want to be there to see it."

"What do you mean manipulate his love life. If it wasn't for me, he wouldn't have one."

"You shotdodger. Here we are sitting in your car with a big disappointment on a major case and you are in a silly, kidding mood."

"Right now if I think about our disappointment, I will probably say something that I might be sorry for later. I am more disappointed in my gut feeling than anything else. I can always count on my gut feeling and this time it has let me down. I was so sure that Tanner or Samuels owned the warehouse. Let's go to the farm and talk with Tim to make sure that we have the right warehouse."

When they got to the farm, they went in the back way to keep Mama E and Sara from seeing them. As they were coming to the barn, Jake came out of the barn and saw them. When they stopped the car, he went over there because he knew that something was up. "Hey, you guys, anything wrong?"

Cody said, "We just want to talk to Tim a minute. Is he around?"

"Yes, I'll get him for you. You don't need me, do you? I am in the process of delivering a baby calf."

"No, Jake, you go and do what you need to do. We won't be long. See you later."

"O.K., I'll send Tim out. They are some mighty fine boys. They work good, too. Just wanted to throw that in for now." Cody smiled. He knew that Jake was always trying to help some youngster if he could.

A minute later, Chip and Tim came out of the barn. Chip said, "Nothing is wrong, is there?"

Cody said, "No, we just want to make sure we have the name and address of the warehouse. What did you say the name of the warehouse is and where is it located?"

Tim studied for a moment and then he said, "It is located on the block of Thirty-Sixth Street and Twenty-Eighth Avenue. There is a name on it, but I can't think of it now. Seems like it starts with a 'C'"

Cody asked, "Could it be 'The Crafton Building' and is it painted a light green with darker trim?"

"Yes, that's it. I have heard that name before."

"O.K. Tim, we just wanted to make sure we have the right building."

"Sure, that's it."

"O.K., Boys, you alright here. Jake isn't working you too hard, is he?"

They laughed and Tim said, "No, Jake is a lot of fun. It is a lot better here than where I was before."

"See you guys later. Be careful."

So Nick and Cody drove off down the back road and as they were nearing Nick's place, Nick said, "I think we should go back and talk with Jan."

Cody looked at his watch and said, "By the time we get there, they will be closing the doors. It is later than I thought. You are right, though. We should have waited and talked to her. I'm sorry. I just wasn't in the mood for another disappointment. If Steven can't go by in the morning, we will. I have another thought in mind. Would you like to hear it?" Cody laughed.

Nick looked at him and grinned. "Yes, let's hear it because you are going to tell me anyway."

"What if we pick Wilson up Thursday morning and the rest of the group stake out the warehouse to see who comes in to distribute the drugs."

"That would be neat, wouldn't it? But, it probably won't be the high man."

"No, but we would be one step higher on the ladder. I have a feeling that by this weekend, we will have a lot of evidence. But we have got to get the high man on the Hill."

Nick invited Cody in for a cup of coffee. So while Nick was making the coffee, Cody called Corrie to talk with her. He had not seen her very much lately. When she answered, he said, "Hi, Sweetheart. I was thinking about you and wanted to hear your sweet voice. I'm sorry we haven't had time to be together lately, but I promise as soon as these cases are over, we will."

Right away Corrie knew that Cody was feeling down. "Cody, don't apologize. I understand. I know that you love me and that is enough for me now. Something happened today that disappointed you or did not go right, didn't it?"

"Yes, I was disappointed today, but tomorrow will be different. We are making progress. It is just not going as fast as I want it to. I am too anxious. You know me like a book, don't you? Whenever I feel a little down, I think of you and want to be with you."

About that time, there was a loud crash with glass flying around in the front of the cottage. Nick came running out of the kitchen and into the living room with his gun drawn. Then Cody said, "Honey, I have to hang up. Someone is playing games with us again. Love you. Bye."

"Love you, too. Be careful. Bye." And they both hung up the phone.

When Cody got into the living room, Nick had picked up the rock and was taking the note off of it. The note was written with words from a paper or magazine glued on a sheet of paper. It read, 'BACK OFF OR THERE WILL BE TROUBLE.'

"Nick, did you see anyone or the car?"

"No, I didn't. I will find the son-of-a bitch who is doing this. Now, he owes me for two windows. I just fixed the other one."

Cody looked at Nick and said teasingly, "Evidently, you are not going to back off."

They both looked at each other a moment and then burst out laughing.

"What do you think, Smart Ass?.....That note looks like some kid stuff. He sure doesn't have any smarts, does he?"

So Nick went into the closet off the kitchen and brought out the broom and dustpan. They started picking up the big pieces of glass and then swept up the other smaller ones. Then Cody went to the closet and brought out the vacuum cleaner to make sure that they got all of the glass up.

"I bought two panes the other day. They came two to a package. Want to help me put this one back in now or do you have to leave?"

"No, I'll help you. You come prepared, don't you?"

"Yeah, I guess I do. At this rate, I should have bought the whole damn box."

They laughed again. It seemed as though everything that was said between them was funny this afternoon. They laughed a lot and it made them feel better.

When they had finished with the window and cleaned up the mess, Cody left to go home and told Nick that they would pick him up later. Then Nick went to his mother's for a good meal. He wanted to be with his family for a little while and he, also, wanted to let Corrie know that they were alright. She worried about both of them.

When Cody got home, everyone was there except Tex.

"Has anyone heard from Tex yet?"

Steven answered, "He called about thirty minutes ago and said that he would get a bite on the road and that he would call you or meet you later."

Traci looked puzzled and then she said, "You left him out on the road by himself. You are suppose to be showing him around. One of you should be with him. How dare you?"

Mama E said, "Your sister is right. He doesn't know his way around this town. That is not the way you treat your best friend who is visiting you from out of town."

Cody said, "Mom, he is a grown man and he can find his way around. Besides, he is doing some undercover work for us. It is not good for us to be seen in public with him at this time. Don't worry, he can take care of himself."

Traci's eyes got a bright sparkle to them. She said, "That is why you did not want to go to Johnnie Lee's the other night, isn't it? You did not want to be seen with Tex."

"Yes, it is. Can we discuss this later. I am as hungry as a wolf." Cody gave her a stern stare letting her know that he did not want to discuss it.

Steven said, "Amen to that." And they sat down and started to eat. Traci was still trying to get some more information out of them, but they would not bulge. She was getting so frustrated that they all had to laugh at her.

Finally, Cody said, "Trac, I'll talk to you after dinner. Let it go for now. O.K."

She said in a disgusted voice. "O.K., but you will tell me what is going on later. I demand that."

They laughed.

About that time the phone rang. Traci said, "I am not going to answer that phone again. It has been ringing off the hook since I have been home."

Cody said, "I'll answer it. It may be Tex or one of the other guys."

So Cody answered the phone, but no one would say anything. All he could hear was heavy breathing and then they hung up.

He sat back down and asked, "How long has this been going on?"

"Since about five o'clock, a few minutes after Trac got home. Do you think it has anything to do with your investigations or that Rich would do something like that?"

Cody said, "Mom, yes, it probably does have something to do with this investigation. I will put a monitor on it and we will find out who it is. Trac, do you think Rich would stoop to doing that?"

"No, he wouldn't do that. He called earlier and asked me again about going to the spring dance at the Country Club with him."

"What did you tell him?"

"I told him that I would think about it. I want to go, but I don't know what to do."

"If you want to go, I think you should go."

They all looked at Cody. Then Traci said, "What about Tex? What will he say?"

The others did not see Tex when he came in the back door, but Steven and Cody could see him. Cody said, "Never mind, Tex. He's a grown man, he can take it. Besides, you are not married yet."

Mama E said, "Cody, shame on you. You know how Tex feels about Trac. You sound like you don't approve of Tex and your sister being sweethearts."

Cody winked at Tex and laughed. Tex was enjoying this. Then Cody said, "Yeah, Mom, I approve of Tex and Trac being sweethearts, but I think if she wants to go to the dance with Rich, she should go. Besides, it may make Tex jealous."

Then Tex stepped where they all could see him and he said in a booming voice, "To hell she will. If she goes to a dance, she will go with me. I will take her."

They all howled at the expression on Mama E's and Traci's face.

Finally, Traci caught her breath and asked, "How long have you been standing there?"

Tex came over and kissed her on the cheek and said, "Long enough. If you want to go to a dance, I'll take you." Then he reached up in the cabinet and got himself a plate and fixed himself a glass of tea and set down to the table.

They sat there with Tex while he ate and they had dessert. Sara had baked a juicy coconut cake that day and it was delicious. After she baked it, she put it in the freezer and partially froze it. They all ended up having double helpings of it. Then the guys went out and sat at a table with a cup of coffee in their hands. Traci stayed and helped her mom clean up the kitchen. When they had finished cleaning the kitchen, she went outside with the guys.

As she walked up to them, they were looking at her and laughing. She asked, "What's so funny, you guys, and don't say it's a male thing?"

Cody said, "Come sit down with us, Sis. We want to talk to you."

She said, "That's a first."

So she sat down with them and Cody said, "I have been talking with Tex and he says, very reluctantly, it is alright for you to go to the dance with Rich as long as he can come along with a date."

"What do you mean? Something is not right here. Are you teasing me or trying to pull the wool over my eyes?"

They all laughed. Tex said, "No, Cody is telling you the truth. I don't know how much Cody wants to tell you, so I'll let him explain it to you. But I want you to understand that it took a lot of talking from these two brothers of yours to get me to agree on this. I want you to know that."

Cody said, "Trac, I want you to understand that this is part of our investigation and it should be kept between the four of us. You understand that, I'm sure."

"Yes, I do. You know that, Bro."

"Sis, we have a witness in one of the murder cases who saw the actual killer. She is living in Texas now. That is why Nick and I went to Houston. No one knows about this witness and who she is, except Tex, Nick and I. Steven knows what we have told him and he heard her interview on the tape. The killer possibly lives on the Hill. This witness cannot identify the killer by looking at him, but she may be able to identify him by his voice. She remembers his voice very well. You understand me up to now?"

"Yes, Bro. so you want me to go to the dance with Rich. What good will that do for your investigation?"

"All we want you to do is to agree to go with Rich and invite Tex and his girl to go with you. You and Tex are friends and he is in town that weekend and you can not go unless you can invite him and his girlfriend. Tex will dance with her all the time because he does not want to be away from her at all. She is our gold mine, so to speak, and we do not want to take a chance that anything at all will happen to her. Not even dancing with Rich unless you four are dancing very close. Tell Rich that you and your friends will meet him at the dance.

That way if and when she identifies the voice, Tex can make an excuse and leave and Rich can bring you home or you may leave with Tex. Your choice. If she does not identify the voice, then we will have to look elsewhere. You do understand how important this is to our investigation, don't you?"

She said very excitedly, "Yes, I do. It will be a pleasure to help you in this investigation. I will be glad to do what I can."

Cody said, "Another thing. Don't tell Mom any of this. All she has to know is that you and Tex are going out. You will leave together and then pick up this girl. If her cousin can come with her, they will stay at a hotel or somewhere else. If he can't come with her, then Tex's father will come with her and she may have to stay here. We will figure that out when the time comes. But we do not want her out of our sight. Are you alright with this plan?"

"Sure. I'm fine. In fact, I'm excited about it," she said with enthusiasm.

Steven looked at his watch. "We better get going if we are going to be there by eight o'clock."

"Where are you guys going?"

Steven said, "Sis, we are going to meet some other guys that are helping in the investigation. We are meeting each night to put all the information together. One day, you will be an investigator, and I might add, a very good one." He came over and kissed her on the cheek and said, "Thanks, Sis, you don't know how much this will mean to all of us."

"I'm very glad to be able to do it for the Edwards' Cause." She said laughingly.

The others looked at each other and smiled. *They each were thinking that she did not know how close to the truth she really was. If only she knew.* Then Tex came around to her side and put his arm around her waist and they walked into the house.

Chapter 8

On the way to Kato's place, Cody and Tex filled Nick in on the plans about the dance. Also, that Traci only knew that the girl was a witness in one of the murder cases. They all agreed that they would not mention it to Kato and Marci yet. Their Dad's murder was their case. Maybe later they would tell Kato and Marci.

The guys all arrived at Kato's place right at eight o'clock. They had brought three cartons of beer and a bottle of wine for Marci, pizza and snacks with them.

Kato met them at the door and he noticed that there was someone else there other than the usual. He said, "Well, who have we here. Some more help, I hope. The more the merrier."

Cody winked at Kato, grinned and said, "This is my Little Brother, Steven. He has some good connections whereas females are concerned. He is helping us when he can. He works in Uniform from downtown and is out on the road. You remember those days, don't you, Kato?"

"Yes, I do very well. Glad to meet you Steven. I won't call you Little Brother because I can tell by the look on your face that you prefer Steven." Then he began to laugh. They all laughed. Steven was thinking to himself. *Big Brother, you are getting out of line, and I am going to have a talk with you. He is surely going to hear from me when we get home.*

Then Kato added, "You all come on in and let's have a brew before we get started." They all walked into the kitchen where Marci was sitting. Steven reached over and shook hands with her as he said, "Allow me to introduce myself. I am Steven Edwards, Cody's brother."

They all laughed again.

"Glad to meet you Steven. It would be my pleasure working with you, I am sure," Marci said as she was giving him the eye.

They all got a beer and sat around the table. They shot the breeze a few minutes, so to speak. Finally, Kato said, "Marci and I talked to Garcia today. He wasn't very interested in talking to us. He did say that he and Santino were friends. When I asked him who the hell wanted to be friends with Internal Affairs, he said, 'Sometimes it pays to be friends with the enemy.' When I asked him about Wilson and the drugs, his expression changed and he wouldn't say anything. Marci and I got the impression that he does know about it. When we left him, we went to Santino's place, but he was not in and supposedly would not be back today. So, we didn't get a lot of information today. What about you guys?"

Steven spoke up and said, "He gave you more than he realized, didn't he?"

Marci said, "Yes, he did. His expressions told us that he was involved. We feel he is involved and we know that we will have to connect the dots sooner or later. Hey, I like you, Steven. I'll work with you anytime."

"That will be my pleasure, Ma'am." Everyone laughed because Steven put on his long southern gentleman's drawl.

Kato said, laughing, "I can see why he has a lot of connections with the females. He sure has made a hit with Marci, and I have to say that not too many males do that."

"Kato, I am very choosy when it comes to men and my social life. I have learned that from experience."

They all looked at each other and laughed.

Then Tex said, "I followed Wilson until he went home. He stayed in the office until about four o'clock. He went by the warehouse but did not stop. Just looked around. Then he went straight home, but he was on the telephone most of the time. I thought maybe we would ride by the warehouse on the way back home tonight if the rest of you think we should."

"No, I don't think that will be necessary, said Cody. "I was thinking about Kato's idea today about picking Wilson up just to talk to him Thursday morning just before you all get here with the boys bringing the drugs. That ought to shake up the scene a little. Some of us will stake out the warehouse and see who shows up to pick up the drugs and distribute it to Wilson's boys. What do you all think?"

They all agreed that it was a good idea. Then Cody continued, "Nick and I went to the Tax Office and looked up the owner of the warehouse. Surprisingly, the warehouse is listed as being owned by the county, but we know that it is the warehouse that is being used. I was thinking that maybe Steven could go by in the morning and talk to Jan and find out who is paying the taxes on it. You know how not-so-honest people will do anything to keep from paying taxes or cover up what they own. The county may have owned it at one time and whoever bought it never did change the records for some illegal reason. It will be worth a check. If the county does own it, someone has permission to use it, right?"

Kato laughed, and said, "Steven, you do have a reputation, don't you? It's worth a try."

Steven said, "I talked to Susan this afternoon and she did think about that tag 396. She said Santino reported that tag as being stolen last year. Another tag number was issued to him at his request. Maybe he still has the tag and uses it whenever he does something ....bad."

"That's what I thought," Marci said. "You have a very alert thought process there. And that is a compliment. I don't give them out very often."

"That is a thought. Cody, you asked Marci and I to discreetly get information on Lieutenant Harlan Moss. We found out in a round about way that he does talk to Santino once in a while, but do not socialize with him. Moss' sister is married to Santino's brother, Anthony. From what we could find out, Moss likes his brother-in-law, but do not like Domenic."

"Thanks, I have to make a report to him on this investigation. I just wanted to know how much I should tell him. Nick and I were just beginning to trust him when Roberts, who started this investigation months ago, told us that Moss was a close friend to Dad. The thing that concerns me is that we have information that the killer at Edward's murder scene said that a close friend of Edwards told him that Edwards was getting too close. That was why he had to kill him. The other guy there did not have a clue that the killer was going to kill anybody. Now I know that I have to confront him and get everything out in the open. We can't continue to play cat and mouse with him. I have to know if we can trust him or not."

Kato said, "I would confront him, but not give him any information as to why you are confronting him. Just ask him if he was a friend of your father's and if he says he was, ask him what your father discussed with him about the case. Just to see what he says."

Cody looked at Nick and Nick nodded. Then Cody said, "Good. We will do that."

Marci said, "Cody, Steven, I was very sorry to hear that you have found out that your father was murdered rather than killed in crossfire as was stated. I know it was devastating to find out this way. I promise you both that I for one and I am sure the rest of us here will not stop until we have put all involved under the jail."

They all said, "Amen to that. We will get them no matter how long it takes."

Steven started to say something but couldn't speak, so Cody said, "Thank you, Marci. Steven and I both have always thought that there was something wrong with what was told us, but we never had anything to cause us to think different until now. The witness can identify the voice, but not the face of the killer. I have a plan that I will discuss with you next week on how we are planning to identify him. It is too early now."

"Very good, Cody. I guess you have your reasons for not divulging that now. We will trust you on that."

"Kato, it is not that I don't trust you. I do or I would not be here. Things may change in the investigation this coming week, depending on what we find out. I will tell you when we get ready to go through with this plan. This involves my father and I want it to be kept separate from the other murders right now."

Marci said, "We understand, Cody. You handle it the way you all want, but we are here to help you anyway that we can. Don't forget that. O.K.?"

"O.K., Marci. We won't."

"Our sister does not know about our father being murdered. Neither does our mother. We will tell them in due time. The only ones that know are in this room."

Tex said, "If you all are going to pick up Wilson Thursday, we should let him alone until then. What do you want me to do until Wednesday morning.

Nick said, "Tex, Cody and I have to go downtown in the morning. You go with us and stake out Santino. We will show you what he looks like and his car."

Steven spoke up and said, "I will go by and speak to Jan and find out about the warehouse.

Marci looked at Kato and said, "Why don't you and I find the kids that are selling the drugs. Sometimes, kids say things that they do not know is important."

Cody said, "That's a good idea for you and Kato to talk to them. Nick and I did not want to spook Wilson before, so we did not speak to the kids, but if you do, Wilson will not know that we are involved."

He reached in his brief case and handed Kato a copy of the list of the eleven kids. "You can talk to all of them except Tim. He is at our farm. He came forward and talked with us."

They talked on for another thirty or forty minutes about different things while they had a couple more brews. They were really getting to know each other and enjoying each other's company. The important things to be done was a couple of days away, but until then, they were trying to gather any information that they could to connect the dots as to what they already knew or thought that they knew. But they all were getting antsy because they wanted Thursday to be here now.

Finally, they agreed to meet again tomorrow night which would be Tuesday night.

On the way home, they did go by Wilson's house and his car was home. Then they rode by the warehouse and it was quiet. Finally, they dropped Nick off at his place and they went on home. Everyone was in bed when they got there, so they went quietly upstairs and into their own bedroom. Each had their own thoughts.

The next morning at the breakfast table, Traci said, "I switched on the answering machine last night. The phone was ringing every thirty minutes and no one would say anything. So, if you all want to call anyone, call on the cellular phone. If you want Mom, wait until the answering machine picks up and ask her to pick up the phone and she will. I don't want her to be answering the phone all day. Is that understood?"

They all stared at Traci and said, "Yes." It was not very often that she demanded things, so when she did, they listened.

Then Cody asked, "How late was the last call?"

Mama E spoke up then, "It was about eleven o'clock. Then it rang again around three o'clock several times. That was the last time."

187

Cody said, "I will try to remember to bring a monitor home tonight and we will find out who is doing this. I am sure it has something to do with the investigation."

Steven looked at his mother and knew that she did not get much sleep last night. "Mom, why don't you have Sara stay here with you today. You can go back to bed and let her take care of the house, or she can talk to you and keep you company, whichever you prefer. Don't worry about the calls. Just let it ring. They will give up sooner or later."

Traci said, "I will see Sara this morning and make sure she is here. I don't have to be at work as early as you all do."

"O. K., Sis. That will be your chore for today."

She looked at Steven and smiled. The others got up from the table and carried their plates to the counter. Then they said their goodbyes and left.

Steven stayed a little longer and helped clear the table while Traci went to talk to Sara.

"Mom, why don't you go lay down, Sara will take care of the kitchen and she will stay here as long as you want her to be here."

"I know that, Steven. I will wait until Sara gets here and then I will lay down for a little while. You go on to work. A few phone calls do not scare me."

Steven grinned. "I know, Mom. But you are not sleeping as good as you should lately. Get Sara to take you to see Dr. Smith. Let him give you something to take that will make you sleep at night."

"I still have some of the pills that he gave me before. I will take a couple and lay down after Sara gets here. You kids worry too much about me. I can take care of myself."

"Mom, we know that. Here comes Traci and Sara now. I will leave you females alone. See you tonight, Mom."

"O.K., Son. Be careful."

Steven went outside and got in his car, waved to his sister and Sara and then drove down the driveway. Traci went in and said her goodbye to her mother and then left for work. Sara sat down at the table with Mama E and they had a second cup of coffee. Then Sara gave Mama E a couple of her pills and scooted her off to bed. Then she came back and started cleaning up the kitchen. The phone started ringing, but Traci had told her not to answer it unless one of them called and they would put their name on the answering machine. Sara turned the phone down another notch or two and then went about cleaning the house. It wasn't much to do since she had cleaned it on Friday. Then she sat down with her needle work and started working on the sweater that she had started.

In the meantime, Steven was at his desk, when Traci came in and sat in a chair beside his desk. She was white and upset. Steven took one look at her, "What's wrong, Sis?" He got up and went back of her and put his arms around her shoulders. She was really shook up.

She said in a shaky voice. "On the way to work this morning, a car tried to run me off the road." She let out a sigh and then took another breath and said, "He hit the side of my car and then took off. I am not hurt. I am O.K., ...but he dented my car."

"What was the description of the car and did you see the driver?"

"The car was an unmarked dark car and the driver was dark. Dark skinned face, dark hair. I think his hair was short, but not real short. I had to keep my eye on the road. I only had one look at him and that was when he was beside me."

Steven walked to the cooler and brought her a glass of water. She sipped some of it and just sat there for a moment.

Then Steven said, "Come on and show me your car." He helped her up and held his arms around her waist and they walked out the door to the parking lot. She sat down in the car while Steven looked at the dent on the front fender. She had calmed down quite a bit by then. Then he asked her if she wanted to go home or if she felt like working. "If you want to go home, I will take you. O.K."

"I will be just as well off here as I will be at home. I will stay here. If I go home, Mom will worry too much."

"You stay in your office. Don't leave to go anywhere outside your immediate area. Give me the keys and I will have the Crime Lab look at the dent and see what they can come up with. I'll come by later and see you and take you to lunch. How is that?"

"Gee. Thanks, Bro. I would love to have lunch with you." She then gave him a hug and her keys.

He walked her back inside to her desk and told her in no uncertain terms not to move from there. He did not want her walking up and down the hallway or out of her office. Then he went to the Crime Lab hoping that Cody, Tex and Nick were there. He knew that they would be checking on the bullets. They were not there when he got there, but while he and Hal were outside looking at Traci's car, they drove up.

As soon as he stopped the car, Cody jumped out and asked, "What happened? That's Traci's car."

Tex said with a frightened voice, "What happened? Is Traci alright?"

Steven smiled to let them know she was alright and then said, "Yes, she is. Someone tried to run her off the road this morning. She is a little shook up, but she said she wanted to stay at work. I'll check on her later."

Cody asked, "Did she see who did this?"

"She said that the car was a dark unmarked car and the driver was dark also with medium short dark hair. She only had one good glance at him. She was trying to keep her eyes on the road."

Nick looked at Cody, "Let's go check out a car before he can take it to a shop. Hal, I'll be back to get the report."

"If you find the car, call me and I'll be glad to check the paint on it."

So Nick, Tex and Cody took off to the parking lot where Santino parks his car. Sure enough it was there and had a dent with blue paint on it. Cody got on his cellular phone and called Hal. Hal and Steven were there in less than five minutes. Hal was shocked. He said, "This is Santino's car. I can't believe it. It sure looks like a match, though. Hal took out his camera and took pictures of the tag number, the whole car and several of the dents in different directions. Hal took out his kit and took samples of the paint to take to the Lab. He did that right away so he would have them before Santino knew that he did.

When he had finished getting his samples of paint, he said, "You go get the warrants while Cody and Nick make sure that Santino doesn't take the car. I'll be right back with the tow truck."

He smiled at Nick and Cody and said, "Santino must be at a meeting that he couldn't get out of attending. Otherwise, he would have this car in a garage by now."

It wasn't long before everything was in place and Hal and a driver were back with the tow truck to tow the car to the lab. Santino had not showed up at that time. Hal was standing over by the tow truck talking to the driver, while the others were standing by their car.

Cody said, "If we arrest him now, he will be out in a couple of hours. I am worried about Traci since she is his target. Either way he won't be in jail after a few hours. What do you think we should do? Arrest him now or follow him the next day or two and arrest him Thursday morning. Along about the time we pick up Wilson. What do you think?"

Nick said, "Tow the car to the Lab now and wait until later to get Traci to identify him and then arrest him. That will narrow down the people to show up at the warehouse. These two, we know are involved in this drug operation."

Tex nodded as he said, "Yes, I agree with that. He could always say someone else was driving his car. But if Traci can identify him, we will have him. We can pick him up anytime between now and Thursday. How are we going to get Traci to identify him."

Cody thought for a moment and then said, "Steven, go get Traci and she and Tex can stay in his vehicle and watch for Santino and she can get a good look at him. After she does that, she can go back to work and Tex will follow him and see what he does when he comes out and finds his car gone. Tex was suppose to follow him today, anyway. We will stay here until Traci gets here and the car is gone. Nick and I have to go and confront the Lieutenant. Tex, keep in touch with us. O.K. And take care of our sister."

"Sure, Cody. On both counts, especially the last one. Don't you worry about Traci. I'll take good care of her. I have a special interest in her, remember."

"How can we forget."

They laughed.

Hal came over and told them that they were towing the car to the Lab. He would be there all day if they needed him. Then he said, "By the way, Nick, I checked out those bullets and came up with nothing, but I am not through yet. I have some other comparisons I want to do, especially after this. I'll see you all later."

"O.K. Hal. Thanks."

Then Steven left to pick up Traci. When he got there, all the girls were standing around her and asking her questions and telling her how sorry they were that she had to go through that. And that they hoped they caught the guy that did that to her.

Steven walked up and they all spoke to him. He said, "Good morning, ladies. Traci, I need you to come with me. I have already talked with your supervisor and she gave her permission."

The others wished her the best and then went back to their desk. They all were smiling at Steven. Traci got her purse and she and Steven left. Steven explained to her what their plans were. By that time they were already at the parking lot. She got out of his car and walked over to where the others were. Tex put his arm around her waist and kissed her on the cheek, "How are you feeling now, Sweetheart?"

She smiled up at him, "I feel alright. I was a little shook up earlier, but I am fine now."

The others watched as Tex led her to his car.

He opened the door to his car and asked her to get in and sit down. Then he walked back to the others. Steven then handed him a picture of Santino. He said, "I did not show it to Traci. I thought it would be better if she saw him in person without looking at a photo. I am giving you this so that you will know what he looks like."

"Sure, Steven." He looked at it and said. "He is dark skinned and has dark hair."

"Yes, he does fit that description." They each grinned.

Then Tex stuck the picture in his pocket and walked to his car and got in beside Traci and they hunkered down so that they would not be that noticable.

The others got into their cars and left.

Cody and Nick went back by the Lab and talked with Hal and then went into the shop and looked at the car. Hal had found a key with a magnet under the car that would unlock the trunk.

Nick said, "What you bet we find a tag with the numbers 396 on it?"

Cody grinned and said, "Bet we do."

Hal just stood and looked at them. Then he opened the trunk of the car. And sure enough, there was the tag stuck down by the side partially covered up with a small blanket.

Hal said, "How did you all know that?"

Nick said, "Hal, this car had this tag on it when someone shot those bullets into my house. Steven was right last night when he said that he uses the tag when

he does something bad."

Hal said, "I never did like Santino, but that was nothing unusual. I don't like a lot of guys on the department. Especially, the ones that think they can do anything because they have a badge and gun."

Cody said, "Hal, I don't have to tell you to keep this to yourself, do I? We have our reasons for not wanting to arrest him now. We are planning to do that later on this week. Do I have your word that you will not tell anyone, not even your co-workers about this? Don't even make a report on the car until I let you know."

"Sure, Cody. Not a word until you say the word. I am on your side. There are only a few good guys left around here and that includes you all. If this guy is dirty, I would be the first to say 'put him under the jail'."

Cody and Nick both smiled at him, "Thanks, Hal. We'll stop by tomorrow and see about the bullets."

"O.K., you two. See you then." Then he turned around and walked back into the Lab. And Nick and Cody drove off to go to their office and confront Moss on some issues.

When they arrived in their office, Cody made a pot of coffee and then walked up to the Lieutenant's office. He had someone in the office just casually talking.

Cody said, "Lieutenant, Nick and I would like to see you when you finish here. We will be in our office. It will be better to meet there."

"Sure Cody. I'll be there in a minute. We are about finished here, anyway."

Cody walked back to his office and sat behind his desk. Nick was sitting at his desk going through the mail. They both were nervous about what they would learn from Moss. Their desk faced each other and they sat there looking at each other wondering how this talk was going to turn out.

Finally, Cody said, "He will be here in a minute. He was talking to someone."

"Cody, I sure hope we are wrong in what we are thinking. I like the Lieutenant and sure as hell hope that he is not connected in this mess."

"I do, too, Nick. I sure do. Mainly, because he was suppose to be a friend of Dad's. I sure hope he wasn't the one that told someone that Dad was too close in his investigation."

Cody looked up and saw the Lieutenant standing in the doorway. He said very roughly, "Come in, Lieutenant. We have a few things to clear up and we need some answers now." Cody was wanting to get this over with because he liked the Lieutenant and wanted to believe he was not involved in this investigation, but he had his doubts.

Lieutenant Moss cocked his head and looked amazed, then he said, "Sergeant, you sound angry. Hope you aren't angry with me."

Cody, looking him in the face, said very sternly, "That depends on what you have to say, Lieutenant. ....What is your relationship with Santino in Internal Affairs?"

He looked puzzled, but said very calmly and slowly, "Lieutenant Santino is not a friend of mine, if that is what you mean. I speak to him whenever I see him and socialize with him whenever I am invited to my sister's house and he is there. That is all. I do not care to be seen in public with him. I do not say anymore than necessary to him. My sister is married to his brother. They are complete opposites; I might add. ....What is this about, Edwards? I can tell that you are upset about something."

Cody ignored the question and then asked, "Did you consider yourself a friend of my father's when he was alive?"

"Yes, I felt that I was a good friend to him. He acted the same way toward me. ...I certainly considered him to be my friend. He was very helpful to me when I came to this section. ...Are you going to tell me what this is about?"

"In a minute after I get some answers. Did my Dad discuss these cases with you at any time?"

"Not really. He did tell me one day that he was on to something in the department, but he never told me any specific thing about the cases."

"Did you ever discuss these cases with anyone in the office or outside at your sister's house?"

"No, I did not. I do not discuss cases outside the office and only with the ones working on the cases in the office." By that time the Lieutenant was getting very upset. "What do you think I did, Edwards?" He said as he glared at Cody with anger shooting from his eyes and a growl in his voice.

"Lieutenant, I have reason to believe that someone close to my father told someone that is involved with these cases that my father was close to something and that is why he was killed. My sources also told me that you were close to my father. I have to find out if you were the one that my father told that to."

"Cody, Nick, I assure you that I know nothing about who is involved in this corruption. I sure as hell would not have said anything that would get your father killed. I liked him very much and respected him. He was a big help to me when I came into this department. He was the one that recommended me to take his place when he retired. He was planning to retire in another year as you know."

Cody was really getting angry now. "What was wrong, Lieutenant? You couldn't wait for another year?"

Lieutenant Moss stood up and came around Cody's desk with his fist drawn as he hollered at Cody. "Alright, Sergeant. You are out of line." Cody had stood up, too, with his fist drawn back and was ready to let the Lieutenant have it if the Lieutenant made the first move.

By that time, Nick was there, but could not get to Cody, so he grabbed Lieutenant Moss and held him back. After a moment of staring at each other, Cody sat down behind his desk again and put his head in his hands. Nick let go of the Lieutenant and said, "Look, Lieutenant, if you know of anyone or heard anything about this, please tell us now. We need to know that. ..Cody need to know that."

"Nick, I swear to you. I don't know anything about this. I was Captain Edwards' closest friend. He was friendly to me because I was always asking him for help on this or that. He was not friends with any of his men, but they all respected him." He put his head in his hands for a moment, but then he started to raise his head slowly and had an awful look on his face. Then, he said, "Oh, my God. ...Oh, my God. No. It can't be."

Nick staring at the Lieutenant, said, "Lieutenant, what is it?"

By then Cody had raised his head and was staring at Moss.

"My sister invited me and my wife to have dinner with them one night. We were the only ones that were to be there. I always asked my sister if Domenic was going to be there when she invited us over. She knew how I felt about him. We had a pleasant dinner and conversation was lively and enjoyable. Later, Domenic dropped by and we were sitting around the table having a second cup of coffee.

He never did say why he came. I assumed it was about a business that he and Anthony was talking about. I stayed as long as I could without being rude. Then just as I was leaving, the phone rang. Elizabeth came to the door and said, 'Harlan, there is a Captain Edwards on the phone. He wants to talk to you. I went to the phone and spoke to him. He asked me something about a warehouse, and I answered him with, 'there is a warehouse on such and such street and avenue.' Then I said, 'getting close, huh.' And he said 'yeah'. Then we hung up and I said goodbye to my sister and then walked out the door." Then he put his head in his hands again and cried, "Oh, God, No. Domenic was there and could probably hear the phone conversation. I don't know if he did or not. Oh, Cody, if that was it, I am sorry. I had no idea. I don't trust Domenic, but I never thought about him being mixed up in these cases. You mentioned being friends with Domenic. You suspect him in this corruption, don't you?"

Cody nodded.

By then, Lieutenant Moss was actually crying and saying, "I'm sorry, Cody. I'm sorry." Cody was crying, too, and could not say anything.

Finally, looking at the Lieutenant and feeling sorry for him, Nick said, "Lieutenant, you had no way of knowing. I'm sorry that we had to be hard on you, but we had to get some answers. We have to know who we can trust."

"I'm so sorry. If Domenic is mixed up in this, I hope to God you get him. I will do anything to help you get to the bottom of this investigation."

By then, Cody had his voice back and he said, "I'm sorry, Lieutenant. I had to know. ....I had to know."

"That's alright, Sergeant. You are just doing your job and a damn good job of it. I am so sorry. I had no idea. Sergeant, if Domenic is involved in this, I would like to be the one that arrest him. That is the least I can do for your father."

Cody said, "Lieutenant, you and I both will arrest him together."

"That will be a pleasure for me. You two go get him." Then they all shook hands. And the Lieutenant went back to his office feeling very distraught, and Nick and Cody left the office. Cody did not want to stay there any longer that day.

Cody said, "I wonder if Tex has had any luck with Santino. Let's take a ride by there." Then Cody turned the car in that direction. When they got to the parking lot, Tex was no where to be seen. Then they rode around the parking lot and then decided to go to this out-of-the-way diner. They liked to go there when they were not in the mood to see anyone that they knew. It was a quaint little barbecue place called, 'Smokey's Q'. It was located out in the country, not far from town, but yet, it was quiet and relaxing. While they were eating, Cody's phone rang. It was Tex so he stepped outside in the car to talk to him. After he finished the conversation, he went back inside the diner.

Cody laughed and said, "Santino is giving Tex and Traci a ride for their money."

Nick laughed. Then he said, "I bet he is going crazy trying to find his car."

"He is. He came out and looked all around and then went back inside. Then he came out again and looked all around. Then he went back in and came out with a uniformed officer and, evidently, made a stolen report on it. The officer wasn't too enthused about it."

"Do you think we should tell the officer or just let them look for it?"

They both laughed.

Then Cody said, "By the way, Traci did identify him as the one that ran her off the road. According to Tex, Santino led them to Wilson's place and to the warehouse. Then he led them to Samuels building. Santino went in the building and a few minutes later, he and

Samuels came out of the building and stood by Santino's car. By the way, Santino's new car, or the one that he is using, has the tag number 388. So Samuels is involved in this somehow."

"Yes, I agree with you. Don't worry, Cody. we will get him and all the others. I'll write his tag number down in case we need it for future use. Where are they now?"

"He said that Traci just went to the bathroom. She was puzzled and a little upset as to why he would go to Samuels place. He thinks we should tell her more about what is going on. Santino went back to his office and they are at the diner down from the sheriff's building having lunch."

"How long are they going to stay on him?"

"Tex said until he goes home. And I think that is a good idea. He wants Traci with him to keep him company."

Nick laughed, "It would be nice to work like that." Then they both laughed.

Cody continued, "Tex feels that Santino may lead them somewhere else when he gets off work. He, also, said for me to tell Mama E that they would not be there for dinner."

They laughed again. Then Nick said, "Tex is really something, isn't he? Cody, I like him a lot. I am glad that you introduced me to him. ....At first I thought that him being from Texas, he would be a showoff and bigmouth, but he isn't. He is a lot of fun. I like his father, too." Then he grinned, " I might even like his sister, too, if I could meet her."

Cody said, "I'm glad, too, Nick. He and I hit it off right away. The other friends we had in college were friends, but Tex and I were more like brothers. By the way, I do think you would like his sister. She is somewhat like Traci as being outspoken and family orientated. She is a lot of fun, too. They both take after their father, evidently."

By this time, they were through with their lunch. They paid their bill and left.

Cody said, "Let's check the courthouse and find out if Steven has been by there yet. If not, we will talk to Jan.

"That's a good idea. The best you have had in a long time." Nick looked at Cody and grinned teasingly.

He knew that Cody had come up with some great ideas and he enjoyed working with him. He was learning and knew that he would learn the right way with Cody.

As they were pulling into the parking lot at the courthouse, Steven was walking to his car. They pulled up beside him and he laughed.

"I got your information for you. And I, also, got a date for tomorrow night. Thanks to you."

"Bro, you have a lot to thank me for. What did you find out?"

"Jan took me in the back room and we studied the records of that warehouse. Mmmm Ummmm. She is quite a gal. The others were out to lunch, so we had the place to ourselves. We found out something that she didn't know."

"Nick said, "Steven, you were there to get information about the warehouse, not to expand your love life."

They laughed.

"Oh, yeah, O.K.. You were right about the books. They were never changed. The warehouse is actually in Richard Samuels' name, but is spelled, first name: Drahcir; last name: Sleumas. In other words, he is using the name of Drahcir Sleumas. Richard Samuels spelled backwards. Everything that he has that is derived from the drug money is probably in that name, even his secret bank account. That would be my guess because he is using a different bank. We dug back to the transaction where he bought the warehouse from the county at a very low price with a stipulation that he was to tear it down and build a new building there. That was two years ago. There were two banks listed. The First Bank of Littleton was the bank he wrote the check from to buy the building. The check was for a larger amount than he actual paid for the building. But he deposited some of the money from the transaction into the other account at North Merchants Bank. It is all on these copies. Jan made a copy for me "

"Little Brother, you did good, real good. Thank Jan for me."

"I will be glad to, Bro, tomorrow night."

They all laughed.

"Steven, are you planning to go with us over to Kato's tonight?"

"Yes, I want to be involved as much as possible, but like I said, tomorrow night I have a date. I feel like we are getting somewhere now. It is getting very interesting."

"Yes, it is. We'll see you at home. And thanks. You have been a big help.

Then Steven said, "I guess Traci will stay with Tex as long as he is out. Before I leave, I will call her to make sure that she is not back in the office and that she does not go home by herself."

"No, there is no need to call her. She will be with Tex until tonight. In fact, Tex said not to wait dinner for them. So, I assume that they plan to eat out tonight."

"See you two tonight." Then Steven threw up a hand to both of them and walked on to his car and then drove off. And Cody and Nick decided to go and get a warrant to check the records of Richard Samuels. They would get the warrants today, and then go to the banks to check on Drahcir Sleumas' account. They knew the bank that he used for his family's business, but they were more interested in the account at The North Merchants Bank across town.

After they got the warrants, which would be good for several days, it was getting late so they decided not to go to the bank just yet, but decided to go home and relax for a little while before dinner. Cody dropped Nick off at the station to get his car, but he did not go in the station. He was not in the mood to talk to the Lieutenant at this time.

When he got home, Mama E and Sara were sitting in front of the television watching some story that they were interested in. Mama E looked up and said, "Cody, you are home a little early today. Is anything wrong?"

"No, Mom, we had a full day, so Nick and I decided to relax a while before dinner. Have you heard from Traci today?"

"Yes, she called me earlier and said that she was with Tex and they would be late. She told me about someone trying to run her off the road this morning, but said that she was fine now. Did you know about that?"

"Yes, Mom, we checked the cars and we know who did it. That is why she is riding with Tex. One of us will take her to and from work until this is over. Were there anymore unwanted phone calls today?"

"Maybe a few, but not many today. They may start again a little later. They didn't start yesterday until around four-thirty or five o'clock."

"I brought home a monitor to put on the phone. If it continues to ring tonight. We will use it." Cody then turned on the answering machine to play back the messages. There were two early this morning, but none since then. Then he went upstairs and took a shower and laid down across the bed. The next thing that he knew was Steven had knocked on his door and since he didn't answer, he opened the door and Cody was sound asleep. He said, "Bro, I hate to wake you, but dinner is ready." He knew better than to shake him. Cody didn't make a sound. So he said a little louder, "Big Brother, wake up, dinner is ready." Then Cody started to stir about. Finally, he opened his eyes. When he saw Steven standing there he asked with a worried look on his face, "Is anything wrong?"

"No, you were sleeping so soundly and peaceful, I didn't want to wake you. But dinner is ready and I knew you would want to wake up and eat before going over to Kato's."

"Yeah, I do. I'll just have to wash my face. Then I will be right down. Oh, by the way, Nick and I got the warrants to check out the two banks, but we are only interested in the one that Samuels is using under that other name. It is good for several days so we are just waiting for a good time."

"Good. Come on down. Tex and Traci haven't come in yet. I don't expect them until late tonight."

They laughed. Then Cody said, "No, probably not. There is no telling where they are. Tex is probably trying to convince her what a good husband he will be. Even though he knows Traci doesn't love Rich, he is still jealous of him."

They laughed, picturing Tex in their mind. Then Steven started toward the door and then turned around grinning. "You know, Bro, it will be nice to have another brother around. He will have to live here because I know Traci will not consider moving to Texas. At least, I hope she won't."

They both laughed, thinking about Traci and Tex being together. Then Cody said, "Well, Bro, love can change things, but let's hope that they will live here." They looked at each other for a moment, and then Steven went out the door and down the stairs to the kitchen. As he came into the kitchen, he said, "Mom, Cody will be down in a couple of minutes. Looks like it will only be us three tonight."

"It is enough for Tex and Traci whenever they get in if they want to eat. I know they said they would be late, but you know how you all come in and start raiding the refrigerator late at night."

They shared a laugh together. Then she said with a smile on her face, "Steven, it seems as though he and Traci are already a twosome and they haven't really had a date yet. She said something about helping Tex on some type of stakeout."

"Yes, Mom, they are following the guy that tried to run her off the road to see where he goes and who he talks to. He is a part of this investigation. That is why Cody does not want him arrested yet, but he will be soon."

"I see. I know Tex will take care of her, though. He won't let her get into anything dangerous."

"Yes, Mom, you are right. Neither will we let her do anything that might hurt her."

"I know, Son. I know."

Cody had come into the kitchen and he sat down to the table. "Mom, Traci is stronger than you think. And if she is thinking about changing over to a police officer, she should get her feet wet before she actually does. This will be good experience for her. Besides, Tex is going to be busy the next few days. In fact, he is going to be out of town for a couple of days. Today and tonight will give him a chance to talk to her and explain some of the remarks that he has been making. I think she is somewhat puzzled and not sure of what to make of it. In fact, it was a complete shock to me the first time he made a remark about Traci." Then he and Steven looked at each other and laughed. Then Mama E joined in with them. Then she said, "I think he shocked all of us, maybe himself."

The phone started to ring and Mama E started to get up to answer it, but Steven said, "No, Mom, let the answering machine pick it up. If it is anyone you want to talk to, all you have to do is pick up the receiver before they hang up." So she sat back down. It was the crank call. They were starting again, but they learned to ignore them. They were ringing every few minutes now. So Steven got up and turned it down a little more.

After Steven had set back down, Cody said, "Mom, Steven and I will be going to a meeting tonight. I am going to call Sara and ask her to come over and set with you for awhile. But before we go, I will hook up the monitor to the phone."

"No, Son, I will be alright. I don't need anyone here with me. I will keep the doors locked. Tex and Traci will be coming in later. Don't worry about me. I don't like to take advantage of Sara so much."

"Mom, you are not taking advantage of Sara. She enjoys your company. She likes watching television with you because you two watch the same things. Jake likes to watch other movies. I know you will be alright, but we will feel better if we know that someone is here with you."

Just as they were getting the table cleared away, Jake and Sara came in. He said, "Ms. Claire, I hope you don't mind if two old crankies come in to watch television with you, do you?" Jake was looking at Cody and winked at him to let him know that Sara did not want to leave Claire by herself."

Cody said, "We were just talking about asking Sara to come and sit with Mom for a while. We are glad that you came. Tex and Traci may be late tonight, but Bro and I won't be too long. It will be a short meeting tonight."

"No, stay as long as you like. We got all night." He winked at Cody and Steven. "It has been a long time since me and the old lady has been out all night. It might feel good for a change. Since those two boys have been here, I haven't had to do very much. They sure are some fine boys. I just wanted to let you know that."

They all laughed. Then Steven said, "I'm glad to hear it. Maybe we can use them all during the summer with the hay and all. I know that Chip is trying to save some money to help his Mom pay his college starting in September."

"Yes Sir. They are two fine boys. All they needed was someone to guide them. I wouldn't mind adopting them, myself."

Sara spoke up, "Yes, Jake, you are the right one for that. He always wanted a boy, but we never had any children."

During this time Cody was fooling with the phone and when he had finished, he said, "Well, we will get going so we won't be late. Jake, Sara, glad you two came over. We will see you later. Oh, I put a monitor on the phone. I will check it when we get back. Don't answer it. It is turned down real low."

Steven said, "See ya."

On the way to the car, Steven said, "I don't know what we would do without Jake and Sara. They have really been a life saver for us, even when Dad was living. I know Dad set up a retirement account for them years ago, but we should check on it. They very seldom take any time off and never go on vacation anywhere."

"Yes, when this is over we will check it out and talk it over with Mom. Maybe we will send them on a vacation for a couple of weeks when it is slow on the farm. That's a nice thought, Steven."

"Well, they are always there when we need them and they are always doing things for us even when we haven't asked them."

"You're right. We have to make it a point to do something for them."

A few minutes later, they were at Nick's. He was waiting on the porch and when they drove up, he came on out to the car.

Nick said, "Well, between the three of us, we accomplished a lot today. I hope Kato and Marci found some answers. Are Tex and Traci still following Santino around?"

"Yes, the last that we heard after I left you was that they would be out late. How much of that is work, I can't answer."

They all laughed.

A few minutes later, they were at Kato's place and setting around the table with a couple cartons of beer with chips and snacks.

Cody said, "I guess you heard what happened to my sister this morning."

Kato said, "No, we didn't hear. We were out rounding up the kids and talked to almost all of them. But, before we get into that, what happened to your sister, nothing bad, I hope."

Steven said, "She came to my office and sat down at my desk right after she got to work. She was pale and was pretty shaken up. Someone tried to run her off the road. It didn't hurt her, but she was shaken up at the time. She said the car was a dark unmarked car with a dark man with dark hair driving. She didn't get the tag number. When we checked out the car, there was a dent on it with dark paint on it. By that time, Cody and Nick showed up. I told them about it and the first place we looked was in the parking lot where Internal Affairs' people park. Hal was with us. And sure enough Old Santino's car was there with a dent on it with blue paint on it."

Kato hollered, "Hooray. Hope you guys got him."

Cody spoke up, "Evidently, he was in court or in a meeting that he couldn't have the car fixed before anyone saw it. Hal had it towed to the Crime Lab and Tex and Traci have been following Santino ever since. The last we heard he had gone to Samuels building and they came out and stood by the car that Santino had driven there and talked for a few minutes. But before that, he went to Wilson's place and then by the warehouse. Traci has identified him as the man driving the car to Tex. We thought we would pick him up Thursday morning along with Wilson, but do it separately so they will not know the other one has been picked up. If we pick him up on this, he will be out in an hour. We want to connect him to other things before we arrest him so he won't be able to get out of jail now. Also some one has been calling our house and hanging up without saying a word. I put a monitor on it before we left to come here."

"Great. Things are looking up. Marci and I had a long talk with some of the guys. They are smart kids, you know. Several of them have tried to get out of selling drugs, but Wilson won't let them. He threatens them with jail."

Nick spoke up, "Were they Doug Ward, Johnny Lowe and Tommy Downey? Those are the names that Tim gave us that really wanted to quit, but Wilson wouldn't let them. In fact, Tim asked us if we could help them when this came down. We told him that we would try."

"Yes, those are the ones. I wrote their names down as being cooperative and pretty good kids, considering," said Marci. Then she continued on, "Most of them were scared at first, but after talking with them a little while, they opened up and told us about what you all already knew. The three good kids said they would testify against Wilson if they had to. By the way, we talked to them separately so that the other tough, smart ass kids would not hear what they were saying. They are all afraid because of the other two being killed because they went to the police. Kato told them all to call us if they heard anything."

Nick said, "By the way, going back to Santino, we opened up the trunk on his car and there was the tag that we have been looking for all this time."

"Wow, Santino really gave you all some information today, didn't he?" said Marci.

Cody said, "That's not all. Steven tell them what you found out today."

So, Steven started telling them about what he and Jan found out about Samuels buying the warehouse from the county. The name that he used and the other bank account.

Then Cody showed him and Marci the copies of the transaction that took place between Samuels and the county. Then he said, "Nick and I have the warrants to check both accounts. We plan to go to the suspicious bank account first in the morning."

"Good. Now, what about Tex? Will he be ready to go to Savannah with Marci in the morning?"

"He said that he would call here tonight to find out what time Marci wanted to leave. So he will be ready when you are, Marci. What time do you have in mind to leave?"

"Just tell him that I will meet him here in the morning around seven o'clock and I will have the equipment and cameras that we will need. Another thing, should we have the GBI take the boat after we leave Savannah and then arrest the two guys after they arrive here?"

Cody said, "I would suggest that you all call us about an hour before you get here. Some of us will be at the warehouse staking it out. We are planning to have Santino and Wilson brought into the station, but not let them know the other is there. In other words, we plan to screw up their regular routine to see who comes to the warehouse when the drugs arrive. We will have the two lower guys at the station. Also, you may want to have the GBI on standby in Savannah in reference to the boat. It will probably stay at the dock for a while before going back to wherever they came from. When you contact us, we will let you know then.

Kato said, "That sounds good to me. Steven, what do you and Nick think about what Cody said."

Nick said, "Sounds good to me. We don't want to rush things. We want to make sure when we go to court that everything is right and that they cannot get off on any technicalities. What is in the back of my mind is that because they show up at the warehouse, will that be enough evidence to make the arrest stick?"

Kato said, "When an officer is buying drugs from a dealer, it is better to buy more than one time. But this will be fine because of the amount and the exchange of money and drugs."

"O.K. I just wanted to be clear about it. I know sometimes it is alright and sometimes, it is thrown out of court."

"Thanks for clearing that up, "Steven said as he was looking at Kato. Then he asked, "Do you know the GBI men in Savannah? Will they wait or will they try to be heroes?"

They all laughed. Then Kato said, "You are right about some of them, but we have worked with a couple of them in Savannah and they will listen and do what is best for the investigation, not for their ego."

Marci said, "I know how to contact them and who to contact."

About that time Cody's phone rang. It was Tex. He put it on the speaker phone. They were all laughing.

He said, "Hey, where the hell are you?"

"Never mind where I am. Traci and I had a ...."

"I don't want to hear what you and Traci did. She is my sister, remember."

"How well I know. How well I know. You taught her well. But to get to what I called about. We followed Santino when he left work. He went by Samuels building again and then he went to a restaurant close to where he lives. Then he went home. We waited there for about two hours and he did not come out so I figured that was long enough. By the way, the building he lives in is very expensive. He can't afford that on a policeman's salary unless his family has money or your police department pays a heck of a lot more than Houston. Traci and I are heading home unless you have something else for us to do tonight."

"No, not tonight."

Marci said, "What time do you want to leave in the morning. I told Cody to tell you around seven o'clock. I can meet you here at Kato's. He gets up early. Is that O.K. with you?"

"Sure, that will be fine. I can find my way there. So, I'll meet you there at seven."

"O.K., Tex. We'll see you a little later."

They hung up the phone and Nick said while he was grinning, "It would be great for Tex to be working with us all the time. He is a character."

Steven said, "From the looks of things, he may be later. Evidently, he has his eyes on Traci and I know she is not going to leave the farm. And then, again, she may surprise us."

Kato said halfway laughing, "He let me know to stay away from her right away. ......As for tomorrow, I guess we lay low until Thursday morning. Then we go to the warehouse and stake it out. Then the three of us will meet tomorrow night. Anything else."

Nick interjected with, "You watch the warehouse starting probably around ten o'clock to see who comes around. Actually we need two, one for the front and one for the back."

Then Steven spoke up, "I can take off Thursday and help Kato stake out the warehouse. You and Cody pick up Santino and bring him to the station and then pick up Wilson. Is there anyone at the station that you could get to keep them separated there?"

Cody said, "Yes, we can get the Lieutenant to keep Santino in his office since they are brother-in-laws or in one interrogation room and the other in our office or the other interrogation room depending on who is out front when we bring them to the station. They would not be able to see one another. I think Roberts would help. He has been helpful to us and I believe we can trust him. The only thing is that Garcia would be in the front room. Nick and I will work something out so that they both will not be able to go to the warehouse on Thursday. As Kato said, we can lay low tomorrow unless something comes up and we need to attend to it."

Kato was looking at Cody with a strange look on his face. "Cody, did you talk to your Lieutenant yet and can you trust him?"

Cody said very sincerely, "Yes, to both of your questions, Kato. We got that straightened out. I don't want to talk about it right now. Maybe some other time. O.K."

Then Kato said, "Good, Cody. Whatever you say. .....If nothing comes up tomorrow, I will follow Santino since Tex will be gone. It may not turn up anything, but at least it will be better than setting around here. The big deal is for Thursday morning. That should shake something loose."

Steven said, "I have a date tomorrow night, but Cody can tell me what he wants me to do Thursday. I will take a vacation day so I will be off to help without wearing my uniform."

"Cody and I will go to the bank first thing in the morning." Then Nick stopped because Cody was shaking his head.

Cody said, "I was thinking maybe we should wait until after the dance to do that because someone at the bank could tip Samuels that we are wise to him. When we go in the bank, we should freeze the account. At the dance for the following week, we will have the witness here to identify the voice. I don't want to do anything to mess that up."

Kato said, "That makes sense. So what you are planning to do is have all of this come down after the dance on Friday. That will be almost a week and a half away."

"Yes. Thursday will be the beginning if we can make Wilson and Santino talk. Also, Nick and I need to go by the Crime Lab and talk to Hal to find out what the scoop is on the bullets and if there are matches on some department guns."

Marci stood up and said, "If we are about finished here, I have to go and get ready for the trip in the morning."

They all agreed that they were finished for now and said their goodbyes and left with the understanding that Marci or Tex would call tomorrow night while they were at Kato's and Nick and Cody would be there. Steven had his date with Jan.

On the way home, Nick said, "Cody, you keep switching plans on me. I thought that we were going to the bank in the morning. I felt a little awkward tonight."

"We were, Nick, but after thinking about it, we don't want to act too fast. I want the dance to be tonight so we can find out if Casey can identify the voice. It's my fault, not yours. I am just anxious to get Dad's murderer and I think one thing and then when I am calm and think like a cop, I see things a little differently. I have to put Dad's involvement out of my mind and think like it is any other case. It is hard to do. I'm sorry, but I hope you understand. I am not trying to confuse you or make you look bad. You are a good police officer and a good friend. I would never do anything to make you look any different. In fact, I keep thinking about picking up Wilson and Santino. If it is the right thing to do. That's something we both need to think about and decide by tomorrow night."

"I'm sorry. I didn't mean to imply that you were doing it intentionally. I know you wouldn't do that. I just spoke out of turn back there, but what you said about waiting on the bank account does make more sense. The other, I don't know. I wish we had more evidence on Santino so we could put him away without him getting out on bail. But we'll get together on that."

"No, you didn't, Nick. You should not feel bad. No one thought anything about it. I know, I didn't, and Marci and Kato did not give me the impression that they even thought anything about it," said Steven. Then he continued, "I know how Cody feels, though. I want to rush ahead about Dad's murder and forget about the other three. I have to remind myself that the other three are just as important to their families as Dad's is to us."

Cody said, "You're right, Steven. But if everything works out like we think it will, we will have all of them by next Friday night. That will be our goal, but we may have to change things from day to day as we get new information. You both be thinking about Wilson and Santino. If we need to just take pictures this time and pick them up next week. I keep getting that gut feeling that we should wait, get pictures first because they will not talk. I have that feeling."

"Cody, If you feel that way we will discuss it tomorrow night at the meeting. Tell Tex, just to take pictures. If we need them, we will have them. When they call one hour before arriving here, we can tell them the plans then. We certainly don't want to rush things. Right."

"Right."

"I am really glad that you have me to help you with this investigation. I don't know what you would do without me," Nick said halfway laughing.

"I am too, Nick. I don't know anyone else that I would want to work with me on this." Then they smiled at each other and Cody laughed and said, "Who else could I trust? Or keep me straight?"

They all laughed and by the time they got to Nick's place, they had forgotten about Nick's little insecure feeling he had at the meeting. They were now in a jolly mood. Then the subject was changed to Tex and Traci making comments as to how Tex was explaining about him going on a trip with Marci and how Traci was feeling about that.

Nick said, "I can see him now saying, 'Trac, Honey, Darling, we are going to have separate rooms. It's just one night. It's just business and I will be thinking about you the whole time.'"

Steven laughingly said, "Yes, and I can hear Trac saying, 'Yeah, I bet. Don't tell me you wouldn't sleep with her. You men think alike. women, women, women.'"

Nick said in all earnest, "No, Steven, you have Traci thinking like most females and she doesn't. You have to give her more credit than that. She had good teachers from her brothers. Although, Steven, you may be an exception here."

They all laughed.

"Nick, are you saying that I am a bad influence on my sister?"

"No, I was just teasing you. Your sister will be fine knowing that Tex is going to Savannah with Marci. She knows more than you think about cops. That is, good cops. She trust males because of her brothers, maybe too trusting for some."

Cody said, "You're right, Nick. She is too trusting sometimes, but we keep an eye on her without her knowing it. She thinks of Tex as a part of our family and I know that she trusts him, too."

Nick then got out of the car with the understanding that Cody would pick him up in the morning around eight o'clock and they would go to the Crime Lab and talk with Hal.

Chapter 9

When Cody and Steven got home, they found Tex and Traci outside sitting in the hammock. They walked to the back door and went inside because they felt that they wanted to be alone. He and Traci needed to have this time alone together. Neither Cody nor Steven could go to sleep right away. So much was beginning to happen now. It was some time that they were in bed, they heard Tex come upstairs and go into his room.

But Tex had a hard time going to sleep, too. He kept thinking about being away from Traci even though it was only for two days. *She felt so good in my arms and when I kissed her, I was delirious. It was as though I could not get enough of her. I hope I didn't scare her. She didn't seem to be frightened. Her response really shook me. He knew he had to take it easy because of who she was and how much she meant to him.*

Meantime, Traci was having the same problem. She understood about him going to Savannah with Marci. She didn't know Marci, but she felt she knew Tex enough to trust him. *Gosh, it felt so good being held by him and when he kissed me, I thought I would die. I wish it was me going with him to Savannah. Maybe when I become a police officer, we can work together, whether it be here or in Houston. I don't want to think about moving from here. I won't think about that now. I'll deal with that when the time comes. Today was great. I will think about that.* That was her last thought before she closed her eyes and went to sleep.

The next morning she was up earlier than usual because she wanted to see Tex before he left. In fact, when he came downstairs, he had not intended to eat breakfast because he did not want to see her this morning. It would be better this way. He looked into the kitchen and there was Traci with his breakfast already on the table, ready for him to eat. He could not decline then. He went into the kitchen as though he was expecting her to be there.

He stood inside the doorway looking at her for a moment before he walked over to her and gave her a good morning kiss. She smiled and said, "I just couldn't let you go off without something to eat."

And he smiled at her and said, "I just couldn't go off without seeing you this morning. The food looks great. Why don't you set down and eat with me?"

"I am. I am getting my plate now. You can pour the coffee."

So he got the coffee pot and poured the coffee and then they both sat down to eat. It was an enjoyable breakfast for both of them. But by the time they had finished eating, Mama E came in and poured herself some coffee and sat down with them. She said, "You all are up early this morning."

"Yes, I will be going out of town this morning. I will be back sometime Thursday. In fact, I have to go now. He got up from the table and placed his dishes on the counter by the dishwasher. Then he bent over and gave Mama E a kiss and said, "Thanks for everything. See you sometime Thursday." Then he picked up his bag and started out the door. Traci followed him outside. He pulled her close and said, "I can't call you while I am gone, but I will be thinking about you." Then he kissed her very lightly and then looked into her eyes. Then he pulled her tight against him and hugged her tight and kissed her long and passionately. When they pulled apart, they both were shaken. Tex said to himself, "*I have got to get out of here*". Then he got into the car and drove away. She watched him until he was all the way down the driveway. Then she walked slowly into the house and started helping Mama E fix breakfast for the others.

By the time that they had breakfast on the table, Cody and Steven appeared in the kitchen.

Steven said teasingly, "Gee, Sis, you are up early this morning. You got up just to fix my breakfast."

"No, you are not her only brother, she got up early to fix mine."

Mama E smiled and said, "No, she got up to fix Tex's breakfast. In fact, they were through eating when I came into the kitchen." She winked at Cody and Steven and said, "It made me wonder if they were up all night or not."

Traci looked at her mother with an 'I can't believe you, Mom' look. "Mom, I hope you are not serious. I have never stayed out all night."

"No, you haven't, Honey, but you haven't been out with Tex before." Then she laughed. They all laughed.

Cody said, "Mom, I believe you are feeling like your old self again. I have to say that it sure sounds good to hear you laugh again. It seems that Tex can do it everytime."

"No, Son, it isn't only Tex that makes me laugh. All four of you make me laugh. When you all are feeling good, I feel good. It is just that once in a while it is a little rough for me without your father. You four make me think of how good it is to be alive and see you all living your lives and being happy. I only wish that Thomas was here to see you."

Steven said, "Mom, you don't have to explain anything. We know how you feel, but it sounds good to hear you say it once in a while, though. As for Dad, I feel that he knows how we are and what we are doing and is still guiding us. He is looking down on us at all times. But Cody was just teasing you."

"I know he was, but I just felt like saying what I did. Now you all come on and sit down and eat your breakfast before it gets cold."

So they all sat down and ate their breakfast, while Traci had another glass of orange juice. She would be riding in with Steven, so as soon as she finished her orange juice, she said, "Steven, I'll be ready in a few minutes." And she got up from the table and went to her bedroom to finish dressing. When she came back, Cody had gotten the tape from the monitor and had already left and Steven was waiting for her. Sara had come in and was sitting at the table with Mama E having a second cup of coffee. They said their goodbyes and Steven and Traci left.

When Traci got to her desk, her phone was ringing. It stopped by the time she got there, but she thought to herself that they would call back. So she put her purse away and got out her coffee cup to go and get a cup of coffee before she started her work. As she got up from her desk, the phone started ringing again. When she answered it, no one would say anything. She put the receiver back on the hook and asked the girl at the desk next to her how long her phone had been ringing.

Gail said, "It has been ringing off the hook the last fifteen minutes. I answered it a couple of times but no one would answer. So I didn't answer it again." Then she smiled and said, teasingly, "I thought it might have been your boyfriend and he didn't want me to know who it was."

Traci said, angrily, "No, I don't have a boyfriend, especially one that acts like that. I have been getting these phone calls at home, too."

"Trac, I was just kidding you. It probably is the same person that tried to run you off the road yesterday morning. Did you find out who tried to run you off the road?"

"My brothers are working on it. You're right about it being connected to that. It has to be. Well, I am going to turn my phone off here and go to another desk and work today. I am not going to put up with that."

"I don't blame you. If there is anything that I can do to help, just let me know."

"Sure, Gail. Thank you. Thank you very much."

Gail went back to her desk and Traci unplugged her phone and then went to her supervisor. After talking with her, Traci went to an empty office and started her work there. She called her mother and gave her the phone number at this desk in case she needed her. Traci was going to work there until the phone calling stopped.

In the meantime, Cody and Nick had decided to go to the Crime Lab and talk to Hal. When they arrived at the Lab, Hal was out, but would be back in a few minutes. They decided to wait around for Hal. So, they went into an office and sat down, but did not discuss the cases they were working on because there were some officers going back and forth.

Finally, Hal came back and came over to see them. As he came close to them, he said, "You guys have really stumbled onto something. I don't want to discuss it here. You all come on back into my office. We will have more privacy there."

Hal led them back to his office. As they sat down across from his desk, he put his finger to his lips to tell them not to discuss it. He said as he pushed some reports over to them, "Here is what you wanted, I think. I don't have the other one yet."

As Nick and Cody read the reports together, they could not believe the information that Hal had gotten. They knew in their gut that Santino was one of the killers, but they didn't know which murder or all of them. Santino had killed both the young boys. His 9MM shot on file matched the bullets that killed them. This was the evidence that they needed to keep him in jail without bail.

Cody looked at Nick and said, "We can take him off the streets now. We will go through with what we had planned for tomorrow. I can't wait to see his face when we arrest him. Wait until Lieutenant Moss sees these reports."

Nick said, "Yes, I see what you mean. We are getting there, Pardner." Then he looked at Hal and said, "Hal, when this is over, we are going to take you out and buy you and your wife a dinner that you will never forget."

They all laughed. Then Cody said, "You bet, Hal. You don't know how much we appreciate this. We will make it up to you."

"You don't owe me anything personally. You just go get the bastard and that will pay me back ten fold. I have never liked him, anyway. He has not been around looking for his car. I guess he thinks someone stole it, especially since no one has arrested him."

They sat there for a few more minutes just shooting the bull with Hal. Cody put the reports in his brief case, and then he said, "Hal, it has been a pleasure doing business with you. Right now, we have a lot to do, but we will keep in touch." Then they shook hands and left.

When they got in the car, they just sat there and looked at each other, each not believing what was happening, but, also, very excited about it. Neither of them could say a word. Then they both burst out laughing. Finally, Cody said, "Nick, we will go through with the plan that we were discussing last night. This was what we needed. That means that we need to get a warrant to search his house, car and person for his 9 MM. While we have him at the station, we will have someone searching his apartment. And if we see a .38 Caliber, we will take it, too. The 9MM will solve two of the oldest murders, and, hopefully, by next weekend we will solve at least one of the others, if not both of them."

Nick said, "Let's contact Kato and meet now to plan what we are going to do tomorrow. And, I also, think we should wait until in the morning to get the warrant. We don't want to take any chances in someone warning him. We still have the two judges that we don't know if we can trust or not, plus Garcia. We need to think about what we are going to do with him. How are we going to tie Garcia in with the operation? Or prove he destroyed the files?"

"You're right. We need to talk to Kato now. We have too much to talk about to wait until tonight." So Cody started the car and they headed to Nick's place. "We will call Kato from there and have him come over to your place if you don't mind."

"No, it's fine with me. I feel more comfortable discussing things in my place, anyway. I'll probably have to go to the store and get some coffee."

"No problem. I'll drop you off and I'll get something for lunch. What do you feel like eating? We may be here for a while."

"Something for sandwiches will be fine with me. I am tired of pizza and take-out food. Get whatever you feel like eating."

They both laughed.

Cody said as he pulled up to the curb, "Call Kato and keep your eyes open. I will be back shortly with a good meal fit for a king."

After about thirty minutes, Cody came back with lettuce, ham, turkey, tomatoes, mayonnaise, potato salad potato chips, baked beans and peach cobbler. Also, he had some tea, coffee and beer. So, when they finished with their days work, they could have a few cold ones.

"My goodness, Cody, what did you do, buy the store out. I didn't mean for you to get all of this. I do have some groceries here."

"I know you do, but I have eaten off you for some time now and it is time that I paid you back."

"Oh, Man, are you going to start measuring what we do for each other? If you are, I am afraid that I would be in the hole."

"No, you wouldn't. And I am not measuring anything between us. Friends don't do that. In this particular instance, this is business. So I am just doing my part. O.K."

"O.K., this time. I called Kato and he will be here anytime. He is anxious to hear what we have to say."

Cody started making some coffee, while Nick was getting down some plates, cups and utensils.

By the time that they had the table ready for lunch for the three of them, there was a knock on the door. Thinking that it was Kato, Nick hollered out, "The door is open, come on in. We are in the kitchen."

They heard the door open and someone come in the door, but, in an instant, they knew that it wasn't Kato. Just as they looked at each other with puzzlement, they drew their guns and stood by the wall at the door waiting for the person to come to the door. Then all of a sudden, Corrie was standing in the door. They drew a breath of relief and Cody pulled her in the kitchen and hugged her. He said, "This is a wonderful surprise." Then he kissed her.

"Who were you expecting that you would call out like that? I know Nick doesn't usually do that."

"No, I don't. We were expecting Kato right about this time. I was wrong in doing that, but I am glad that it was you. By the way, what are you doing home at this hour and what are you doing here?"

"My, you are full of questions, aren't you? First of all, I am on a vacation day because Mom wanted me to take her shopping and do some things around the house. She doesn't like to go by herself. She prefers that I go with her. And, second, I was going to the grocery store to pick up some items for her that she forgot. I saw the cars here and thought I would stop and say hi since I don't see either of you very much anymore."

In the meantime, Cody still had his arms around her and kissed her again. Then he said, "I sure am glad you did. I have really missed you. I promise that when this is over, you and I will get tired of each other."

"Oh, no, we won't. Don't you ever say that again and I don't want you to promise me anything. I know that you all are working on these cases and I don't want to do anything that would take away from that. I know what it means to you both."

Then they heard another knock on the door. Nick said, "I am going to the door this time." And he walked to the front room to the front door. This time it was Kato.

Kato said, "You guys sounded like you have found something good. And I might, also, add that I am ready for lunch. I didn't eat much breakfast."

As they came into the kitchen, Cody and Corrie were kissing. Kato said, "You didn't tell me that this was going to be a party."

Cody laughed and said, "Kato, I want you to meet Corrie, Nick's sister and my fiancee. She saw our cars here and stopped by today. She took a vacation day to help her mother."

"Lucky for you. I don't have that type of luck. I am stuck with Tony and/or Marci or by myself. How do I get into your group?"

They all laughed. Then Nick asked, "Corrie, would you like to eat with us. Mom is not expecting you back soon, is she?"

"No, I told her that I may go by and see Aunt Rosa while I was off. I haven't seen her in some time."

Cody said, "Come on and sit down for awhile." He put his hand on the chair next to him.

She said, "You all probably want to discuss some important issues. I'll go now and if the cars are still here when I come back this way, I'll stop."

"Sure. Do that. We will be here for a while." Cody got up and walked her out to her car and they kissed and talked for a minute or so.

When Cody came back in, he sat down at the table. Nick said, "I haven't told Kato anything. I was waiting for you to tell him."

So Cody took out the reports Hal had given him and gave them to Kato. Then he said, "We have Santino by the kahonees (ka-honees).'' Then they were quiet until Kato looked up. He had the biggest grin on his face. He said, "I can't believe it. It says here in the report that Santino's 9MM is a match to the murder of the two young boys."

Cody showing his excitement, said, "Yes, Hal is checking the .38 Caliber for the last two. Dad was killed with a .38 Caliber. The reason we called you was to tell you this and also to decide what we want to plan for tomorrow. Until we got this information, I was about to decide not to bring Santino and Wilson into the office and just make pictures and get evidence. But now, I think it will be a good idea to go ahead with the plans. We need to get him off the streets. We can pick Santino up on these two murder charges. When we pick him up, I want to have warrants to search his car and apartment for the 9MM. If we find a .38 Caliber, that would be fine, too. But, if we pick Santino and Wilson up, that will alert the others that we have some information. So, I suggest that we have Tex and Marci have the boat seized and arrest the crew after they leave Savannah, of course. Then when they get here, we will arrest all that are in the warehouse. What do you think? Nick and I are in agreement."

Nick said, "Yes, I think we should. If we wait till the dance and do all of this next week, other things could go wrong and that means that there are more drugs in the area. A lot could happen in a week with Santino, especially, on the streets."

Kato said, "Yes, it will give them more time to get the information that we are onto them. I was feeling like Cody about this. I thought we may have been rushing things before, but with this new information, I don't think we should wait. ......And, Cody, you say you have a witness that saw your father's murder. Since he and the other victim were killed with a .38 Caliber, the witness may solve both of those murders. If we can get the killers now, we can work on getting the higher ups that are involved in the drugs. I would say that is the priority now. We can leave the drugs out of the charges on Santino now and just arrest him for murder and then next week add the drug charges. That way the higher ups will not know that we are onto them or at least have doubts or be confused about it. I think it is worth taking a chance."

Nick said, "Then you are in agreement with us that we should act now."

"Yes, I feel very strong about it now with this new information. Now we have to plan what we are going to do in the morning and make sure that we don't overlook anything."

Cody said, "We will need a warrant for Santino's place first thing. Someone to pick up Santino. I did promise Lieutenant Moss that if Santino was involved in this, he and I would arrest him together. So, Moss and I will pick up Santino and take him downtown. Nick, you and Steven pick up Wilson and bring him to the station. I think Roberts will keep him there as long as we can hold him. In the meantime, Kato, you get the warrant for Santino's place and car. Then contact Nick and Steven to meet you there. That leaves Garcia. What should we do with him? We have nothing on him unless Wilson will talk."

"Maybe we can talk Moss into sending Garcia somewhere in the morning so that he won't know what is going on," said Nick. Then he added, "Cody, do you trust Moss enough to give him this information today or should we have him standby for early in the morning?"

"He seemed so sincere and so innocent the day that we confronted him when he was talking about my father. My father evidently trusted him, and I want to trust him, but I sure don't want to have our plans spoiled. What do you think, Kato?"

"Why not wait until first thing in the morning. Call and tell him that you need him first thing in the morning and you wanted to make sure if he was going to be in the office. If he says he is, just tell him you will be in his office at a certain time. Then tell him what the plans are and make sure that he stays with you the whole time. He doesn't know about any of this information, does he?"

"No, he doesn't know about any of it, even about Santino running Traci off the road. I am very anxious to pick him up and I don't want anything to go wrong. That is a good idea, Kato. Remind me to call him a little later."

227

Nick said, "Then we need to talk to Tex or Marci and let them know what to do."

"I'll call Marci tonight. I am sure they are not in their hotel rooms now."

Nick and Cody looked at each other and burst out laughing. Then Kato started laughing, too. Then he said, "You all may have something there." Then he said, "No, I know Marci. She is a real professional when she is working. Now, when she is not working, that may be a different story." Then they all laughed again.

Nick and Cody were wondering just how close Kato and Marci really were. But it was none of their business so neither one of them said anything. Kato seemed like a lonely man, though.

Cody said, "Oh, Kato, I forgot to tell you, but Santino's car that he used the tag 396 and tried to run Traci off the road, it is still parked at the Crime Lab. You would have to see Hal in order to see the car. The officers are probably still going crazy trying to find that car. We decided not to tell them where it was. I want the car that he is using now listed on the warrant in case he has a gun in there."

Kato reached over and got himself another helping of potato salad and baked beans. He said, "I don't know about you guys, but I was hungry today. This sure hits the spot. I am making a pig of myself. I can't eat with you guys much if I want to keep my trim physique."

"Don't fill up on that. Cody brought a big peach cobbler for later with coffee. Also some beer for when we quit work." They all laughed. They had not seen Kato enjoying himself like he was today. It was good to see him laugh.

"You guys are planning to make a long night of it, aren't you?"

"Just in case. Just in case. We didn't want to run out," said Cody. Then he added, "Can either of you think of anything else we should be doing now or will need to do in the morning? We sure don't want to mess this thing up."

Then Kato spoke up, "Before you called, I was out talking to the kids, and I, also, went by to see Jeanne. I was just riding in that neighborhood to see what was going on there. Jeanne is doing fine. I talked with Mrs. Stevens. Jeanne was in school. The kids didn't have anymore information for me, but they were a little more friendlier today than before. Some of them are good kids."

Nick said, "Yes, some of them are. All they need is a chance."

"O.K., Kato, you call Marci or Tex and let them know that we are going to wrap this part up tomorrow. I will contact Moss, and, Nick, I'll tell Steven to meet you here in the morning. Is that all that we have to do today?"

"I'll call Marci now and let her know to go ahead and have the slime down there arrested after they leave Savannah."

Then Kato got out his phone and dialed Marci's cellular phone. After a couple of rings, Marci answered her phone with a "Hello".

Kato said, "Hi, we were wondering how you and Tex are making out." He laughed. Then said, "Have you all had any luck down there?"

"Tex and I are fine. Ha. Ha. A little luck, but nothing that I can report now. Will let you know later. How about there? Anything that we should know about before we get there?"

"Yes, Go ahead and wrap things up down there. I mean everything. We don't want to have to go there again. We have had some luck here. So we are going to wrap up some of it here. Call just before you get here. Understand?"

"Sure, we'll see you later. Bye."

After he hung up the phone, he said, "Marci said that they have found out a little and she understood what I was saying."

Then Cody said, "I think I will call Lieutenant Moss and get that out of the way. So he got his phone and called the Lieutenant.

"Hi, Lieutenant. I was wondering if you are going to be in the office first thing in the morning. I need to talk to you for a couple of minutes."

"I had an appointment around nine o'clock, but I will cancel it if you think I should."

"I think you should. I wouldn't ask you to do that if I didn't think this was important. ......I really appreciate it, Lieutenant."

"Sure, Cody, I'll be here the usual time, about eight o'clock unless you want me to be here earlier. I assume that this is about the investigation."

"Yes, it is. And no, Lieutenant, that will be early enough. See you then. And thanks."

"Sure, Cody." And they hung up the phone.

The three of them talked on a little longer and then, finally, Kato said, "I need to go home and get some paper work done. Do you all want to meet tonight just for the fun of it or do you have other plans? I don't have anything else to do, myself."

Nick sensing Kato's loneliness, said, "Sure, it will be good for all of us to get together and not discuss work for a change. We could all use some relaxation. Bring a date, if you wish. We will just have a little get together. Cody bought enough food for an army. We will meet here if it is alright with you all."

"Sure, Nick. Maybe we can invite the girls and just relax before tomorrow. I know that I sure have missed Corrie."

They all laughed.

Kato said grinning, "Yes, I could see that when I came in earlier. I'll see you all later." Then he walked to the door and left. He seemed a little down as he walked out to the car.

"Nick, did you notice the expression on Kato's face when he left. When I mentioned inviting the girls, he had a different look.

"Yes, I noticed that, too. You know, his other partner, Lisa Gardener, was killed a couple of years ago in North Georgia. I had heard rumors that they were living together, but you know how rumors can get started sometimes."

"Yes, Nick, I remember that. I have worked with him off and on for about a year and a half and I have never heard him mention a girl. Other than the other night when he said he would like to meet Traci. I did notice that Marci looked at him and had a supprised look on her face when he said that. That is odd."

"We'll see tonight if he brings anyone. I'll call Angie and see if she wants to get together. She may have other plans, but I'll call her anyway."

"O.K. Nick. I am going to take a ride by Casey's Mom's place and then check out the neighborhood before I go home. We'll see you tonight." And with that he left and walked out the door still thinking about Kato and what was going on with him in his personal life. He got into his car and pulled away from the curb and headed toward Mrs. Branson's place. He was thinking of Kato and Liza and then he turned his mind to Corrie. *God, I miss her. She is so sweet and accomodating. She knows me inside and out. She knows when I am down and when I need her. She is so good for me. The smell and taste of her sends me into tenth orbit. She means everything to me. We are going to have to set a wedding date soon. I'll talk to her about it soon.*

Everything seem to be in order in the neighborhood and at Mrs. Branson's. So he turned toward home. When he got home, Sara and Mama E had gone shopping. No one was there, so he went upstairs and laid down across the bed for a while just running things through his mind to make sure that they had covered everything. After a few minutes, there was a knock on his door.

"Cody, may I come in for a little while."

"Sure, Sis, I'm awake." She walked in and sat on the side of the bed. "You look tired or like you are feeling down. I don't know which. You want to talk about it, Bro."

"No, yes, some, Sis. What I tell you is between you, me and Steven. O.K."

"O.K."

"Now, don't be frightened. Steven and I will keep you safe. Alright."

"Sure, Bro, I am not frightened."

"Alright. You know Santino, the one that tried to run you off the road. Well, we found out that his gun is the one that killed the first two young boys. We are going to pick him up in the morning. We don't know about the other murder yet. While we have him at the downtown building, we will be searching his apartment and car for the gun. We have to get the gun. Otherwise, he can say that it was stolen. But another thing is we have you to identify him as the one that tried to run you off the road. Also, someone shot into Nick's place a couple of times. We, also, have the tag 396 from Santino's car as the one that shot into Nick's place. Hal has not come up with the match on that yet. In other words, tomorrow about this time, we will know for sure a lot more than we know now. Tex and Marci are following the drug runners and they will be arrested when they get here tomorrow."

"Cody, I didn't know anyone shot into Nick's place. I'm glad you told me this much, though. I know that you are still holding back on some of it, but I understand. What about at the dance? Do you still want me to go? I am asking because Rich called me again today and was practically begging me. I felt sorry for him, and I was planning to tell him I would go, but he wouldn't give me a chance. Finally, when he stopped going on and on, I told him that I would go, but my cousin would be here for the weekend and I would have to bring her and her date." She smiled at Cody because he was smiling at her, and then she said, "He was so happy that he said that would be fine. The more the merrier. So we are going to the dance next Friday night."

"Sis, I appreciate this very much. You don't know how much it will help us in this investigation. I just hope that Casey can identify the voice. If she can, then we will have ......the other murder solved." He almost said we will have Dad's murder solved, but he caught himself just in time. He did not want to reveal about their father to her yet.

She leaned over and kissed him on the cheek and said, "I sure hope she can. And, Bro, if she wants to stay here, she can stay in my room with me. If she is my cousin, that would be better, wouldn't it?"

"You may be right. We'll see when Tex calls his father and let him know when to come. Thanks, Sis."

"You are welcome, Bro, and thanks for sharing this with me. I will be glad when this is all over. I'll go and let you get some rest. I think Mom and Sara are back. They may need some help."

"Sure, I'll be down in a few minutes. When Steven comes in, tell him that I want to see him. Oh, and by the way, I checked the phone monitor. The numbers belong to Santino and Wilson, a probation officer, and a pay phone. After tomorrow morning, the calls should stop."

"Thanks, Bro. And I'll tell Steven. You get some rest now." Then she closed the door behind her and went downstairs to help her mother. She was missing Tex. He had only left that morning, but it seemed like a long time. *Oh, Tex, I do miss you. You have made me very happy. I am looking forward to our talk. I think I do love you. But I have never been in love before. If it is not love, it sure makes me feel like it is. It's gotta be.*

By the time Steven got home, Sara had helped them with most of the dinner and had gone home. She took some of the food with her for her and Jake and the boys. She did that sometimes when they prepared a big portion of one thing or another. It was nice cooking together sometimes.

"Oh, Steven, Cody wants to see you. He is upstairs in his room."

"Thanks, Sis. I am going upstairs to unload all this gear. I'll look in on him." And he headed up the stairs to his room. After he put his things in their proper place. He went to Cody's room. The door was open and Cody motioned for him to come in and he set on the bed for a minute.

"Steven, I haven't talked to you today, but we found out that Santino's 9MM matched the bullets that murdered the two young boys. So we plan to go through with the original plan. I have a meeting with Moss in the morning. He doesn't know it yet, but he and I will pick up Santino and arrest him. He asked me to let him do it when Nick and I confronted him before. You and

Nick will pick up Wilson and bring him in and I may have to ask Roberts to help. Kato is going to get a warrant and search Santino's apartment. Then he will meet you and Nick at the warehouse to stake that out until the drug runners get here."

"Wow, Brother, things are really looking up. I can tell that you feel a lot better about going through with your plan now. That will be great. Now, if Casey can identify the voice at the dance. Are Tex and Marci going to put a hold on the boat and have the crew and whoever arrested?"

"Yes, Kato talked to Marci today and she knows what to do. Also, after tomorrow, Tex will call his father to make arrangements for Casey to be brought here. I haven't said anything to Chip about her coming. I don't want him to know until she gets here. Another thing, Nick, Kato and I met at Nick's place today and had lunch and talked this over. We had enough food left over that we are going to meet there tonight and bring our girls. I know that you have a date, but if you want to drop by, we would be glad to have you and your date. Sort of a little support party to get everyone in the mood for tomorrow, I guess. I am inviting Corrie and Nick is going to see if

Angie will come. I thought about asking Traci to go, but I don't want to leave Mom alone right now with the phone calls and all. They should stop tomorrow morning. The numbers on the monitor belonged to Santino and Wilson and a pay phone. I told Traci what some of our plans are for tomorrow."

"That's good. I don't like leaving her out of this investigation. She has a right to know, but I understand why she shouldn't know some of it at this point. Jan and I are going to the Red Lobster. She likes seafood. We may come by later if you all will be there."

"We will not be out too late, probably no later than one o'clock, but, stop by if you can. Oh, by the way, Rich called Traci again today and begged her to go to the dance. She told him that she would go if her cousin could go. Her cousin would be here for the weekend and her date. He said it would be fine. So that is working out alright."

Then they heard Traci call from the bottom of the stairs that dinner was ready.

Steven hollered, "We're coming."

Then they went downstairs and they sat down to eat dinner. Cody told Mom and Traci about the get together tonight at Nick's and asked Traci if she wanted to go.

"No, I think I will pass on this one, but I will make sure that I am there for the final party."

"You make sure of that, Sis. You, too, Mom. We are going to have a blast. I want Jake and Sara there, too," said Steven. Then he continued, "Cody, I know that we said we were going to wait until after the investigation was over. But, Mom, Cody and I were talking the other day about Sara and Jake. They do so much for us. Things that are not expected of them. They are true friends of the family. Actually, a part of this family. I know that Dad has an account set up for them when they retire, but what about time off or vacations. Do they ever get any vacation time?"

"No, not a specific time each year, but Tom always told them to plan a vacation and he would make sure that there was help here to carry on while they were gone. But they very seldom ask to go anywhere. Every time he would ask them about it, they would say that they would rather stay home. That they were not the traveling type. There was nowhere in particular they would like to go."

Steven said, "Mom, will you try to find out from Sara in a round about way where she would like to go or what she would like to do. When this investigation is over, we will surprise them with something. They have been so good to this family over the years and, especially since Dad died. I think we should do something for them."

Mama E was really moved by Steven's concern for Jake and Sara, said, "Why, Steven, that is very thoughtful of you. I am glad that you brought it up. We will plan something for them. I'll see what I can find out."

Then Traci said, "That is a good idea, Steven. We should do something nice for them. We count on them so much, especially lately. I don't know what we would have done without them at times."

"You are right, Trac. They have been a life saver for us most of the time. Sara has really been the best friend that I could have," said Mama E.

Cody said, "Well, I hate to leave this good conversation, but I have to get ready for a get together tonight. Mom, I will be over at Nick's place if you all need me."

"I have a date, but I have my cellular phone with me. We may end up over at Nick's later. I told Jan that I would take her to the Red Lobster. She loves seafood."

Traci said, acting angrily, but grinning, "I love seafood, too, but you don't invite me to go to the Red Lobster."

"Trac, you can thank our dear brother for this. He is the reason that I am taking Jan out tonight. Not that I mind. She was a big help to our dear brother. He is playing havoc with my love life. He makes these dates for me," said Steven, laughing all the time he was talking.

Cody said, "I have really got to go now before our brother thinks up something else." With that, he went upstairs, leaving the others laughing.

After taking his shower and dressing in his clean jeans and shirt, he felt good. *He never did like to wear dress pants, jacket and tie. He would be with Corrie tonight, and no work would be discussed. He would see to that. If anyone said anything about work, he would stop them. Tonight was going to be an enjoyable night.*

Chapter 10

When Cody got to Nick's place, Angie was already there helping Nick set things up.

"Nick, Corrie told me that she was coming over early to help you. Does she want me to pick her up?"

"No, Cody, she called and said that she would be a little late. She had to help Mom with something and would drive her car over because she wasn't sure what time she would finish. She was helping her make a cake, a wedding cake that has to be finished by tomorrow morning. Mom over extended herself again. She can't say no, especially to her friends."

"How about Kato? Have you heard from him?"

"No, but it is a little early. He'll be here."

"I couldn't talk Traci into coming. She won't leave Mom by herself, but she said that she will make sure that she is at the big party. Steven said he and Jan may come by later. He promised to take her to the

Red Lobster."

He and Nick laughed. Angie just stared at them angrily, and asked, "What is so funny about Steven taking Jan to the Red Lobster? I think that is very sweet of him to take her. There is nothing funny about that."

Nick came over and put his arm around her and then looked at Cody. Should we tell her?" They both laughed again.

"Well, I'm waiting. How did Jan get Steven to take her to the Red Lobster? I can't get you to take me anywhere these days. If they come by later, I'll have to ask her to give me some tips." Then Angie started smiling. They knew that she was kidding.

Nick looked down at her and said, "I don't think you want to know." Then he said, "Cody gets these girls that work in the government complex to help him on this case we are working on by giving him reports or information that is available. Then he tells Steven that he promised this one and that one that Steven would take them out. All the girls love Steven and want to go out with him. This is Cody's way of giving the girls a chance with his brother, and playing havoc with Steven's love life. Steven has not wised up to it yet. We keep waiting for him to say something, but he hasn't yet."

Angie said, "Maybe Steven is the wise one and he knows when to keep his mouth shut."

They looked at each other and then Nick said, "Hey, you've got a point there." Then he leaned down and kissed her on the cheek. Then he said, "If you want to go to the Red Lobster, we will soon. O.K."

"I was just kidding. I know that you all are busy now and you have a lot on your mind. But ask me when this is over and see what I say," Angie said grinning.

About that time, they heard a car drive up and Cody went to the door to see if it was Corrie. It was just getting dark and he did not want her out by herself even if it was only a couple of blocks. He came back in and said that it was a car going along the street. He then waited a few minutes, but could not wait any longer. Then he said, "Nick, I am going to pick Corrie up. I don't like for her to be out by herself at night. I'll be back in a while."

"O.K. Cody. I don't like it myself. I told her to call when she was ready and that you or I would pick her up, but you know women. They want to be independent, but yet, dependent on men. I am not sure what they want." Angie hit him on the arm when he said that and they laughed.

As Cody was going out the door, two cars had driven up and Corrie was getting out of one of them and he saw Kato starting to get out of his car. As Cody went down the walk to meet Corrie, a car went by slow and a shot rang out and the next thing that he knew Corrie was on the ground. Then he heard Kato holler, "Cody, I got him. You take care of her." He bent down and Corrie was laying there very still. He started crying her name. saying, "Corrie, talk to me. Talk to me." Then he saw Nick and Angie standing there. Nick was on the phone calling 911 as he was running for his car.

Cody hollered, "Kato went after him. I didn't see the car, but Kato did. They went that way." Then he looked back down at Corrie. She moved in his arms. He grabbed her tighter. "Hold on, Sweetheart. The ambulance is on the way."

She tried to speak, but he shushed her, saying, "Don't talk now. You will be alright." Then he saw the blood on her left shoulder. He looked up and Angie was standing there with a towel and blanket. She handed him the towel and then she spread the blanket over Corrie. Cody found the wound and put the towel over it and then pressed it to stop the bleeding. He knew then that she would be alright. By then she was more alert. She kept asking "what happened. What happened."

Cody held her tight and said, "Sweetheart, you were shot, but you are going to be fine. The ambulance is on the way." By that time, they heard the siren and Angie went out in the street to direct them there.

When the ambulance arrived on the scene, they took over, but Cody stayed as close to her as he could. He told Angie to go in the house and lock the doors. Nick would be back shortly. But Angie had other ideas.

She said, "I will go get Corrie's mother and bring her to the hospital. I know that she would want to be there and she will be very angry if we do not let her know."

"You're right. I wasn't thinking clearly. Of course, she would want to know. Be careful and we'll see you there. She will be alright. It is a shoulder wound. Don't worry. Nick and Kato will get him. If they don't get him tonight, I promise that we will get him. Thanks, Angie. You've been a big help tonight."

Angie then walked in the house and put the food in the refrigerator and made sure that everything else was alright and then she came out the door and locked it. Then she got into her car and went up the street to Mrs. Carillo's house. When she arrived, Mrs. Carillo said, "Angie, what is wrong? You are as white as a ghost."

Angie walked over to Mrs. Carillo and put her arm around her and said, "Mrs. Carillo, I came to take you to the hospital. Corrie was shot a few minutes ago, but she will be alright. It was a shoulder wound. Cody went with her in the ambulance. She was alert when they left."

"And Nick, where is he?"

"Nick and Kato went after the shooter. Kato had a good start. He was right behind him when he took off. Nick followed them, but, right now, we should go to the hospital."

By then Mrs. Carillo was crying and shaking. She had just realized what Angie was telling her. She cried for a few minutes and then she said, "Angie, I do want to go to the hospital. You said that she will be alright, didn't you?"

"Yes, she will be alright. It was a shoulder wound." Then, Angie got her purse for her and helped her into her car. And by the time they got to the hospital, Mrs. Carillo had straightened up and was more calm. They walked into the emergency room and finally found Cody sitting in a room by himself with his head down.

When Mrs. Carillo spoke to him, he looked up and got up and hugged her. He said, "She will be alright. It was a shoulder wound. She is in surgery now. She asked about you on the way to the hospital." He then led her to a chair and asked if she wanted some coffee or hot tea.

She said, "I would like some hot tea with lemon in it." She started to open her purse, but Angie stopped her. "No, Mrs. Carillo, I'll go get it. You stay here with Cody. The doctor may want to talk to you." Then she turned to Cody and asked, "Would you like something to eat or drink."

"I'll just have some coffee. I ate dinner before I came over to Nick's.

Before he could get any money for her, she had gone out the door.

Cody looked at Mrs. Carillo, "Mama C, she will be O.K. ....Angie has been a big help tonight. She was right there to cover Corrie with a blanket and gave me a towel to stop the bleeding. She was the one to think of you. My mind was a blank of everything around me. All I could think about was Corrie, and then she moved in my arms and I knew then that she would be alright. Nick and Kato went after the shooter. Kato was still in his car when it happened, and he took off right behind him. Don't worry, they will catch him."

"Yes, that is what Angie told me on the way to the hospital. You know, we have been very fortunate as a family. Nick nor Corrie have ever really been sick or had broken bones. They had the regular childhood sickness, but nothing out of the ordinary. They take after me, I guess. I haven't really been sick much during all my years."

"Oh, now, Mama C, you are not that old. You and Corrie look like sisters."

She laughed, "Now, Cody, I don't know whether you think that I am that young or if Corrie is that old. She knew that she was frustrating him and that was what she meant to do. She liked Cody very much."

He laughed. "I see what you mean. I put my foot in my mouth, didn't I? But what I meant was that you look as young and beautiful as Corrie does."

Angie walked in with a couple of sandwiches and coffee and tea. She saw them laughing. "Evidently, I missed something funny," she said smiling.

Then Mrs. Carillo told her what they were talking about. They all laughed.

Cody said, "I forgot. I should call Mom and let her know. She will be angry with me if I don't."

So he pulled out his phone and called Traci. He explained everything to her. Traci was upset, but Cody assured her that Corrie would be O.K. He promised her that he would call back as soon as they talked to the doctor. Then he said, "Oh, Trac, would you mind calling Steven and tell him what happened and where we are. He had said that he might come by Nick's later."

"Sure, be glad to. He would want to know right away. I'll call him as soon as we hang up. You be careful. Anything that we can do, let us know."

"I will, Sis. I'll call as soon as I hear anything. Bye."

Angie got Mrs. Carillo to eat a sandwich because she knew that she had not eaten anything. She had seen the sandwich on the table that Mrs. Carillo was just before sitting down to eat when she came in with the news of Corrie being shot.

About forty minutes later, in walked Traci and Mama E. Traci said, "I'm sorry, Cody, but I couldn't keep Mom home. She had to come here. I wasn't sure she felt up to coming out tonight, but she would not listen to me."

"That's O.K., Sis. It may do her good." Thinking that she was acting more like her old self again. Traci got the meaning by the way he was looking at her. He got up and went over and hugged her. "Mom, I'm glad you came, but are you sure that you feel up to this?"

"Yes, Son, I'm fine. I had to come and be with Elizabeth. She did so much for me when Thomas died. I am feeling fine. Have you heard from the doctor yet?"

Elizabeth said, "No, not yet, but hopefully it will be soon. It seems like it has been hours, but actually it has only been about an hour. Cody said that it was a shoulder wound and that she would be alright."

"Yes, I'm sure she will. When you are sitting in a hospital waiting for someone to tell you something, time passes so slow."

Cody said, "I think I will take a walk and see if I can find out anything." So he got up and walked out the door and down the hall to the nurses station. He talked to a couple of the nurses that he knew. One of them said she would try to find out what she could. So she went up the hall and was back in about ten minutes. She said, "The surgery is almost over. She came through it fine. The doctor will be out in a few minutes to talk with you all."

"Thank you very much. I guess I better go back to the room before he gets there. Thanks again." Then he turned around and walked back up the hall. But before he got to the door of the room that they were waiting in, he saw Steven and Jan walking to meet him. He then stopped and waited for them.

Steven said, "Have you heard anything yet?"

"A nurse just checked for me and said that the surgery is almost over. She came through it fine. The doctor will be here in a few minutes to talk to us. Mom and Traci just came in a few minutes ago....Hi Jan. I'm sorry. I am not thinking very good tonight."

"That's O.K., Cody. I understand."

Then Steven said, "I'm surprised that Mom came to the hospital. She wouldn't come a couple of weeks ago when a friend of hers was here. ... Before we get to the room, we went by Nick's place and they were there. I told Nick what Traci had told me reference Corrie. He was really worried. He had not heard anything and could not leave because he had to stay there. They caught the guy. He had to stop at a red light. He had nowhere to go. Kato was right behind him all the way and he jumped out of the car and arrested him on the spot. It was Santino."

"I'll kill the Son-Of-A Bitch when I get my hands on him. ....I'm sorry Jan. That guy has given us fits this week."

"That's alright, Cody. I understand how you feel. I was just shocked when I saw him. I couldn't believe we have someone like him working in our department and so high up, too. Don't worry. I won't say anything to anyone. Steven has explained some of the things to me."

Cody said very angrily, "Believe it. We were going to arrest him in the morning. Now I won't have the pleasure of doing it."

"I explained to Jan that he was the one that Traci identified that tried to run her off the road."

Cody knew that Steven was telling him as to what Jan knew. It was a sign for him not to say too much more. Cody saw the doctor coming their way so he said, "Here comes the doctor. Let's go in the room and hear what he has to say." So they walked up the hall to the room where the others were waiting.

As they walked into the doorway, Cody said, "The doctor is on his way here."

Steven introduced Jan to everyone. And then he said, "Nick and Kato caught the guy that did the shooting. They were taking him to jail when we left them. They are tied up right now with all the necessary paper work. They will be here as soon as they complete it."

By that time the doctor was standing in the door. He said, "I am Dr. Bernard. The surgery went well and the patient came through it fine. She is in Recovery now. It was a little more extensive than we thought, but she will be alright. It will take some time for her to heal completely. The bullet was lodged deep in her chest area, but we got it out."

Cody asked, "Do you have the bullet, Doctor? I need it for evidence."

"Yes, I have it in my office. I was holding it for the police."

"I am Sergeant Edwards and I am working on this case. The man that did the shooting is already in custody." And Cody pulled out his badge and showed it to the doctor.

"If you will follow me when I leave, I will turn it over to you. You will have to sign for it."

"Yes, Doctor. I will be glad to."

"Good, Sergeant. That was fast work. If I have any problems, I'll be sure to call you." He smiled.

"Where the shooting occurred, another officer was just getting out of a car. He heard the shot and took off right behind the shooter. Then Corrie's brother took off to help him. They got him a few blocks up from the scene."

"Corrie will be sleeping for awhile. If you all would like to leave and come back later. It will be a couple of hours before she will be awake."

Mrs. Carillo spoke up, "We'll wait here, Doctor. Thank you very much."

"You are welcome, Mrs. Carillo. If there is anything that we can do, let us know." Then he said, Sergeant, if you will come with me, I will transfer the bullet to you."

Cody followed him out of the room and down the hall to his office. He then signed the transfer paper and the doctor turned the bullet over to him.

As Cody turned to walk toward the door, Dr. Bernard asked, "Are you related to the patient, Sergeant? You seem more concerned than this just being a case you are working on."

"No, Doctor, she and I are engaged to be married. I have known her several years. Our families have been friends for that length of time."

"Sergeant, are you related to Captain Edwards, who was killed about six or seven months ago. You look a lot like him."

"I am his oldest son. The other male in the room is my brother. My mother and sister are also back there in the waiting room."

"I thought so. I knew Captain Edwards. He was a good man. I was so sorry to hear of his death."

"Thank you, Doctor. ...Will we be notified when we can see Corrie? It seems that we will be waiting in the waiting room with Mrs. Carillo."

"Yes, I'll make sure of that. And Sergeant, she will be fine. At first, it was touch and go, but she made it just fine. There is always a risk when you are trying to get a small piece of metal out that is imbedded so close to a main artery. Hers was. But, like I said, she will be fine. By the way, I didn't say that in front of Mrs. Carillo. I didn't want to upset her anymore than she is right now. I will tell her that later when Corrie is feeling better."

"I understand. Thanks again, Doctor."

Then Cody walked back up the hall to the waiting room that they had occupied. They were lucky that it was available and did not have to wait out in the other waiting room which is always crowded. As he approached the door, he saw Nick and Kato standing outside. Cody walked up to them and said, "I hope the Son-Of-A Bitch rots in hell."

Kato said, angrily, "He may have some bruises and be sore in the morning, but he should not have resisted arrest. I didn't know until tonight that he was such an arrogant ass. He evidently thinks that he is smarter than anyone else and can get by with anything that he want to do because his attitude stinks."

Nick said, "He is an arrogant bastard. I wanted to kill him so bad. ...Well, we won't have to arrest him in the morning. Cody, I called Lieutenant Moss and told him. He met us at the station. I only told him about what happened tonight. I, also told him that you would want to talk to him in the morning. He said he would be in the office early. By the way, he also said, 'Good work, guys, I am very proud of both of you.'"

Then Kato spoke up, "He really acted as though he was happy about the arrest. Cody, I really believe Moss is innocent in all of this."

"Thanks, Kato, for telling me. I want to believe it, and if he said that and meant it, then I will try to believe it."

"Cody, are we still on for the plans for tomorrow?" asked Nick.

"You bet. More than ever. The doctor said that all Corrie needs now is rest. She will be alright. It will take her some time to heal, but she will be O.K. Kato, I will go talk to Moss early in the morning and then meet you at Santino's apartment, or did you get the gun?"

Nick laughed then, and said, "Yes, we got his 9MM and his .38 Caliber was in the car. I don't think we need to search his apartment."

Cody laughed, and then he said, "All we have to do now is add the murder charges to his other charges. That will take care of him. So, Kato, you and Steven. Oh, is Steven still here?"

Nick said, "No, he left so he could follow Traci and Mama E home and then he was going to take Jan home. He said he would see you at home."

"Oh, O.K., Kato, you and Steven can go to the warehouse and stake it out. Nick and I will pick up Wilson and take him to the station and we can talk to Moss then. He can keep Wilson busy. Our only other problem is Garcia. We will take care of that with Moss or Roberts. Then Nick and I will meet you at the warehouse and wait for Tex and Marci to call and then show up. Does that cover it all?"

Kato said, "Sounds good to me."

"I had better take Angie home. I know that Mom is not going anywhere until she sees Corrie." So Nick walked into the room and Mama C was laying on the couch sound asleep. Nick motioned for Angie to come outside and she did.

"Angie, I'm sorry. I know you are tired. Let me carry you home. I'm sorry that none of the food was eaten after you had prepared the table. It is probably spoiled by now."

"No, I put it away before I went to pick up your mother and locked the door for you."

"You are so sweet. What would I do without you?"

She smiled and then said, "Nick, I know that you all have big plans for tomorrow, so, let me stay here with Mrs. Carillo and you all go home and get some rest. I'll call you if anything at all changes."

"Angie, I can't let you do that."

"You are not letting me. I do not have to work tomorrow and I am inviting myself to stay right here. We will be fine."

Kato said, "Well, I think I will leave. Can I give either one of you a ride?"

Cody said, "I don't have a car here, but I would like to stay a little longer."

"Kato, you go on and get some rest. I'll wait here with Cody a while longer and then we will leave. We'll see you in the morning."

"O.K. If there is anything that I can do, please don't hesitate to let me know."

Cody said, "You done great. I am so glad that you were there and could catch the slime before he got away. Thanks, Kato." Cody reached over and hugged him around his shoulders as he grabbed his hand and shook it.

"Glad I could. See you two in the morning." And he turned and walked down the hall and out into the fresh air. *It felt good outside. He was getting hot in the hospital. He never did like to be cooped up in a place for long. The air smells fresh and nice. Oh, Lisa, I miss you so. I can't seem to get interested in anyone else. There is no one else like you. Why did you have to go so soon. You have such a hold on me. I don't know if I ever will let go of you.* He was feeling sad as he got in his car and drove home to an empty house.

Cody and Nick stood there and watched him walk down the hall on his way out of the hospital. He looked so lonely.

Cody and Nick walked into the room. Mrs. Carillo was still sleeping. Angie had put a blanket over her. And Angie was laying back in a chair with her eyes closed. Nick walked over sat beside her in the other chair and Cody sat in another across from Nick. They were silent for a while, each one thinking their own thoughts. A little while later, Doctor Bernard came to the door and said that Corrie was in Intensive Care for now just for precautionary measures. He smiled and then said, "Besides, we don't have a private room tonight, but she will be put in one tomorrow morning. I thought it best for her to be in Intensive Care rather than in a semi-private room for now. She is doing fine under the circumstances. You may go in and see her, but no more than two at a time and not for long. She is still half asleep, but she is coming out of it earlier than we thought."

Nick said, "Thank you, Doctor. Thanks for everything. We know that you are doing everything possible and that you are also considering our comfort. We could not ask for any better." And Nick shook hands with the doctor and then Cody shook hands with him.

Cody said, "Thanks, Doctor."

Nick looked at Cody and said, "Cody, why don't you go in and see her. I'll go next and then we will wake Mom and Angie and they can see her a little later."

Doctor Bernard said, "That will be fine. Just don't try to get her to talk. We'll see you tomorrow." Then he turned and walked out of the room.

Cody looked at Nick and said, "Thanks, Nick. I won't be long." And he walked out the door and upstairs to Intensive Care. When he walked in and saw her lying there. *She looked so white. Almost like she was dead. He was thinking how beautiful she was. And, also, how lucky she was that she was still living. He was so thankful that he bowed his head and said a prayer of thanks before he said anything to Corrie. My sweet Corrie.*

Cody reached over and held her hand. Then he put his lips on her cheek and kissed her lightly. He felt her squeeze his hand. He leaned over a little more and looked into her eyes. She had opened her eyes and was trying to smile at him. She started to say something, but he put his fingers to her lips and said, "Don't try to talk now. The doctor said that you would be fine. Don't try to rush it. Save your strength. Just listen to me now and you can talk later when you feel up to it. O.K."

She blinked her eyes.

"Sweetheart, I love you so much. I have wished a thousand times that it had been me instead of you. We should have taken the warning shots more seriously. We had planned to arrest him in the morning. If only we had arrested him before today." She was nodding her head to say 'No'. But he stopped her again. Then he continued, "Kato was

251

getting out of his car when this happened, and thank God, he was there, because he took off after him and caught up with him at a red light. He and Nick have arrested him and he will be put away for a long time. Well, Sweetheart, I have talked too long on something that can wait, but I wanted you to know that he has been arrested. Nick is waiting to see you. I love you and I'll see you sometime tomorrow. We have a full day planned that we have to take care of and we can not put it off. I will see you as soon as I can. O.K."

She whispered, "Yes, I love you, too." And she squeezed his hand and he squeezed hers back. Then he leaned over and kissed her again and she had closed her eyes like she was sleeping. He looked at her a moment or so, then he left.

When he got back to the room, Nick had awaken Angie and told her that he had found a room on the second floor that was closer to Intensive Care. He was waiting until Cody got back to take them there. When Nick saw Cody, he woke up his mother and told her what the doctor had said, and also about the other room. So Cody and Nick picked up their things and they went upstairs to the other room that was available. After they were settled in that room, Nick went in to see Corrie for a few minutes. When he came back, he said, "Mom, you and Angie can go in and see her when you want. She is a little tired right now and it is hard for her to keep her eyes open. Cody and I went first because we have to leave now. Angie is going to stay with you. If you need anything at all, or if there is a change, call me on my phone. I will have it with me at all times. We will stop by and see you in the morning before we go to work. Alright."

"Yes, Son, I understand. Angie and I will be alright. We'll just go in and look at her. I won't wake her. She needs her rest more than anything now." She looked at Angie and smiled. Then she said, "She is so sweet, isn't she?"

Nick smiled at Angie and said, "Yes, Mom, she is."

And Nick went over and put his arms around her and then kissed her and thanked her. Then Nick asked, "Can we get you two something to eat before we go or anything at all?"

They said no that they weren't hungry, but Cody and Nick went down to the cafeteria and brought back some coffee, a couple of warm egg sandwiches and a few snacks that they could munch on whenever they felt like it.

Nick said, "Mom, I do want you and Angie to eat something. Eat it now while it is warm. Then go in and see Corrie. You'll feel better." Then he leaned over and kissed his mom and said again, "We'll be back early in the morning." Then he and Cody left the hospital and went home to get a couple of hours sleep. But as it ended up, neither of them slept that night. They both were thinking of what happened that night and what was going to happen the next day.

Cody was already awake when Nick called him about six o'clock. "Cody, I hope I didn't wake you, but I haven't slept any, and I have a feeling that you didn't either." Then he jokingly asked, "Did you?"

"No, you're right. I haven't. When I got home, Mom was waiting up for me. She wanted to know what the latest news was and I told her. Then we both went to bed, but I couldn't go to sleep. I kept seeing Corrie laying on the ground before the ambulance came. I tried to focus on her in the hospital when I talked to her, but my mind kept going back to her laying on the ground. I guess I was trying to see if I could have done something, but I couldn't think of anything. I assume that the reason you called is that you want to go to the hospital before going to work. That is what I want to do."

"Yes, I was thinking about the same thing. We can go to the hospital and get something to eat between there and the station. I'll make some coffee so we can have a cup before we go."

"That sounds good to me. See you in a few minutes, and make that coffee strong. I need a big boost this morning."

They laughed.

Cody got dressed and eased out of the house trying not to wake anyone, but Traci was in the kitchen preparing breakfast for all. Cody talked to her a couple of minutes and told her that they were going to eat on the way to the station. He also told her that they will have a long day and not to expect him nor Steven for dinner tonight.

"Alright, Bro. Steven and Mom will be up in a few minutes. I think Mom and Sara are going to the hospital a little later and try to talk Mrs. Carillo into going home so she can get some rest for a few hours. If anything changes, please call me."

"I will, Sis. See you later." Then he was out the door and into his car headed toward Nick's place. When he got there, Nick handed him a strong cup of coffee and he took a sip of it. He said, "Gee, Nick, Old Buddy, I think I will live now. Let's go see Corrie." Then they got into Cody's car and headed toward the hospital.

When they got to the hospital, they found Mama C and Angie in the cafeteria eating breakfast. Mama C saw them first and motioned for them to join them. When they sat down at the table, she said, "Corrie was awake this morning when I went in to see her. She talked a little, but I wouldn't let her talk too much. She is looking a little better. She had more color to her face this morning. They are bathing her now and doing what they have to do, so we thought this would be a good time to get something to eat."

Cody said, "We just wanted see her before we left for work because we may not get a chance to come by for quite awhile. By the way, Mom and Sara are coming to stay with Corrie so you and Angie can go home and get some sleep and don't argue with Mom because, take it from me, she will not take no for an answer."

They all laughed.

"That is real sweet of them to come, but I slept some last night. Not very much, but some. I'll go back in later to see Corrie, and then I may take your mom up on her offer. I don't feel like arguing right now. A few hours can make a big difference in some patients and I think you will see that difference in Corrie when you go in to see her this morning. She is a survivor. My daughter. She is stronger than she looks."

Nick said, "She is a lot like you, Mom. You are a survivor, too. Don't you forget that?"

"I won't, Son. We all are survivors."

Since they could not go in yet to see Corrie, Nick and Cody ordered breakfast when the waitress brought coffee for Mama C and Angie. A few minutes later, they all were eating a good breakfast. Cody and Nick did not know when they would get to eat again that day. So they ate a big hearty breakfast and had another cup of coffee before they went upstairs to wait to see Corrie.

A few minutes after they arrived, a nurse came in and said that they could see her before they moved her to a private room. So, Cody went in to see her and he knew right away what Mama C was talking about. When he entered the room, she was wide awake and looking at him as he walked to the bed. He stood there for a moment just looking down at her. She smiled and said, "Good morning."

He bent over and kissed her softly and then said, "Good morning to you. You sure look good this morning and smell good, too." He grinned.

"I still feel drowsy, but I feel better than I did last night. They just gave me a shot to make me go to sleep again. The nurse said that I needed to rest as much as possible, so they will be giving me shots for a day or two."

Cody bent over and kissed her again, a little more passionate than before, and then said, "In that case, I better go so Nick can come in to see you. We will have a full day today, so I probably won't be back until tonight. But, I will be thinking about you. O.K., Sweetheart."

"Yes, I love you, too." She smiled and waved her hand as best she could when he turned to look back as he started out the door. They both smiled at each other and then he was gone. *He felt so good because she did look so much better to him. Mama C was right. A few hours can make a big difference, but she has a long way to go yet.*

When Nick came back from seeing his sister, they left to go to the station to talk to the Lieutenant. Because it was early, they decided to go to the station first and pick Wilson up somewhere between eleven and eleven-thirty.

On the way to the station, Nick commented on how much better Corrie looked this morning compared to last night.

"Yes, Nick, I could see quite a difference, too, but she has a long way to go yet. Honest to God, Nick, I wish it had been me instead of her. It breaks my heart to see her laying there in that bed."

"I know what you mean, Cody. I have wished it, myself, but we can't change what has happened. We can only hope for the best. But we can make these sleezy Son-Of-A Bitches pay, and that is what I intend to do today and next Friday night."

"That is my intention, too. That is why I want to do this as close to the book as possible. I certainly don't want any of them to get off on a technicality, especially one that I may have made."

"Yes, that is why I am glad that you are leading this investigation. You have more experience than I do, and I might add that I have learned quite a lot from you the last couple of weeks. Yes, it is good to be working with someone you can trust and know that will not lead you wrong. I can't say that about some of the guys."

Cody looked at Nick with a halfway grin on his face, "You know how to make a guy feel good, don't you? Pardner, I picked you because I knew that you had it upstairs and could be my equal. Meaning that we could follow each other toe to toe and know exactly what the other was thinking and doing. And I don't think I made a mistake."

They laughed at each other. And as they were nearing the parking lot, Cody said in a gruff voice, "Let's go get'em, Pardner. Our full day is starting now. The first thing to do is talk to the Lieutenant and then we will go from there. I hope Garcia is out today for some reason or another. I don't want to deal with him now, but I am wondering what his part in this mess is other than destroying files."

"Well, you may not have to. I don't see his car, but that don't mean anything. Another thing, Pardner, we will have to prove Garcia is involved unless one of the others talk. We know that he is, but we have to have evidence."

They walked in the front door, but very few of the men were there. They proceeded down the hall to their office. After they were settled in their office, Cody went to the Lieutenant's office. He was alone, but he had a stack of papers on his desk that he was reading.

"Good morning, Lieutenant. May we talk to you for a few minutes?"

"Good morning, Sergeant. Sure. I'll come to your office as soon as I finish signing these papers. It would be better there."

"Sure, Lieutenant." Then Cody turned and walked back to his office. Nick had just finished getting a pot of coffee ready to brew.

A few minutes later, Lieutenant Moss walked into their office and sat in one of the chairs where he was facing both men. "Before we get started on what happened last night, how is Corrie doing?"

Nick said, "She looks somewhat better this morning. The doctor said that she would be alright. She will need a lot of rest and that it would take time. She was awake this morning and talked a little."

"Good. I am so sorry that it happened. But, I do want to congratulate you both. Our dear Mr. Santino is locked away until his lawyer can get him out."

Cody spoke then, "Lieutenant, we talked with Hal in the Crime Lab yesterday morning and the bullets that killed the two young boys matched Santino's 9MM. We had planned to arrest him this morning and search his apartment for the guns so that he could not say that they were stolen or something. We wanted to surprise him, but as you know, it didn't work out that way."

"That Son-Of-A Bitch. I hope he rots in jail. I am only sorry that I wasn't the one to arrest him. You had better go and add those two murder charges before his attorney shows up. You do have his gun, don't you?"

"Yes, Kato and I took both guns from his car, the .38 Caliber and 9MM, when we arrested him last night. Hal is checking out the .38 Caliber because the other victims were killed with a .38 Caliber," Nick said as he got up to get a cup of coffee and offered the others a cup also. He poured three cups and handed one each to Cody and Moss and then sat down at his desk with his cup.

After the Lieutenant had absorbed that information, then Cody said, "Lieutenant, I would like to bring you up to date on what we are planning today. We know that the drugs come from Savannah on Thursday or Friday and arrive here somewhere around twelve noon or twelve-thirty because Wilson picks it up at a warehouse and distributes it to his boys to sell in the afternoon. A friend of mine from Texas is working with us. He and Marci, GBI Agent, have been in Savannah since Wednesday morning checking things out. They are following the drug carriers here to this warehouse. When they leave Savannah, the boat, "My Fantasy" will be seized along with the crew and arrested by the GBI there. Tex or Marci will call us when they are about an hour away from here. My brother, Steven, and Kato are going to the warehouse and stake it out somewhere around ten this morning. Nick and I are going to pick up Wilson around eleven or eleven-thirty. Since Wilson will not be at the warehouse to receive the drugs, we will be staking it out to see who shows up to distribute it to the boys. With Santino in jail and Wilson here, it will leave Garcia. We know that he is involved, but we have no evidence of what his part in this mess has been. We only hope that Wilson will talk this time. We would like for Garcia to be out of the office or at least not know that Wilson is being held here. Also, somewhere that the higher ups in the drug business cannot get in touch with Garcia and send him to the warehouse. We want the big boys or at least as many of them that we can get to be there. What do you propose that we do?"

"Well, Cody, you guys have really been busy. You don't know how proud I am of you guys. I knew I could count on you two. I shouldn't be, but I am surprised that you all have done so well on what you had to go on. This has really been fast. No problem with Garcia, I'll hold him in my office doing things with me so that he won't know that Wilson is here. Do you trust Roberts?"

"I had thought about Roberts. He did give us some information he had when he started the investigation six or seven months ago. If he could hold Wilson in our office or in the interrogation room and try to get him to talk and don't let him out until we clear it, it would be a big help."

"Don't worry about those two, Cody. I'll take care of them. But you two had better go add those two murder charges before the Judge lets Santino out on bond. And thanks again, guys, for a job well done."

Cody smiled and said, "Lieutenant, it isn't done yet, but by tonight we will know if our plans worked. Also, Lieutenant, we need to make sure that Santino does not go before Judge Turner or Judge Mason for a Bond Hearing. We have reason to believe that at least Judge Turner may be involved. We are not sure about Judge Mason."

"Cody, I'll check on that, but when you go to the D.A.'s office make sure that they know."

"We will, Lieutenant."

They shook hands and the Lieutenant walked back to his office with a happy smile on his face and Cody and Nick went to the District Attorney's Office. When they had finished there, they went by the Crime Lab to talk with Hal. Hal was in Court and would not be back to the office before lunch time. Cody looked at his watch and said, "Steven and Kato are probably at the warehouse by now. So they decided to check with Steven and Kato to see if anything was happening. Cody called Steven on his phone. When Steven answered, Cody asked, "Hey, Bro, where are you all now?"

"We are sitting in a diner across the street from a big building. I don't know the name of the diner. What are you two up to now?"

"We have taken care of our business and we are now on our way back to Nick's place to pick up his personal vehicle and head over to where you all are."

"Good, we'll see you then."

When Steven hung up the phone, Kato said grinning, "You know, Steven, you may make an investigator yet."

"What do you mean?"

"The way you told Cody where we were. I would work with you anytime. It is wise to be discreet on the cellular phones. You never know who may be listening. The name of the diner is in big letters right in front of you. But, of course, the waitress has been flirting with you. You probably didn't realize it was there. You have a way with females. I need to stick with you and maybe some of it would rub off on me.

They both laughed. They had finished their second breakfast and were now drinking about their third or fourth cup of coffee since waking up this morning. They both had breakfast at home, but this diner was in a good place because they could see the front and one side of the warehouse across the street and they had a lot of time to pass before they really got serious with what they were going to do. Now, they were waiting for Cody and Nick.

After about thirty or thirty-five minutes, Cody and Nick walked into the diner and sat down with Steven and Kato. Steven asked, "How are things going?"

Cody said, "Everything is fine. Moss said he would take care of the office while we are here....I think you are right, Kato. I do believe that Moss is on the level and want to get to the bottom of this even though his brother-in-law is involved."

Then Nick spoke up and asked, "Have you all checked the building yet?"

"Yes, we did when we first got here. All the doors are locked, but we found some good hiding places where we can see who enters the building and who comes out." Steven then took a sip of coffee and continued, "The side door would not be hard to break down if we had to. It shook real easy. Besides, I have a little kit...."

Nick started smiling and shaking his head from side to side. Steven stopped talking and everyone looked at him. Nick said, "Steven, we don't want to hear about your kit. But I must admit. You think of everything, don't you? Just keep it handy in case we need it."

Everyone laughed. Then Cody said, "All we have to do is pick up Wilson, and we are waiting a while yet. We don't want Moss to have to deal with him no longer than he has to. He is also going to take care of Garcia during this time. So, now, we just set and wait."

Kato had been quiet, just listening to the others. Finally, he said, "You know, you guys, I love working with you. Sure wish all three of you were with the GBI. We would have a time of our life."

They all laughed again and ordered another cup of coffee. Cody looked at his watch and said, "We have about thirty minutes to go. By that time, we all will be going to the bathroom so much, we won't have time to do anything else." They all laughed again. They all were feeling good about what was happening today and just wanted to get it over with and hope that they could get everyone involved. Although they knew it was not possible that they would get all of the higher ups, they were determined to get as many as they could. It was like being on a high.

Steven said, "Hmmm, look, there are some kids hanging around the warehouse. Are they the ones that are under Wilson?"

Kato looked and then said, "A couple of them look like the kids we talked to but I can't be sure. How about you, Nick and Cody?"

They both looked but couldn't be sure, either. Then Cody said, "We'll just watch them from here. Nick and I will have to leave in about twenty-five minutes. If they are still there we will go over and talk to them and make sure that they leave. I hope they leave on their own, though."

All four of them kept watching the kids, but trying to make it seem that they were not really interested. Finally, it was about time for Nick and Cody to leave, so they got up and Cody said, "Thanks for the coffee, Little Brother. I'll repay you sometime." They all laughed at the expression on Steven's face.

"The way you repay me can stop for now. If you keep repaying me, I'll be in your debt for life."

They all laughed, trying to make it a normal outing so that the people in the diner would not get the impression that something was going down. Nick and Cody walked out of the diner and got into their car. The boys were still there in front of the warehouse. Cody drove over to where they were standing and he said, "Hey, you guys, aren't you suppose to be in school this time of day?"

One of them looked at him and said, "No, we don't go to school. We dropped out a few months ago."

Cody looked at them and recognized that three of them were the guys that Tim had asked them about. What are your names?"

They all seemed a little nervous, but the one that had spoken said, "I am Doug Ward and this is Johnny Lowe and that is Tommy Downey. We are suppose to meet someone here."

"Who might that be?"

"Our probation officer. His name is Wilson."

"I see. Why are you meeting him here and not in his office?"

"I don't know. He said for us to meet him here at twelve-thirty. We are early, but we didn't have anywhere else to go so we came here hoping that the warehouse was open, but it's locked."

"I tell you what. Do you know Tim Carson?"

"Yes, he is a good friend of ours, but we haven't seen him the last few days. He is suppose to be here, too. Has anything happened to him? He isn't dead, is he?"

"No, no, nothing has happened to him. He is fine, but he won't be here today. You guys, do you remember either of us?"

"Yes Sir, you are with the Sheriff's Department. We talked to you before, and also, the other two guys in the diner. The one with the beard talked to us a couple of times. He is real nice. He promised to help us, but he hasn't yet."

"I see. Why don't you three get in the car and we will take you to see Tim. He will be very glad to see you. He spoke very highly of you three."

"Oh, no, we can't. If we are not here when Wilson shows up, we will be in deep trouble."

"If you are not here when Wilson shows up, we will make everything right. O.K."

Nick got out of the car and opened the door for them. While they were getting into the car, Nick waved to Steven and Kato to make sure that they saw them. The boys were nervous and frightened.

Nick said, "Don't be frightened. We are not going to hurt you. We are going to help you. Don't worry about Wilson. We will take care of him."

They were quiet for a few miles, then Cody said, "Tim is staying at my farm. We are taking you three there to keep you safe for now. So, there is nothing to be afraid of. When we get there, Tim and Chip will explain everything to you. O.K. We are helping you because we

263

know what Wilson expects you to do and Tim is a good friend of yours. He told us that you three were selling drugs against your will and asked us to look out for you."

All three, sounding happy now, said, "Yes Sir. We will do whatever you tell us to do. We just want out."

"Don't worry. You will get out."

Then they became quiet wondering what was going to happen to them. They wanted to ask questions, but was not sure if they should. They were quiet until they got to the Edwards farm. Cody drove in the back way and right away saw Tim and Chip. They came over to the car smiling.

Cody said, "We brought three guys to help you with your chores. You two can show them around the place and fix a place for them to sleep tonight. Also, you can explain things to them. They are a little frightened right now. Where's Jake?"

Tim looked in the back seat and grinned from ear to ear. Then he said, excitedly, "Al...right, you guys." By that time, Nick was out of the car and opening the back door for them to get out.

Chip said, "He is in one of the stalls, I'll go get him." And he took off to find Jake.

Tim was hugging them and telling them that he was so glad to see them. They all were laughing now. Then he said, "Sergeant Edwards and Corporal Carillo is helping us like they said they would. You will be happy here. We won't have to sell drugs anymore, will we, Sergeant Edwards?"

"No, you won't."

A minute or so later, Chip and Jake came around the corner and walked up to the car. Jake was grinning. "I see you brought me some more help."

Cody said, "Yes, you think you can take care of them for a couple of days. I know sleeping arrangements might be a little scarce, but do you think you can make do for tonight?"

"Sure, we have that other room. They can clean it up and we have some cots. They will be alright. Don't worry about them."

Then Cody looked at Nick and said, "We have to get going. Jake, I told these three that Tim would explain everything to them. You make sure that they understand what Tim says and they do what you tell them. They are a little frightened right now because they were waiting for Wilson when we saw them. If they need to call home, let them, but no telling of where they are."

"Don't worry, Cody. I'll take care of them. We can always use more help." He laughed.

"Thanks, Jake. We owe you plenty. We'll see you later. Hopefully, it won't be much longer."

"No problem, Cody. Glad to help out any youngster that we can if it will start them on a good solid road in life."

Then Cody and Nick drove off and left the five boys with Jake. He knew that Jake meant what he said and that everything would be alright.

On the way to pick up Wilson, Cody called Moss and told him that they were on their way to pick up Wilson. "Lieutenant, is everything there working out alright?"

"Yes, everything is fine. Oh, by the way, Roberts took Garcia with him to pick up a prisoner in Carlton. They will probably be back sometime around quitting time this afternoon."

"Good. Lieutenant. Then we will bring Wilson in to see you. Right."

"Right. Sergeant. We'll see you then."

265

"Sure, Lieutenant." Then Cody hung up the phone and said, "Roberts has taken Garcia to Carlton to pick up a prisoner. They won't be back until quitting time."

Nick laughed and then Cody joined in with him.

"Well, Cody, it looks like the Lieutenant is on our side, doesn't it?"

"Yes, it does. If he continues to work with us, I will owe him a great big apology."

"We both will. Maybe we'll invite him to our celebration party," Nick said as he was grinning.

Cody knew that they were running later than he had intended to, but he had a chance to get the boys out of danger and took it. So, just as they were pulling into the parking lot, Wilson was coming out of the door going to his car. Cody pulled up beside him and Nick jumped out of the car. "O.K., Wilson, get in the car. We are taking you in for questioning."

"You can't take me in now. I have an appointment that I can't miss."

"O.K., Wilson, if that is what you want. I guess you heard about Santino being arrested last night for trying to run my sister off the road and then shooting my girlfriend last night. From what I hear, he is talking his head off. Now, do you want to take the fall for him or do you want to defend yourself?"

"What do you mean? Santino was arrested. I have not heard anything about it."

"I haven't tried to run anyone off the road and I haven't shot anyone. He can't lay that on me."

"Oh, he isn't laying that on you. We have a couple of witnesses to that, but we have two murders that you have probably forgotten about. You remember the two young boys that were under your supervision. They were murdered or do they mean anything to you."

He turned white as a sheet and Cody thought he was going to fall out. Nick was standing beside the car. He said, "Wilson, can you make it in the car or do you need some help?"

When Wilson was able to talk, he said, "I am not going to take no rap for murder. Like I said, I never shot anyone." He walked over to the back door and got in the car before he realized what he had done. When he realized that he was in the car, he said, "Hey, I can't go downtown with you. I have an important appointment that I can't miss." He started to open the door, but realized that there were no handles on the inside of the doors in the back seat. "Let me out. Let me out."

Cody looked him right in the eye and said, "No, we are not going to let you out because as soon as the phone rings and give us the go ahead, we are going to arrest you for the two murders. Santino is being questioned as we speak. Is that what you want?"

"No, no, I'll go. But I tell you that I have not murdered anyone."

"Then you go to the station and make your statement in writing."

"Alright. Alright. I will go with you. I didn't kill anybody."

Nick looked at Cody and smiled. Then they got in the car and took off for the station. Wilson was quiet during the ride into the station. At one time Nick asked him, "Wilson, what kind of an appointment did you have? You are welcome to use my phone to cancel it, if you want." Then he picked up his phone and offered it to Wilson.

"I don't need your phone. I will call when I get to the station. Besides, I won't be there long. I did not kill anyone. I don't care what Santino says."

Nick looked at Cody and smiled again. Then he put his phone back into his pocket. Cody knew that Nick was trying to lead Wilson on to see what he would say. Just before they got to the station, Cody's phone began to ring. Wilson looked up and had a frightened look on his face. Cody said, "That must be the Lieutenant." Cody knew that it was probably Tex, but he wanted Wilson to think it was someone from the station calling. Cody said, "Hello, Sergeant Edwards speaking." Then Tex answered, "Hello, Old Buddy. We are about an hour from there. Everything has gone as planned." Then Cody said, "Good. We are bringing Wilson to the station now. See you in a little while. Bye."

Wilson asked, "Does that call mean that I will be arrested for murder? Is that what that Son-of-A Bitch said?"

Cody said, "Not one murder but two, Wilson. We are taking you in to see the Lieutenant. He will take care of you."

"You don't have any evidence that I murdered anybody because I didn't. You can't take Santino's word for anything. He is lying if he said I had anything to do with it. He is the one that took care of that part of the operation."

Nick looked at Cody and then looked back at Wilson and asked, "What operation are you talking about?"

"I ain't talking now. I want a lawyer before I say anymore. You are not going to get another word from me until I have a lawyer present."

"O.K. if you feel you need one. The Lieutenant will be taking care of you. You talk to him."

By that time they were pulling into the parking lot of the station. Cody stepped out to the car and opened the back door. "Do we need to handcuff you Wilson or are you going to walk in peacefully?"

"I'll walk in peacefully. I am here, ain't I?"

Nick said, "My, my, Wilson. What grammar you use."

They walked into the front office and very few of the men were inside today. Most of them were working out in the field. The Lieutenant was waiting for them.

Cody said, "Lieutenant, we brought Wilson in. I understand that Santino has been talking. But Wilson says that he has not killed anyone. He also said that 'that part of the operation was Santino's. He wouldn't say what operation to us, but I assume that you will be able to get it out of him. Oh, and by the way, he wants a lawyer present."

Lieutenant Moss smiled and said, "I see what you mean. Do you want a lawyer present, Wilson?"

"Yes Sir, I do. I am not admitting to nothing. I ain't going to say nothing until he gets here."

Cody said, "Wilson, you will have a long time to work on your grammar."

The Lieutenant pointed to the phone and said, "Go ahead and call your lawyer. We got all day. I am waiting for Thompson to finish writing his report because he is going to join us before any questioning is done."

"Lieutenant, May I use a phone in private?"

"No, you may not. You may use this phone or not at all."

Then Cody said, "Oh, Lieutenant, I almost forgot. Wilson has an appointment. He also said he needs to call and cancel it." He smiled at the Lieutenant.

The Lieutenant smiled and said, 'Wilson, go ahead and use the phone before we get started." Thompson came to the door and Moss motioned for him to come in. Cody and Nick spoke to him. They had seen him around the office and thought he was a pretty good guy, but neither of them had worked with him before.

Cody said, "Well, Lieutenant, we have to leave now. You all take good care of Wilson."

Thompson said, "We will. I am glad that Lieutenant asked me to help. The more scum that we can get off the streets, the better. I appreciate a chance to help."

"Thank you, guys, you have done a good job. I'll take it from here."

Chapter 11

So Cody and Nick left to meet Kato and Steven at the warehouse. When they arrived, Kato and Steven were sitting in Steven's personal car across the street facing the side of the building. They could see if anyone went to the front or back door. They had another thirty minutes or so to really get into position.

Cody and Nick pulled up in front of the diner and noticed that it had a closed sign on the door, but there were a few people still in there. They did not want to go where Kato and Steven were parked or to arouse any suspicion in the area. About that time, Cody's phone rang. Cody answered, and Steven said, "Bro, the diner is going to close as soon as the other people leave. They should be ready in about ten minutes. We talked to the owner and he told his customers that he had received word that the street in front of the diner would be closed in a few minutes so they would have to leave as soon as possible. We have made arrangements for some officers to block both the streets after the white van passes and is out of sight. We are just taking precautions, that's all. Have you heard from Tex?"

"That's good, Brother. Yes, about forty minutes ago. He said that everything had gone as planned. They should be here in about twenty-five to thirty minutes. I think we need to get the rest of the people out of the diner. You and Kato take the back. We will be out front."

"O.K. Brother. Take care."

"You, too, Brother."

After Cody hung up the phone, he and Nick got out of the car and went to the diner and knocked on the door. The owner came to the door and said, "We're closed." Cody showed him his badge and said,

"It's time to evacuate the building. Are your customers about finished with their lunch?"

"Yes, they will be out in five minutes. I talked with the other officers and they said I could stay here as long as I stayed in the back."

"It could be dangerous. I think you need to leave, too."

"Officer, I explained to the other officers that I am a retired military man and can handle myself. I assure you that I will not get in the way. I have worked with Kato before."

Cody looked at Nick and then said, "If Kato said you could stay then so be it."

The owner smiled at them and said, "I'll have these people out in five minutes."

They shook hands and Cody and Nick went back to the car to wait, and sure enough, a few minutes later the diner was empty. Then Cody moved the car and they found a good place to stay on the side of the building. There was a small room built on the side of the building which had a platform on top of it. So they climbed on top of it and hid behind a box that was already there. It was close enough that they could see and hear what was going on at the front door.

Kato and Steven had already looked around and found their hiding place. Now they were in place and all they had to do was set and wait.

Finally, they saw a white van pull around to the back of the warehouse. A couple of minutes later, they saw Tex and Marci pull up to the curb about a half of block up the street. Cody flashed his badge against the sun and Tex saw them. Tex and Marci walked up to the side of the building where Nick and Cody were, and then, they walked against the wall toward the back of the building. There they found Kato and Steven who could see the two men at the back door.

The men were very frustrated and angry because they could not get into the warehouse. One of them pulled out a phone and made a phone call. Then they heard him say, "How the Hell do I know. Wilson was suppose to be here and have the doors open." A minute later, he said, "O.K., we will wait, but call me back if you can't get Wilson." Then he hung up the phone and they got back into the white van and waited.

Finally, the phone rang again and they heard him say, "O.K. but make it fast. We don't want to be here any longer than we have to be. Damn Wilson." Then he hung up the phone again and told his partner that someone would be there shortly.

After waiting about fifteen minutes more, a car drove up with two men in it. They got out of the car and one of them said, "I don't know where Wilson is, but I am going to find out why he isn't here. He did not pick up the money, either. We are suppose to be halfway to Savannah by now."

One of the guys from the white van said, "I sure don't want this to happen again. It makes me very, very nervous to wait around like this."

"Well, let's get this over with because Robert and I are late for a special meeting in Savannah."

By then the door had been unlocked and they drove the van inside leaving the door open just a little. Tex and Marci eased their way up to the side of the door listening for the transaction to be completed. Since Tex was wearing the wire, he was to get as close as he could and Marci second. Kato was also wearing a wire just in case. He and Steven had made their way to the other side of the door.

Cody was at the side of the front door and Nick was at the corner of the building watching the side door in case anyone tried to come that way. They all were waiting for the sign.

Then Tex heard one of the men say, "Well, that takes care of that. This is Wilson's bag and there are the other two bags that we will take care of when we get back from Savannah. I'll call Samuels and have him come by here and pick this up and keep it until we get back. Thank you two for being patient. We will find out what happened to Wilson and rest assured that next week we will make sure someone is here and has the warehouse open."

"I hope so, because if this happens again, I am out of here," said one of the men as he was getting into the white van.

About that time Tex pushed the back door open and as he came through the door, a bullet hit him in the chest and he fell down. Marci was right behind him and fired a shot at the guy who had fired the shot. He went down. She said, "GBI agent. Hands up or I'll shoot." Tanner had turned and started running to the front door. By then, Kato and Steven were in the building with their guns drawn. They let him go because they knew that Cody and Nick were there waiting for him. Marci bent down to check out Tex. He was out cold. She saw where the bullet hit him and knew that he had on his vest and she did not see any blood so she knew that he was O.K. She nodded to the others to let them know that he would be fine. She stayed there with him. Cody and Nick walked Tanner back inside just in time to see Marci give the sign that Tex was O.K.

After everyone was handcuffed, Cody and Nick looked at each other and laughed. They had two of the higher ups, Robert Tanner and Attorney Larry Collins. They would get them one at a time if they had to, but they would get them. Then Cody walked over to Tex and said, "Hey, Texas Boy, wake up. Can't you keep up with us, Georgia Boys."

Everyone laughed. It helped to get the tension out of their system.

After a moment Tex raised up his head and looked around. "What in the world happened?"

They all laughed again and were shaking their heads.

Cody said, "You got shot or at least your vest did, but don't worry. Marci took care of him for you. I wouldn't mind having her for a partner anytime."

They all laughed again. It felt really good to have that behind them, but they knew that there were others involved. They still had work to do.

Tex just lowered his head, grinning and then he raised up and leaned over to Marci and kissed her on the cheek and said in his Texas drawl, "Thanks, Pardner. We make a good team, don't we?"

She smiled and said, "Yes, we do. I"ll work with you anytime."

Then Tex looked at Cody, grinning, "I'll never live this down, will I?"

Cody said, "No, you won't. I will make sure of that." And Cody put his hand out to help him up. When Tex stood up, he slapped Cody on the back and said, "We have made a start, Brother." They all said, "Yes, we have and more to come."

Nick got on the radio and called the officers that were at the barricades to come and pick up the prisoners, and, also, have the tow truck to get the cars. After the officers had picked them up and left, Cody and Nick gathered the money and drugs up and took it downtown to be processed as evidence. When they had finished there, Cody and Nick went by the station to see Lieutenant Moss. The others went to Kato's place and Cody and Nick were to meet them there. As Cody and Nick walked into the front office, they saw that it was almost empty. Lieutenant Moss and Thompson were in Moss' office and when Moss saw them, he motioned for them to come in.

As they walked into his office, he said, "By the smiles on your faces, I can see everything went well."

"Yes, Lieutenant, it went very well. With the help of a friend of mine, Sergeant Tex Tyler, who is visiting and helping us with this investigation. Also, Kato Delgado and Marci Fernandez, GBI Agents, have been working with us."

"No, I didn't know who was working with you, but I knew that whoever it was would be someone that would help you get the job done. That is why I did not want to interfere and wanted you to carry the ball all the way. Evidently, I was right." Then he introduced Andrew Thompson to them.

Cody thanked Thompson for helping with Wilson and Thompson said, "You are quite welcome. It was a long time coming. I have tried to get him before, but he always found a way to get out of it. I hope it sticks this time."

Cody said, "It will and it may surprise you as to who we met at the warehouse."

Moss said, "I have no idea, Cody. Wilson declared that Santino was the one that killed Douglas and Koster. And, of course, you know that Santino's gun showed that to be true. But his .38 Caliber was not the one that killed Harris. We locked Wilson up on Distribution and Sale of Drugs. That will hold him for awhile. Who did you all arrest?"

Cody and Nick smiled at each other and then Cody said, "Robert Tanner, Wilson's Uncle, Larry Collins and one of the drug carriers. The other one was a little trigger happy and shot Tex in the chest, but Marci got him before he could fire off another shot. Larry Collins is the attorney that defends all the kids when they are arrested. They met the men from Savannah with a bag full of money to exchange for the drugs. We have it recorded. Also, Marci and Tex had the GBI to arrest the boat crew in Savannah after they left and followed the two drug carriers here. Also, two men were arrested that were involved there in buying drugs from the boat. The Savannah men will take care of them. We found out about them a little while ago from Marci."

"I see, Sergeant. That's great. I am surprised that an attorney would be the one there to deal. I would have thought he was smarter than that. But Thompson and I were discussing this and he was telling me before you all came in that he had a feeling that the attorney was involved because of him always representing Wilson's kids."

Thompson spoke up, "Yes, I noticed that everytime I was in court for one case or another, Collins was there when it involved drugs. I am glad you got the Slime. Good job, you guys. I am only sorry that I wasn't there to arrest him and anyone that is involved with drugs."

Cody said, "Thompson, thank you again and I'll remember that next time I need some help. .....By the way, there were three big bags of drugs already bagged and ready for sale. Each one had a name on it. One was Wilson, one was Garcia/Tanner and the other name was Samuels. Wilson was not the only one selling the drugs. I am wondering who is selling for Garcia/Tanner and Samuels."

"Sergeant, that remains to be seen, but I am sure you will be able to find out."

"Lieutenant, we are going to do our best to get as many as we can." ...And then he continued, "Lieutenant, if it is alright with you, we will write up the report at Nick's place and give it to you tomorrow. I have got to set down and get my mind straight before I start writing this all down.

"That will be fine, Cody. Have you heard from Corrie since this morning?"

"No, evidently, she is doing as well as to be expected. Mrs. Carillo was to call us if there was a change and we haven't heard from her. The doctor says that what she needs now is rest and a lot of it.

Cody looked at Thompson and asked, "Thompson, I may call on you next week. We may need your help."

"Do that, Edwards. I'll be glad to help on or off duty. Just give me a call." He handed Cody a card with his home phone number on it.

"Thanks."

The Lieutenant looked at Cody and said, "You mean that this is not the end of this investigation?"

"No, Lieutenant, we still have another murder to solve. You haven't forgotten the Harris murder, have you?" *But Cody wasn't thinking about the Harris murder, he was thinking about his father's murder. He had a good feeling about Thompson, though, and felt that he was on the level.*

"I'm sorry, Cody. I am so thrilled with the result that you all have done, I completely forgot about him."

Then Thompson spoke up and said, "Cody, what about the other two bags, Garcia/Tanner and Samuels? If I can help you find their sellers, let me know."

"Yes, that is right. Since we just found that out today, we'll have to think about how to proceed. I'll have to call you later. The plans are not complete yet. Will that be alright with you?"

"Sure."

"O.K,. Thompson, I'll give you a call later. ..... Oh, another thing. Samuels is bound to find out about Tanner and Collins arrest. We will have to figure out how to handle him. I don't want him arrested until after next Friday. That is a must."

Nick spoke up, "Cody, maybe we should stake out the warehouse until tonight. I feel that Samuels and Garcia have someone else pick up their bags."

"You may have something there, Nick. We will take a ride by the warehouse and wait there awhile."

Thompson said, "If the Lieutenant is finished with me here, I'll be glad to watch the warehouse for you. I know the area, but am not sure where the warehouse is, but I can find it."

"Sure, Thompson, that would be great. That's a good idea. While you are there, we can write up the reports and then check back by with you."

The Lieutenant nodded that they were finished. So Andy Thompson followed Nick and Cody to the warehouse. The officers were just finishing up with their work at the warehouse, getting fingerprints and whatever evidence that they could find. The officers locked it up and gave the keys to Cody and left.

Cody gave the keys to the warehouse to Andy and Andy parked his car across the street at the diner so he could see the side that had the driveway to the back.

Cody and Nick gave him their card with their phone number on it and told Andy not to use the radio. Andy told them that he understood and would stay there until he heard from them or saw something.

And with that Nick and Cody walked to their car and they left for Nick's place. On the way, Cody said, "I have a good feeling about Thompson and I think we should give him a chance to work with us this week. We may need more men because there are a lot of doors at the Country Club."

"I agree with you. He seems like a nice guy, a regular family man. He certainly does not seem like a man that would be involved with drugs. You know he has about five kids from what I have heard."

"No, I didn't know that, but we do need some help and he is willing to do anything to help."

By this time they were headed toward the hospital to see Corrie. But before they arrived at the hospital, Nick called Kato on his cellular phone to let him know that they were going to the hospital and then home. And asked him to advise Tex and Steven that they would not be coming by. They would see him first thing in the morning. That he and Cody had some reports to write up tonight. And Kato said that was fine. He had plans for the evening, too.

At the hospital, Cody walked into Corrie's room and she had her eyes closed. He walked over to the bed and picked up her hand. He held it for a few minutes and then he leaned over and kissed her on the forehead and then on the lips lightly. She then opened her eyes and looked up at him and said, "Hi, Sweetheart, how long have you been here?"

"Only a few minutes. We are finished for today, except, Nick and I have some reports to write up. We got what we were after today, but there is still one more big fish to catch."

"Is everyone alright?"

"Yes, Darling. Everyone is fine and everything went as planned. We have one more big job to do and that is next Friday night. We will be doing some work this coming week, but not like before."

"I understand. You all be careful."

"We will. We always are." *He didn't want to tell her yet exactly what had occurred and about Tex getting shot. He would wait until she came home and everything was settled.*

Then he said, "Nick is outside and wants to see you, so I'll go and let him come in for a few minutes. I'll try to get by to see you sometime tomorrow. O.K."

"O.K., but if you don't, I'll understand."

He bent over and kissed her full on the lips and lingered for a little while. Then he squeezed her hand and said, "I'll see you tomorrow if I can." She smiled at him and then he turned and walked out the door.

After Nick's visit with his sister, Cody took Nick home and then he drove home thinking about Corrie. When he got home, Tex and Steven were there.

Tex said, "I talked to Dad a few minutes ago. My sister is having problems with the oil business and he feels that he should not leave her to deal with it alone right now. He feels that he should be there with her. But if they get it cleared up this coming week, he will come. He had talked to John, Casey's cousin, and he said that he could come anytime with Casey. Just let him know. Mama E said that they could stay here and I think that is best, too. What do you think?"

Cody laughed, he started to say something, but stopped.

Tex said, very sternly, "Don't you dare, not now, anyway."

Steven and Cody burst out laughing. Then Tex joined them. Mama E did not know what to think. She just stared at all three of them. Finally, she asked, "What is so funny?"

Steven said, "Oh, Mom, we will wait and let Tex tell you later, but I don't think he will be bragging so much about the Texas boys as he did before."

They laughed again.

Then Cody said, "That's a good idea, Mom. I think Casey will feel safer here than at a hotel even though she will be with her cousin."

Mama E said, "John can use the guest bedroom upstairs with you guys and the girl, what's her name?"

"Her name is Casey, Mom."

"Casey can use Traci's room and Traci can sleep in my room. My bed is kingsize and she and I can sleep on it. I am sure she won't mind just for a night or two."

"Thanks, Mom. We really appreciate it. I might add that I think you will love this girl once you get to know her. She is being a jewel about this investigation and we all will owe her quite a lot when this is all over."

"Son, I will do anything to help my children. You don't owe me any thanks."

Cody said, "Tex, I hope the problems that your sister is having will work out. Would like for your dad to visit with us. He has never been here before."

"Oh, they will. One of the accounts doesn't want to pay his bill. Dad has had problems with him before. He should know by now that Dad is not taking this sitting down. When Dad gets through with him this time, he will wish he had paid up in the beginning. No one pulls anything over on Dad."

"I'm sure he can handle it. I sure don't want to be on the wrong side with your father," said Cody.

"He did say that when he solved the problem, he wanted to come to Georgia for a few days and see what was so interesting here. I told him to come on and we will show him."

They all laughed.

Then Tex noticed that Traci had driven into the yard. He got up and said, "I'll see you later. I have some important business to take care of. If Dad was here now, he could see what is so interesting here in Georgia."

By the time he got outside, Traci was out of her car and was headed for the back door. He caught her around the waist and turned her around and they walked over to where the hammocks were with his arm around her waist and kissing her all the way. They sat down in a hammock with her leaning on his shoulder. They were silent for a while. *He was thinking of how glad he was that he had come to Georgia at the right time. He was so glad to see her. He sure had missed her.* He finally said, "I have never missed anyone as much as I missed you the last couple of days."

"I missed you, too.....Did you all accomplish all that you had planned to do?"

"Yes, we did. I'll wait and let Cody tell you about it. Our witness who is coming for the dance will be coming in next week. Mama E would not hear of her staying at a hotel. She insisted that she stay here, so I think her plans are for you to sleep with her and give your room to Casey. Casey will only be here one night, two the most. We all think that it is a good idea for her to stay here. She will be safer here than in a hotel room. Are we taking too much for granted by doing this?"

"No, you are not. I don't mind. Mom's room is bigger and she has a kingsize bed. That will be fine. Besides, it may be fun to have a sister for a couple of days."

"I do think you will like her when you meet her. She is only eighteen, though. Maybe, you can teach her some things that a big sister would teach her younger sister. It may be an inconvenience now, but I think you will be proud that you did when this is all over."

"Anything to help you and my brothers." She leaned over and kissed him full on the lips.

"Hey, that was a good surprise. Let's try that again."

They both laughed.

Traci said, "We better go in the house. Mom is probably waiting for me to help prepare dinner."

"No, she is not. She and Sara have already prepared dinner. We are having baked chicken with rice and broccoli, and a squash casserole. And guess what Sara made for dessert?"

"Mom's favorite. Blackberry cobbler."

He nodded. "Yes, you're right. Your Mom sure loves blackberries."

"Yes, when I came home from school, she would send me down to the fence near the garden to pick her blackberries so Sara could make her a blackberry cobbler.

Since I have been working and get home later, Jake is the one that inherited the picking of blackberries. ....Oh, did Cody tell you about Corrie getting shot?"

"Yes, Steven and Mama E told me. I really haven't had time to talk to Cody. He only came in a few minutes before you did. I was sorry to hear about Corrie, but I am glad that Kato was there and got the Son-Of-A-Bitch. He was the same one that tried to run you off the road, too. It is a good thing that I wasn't here, I would have killed him."

"Do you think Cody was wrong in waiting to arrest him before? If he had arrested him then, He would not have shot Corrie."

"No, now, don't go second-guessing Cody. He was right in what he did. If Cody had arrested him on that charge, Santino would have been out of jail, anyway. Don't worry, Cody knows what he is doing. Don't ever try to second-guess him or Steven........nor me." He laughed. "They both are good investigators." He grinned and then said, "So am I."

She laughed with him. Then they heard a voice coming toward them. Tex looked up and Cody was saying, "O.K. enough is enough." They all laughed.

Tex said, "Cody, Mama E and Steven told me about Corrie. I am really, really sorry. Did you see her today?"

"Yes, Nick and I went by the hospital before I came home. She is doing O.K. The doctor says that what she needs now is a lot of rest. She is in good spirits."

"Good. Glad to hear that."

"I came out to tell you two that dinner is almost ready." Traci started to get up, but Cody nodded for her to stay put. "Steven is helping Mom. They need some bonding time. He will call us when it is time to go in."

Traci sat back down. Then she said, "Bro, Tex told me about Casey staying here. I'm glad. It will be nice to have a little sister for a couple of days."

"Thanks, Sis. It is well appreciated. She seems like a very sweet girl. Chip made a good choice, I think. By the way, does Chip know that she is coming?"

Tex said, "No, I haven't told anyone except us."

"I'll tell him later in the week. He won't be able to sleep for the next week if I tell him tonight. And he will probably want to go to the airport to meet her, but that would be a bad idea. We would have to discourage that."

"Her identification of the person she saw means a lot to you, don't it, Bro?"

Cody answered her in a slow drawl, "Yes, Sis, more than you know. More than you know. ...Before you go to the dance next week, I want to talk to you. O.K."

"Sure. I know what I am suppose to do. Don't worry about that. I know that Casey has to be looked after and kept safe."

Steven then ducked his head out the door and called them in to dinner.

During dinner, Traci talked about Casey being there and how much she was going to enjoy her company. She had always wanted to have a little sister. Cody, Tex and Steven let her talk because that kept Mama E from asking any questions. She just sat there eating and listening to Traci.

Finally, she got an edge that she could ask Tex what happened in Savannah. So she butted in with, "Tex, did you accomplish everything that you wanted to do in Savannah the last couple of days?"

He looked at Cody and Cody nodded 'no'. Then he looked back at Mama E and said, "Mama E, everything worked out fine. Hopefully, after the dance next Friday night, it will all be over until court time."

"Well, I am glad to hear that. Maybe when it is over you all will explain everything that has been going on around here. You guys are just like Thomas. He kept everything a secret until after it was over with and then he would tell me some of it."

Cody said, "Mom, we don't want you to worry. We can take care of ourselves. Besides, the less people know what we are doing, the better, not that you would tell anyone, but it is best to keep quiet until it is over. Then we will explain everything and we are going to celebrate, O.K."

"I understand how it is, Son. When you get ready to tell me, you will. O.K., who is ready for dessert?"

Steven said, "I am." And he got up and started fixing the dessert for everyone.

Later, Tex, Cody and Steven left to go to Nick's place. Nick and Cody sat down and started writing the reports that they had not finished. Tex and Steven helped them. Just before they finished the reports, Nick called Kato and asked him to come over and help eat some of that food that was left from before and to bring Marci with him. They arrived about forty-five minutes later.

After a few minutes of laughing and making gestures about Tanner and Collins' surprise facial expressions when they came in the warehouse, they settled down to prepare the table with the food.

Cody said, "It was a pleasure to write these arrest reports. It will be even greater pleasure to write the one after the dance."

"Amen to that," they all remarked.

Then they started talking about the dance.

Tex said teasingly, "I will already be inside with Casey and Traci enjoying the dance."

Then Cody said, "Hey, I need to check in with Andy Thompson. He is watching the warehouse. He volunteered to stake it out for a while because of the other two bags for Samuels and Garcia. We felt that someone would be coming to pick those up. All this time we were just planning for Wilson to pick up the drugs, but there are more people involved here. There are some drug pushers out there other than Wilson's kids. We need to concentrate on them this week while we are waiting for the dance."

Nick said, "I'll call Andy. You tell Kato and Marci what we plan for the dance." Then Nick walked in the other room so he could hear over the phone.

Kato said, "Hey, let's start at the beginning. You haven't discussed any of this with us. Cody, you said you would later. Well, it is later, and we would like to be in on this arrest, also."

"You will," Cody answered. Then he started to explain to Kato and Marci. "Yes, we do want you to work with us on this. Here is the plan: Tex, Traci and Casey (our witness) will meet Rich, Traci's date, at the Country Club. All of us will be outside watching the entrances to the building and waiting for a signal from Tex to let us know that Casey has identified the killer. As soon as Casey identifies the killer, Tex will lead her outside and take her to our place for safekeeping. Nick, Steven and I will rush in. Steven will find Traci and get her out and Nick and I will arrest the Son-Of-A Bitch. We will need at least one person at each doorway. I think there are three entrances. The front door is a double door, perhaps we should have two people there. One on each side."

Marci spoke up and said, "Yes, you are right, Cody. I have been there once. We would need four or five people outside."

Kato laughed and said, "Oh, maybe we should investigate you. How did you wrangle a visit to the Country Club?"

They all laughed. Then Marci said, "Have your fun, but, believe it or not, I did date a guy with money, and it was legal money. I checked that out, myself. The only problem was that we lived in two different worlds."

Kato said, "I was just kidding, Marci. We don't need to know your personal life."

"No, you don't, and I am not going to tell you. I just wanted to explain how I came about going up on the Hill one time."

They all laughed.

Steven winked at Marci and said, "Don't let them get to you, Marci. I have been there, too. They are just jealous because they haven't been to a dance on the Hill."

"You're probably right, Steven," said Kato.

Then Nick walked back into the room and said, "Andy said that Garcia came by the warehouse, went in and then a few minutes later came out again. He took a few pictures of him going in and coming out and made sure that the name of the building was on the pictures. He then followed him to his house and everything was quiet. He then went home."

"Good," said Cody. "Now we need to figure out a way to start over and find out who is selling for Garcia and Samuels. Anyone have any suggestions."

Then Tex said, "Alright, let's get serious now. We had the boat crew that was bringing the drugs into Savannah arrested. And, also, two men that bought drugs from the same crew there in Savannah were arrested by the GBI. And, Marci, Kato probably told you that he and Nick have arrested the one that tried to run Traci off the road, shot Corrie. He is, also, the one that killed the two young boys a few months ago. So, we all have accomplished a lot the last few days. That is all of the old business. Now let's start with the new."

Cody said, "We have to concentrate on the drugs this coming week. We know what we will do to get the other murderer. Following Garcia and Samuels would be one start. Do any of you have another suggestion?"

"Kato, Tex and I can follow those two," said Marci. They don't know us. "That will leave you three to do something else. Maybe talk to the kids about the other drugs. We never asked them about that because we didn't know there were others selling drugs in this operation."

Steven said, "Nick and Cody can do that and I will check on the computer and see what adults are being arrested for drugs and if they go before Judge Turner or what Judge. And, also, if Larry Collins represent them on these charges."

"That's a good suggestion, Bro."

"Cody, I told you I was a good investigator. I don't know why you all don't believe me."

They all laughed. ....Then Marci said laughingly, "Steven, I will work with you anytime. You just contact me when you need a partner."

"Uh, oh," Kato said, ""I believe she has her eye on you, Steven. We are going to have to watch you two."

"I've got my eye on her, too," Steven said as he winked at Marci.

They laughed again.

"Wouldn't it be nice if all of us could work together all the time. We would clean up this place," said Kato. Everyone was looking at him and thinking of how happy he seemed to be while working.

Tex asked, "Should I come here or should we meet somewhere in the morning? Maybe I should follow Garcia and not Samuels because I will be at the dance Friday night."

"Tex, Marci can go with you since you are new in town and follow Garcia. I will take Samuels. We need to watch him closely because he probably knows by now that Tanner and Collins have been arrested. Then again he may not. They were on their way to a meeting in Savannah. He may think that they are in Savannah. It is going to be slow and we will probably be sitting in our cars and just waiting because it is a Friday and they will be working most of the day. But we need to follow their moves and take pictures when we think it is important to the case."

"Do you all think we should meet tomorrow night like we have been?" asked Nick.

Cody said, "Not unless something happens that we should know about, but we can always use the phone. Unless something comes up that we have to take another course, we will continue following Garcia and Samuels and hope they will lead us to someone else."

Nick said, "We will take it day by day. Who knows. Santino or Wilson may decide to talk."

"Yeah, right," said Kato.

They all laughed. And then Cody said, "We will do what we said for tomorrow. If nothing turns up, we will continue it the next day. If anything at all turns up, call Nick or I and then we will decide what to do next. Agreed."

"Agreed," they all said.

Kato said, "Well, if there is not anything else to discuss, I am going home. Good goings today, you guys." And he got up and said his goodbyes.

"Wait a minute, I rode with you."

Kato said, "I'm sorry. Are you ready to leave, Marci?"

"Yes, Kato. I have some things to do before going to bed." So she said her goodbyes and they left.

Then Cody, Tex and Steven helped Nick clean up his kitchen and put the remainder of the food away and then they left with the understanding that Cody would pick Nick up the next morning.

The next morning things went the usual. They each were doing their job assignment, except for Steven. He was on regular duty at work, but he took the time out to check the main computer to get his list. He looked over the list, but it did not show anything that would catch his eye. Several of the names on the list had been arrested more than one time, but two of the names had gone before Judge Turner and had gotten probation each time. Steven thought that might be worth checking out. He then went to the courthouse and had the clerk to pull the two files. He sat down at the table and studied the files. He wrote down their address and information that he thought Cody might need and then returned the files and left.

Meanwhile, Tex and Marci had followed Garcia from the station to Samuels' office. He was there for about thirty minutes. When he came out of the building, he seemed to be worried by the expression on his face. Tex was watching him with the binoculars when he could see his face. While they were waiting for Garcia outside Samuels' office, they saw Nick and Cody setting across the street waiting for Samuels to come out, but so far, he hadn't. Tex and Marci then followed Garcia to his home and waited abut fifteen minutes and then a few minutes later they followed him back to the station.

A few minutes after Garcia left, Samuels came out of the building and Cody and Nick followed him home. He was there for about forty-five minutes and then he left and went to the warehouse and was waitiing there for about twenty minutes when two men pulled up. Cody and Nick got out of the car and walked close to the building toward the back so they could hear what was being said. When they got close enough to hear, Samuels was saying, "I don't know what happened. Wilson did not show up yesterday and no one has heard from him. Tanner and Collins are in Savannah and I can't reach them. Garcia said that he had to go out of town yesterday. He wasn't here to get the drugs. Where in the hell could the bags be?"

One of the other guys said, "Do you think that Wilson got greedy and took off with the bags?"

"No, I don't think that Wilson has the brains to do something like that. You two guys just lay low and tell the others to do the same until we can figure out what happened."

"Alright. We will just wait until we hear from you, but I need the money. I am broke."

Samuels said, "What the hell do you do with your money for you to be broke now. Tanner gives you your cut every week."

"It just goes."

The other guy said, "He is just living too high on the hog. Too many babes and booze. You need to put some of it up like I do. You never know when you may need it."

Samuels said, "That's right. Here, there is a hundred dollar bill. Don't spend it all in one place. O. K., you two, lay low until you hear from me." And then he got into his car and took off back to the office and the other two got in their car and left.

Nick and Cody decided to follow the two because they felt that Samuels was going back to his office. Besides, they knew where they could find him. The other two, they didn't know about. So they followed them to a bar. They took pictures of the bar and street signs. Also Nick wrote down the name of the bar and where it was located. When they came out, Nick got a couple of good shots of them with the camera. Then they followed them to a house that they assumed that one of them lived because one got out and the other one drove on up the street a couple of blocks. After Nick wrote down the addresses of both houses, they drove back to Samuels office. His car was there so they decided to get some lunch at a restaurant a couple of blocks away.

After they had sat down at a table, Nick said, "You know it is strange that they are wondering what has happened and have not yet called the jail to see if they had been arrested. I wonder why Santino or Wilson has not called them to let them know."

"They are so sure that they cannot be arrested that they probably have not thought of it and they are too embarrassed to tell Samuels they are in jail. Besides, their lawyer is in jail with them so they don't need to call outside." Then Cody began to laugh and Nick joined in laughing, too.

"I know, but you would think that Tanner would have called his wife and she would have told Samuels."

"While we were there at Samuels house, the Tanner house looked like no one was home. Maybe she is on vacation or out of town visiting someone and she doesn't know it yet."

"That's a possibility. Anyway, if that is true, it sure is working in our favor. We are grateful for any help that fate will give us.

"Amen to that, Nick."

After they finished their lunch, they went back and parked across from Samuels building. His car was still there.

"You know something, Nick. This is the part of investigations that I find very boring. I know that it is necessary, but it is still boring."

"You mean that I am not interesting enough for you and you are bored," Nick said laughingly.

"You know what I mean. Just sitting here waiting for someone else to make a move."

"I know what you mean, Cody. Tex had the right idea. It would be more exciting if Corrie and Angie were here with us, right."

"You've got it, Pardner. That would be very nice. I have missed her the last couple of weeks. I vow that I am going to make it up to her as soon as she is able to get out and go places. Maybe we will just go on a vacation somewhere and then come back and plan the wedding. I don't think I can wait until the wedding is planned and then go on a honeymoon."

"Oh, what you want to do is go on your honeymoon and then get married. Are you asking for my approval since I am her brother?"

"No, I am not asking for your approval. I am just thinking out loud. But I plan to get her approval. I think we need a vacation away from here for a few days. Don't you think that would be nice?"

"Yes, I think that would be nice. If you want to know what I think, I think you and Corrie should go on a cruise or vacation to some island for a few days when this is over. That would be wonderful for you to suggest that to her." Then he grinned.

"O. K., Smart Ass, I am. I am going by the hospital tonight and ask her. How about that?"

"Good. I am glad that I suggested it."

"You suggested it. You really are a Smart Ass. You know that. I thought of it first and then you chimed in with your two cents."

"At least, it is not boring now, is it?"

"Nick, I have to hand it to you. You do make a good partner, thinking about everything, even boredom. ....Have you talked to Katie yet?"

"No, I haven't. You have kept me so busy that I have not had time. I do not want to call her on the phone. I would rather go by and talk with her and I will do that after next weekend. That is, if that meets your approval?"

"Since when do we have to meet each other's approval for anything."

"Cody, since you started dating my sister."

They both laughed. They were getting into a silly mood now. Finally, Nick said, "I think just sitting here is getting to both of us. Let's take a run to the Tasty Freeze and get an ice cream cone."

"That's a good idea. I love ice cream."

So Cody started up the car and they went a few blocks to the Tasty Freeze and got an ice cream cone each. Then they drove up to Samuels building and parked in a different place. Nothing was happening but they sat there and waited until Samuels left the building at five o'clock and they followed him straight home. They also noticed that the Tanner house was still quiet as though no one was home. So they decided to go by the hospital to see Corrie before they went home. They stopped by and got her a couple pieces of chicken and some salad. She loved chicken and they did not see why she could not have some. The hospital food was not always what a person wanted to eat.

When Cody went in to see her, she was sitting up and watching television. "Hi, Sweetheart, you must be feeling better if you are setting up now." He bent over and kissed her and caught her hand.

"Yes, I am feeling better. The doctor wants me to get up and walk as much as possible. Hi, Nick. You all through for the day?"

"Yeah, Sis. We decided to come by and see you before we go home and to bring you some fried chicken. I don't know if we are going to meet tonight or not. Glad to see you sitting up, though. You look almost like new." He grinned.

"Yes, the doctor said that I may be able to go home by Sunday if I promise to take it easy and not lift anything."

"That's good, Sweetheart. I know you promised him that, didn't you?" Cody said grinning.

"Yes, I did. Although, I am enjoying all this attention that I am getting here. I may just get shot again."

They laughed.

"Oh, no, you won't. Not if I can help it. You don't know how I felt seeing you laying there on the ground. I don't want to have that feeling again."

She smiled up at him.

Cody leaned over and kissed her again and then said, "We have to go now. If we don't have a meeting tonight, I will call you. O.K."

Just then a nurse came in the room to take Corrie for a walk up the hall and then to put her back to bed.

"Sure. See you guys later."

So they left for home. Cody dropped Nick off and told him that he would call him if they decided to meet. It would be depending on if and what the others found out today.

When Cody got home, dinner was almost over. So, he got himself a plate and a glass of tea and sat down to eat a bite. He really wasn't very hungry. He had his mind on Corrie and what they should do tomorrow about the two guys.

Mama E, Traci, Tex and Steven were having their dessert while Cody was picking at his food. After a few minutes, Tex noticed Cody was thinking about something.

Finally, Tex said, "What's wrong, Cody? You look like you have something on your mind."

"I was just thinking about Corrie. Nick and I went by to see her before I came home."

"She is doing alright, isn't she? I talked to Elizabeth this afternoon and she said that she was coming along just fine."

"Yes, she is, Mom. I just feel bad everytime I see her laying there in the bed. Only today she was sitting in a chair. She is getting her color back and is looking better. Another thing is that Nick and I followed two guys from a warehouse that has been a distribution center for drugs. We followed them home and got their addresses. We found out that there are other people involved in selling drugs other than we thought. We thought we had solved most of the drug operation and two of the murders, but there are a few more that we need to put behind bars."

Mama E. said, "Oh, you have solved the cases that you were working on the last few weeks."

"No, Mom. Not all of them. So far, we have solved two of the murders and have him in jail. We also have two others that are involved in the drug operation in jail. There are others that we hope to get next Friday night at the dance. But, Mom, this is all still confidential. I am just thinking out loud. Do not tell anyone, not even Sara for now. O.K."

"I understand, Son. I won't say a word. but I do want to hear about all of it when it is over. Alright."

"Yes, Mom. You will know all of it when it is over because we are going to have a big celebration right here with a big BBQ. All the people that were involved in the investigation and the relatives of the victims will be here."

"Oh, my. That sounds like a good idea. Let me know in plenty of time so we can plan everything."

"We will, Mom."

When they had finished eating and cleaned up the kitchen, the three guys went out into the yard and was sitting under the trees discussing what had happened that day.

Steven said, "Cody, you said two guys came to the warehouse and you and Nick followed them. I have some paper work in my brief case that list adult drug dealers and there were two that had gone before Judge Turner and was put on probation. They may be the same two guys."

"Could be, Bro. Nick took some pictures of these guys. I didn't want to say anything in front of Traci and Mom, but the two guys met Samuels at the warehouse. We heard some of the conversation. Evidently, they still do not know that Tanner and Collins are in jail. Also, Tanner's wife is evidently out of town or surely he would have called her by now and she would have told Samuels. They think that Tanner and Collins are in Savannah on business because Samuels told the two guys that he had tried to reach them but couldn't. So far, it is working for us. We will get the names you have and see if they are the same ones in the pictures. Tex, how about you and Marci? Did you have any luck with Garcia?"

"No, other than he went to Samuels and he had a worried look on his face. He stayed in the office the rest of the day."

Then Cody said, "I wonder what Kato found out from talking to the boys. I think I will give him a call."

Steven got up and said, "I'll go get the list that I got today and I'll call Kato and see if he found out anything and if he want to meet tonight."

"O.K. Steven, really appreciate it. Right now I don't feel like moving. Setting in a car most of the day is not a good thing to do. It is not my thing, anyway."

After Steven left, Tex said, "He would make a good investigator. You may try to get him in your division when this is over. I believe he would be happier during investigation work than on the road like he is now."

"Yes, I am sure he would, but you know we all have to go through a period of being on the road when we first come on the department."

"If I decided to move here, do you think we could work together?"

"Oh, are we getting serious now, Pal?"

"Laugh, if you want to, but I told you that you will wake up one of these days and find out that you have another brother." They laughed. Then he continued, "I am just thinking in my head of different things. Nothing definite now. Besides, I haven't talked to Traci yet."

"Yes, you better talk to her first. She has a mind of her own. But I am glad that you are confiding in me. If you all did decide to live here, it would make all of us happy but what about your father and sister?"

"Oh, he would not say anything to discourage me from moving here as long as my sister is there with him. I do know that he prefer that we all stay together. But who knows, when he comes here for a few days, he may want to move."

They laughed.

"That would be something, wouldn't it. But he would never leave your sister in Texas alone."

"True. True. Traci and I have a lot of time yet to talk and decide what we want in life. Who knows, she may not marry me."

"I think she is as much smitten with you as you are with her. I might add that this is a shock to me. I always thought you would get hooked on an oil heiress and live happily ever after."

Tex laughed. "No, I am not looking for wealth. Most of your wealthy women are shallow and temperamental snobs, or at least the few that I have known. Now you take Traci, I would put her on a pedestal before anyone else that I have known before."

"Like Mom said before, that is about as good of a compliment that I have ever heard."

"It's true. She is a true jewel."

299

"Well, to change the subject, do you think there is any need in meeting tonight?"

"No, Cody, I don't. But let's wait until Steven comes back out and see what Kato has to say."

"Sure."

They were silent for a while each in their own thoughts. A few minutes later Steven came out of the house and walked over to his car and got the papers from his brief case that was in the trunk of his car. Then he strolled over to where they were and he handed the list to Cody. "Here is the list that I got today. I marked the two names on the list. Also, Kato said that he talked with four of the kids and the information that he got was that they knew someone else was selling, but they didn't know their names. They had seen four different men at the warehouse at different times. The two names that they had heard was Snuffy and Cheech. That is probably their street names. They never said anything to them. They work for the man that live on the Hill. Also, Kato said that he would try to find out about them tomorrow. I gave him the two names that are on this list. I also told him about the two guys that you saw at the warehouse. He said that if you will call him sometime tonight and give him the addresses that you have just in case that the three of you are looking for the same guys, there would be no need to meet tonight. I told him that you would call and let him know what you were going to do tomorrow."

"Good, Steven, I really did not want to go anywhere tonight. God, it feels good just to lay out here and relax. I will call Kato when I go in the house and tell him that he and Marci can relax tomorrow. I think that the four of us can handle this for this weekend. Steven, you are off, aren't you?"

"Yes, I am off until Tuesday morning and I have no definite date or plans this weekend."

"Good, because you and Tex can stay on Samuels and if Garcia gets in the way, watch him, too. Whichever one that will lead you somewhere. Tex, I don't think it will matter if Samuels gets a good look at you or not. You will be with Steven so that will be alright, but to be on the safe side, try not to let him get a good look at you. Nick and I will check out the pictures that we took and the addresses that we have on the two men. If anything pops up, we will call one another. Right."

They both said, "Right."

Chapter 12

After a few minutes of being quiet and listening to the birds, they started teasing Tex about being shot and him bragging about Texas. They were laughing and kidding each other when Traci came out and sat down with them.

Traci said, "Alright, you guys, what is so funny? Every time I come walking up to you all, you are laughing. Are you laughing at me?"

"No, we are not. We will laugh with you, but not at you. Come over here and set with me. I missed you today."

Cody said, "Steven, I think this conversation is going to get mushy. Do you think we should leave?"

"Hell, no. I think we should make him miserable."

"Bro, that is no way to treat company, especially Tex, your best friend."

Tex laughed and said, "You're right, Sweetheart. Little Brother has no manners. We will have to teach him some. Manners, that is."

Mama E stepped out the back door and called Cody to come to the phone.

Tex laughingly said, "Sweetheart, at least Mama E is on our side. Now if we can get rid of Steven." He winked at Steven.

Steven said, "I think I know when to make my exit. I am going in and take a shower. I may just take a ride somewhere. Anyone want to go with me?"

"No, thank you. Tonight is a relaxing night at home. Maybe tomorrow night we all can go out," said Tex.

Cody and Steven got up and went into the house and upstairs to their own rooms. Kato was on the phone.

"Hey, Cody, a friend of mine who is very reliable from downtown just called me and said that Samuels has found out that Santino, Tanner and Collins are in jail. Samuels was just there visiting Tanner. It seems that Tanner's wife tried to reach Tanner in Savannah and at home and couldln't get him so she called Samuels. Then Samuels got on the phone and finally called the jail. He overlooked Wilson's name. So they still do not know that Wilson is in jail. What a bunch of creeps. Huh."

"Yeah, they are and more. Did he hear any of the conversation between Samuels and the others?"

"No, other than Samuels was really worried and left in a hurry. So this friend of mine, Skip, followed him and he went straight home. Skip stayed there for about forty minutes and then left."

"Kato, does Skip know about our investigation?"

"No, he doesn't. He works in the jail in Records. Whenever he sees anything happening that he thinks I am interested in, he lets me know. He knew that I was the one that arrested Santino. He only knows what information that is there at the jail. I have not divulged anything that we are working on now. He calls me whenever something comes up there that I might be interested in or would like to know."

"O.K. Thanks, Kato. You think we should take turns following Samuels?"

"Yes, I do. To keep from being bored, we should take turns two at a time. The others can just play it by ear as to what they want to do. If you will give me the two addresses you have, Marci and I can be checking on those."

"Alright, Nick and I will follow him starting in the morning about eight o'clock. Tex and Steven can take over for Sunday. We'll keep in touch. Thanks, Kato."

"Alright, Cody. Talk to you later."

Cody then called Nick and told him what he and Kato had talked about. Nick said, "I'll pick you up in the morning since your place is on the way to Samuels house. I can imagine what was going through Samuels mind. I wish we could have been there."

"Yeah, me too." They both laughed.

Then Cody said, "Well, I am going to take a shower and go to bed. Tex has run Steven and me both away from the hammock in the yard. He and Traci are out there and he let us know that he wanted to be alone with Traci."

They both laughed. Then Cody continued, "Can you believe that I am considering going to bed at eight-thirty on a Friday night?"

"No. I can't. But you know what, so am I. I thought about calling Angie to see if she wanted to go out, but I am really not in the mood to go out."

"Neither am I. See you in the morning, Nick."

"Sure thing."

Cody took his shower and laid down across the bed. He was thinking of Corrie laying in that hospital bed. *Corrie, sweetheart, I wish I could be with you tonight, but not in a hospital. Gosh, I am getting aroused just thinking about you. I did tell you that I would call you, didn't I, but I am not sure this is a good time to talk to you.* But he reached over and picked up the phone, he had to call now because they would not put the call through if he waited until after nine o'clock. *If I am going to call, I had better do it now.*

"Hi, Sweetheart. How are you feeling tonight?"

"Hi, I am feeling a lot better now since I am talking to you. How was your day today?"

"It was boring. Not much happening now. A couple of leads to some other drug dealers. Kato and Marci are going to work on that part. I am just waiting for next Friday night."

"I know you will be glad when it is all over. I know, I will."

"Yes, I just finished taking a shower and was laying across the bed thinking of you. I want you here with me so bad. I am getting aroused just thinking about you. I didn't know if I should talk to you or not. Who knows what will happen." Then he laughed. And then she joined in with him.

"I am so glad that you did call. I was laying here thinking of you, too."

"When you feel up to making plans for our wedding, we are going to set the date. I want you every night, not just once in a while. O.K."

"That sounds good.....Well, the doctor just came in. I'll talk to you tomorrow." Smiling at the doctor, she said, "I hope he is going to tell me that I can come home tomorrow."

"Me too. O.K., Sweetheart. See you then."

Cody lay there for a while thinking of him and Corrie together. That was his last thought until about four o'clock in the morning when he awoke. He then turned down the bed and crawled into it. He lay there for awhile thinking about what they need to do for the next several days. They needed to get the other four lowlife drug dealers. He would let Kato and Marci work on them. He finally fell asleep again until Steven was waking him up for breakfast.

"O.K., Brother, I am awake. Wait a minute." He then told Steven what the conversation was between him and Kato last night. And then he added, "If you and Tex do not have any plans today, contact

305

Kato and work with him and Marci today. Nick and I will be making life miserable for Samuels." He grinned.

"Sure, I'll check with Tex and see if he can stay away from our sister long enough to do a little work."

Then Steven left to go downstairs. Cody got up, dressed and then joined them for breakfast.

As they were finishing breakfast, Nick came in and sat down for a cup of coffee and ended up eating some breakfast. Then he and Cody took off and Steven and Tex left to meet Kato and Marci. Steven had called Kato before to let him know that they would be working with them. Kato gave Steven one of the addresses and he and Marci took the other one to stake out.

While Kato and Marci were waiting for some activity in the house, Marci asked, "Kato, I know that this is none of my business, but being a close friend to you, I am concerned about you. You really loved Lisa, didn't you?"

He looked at her with an angry look on his face and said, "You're right. It is none of your business. End of conversation." Then he turned his head toward the window and looked out toward the woods that were across from the house.

"I'm sorry, Kato. I thought you might want to talk about it. I only asked because I am concerned about you. It has been several years and I watch you going farther and farther into a shell. She was the best thing that happened to you and you to her. I am only saying that she would want you to go on with your life. I can tell you are angry with me for still talking about her, but I have to say it. It was not your fault and she would want you to be happy, and right now, you are not. I am only asking that you think about what I have said. If you want to be angry with me, alright, I'll accept that. Now, I say, end of conversation."

They were silent for awhile. She was determined that she was not going to say anything else until he did. If her little speech would help her friend come out of his shell, it would be worth it even if he was angry with her.

Finally, Kato said gruffly, "You stay here in the car. I am going to the door and see if I can buy some drugs. I'll whistle our code if I need any help. O.K. I can't just sit here and wait to see what they will do. I am too restless."

"O.K., I'll be here if you need me. Be careful. Should I call Tex and Steven. They are down the street a couple of blocks.

"Yeah, but tell them to stay put. If it works out here, I'll come down there and try to buy from that low-life. They wouldn't sell to them or you. I look like a drug user." Then he smiled. She grabbed his hand and said, "Be careful, I want to keep my friend."

Marci knew then that she was forgiven for making her little speech and she knew that he would think about what she had said. She watched him walk up to the door and knock two times and then another two times. Most of the time that was a signal for the drug dealers that it was alright. She only hoped that was true this time. Evidently, it was because he let Kato in the house. She then picked up her phone and called Tex and told him what was happening. They decided to keep the open line between them for awhile until they knew that Kato was alright.

A few minutes later, Marci said, "Tex, there are two guys going into the house. Kato is still in there. You guys drive up this way to be closer where I can see you. Kato will whistle if he needs any help. I will be able to hear him."

"Sure. Nothing happening here, anyway." So they drove around the block and up the street and came in across the street from Marci but behind some shrubs. They could not be seen from the house. They waited and waited. It seemed like a long time. Then they saw a guy walking up the street and going into the house. They were beginning to worry about Kato and wanted to go in and bring him out, but Marci said, "No, wait. Kato takes his time. He doesn't rush things so we wait until he whistles. Kato is smart and can take care of himself and us, too." She smiled.

Steven said, "You think a lot of him, don't you?"

"Yes, I do very much. But just to set the record straight, we are not lovers. We are just good friends who care about one another personally and professionally and we work well together. We get the job done."

Tex said, "I can understand that. You two are a great team. I would work with both of you anytime."

They all were beginning to get restless now. They kept watching the door, but Kato did not come out.

Marci said, "No, no. We wait."

After several minutes, Kato walked out the door and up the street to the car. Then he saw Tex and Steven. He walked over to their car and Marci came over and they all got into Tex's car.

Tex said, "Man, we were getting worried about you, but Marci wouldn't let us go in after you."

"Good girl. She knows how I work. I went in and told them that Cooty in Savannah told me that I could make a buy through him. He believed me right away or else he wanted to get rid of what drugs he had. He said that he didn't have much because there was a mix up this week and he didn't get his supply. Two other men came in to buy some from him. They had buyers but no drugs. Then he got on the phone and called his friend down the street and told him to bring what drugs he had. So, now folks, we have enough on them to arrest them for selling drugs. Why don't you three go in and arrest them while they still have the money and I have the drugs. I'll wait out here unless you need my help." They laughed and told Kato they could not believe their luck. They would have all of the little drug dealers unless someone else popped up, but they didn't think anyone would. The bigger fish would come Friday night.

They decided that two of them would go in and arrest the four men. Kato and Steven would stay outside in case they need his help if some of them started to run. Tex still had not been sworn in for authority in the state of Georgia, but Marci would arrest them and he would assist. And that is exactly what they did. The door was not locked and they just walked right in and surprised them. The four of them were sitting around a table. No guns were in sight. It was the easiest arrests that either had ever made. They went willingly and didn't seem to be worried at all. One of them said, "You can arrest us, but we will be out in an hour. We have been through this a couple of times."

Tex said, "Oh, you think so. Huh. We'll see about that."

When they walked outside and saw Kato, they looked at him and one of them said, "We've got your number now. You won't get us again."

Kato said, "No, I won't have to get you for the next several years. Put them in the car."

They all went to the jail and booked them. While Kato, Marci and Steven finished the paperwork, Tex called Cody and told him what had happened. So Cody and Nick decided that they did not need to watch Samuels anymore. They had the ones that they were after and they would get Samuels Friday night. So, they met the others at the diner across from the warehouse and joined them for lunch.

After everyone had settled down at a table, Cody said, "Now, everyone is taken care of except for Garcia. We have to put a lot of pressure on him or Wilson to get one or the other to talk. At this point, proving he destroyed evidence is going to be hard to do. We can try to break him."

Kato said, "You are forgetting something Cody. Two of the guys that we arrested today were selling drugs for Garcia/Tanner and the others were selling drugs for Samuels. Put pressure on those two, also. See what we can get from them. I think they will be willing to talk when they find out that they won't be going before Judge Turner."

"Yes, so the rest of this coming week all we have to do is talk to these guys and hope they will talk. We're getting there. Thanks to all of you. We will finally make it and in a short time frame considering what is involved. We also have Judge Turner to think about."

Tex said, "So for the coming week we concentrate on Garcia and Judge Turner."

"Once they find out that Judge Turner is out of the picture, I think that the dealers we arrested today will take care of Garcia, Tanner and Samuels for us," said Kato. And after a moment, he continued, "If Garcia won't talk about the files, you'll have to break Wilson on that one. Wilson will break when he realizes that he is caught and there is no way out. He is not as strong as he likes to pretend. They usually aren't."

Steven said, "I have an idea. Tonight is Saturday night. Let's go out and celebrate a little to practice for the big celebration. We can go on the other side of town at this country place. It will take about an hour to get there. It is called 'Clancy's Barn. I have been there a few time. It is like Johnnie Lee's except it is twice as large. The only somebody that we don't want to see Tex is someone on the hill. I am sure they won't be there."

Kato winked at Marci and said, "That sounds like a good idea. Marci, would you mind going with an old man and teach him how to dance again?"

She smiled a big grin and said, "You bet I would. I wouldn't miss it for the world." And she reached across the table and squeezed his hand. They smiled at each other.

The others were wondering what was going on, but, yet, somehow, they knew and was happy to see Kato come alive even if it was just a start. It was a start.

Then Kato said, "Steven, we will have to get you in our group. You know all the places to go. That would be great if we all could work together all the time."

"One day I hope to be there. I haven't thought about it too much until the last couple of weeks, but I am going to make it a goal to get into investigations."

"Bro, I will be the first one to welcome you when that day comes."

By this time, they were finishing their lunch and was enjoying each other's company. And didn't realize until they were ready to leave that they were drawing a lot of onlookers. Evidently, they were wondering why there was only one female amongst five males, or they were enjoying listening to their conversation. Either way, it did not matter to them. They were not talking business now. So they all agreed that they would like to go out and celebrate for whatever cause they wanted to call it. And they all agreed to leave about eight o'clock.

After Cody, Steven and Tex got home, Steven called up Jan to invite her to go with him. He felt bad about the date they had before and had to cut it short because of Corrie getting shot. Jan understood, but he still felt bad. She agreed to go with him tonight.

Cody went to the hospital to see Corrie. He was there for an hour or so. She was doing real well. The doctor came in and told her she could go home tomorrow which was Sunday. She understood about them wanting to go out tonight. She refused to let Cody stay all afternoon and tonight with her. Cody had never seen her that angry before when he mentioned about not wanting to go out unless she went with him.

"No, Cody, you have earned it. You are going out with the rest of them and enjoy it. I'll be at the big one. If you want to take someone, take your mother. She use to love to dance and go out with your father. I know it has only been about seven months, but maybe you can talk her into going."

311

He laughed. "I never thought of that. I never thought of asking my mother to go dancing. She does like to dance. I am not sure she feels up to it yet, but I will ask her. Thank you for mentioning that."

He leaned over and kissed her while holding her hand. "I love you."

"I love you, too. And make sure your mother goes and have a good time"

"I will see what I can do. If I can't talk her into it, Tex can. She will do anything that he asks her to do. See you tomorrow."

He leaned over and kissed her again and then walked to the door and turned around and smiled at her. She was so beautiful and was always thinking of everyone else but herself.

When he got home, Steven and Tex had told Mama E and Traci about going out tonight. They were sitting at the table having something cold to drink and talking about "Clancy's.

Mama E said, "Yes, Thomas took me there several times. We danced a lot when we were younger and up to before he died, but not as often. He was the dancer. Everyone said that we danced good together."

Cody looked at her and asked, "Mom, why don't you go with us tonight. We won't be out too late."

"No, Son, you all go and have a good time. My time has passed for that sort of thing."

Tex said, sternly, "That's nonsense. You are going to go with us. I demand it as a guest in your house."

They all laughed. Then Cody said, "Corrie told me to ask you to go. She mentioned about how much you like to dance. Mom, I am asking you to go as my date."

"Now, you can't refuse your son, can you? I would love to dance with you. I bet you can show us a step or two." Tex said.

Then they all started after her about going. Traci went into her closet and picked out an outfit for her to wear while the others worked on her to agree to go.

Finally, she said, "Alright, I will go to be with my family."

Everyone was shocked that she would give in and go with them, but they were happy that she was getting out of the house. She had to make a start sometime. Her face revealed some puzzlement about it and they knew that she was wondering that maybe she should not go. then her face became a smile and she had decided that if her children wanted her to go, she would.

Tex, Traci, Mama E and Cody left early so that they could get a good table and make sure they had enough room. They got there in time to get the large table in the corner which would seat at least twelve people. As it turned out, all were there including Nick, Angie, Kato and Marci. They were late getting there. After the introductions, Kato said, "I'm sorry that we are late. Just blame it on me. I had a hard time finding something suitable to wear. It has been a long time coming."

Marci had a big smile on her face. She was so happy for her friend. "Yes, I am so happy that you came tonight, Kato. It has been a long time since I have seen you smile."

Cody and Nick looked at each other and smiled. They were happy, too, even though they did not know what had happened in the past.

After a few drinks, Kato looked at Mama E and said, "Mama E, it's alright if I call you that, isn't it?"

"Of course, Kato. Any friend of my children is a friend of mine."

313

"Then, Mama E, would you allow an old man such as myself this dance?"

She smiled and said, "Yes, I will, but I must warn you that it has been awhile since I last danced."

"That makes two of us. We will practice together and see what happens."

They all laughed. They were having a good time and feeling good about what they had accomplished on the investigation. Then Cody looked at Marci and pointed to the dance floor. She nodded and they got up and danced. Before the music stopped, they all were dancing.

While Cody and Marci were dancing, she explained to Cody about how Kato had gone into a shell right after Lisa was shot. They were truly in love and Kato blamed himself for a long time for her death, but it was no way any fault of his. "Cody, I would appreciate it if you all would help me keep him from going backward now that he has made a start to go forward with his life. Even though he is in a crowd, he has been lonely for so long. And to answer your unspoken question, I am not in love with him, but he is the best friend that I have."

"Marci, Nick and I thought that something like that was going on with Kato, but we did not feel we should interfere right now. We were hoping that after this investigation that we all could become friends other than co-workers."

"We would like that very much, Cody."

They all danced during the next couple of hours.

The music stopped for awhile for a break. Then they would start up again for about thirty minutes and then it would be over. It was now close to one o'clock, so they all decided that they would leave.

When Cody, Mama E, Tex and Traci got home, Cody and Mama E went into the house. Tex and Traci sat out under the trees in one of the hammocks.

Cody put his arms around his mother and said, "Mom, I am so glad that you went with us tonight. I hope you enjoyed yourself. I know that it was hard at first, but

I was glad to see your face relax and you seem to be enjoying yourself."

"Yes, I did, Son. Your friend, Kato, is very nice. I like him very much. He and I talked for a while. He has been a lonely man the last couple of years. He told me about Lisa and how she was shot. It seem to do him good to talk about it. I know how he feels. It is one of those things that you can talk to a stranger about and you feel better. With friends and relatives, you don't feel free to express your true feelings. It is strange because it should be just the opposite, but I think we both feel better after tonight. I sure hope that he will be able to go forward with his life now."

"I do, too, Mom, and I think I know what you are talking about. I think Dad would be proud of you tonight."

"Yes, Son. I think he would. See you in the morning. I am going to bed now."

"O. K. Mom. Goodnight." And he kissed her on the cheek and then went upstairs to his bedroom. Even though he was tired, it was hard trying to go to sleep. He would close his eyes but he could not go to sleep. *Corrie, I enjoyed myself tonight because Mom went with us. Thank you for mentioning that thought to me. I think she enjoyed herself, although I know she kept thinking of Dad. Kato made sure she had a good time and she made sure he did. Even though Kato is about 25 years younger than she, they had something in common. Losing someone they loved by way of a bullet. It was a start for both of them. Now we are going to have to find someone that Kato can be comfortable with and enjoy himself. Marci is good for him and she will help, too. Corrie, I missed you tonight, but we will celebrate big the next time. You are looking better, Sweetheart. I will see you tomorrow after you get home. That was the last thought as he drifted off to sleep.*

It was late the next morning when they started getting up and coming into the kitchen.

Cody and Tex were first in the kitchen and started making breakfast. "Hey, Cody, seems like old times. Huh. Remember in college when we had to fix our own meals. We had some good times, didn't we?"

Cody laughed, "Yes, we did. It was a good thing that I knew something about cooking or we would have starved to death. When we were young, Dad made us help out with the cooking, cleaning and anything that was to be done around the house. We rebelled then, but I found out why he wanted us to learn everything about living when we were growing up."

"I'm glad he did because I didn't know anything about cooking nor cleaning. You know, you taught me a lot about life. You always seemed to know what to do whenever we were in a jam or something we wanted to do or needed to do. I owe you for that......It is so nice outside this morning, let's eat breakfast out there under the trees. We will surprise everyone and have a lazily, enjoyable breakfast. I'll get the trays and we will load them up and then wake everyone up."

"Sounds good to me." Then Cody turned to the doorway as he heard someone come in. It was Traci. "Gee, you guys, I should have stayed in bed a while longer."

"No, Sweetheart, you can help. You know, we need some female help in the kitchen." Tex said as he walked over and kissed her good morning.

"Looks like we are going to have a party. What's with the trays?"

"Tex thought it would be a good idea to eat under the trees and have a lazily breakfast. It sounds good to me."

"It does to me, too. What do you want me to do?"

Tex still with his arms around her waist said, "You can start by filling up the trays. We will take them all out at one time."

"First, I will go out and wipe the tables and put a clean tablecloth on them. We always go first class here."

"Sis, you do that and, hopefully, Mom and Steven will be up by then."

"Mom was getting up when I left my room. She will be here in a few minutes. I'll go up and wake Steven." And then she turned and walked up the stairs to Steven's door. She heard a noise in the room so she came back downstairs and announced as she walked back into the kitchen. "Steven is up, too." Then, she got a pan of water and wash cloth with two tablecloths and went outside. After she cleaned the tables and got the tablecloths on them. She took the vases and filled them with fresh flowers. Then she went inside and brought out the plates, napkins, knives, forks, spoons, cups and saucers. By the time that the food was ready to be brought out, the tables were ready for it. They all sat down and had a joyous time, talking about the dance and teasing Steven about getting in so late. Mama E was enjoying herself. They felt so good to see her laugh and hope that this was the beginning of her going on with her life, although they knew that she would miss their Dad and would never forget him. Before they knew it, it was almost twelve o'clock, but they had nothing that had to be done. In fact, they were more or less just waiting until Friday night before they had to really go to work. In the meantime, they would keep their eyes and ears open and do whatever they could to get all the corrupt people that were involved.

Later, Cody went to see Corrie at home and stayed with her for about an hour. He did not want to tire her out since it was her first day home, so he left around four o'clock and went back home to spend the rest of the day with his family. They all played tag football and enjoyed the rest of the day for themselves.

On Monday morning when Cody went into the station, Lieutenant Moss was waiting to see him. "Cody, I just got back from the jail. Thompson and I were called in about an hour ago. It seems that Wilson was ready to talk. He found out that he is on his own and he is mad, mad, mad."

"Lieutenant, I sure wish you had called me. I would love to have been there."

"I know, Sergeant, Kato was there and recorded the conversation. My understanding is that he was there talking to some of the other guys trying to get them to talk when one of the jailers came in and told him that Wilson wanted to talk to someone. Wilson told Kato that he did not want to talk to you or Nick. The jailer called here and Thompson and I went, but stayed in the background. Anyway, Kato will be here to see you in about thirty minutes."

Cody laughed. "Good, Nick will be here by then. I had a gut feeling that Wilson would be the one that would talk. He just needed to stay in jail for a few days."

"You were right, Sergeant. I know that you still have work to do on these cases, but I want you to know that I am very proud of you two. You both have done a great job. Needless to say but that makes me look good. I am only sorry that one of them had to be my sister's brother-in-law. She and her husband, Anthony, feel very bad about this, but they have never been close. In fact, Anthony never really had anything to do with his brother. Santino just pushed himself into their lives and they tried to be nice to him."

Cody looked at Moss and said, "Lieutenant, I am very sorry because of you and your sister. I don't know what else to say."

"Thanks, Cody. There is nothing else to say."

A few minutes later Nick came in and Cody explained everything to him while they were waiting for Kato.

Finally, Kato arrived with a smile on his face. "Hi, you guys. Cody, you were right about Wilson. He started talking and I couldn't shut him up, not that I wanted to stop him from talking."

Lieutenant Moss laughed and the others joined in with him. Then he said, "Well, you guys, let's go down to Cody and Nick's office where we can have some privacy and listen to the tape. You go on down. I'll go get Thompson. Oh, there he is now. Thompson, we are having a meeting in Cody's office. Come on in and listen to it. It may be helpful for you since you will be helping them with the rest of the investigation."

Thompson joined them in Cody's office and after all were seated. Kato put the tape in and started playing it. He explained it as they went along.

After the tape had finished playing, Kato said, "It is like we said, Cody. A lot of the time the little people and the middle people don't even know who the boss is, especially in this business. He really didn't tell us anything new, except that he was more detailed as to what each person did in the operation. Samuels owned the warehouse and used his influence with Judge Turner to see that the sellers did not go to jail and were put back on the street so that they could sell the drugs. If Samuels decide not to talk, we can put pressure on Judge Turner and make him resign, anyway. That will get him off the bench, but I think Samuels will talk after the dance Friday night. The drugs were divided between Samuels, Tanner and Wilson to sell. They gave a certain percentage to the top man and they kept a certain percentage for themselves and the rest was payment for the sellers, Garcia, Santino and Judge Turner. Garcia was the person that took over when Wilson could not be there. He, also, is the one that destroyed the evidence in the files."

Cody said, "But, Kato, one of the bags had Garcia's name on the drugs."

"Yes, that was because Tanner was suppose to be out of town and Garcia was going to distribute Tanner's portion to the three guys who was selling for Tanner and Samuels."

"Then, Samuels is the big man and getting money from his portion and from the top, or there is someone else over the three as the big man," said Cody.

Then Kato continued, "Wilson also said that Santino killed the two young boys, but he did not know who had committed the last murder or if anyone else had been killed because of their operation. So I am trying to put things in perspective so we know what we have and what we need to find out."

Nick said, "It sounds like we more or less wait until the dance Friday night, but if any of us hear anything, we need to act on it."

"Yes, you do, and keep me informed, verbally. And Cody, if you all need anything to complete this investigation, just let me know. We have gone too far not to do everything possible to get all of them," Lieutenant Moss interjected.

"We will, Lieutenant. I think we need to question Garcia. The only evidence we have is Wilson's word and his name was on one of the bags. We need to get his reaction on destroying the files."

"You're right, Cody. You all do what you need to do. I'll be here or at home if you need me."

Kato, Thompson, Nick and Cody went to find Garcia. He was signed out to go to the jail. So they left the station and went to the jail.

When they pulled into the parking lot at the jail, they saw Garcia walking toward his car. As soon as Cody stopped the car, Kato was out of the car and walking toward Garcia. Garcia started running to his car, but Kato caught him as he was trying to put his key in the door lock.

"O. K., Garcia. We need to talk. Let's go." By that time, Kato had Garcia by both of his arms pulled back. "Now, do I have to handcuff you or are you going to come peacefully?"

By that time the other three were there to assist Kato if need be. "No, I'll come peacefully." And he started walking toward the door to the jail. They went into an interrogation room and Kato pushed him into a chair. "Alright, Garcia, Do you want an attorney now because we want some answers? Yes or no."

"No, I don't want an attorney."

"Alright, it's your choice. What is your involvement in this drug operation?"

"I am not involved in....."

"Don't give me no shit, Garcia. We know that you are involved. Your name was on one of the bags of drugs and Wilson has been talking. Now, again, what is your involvement in this mess?" Kato said angrily.

"That was not my drugs. They belonged to Tanner, Robert Tanner. He was suppose to be out of town so they put my name on it so that I could distribute the drugs for him. That's all I know."

Cody interjected, "Don't tell me that's all you know. What about my father's files. We already know that you destroyed the evidence. We just want you to admit it. What about it Garcia?"

"I don't know what you are talking about. You know that we can't go in the file room and that the Lieutenant signs out the files."

"That is the way it is now. Back when my father was here, the Lieutenant that was in charge of the files was very lenient with the files. That is why my father took control of them. Destroying the evidence was done after my father's death. Now, I am asking you again. What do you know about destroying the evidence in the files?"

"I don't know. I don't know."

Kato said, "Alright, Garcia, Wilson is talking up a storm. He is already blaming you for the files and there are three murders to consider. That is in addition to selling and distributing drugs. Do you

321

want to take all the glory and let the others go free? Is that your idea of being a hero?"

Garcia looked down and looked very confused. He knew that he did not kill anybody, but he was not going to take the blame for anybody else.

Cody said, "A guy was seen at one of the murder scenes with a police shirt on and you meet that description. It wasn't a good idea to wear a POLICE shirt to a murder scene. Don't tell me that you are going to take the rap for murder and let the other creep go free? That is not in your blood, Garcia? This is your only chance. Talk or take the rap. Your choice."

Nick said, "Awe, come on, you guys. He is going to be a hero. Let's book him now. I have plans for today and it is not staying here at the jail all day."

"You're right, Nick. Let's book him for murder, destroying evidence, distributing and selling drugs. Is there anything else that we can charge him with?" asked Thompson. "I'll go get the forms and start the process rolling. Like Nick, I have plans for today." Thompson started walking toward the door.

"Thompson, you are my friend. You know very well that I could not murder anyone. Wait, tell them that I could never murder anyone."

"First of all, Garcia, I am not your friend. My friends do not do what you have done. As for you not murdering anyone. I know no such thing. I was friendly to you because you were a co-worker. We never were the best of friends. Any police officer that crosses the line is worst than other criminals that we lock up."

Kato, looking disgruntled, said, "Thompson, go get the forms and let's get this over with. This scum bag isn't going to cooperate with us. He wants to play the hero. Evidently, he doesn't mind going to prison for a long time."

"Wait, I'll talk. I did destroy the evidence, but I didn't want to. Cody, your father was good to me and I didn't want to do it. Santino told me that if I did not do away with the evidence that he would see that I rot in prison or he would kill me himself. Santino is the one that was at the murder scene. He is the one that did all the dirty work. He is mad, Man. He even enjoyed it."

As Kato slid a note pad and pen over to Garcia, he said, "O. K., Garcia, start writing and don't stop until you are finished. We will be right outside the door." They all stepped outside and smiled at each other.

Thompson said, "Thanks, you guys for letting me in on this investigation. It does my heart good when we can get scum off the street, even if it is some of our co-workers. They give the rest of us a bad name."

"Yes, they do." They all agreed.

They posted an officer outside the door and then they went down to the coffee room and sat down for a few minutes with a cup of coffee in hand and a smile on their faces.

Kato grinned as he said, "Well, you guys, it looks like we will have a slow week until Friday night. Is there anything that we can be doing until then?"

Everyone looked at Cody, so he said, "No, the only other question is about the Big Man. If Samuels is the Big Man or if there is someone else. My only suggestion is that we meet Thursday night and plan for the dance. Thompson, I am not sure if you are aware of it or not, but Nick and I have a witness to one of the murders. She can possibly identify the voice, but not the face. She will be at the dance Friday night, and, hopefully, she will be able to make the identification of the murderer. If she does, he will be arrested there on the spot. .....Kato, should we meet at your place Thursday night?" *Cody did not want to say anymore than that for now. He was beginning to trust Thompson, but there was no need in taking a chance. He was too close to getting his father's murderer and he did not want anything to go wrong.*

"Sure, ...Thompson, do you know where my place is located?"

"No, but I can find it if you will give me the address."

"Cody will show you. It is not exactly my house, but we work out of it most of the time. It belongs to the GBI."

"I'll see that Thompson gets there," Nick said. "I think Thompson and I live closer than any of you, so we will meet you there."

"Sure, Nick. Then Steven, Tex and I will meet you at Kato's. Oh, Kato, will Marci be able to help Friday night?"

"Yes, she'll be there Thursday night and Friday night. She would not miss it for the world. She is a lot like me. When she starts something, she doesn't stop until she finishes it."

Cody smiled. He was thinking of how fortunate he wa to be working with such good investigators.

They talked on for a few minutes longer and then Cody said, "Do you think Garcia is finished now?" They all laughed and then agreed that they should get back and check out what he had written down.

When they walked in the door, Garcia said as he pushed the pad to the other side of the table, "There, now stop hasseling me. That is all that I know. Do I get a break?"

They all looked at him in disgust. Then Kato said, "Break. You've had a break ever since you crossed the line. You know how this works. It depends on how much you told us and how much of it that we already know and can prove. We'll let you know. Any time you want to add to this statement, just let one of us know." After glancing over his written statement, Kato continued, "Call that officer and let them start processing this slime, fingerprinting, and etc."

As the officer came in the room, Cody had put handcuffs on Garcia and had placed him under arrest and was reading him his rights. When he had finished, the officer led Garcia out and down to the processing room. Garcia never looked back.

After they all had read the statement, they were well pleased with the contents. Garcia knew how to write up a report. He confessed to destroying the evidence in the files. His part in distributing the drugs when Samuels or Tanner were not there. His estimation of the value of the drugs was somewhere in the vicinity of three to five hundred thousand dollars a week, total. His take was not as much as the others, around twenty-five to thirty thousand a week because he was not as involved as the others. He confirmed what they knew about Santino, Judge Turner, Tanner, Samuels, Wilson and his boys and the other dealers for Samuels and Tanner. He did not know who the Big Man was. That was still a puzzle to them as how Samuels could keep his identity as the Big Man a secret from all the rest of the lowlife. There must be someone higher in this operation, but who could it be?

They all decided to go to this Italian restaurant for lunch. It was about five blocks up from the jail. It was very enjoyable and they were feeling good and relaxed. After about an hour or a little more, it was time to leave. Cody, Nick and Thompson decided to go back and report to the Lieutenant. Kato decided that he would go back to his place and go over some reports that he had gotten in that morning. They parted with the understanding that they would meet at eight o'clock Thursday night.

On the way back to the office, Thompson said, "I think I would like to work with Kato. He seems to be an upstanding guy and knows how to handle criminals. Some of the men don't like him. Why, I don't know."

Then Cody said, "I have known him for almost two years and I have enjoyed working with him each time. He is a straight guy. He will tell you like it is whether you like it or not. If you are right, he will stand behind you to the end, but if you are wrong, he will down you, too. Maybe, that is why some of the officers don't like him. They don't like what he says."

"That is probably it. I like that in a guy. You know where you stand. None of this guessing game. The few that I have heard make their comments are not what I consider good cops, anyway. They are just on the department because they can't make it anywhere else. We don't need that kind here." Thompson smiled and then said, "They give us good guys a bad name."

Nick said, "Well, I just met him through Cody when we started this investigation and I would work with him anytime and let him back me up. I trust him completely. He has been a big help to us. I can never thank him enough for catching Santino after he shot my sister. He was after that guy before any of us knew what was really happening."

"That's right. He has been a friend to me in more ways than one," said Cody.

Then they were silent for awhile. Each one deep in their own thoughts. Before they knew it, they were at the station. And after giving the Lieutenant the run-down on Garcia and a general conversation, Cody and Nick left. Nick went to his place and Cody went by to see Corrie for a little while. When he got there, Corrie was sitting up in the living room reading a book.

"Hi, Sweetheart, you must feel better than you did yesterday," Cody said as he went over and kissed her. Then he sat down beside her on the sofa.

"Oh, I do. I was tired from coming home yesterday, but I feel better today. I think Mama's cooking has something to do with that. The hospital food is not the best, you know. Are you off for the afternoon?"

"Yes, there isn't much we can do this week. We are almost ready to clear up this investigation. At least, hopefully, we will this weekend. So, until then, I am free to do as I please. Sure wish you were." Then he grinned.

She smiled and put her arms around him. "I love you so."

"I love you, too. We will have to make some plans when you are able. So, you be thinking about what you want to do."

"Oh, yes, I almost forgot. Tex called to see if you were here. He said that it wasn't important. He would talk to you later. He said not to return his call because he would be in and out of the house."

"That's right. He and Mom have been there by themselves today." He laughed. "Mom has been in her glory. Tex always makes her laugh. She loves him as much as she does us, I think."

"Oh, Cody, you know that is not true. It maybe almost true, but not completely true." She laughed.

"I'm glad she does because he is like a brother to me and I think Steven is beginning to feel the same way. And, Lord knows, Traci thinks he is the greatest. She is in love with him, you know. And he made it known to all of us that she was his."

She laughed. Then he joined in with her.

A few minutes later, Mrs. Carillo came in the back door with a load of groceries. Cody got up and went to help her. After they had finished bringing in the groceries, Mrs. Carillo went in the living room, "Corrie, don't you think you have been up long enough. You know that you need to ly down this afternoon if you are going to be up tonight."

Cody looked at Corrie and said, "I think Mama C is trying to get rid of me. Would you like for me to help you to bed?"

As she looked at her watch, she said, "Yes, I would like that." *Tex told me to keep him here until at least five o'clock. It is now four-fifteen. I do want to surprise him tonight.*

As he helped her into her bed, he said, "Are you sure you don't want me to get in there with you?"

She laughed. "Yes, I would like for you to get in here with me, but I am afraid that wouldn't be good to do now. But you can sit on the side of the bed and talk to me."

As he sat down, "What did Mama C mean by what she said about you being up tonight?"

"Oh, nothing, she knows that I like to sit up at night sometimes."

"Then I had better go so you can sleep for a while. Besides, Tex probably needs to be rescued from Mom for awhile."

"No, please, stay a little longer. Stay with me until I go to sleep."

"Alright, I'll stay only for a few minutes because I don't want Mama C to come in and tell me I have to leave." He smiled and kissed her and she closed her eyes, but tried to stay awake for awhile longer. But it wasn't long before she was sound sleep. He went downstairs and Mama C kept talking to him until it was about five till five before he left.

On the way home he thought about Mama C and what she had said about Corrie getting her rest and then the way she kept making conversation as if she wanted to keep him there longer. It just seemed a little strange, that's all. It's probably nothing. Corrie sure did look good. She is so much better now. It wasn't good for me to see her in bed. I wanted to get in there with her. I am getting aroused just thinking about it. Gee, she is beautiful. It has been longer than usual for us not to have sex. It is so great when we are together. Oh, well, it won't be much longer now.

Just as he was driving in the yard, Traci was there putting tablecloths on the tables and making vases of flowers for each table. "Hey, Sis, this must be Tex's idea. He loves eating outside, doesn't he?" He went over and kissed her on the cheek.

"Yes, he does, but this was our dear mother's idea. Of course, with a few hints from Tex, she came up with the idea." She smiled.

"Why don't you go up and get comfortable. It will be a while yet before we actually eat."

"Think I will, Sis. I will feel better after I take a shower. I dislike wearing a tie and jacket on these warm days. See you in a while." And he headed for the back door, but before he reached it, Tex had gotten the signal from Traci and popped his head around the house from the front. "Hey, Cody, come here for a minute." So Cody started around the house to the front yard.

Tex was finishing up with washing the lawn mower. "How does the yard look. I have been slaving all day in this yard."

Cody looked at him with a puzzled look on his face. "Tex, what's on your mind. I know that you did not mow all of this lawn. The boys just cut this grass two days ago. Something is up. What is it?"

"Well, to tell you the truth,...."

"That's what I want is the truth."

"I had to get out of the house. Mama E was about to talk my head off. I saw a spot here that the boys evidently didn't see, so I thought I would work on it."

"Now I can believe you about Mom talking too much because when she is in the mood, you can't stop her from talking. I have to go and get out of these clothes. I am going to take a shower. When you finish here, come on up and I'll fill you in on what happened today."

"Alright, I talked with my father today, also. It looks like he won't be able to come down this weekend, but I'll explain it to you when I come up."

"O.K."

Then Cody went up the steps and into the front of the house and up the stairs. As he went by the kitchen, he yelled out, "Hi, Mom. I'm going upstairs. Will see you after I take a shower." Then he heard her holler out. "Alright, Son."

Cody was in the shower when Tex came into his room. *Tex was laughing to himself at how well things were going and Cody didn't seem to remember that today was his birthday. Another hour and everything will work out fine. All I have to do is keep him here for another hour.*

A few minutes later, Cody came out of the shower and then he noticed that Tex was in his room. "Wow, I feel much better. When I got into the office this morning, the Lieutenant informed me that Wilson wanted to talk to someone. Kato happened to be at the jail talking with the other dealers that we brought in a couple of days ago. So Kato went to Wilson and got his statement. He gave me all the statements that he got this morning when he came into the office afterwards. They did not say anything new, but confirmed what we already knew, but they are good to have to help substantiate our case in court. So that left Garcia. We asked ourselves what are we going to do about him? So, we checked the Sign-Out Sheet and he had signed out to go to the jail. So we figured that he was going to talk to Wilson. So the four of us headed for the jail and just as we were going into the parking lot, Garcia was coming out of the building. We grabbed him and carried him right back in the jail and into an interrogation room. Finally, he started talking and then he gave us his statement in writing after we threatened to charge him with three murders and all the drug stuff."

Cody continued, "According to him, he was the low man on the totem pole. He did admit to destroying the evidence in the files. That was the main thing that we wanted from him. About the drugs, he only filled in when some of the others were not there. He nor any of the others know who the Big Man is. He told us about how the money was distributed between them, even Judge Turner. Anyway, the statements are in my briefcase. You can read them when you feel up to it. So, brother, it seems the rest of the week is ours to do what we want. ...Now that I have shot my wad, what is this about your father not being able to come down this weekend."

"I talked with him this morning and he said that Kristen was having problems with one of the men. All of a sudden, he doesn't want to work for a woman and he is trying to start trouble. Kristen fired him and had him removed from the property. She then asked all the others if they had a problem working for her. They all said 'No', but Dad thought it was not a good time for him to leave and I can see his point. He did straighten out the other problem."

"Sure, I don't blame him. What about John? Will he be able to come here with Casey?"

"Yes, I talked with John and he said that he could come with her. They will arrive Thursday evening. He will let me know what time to meet them. We thought that was best so that she will have time to get use to being back and can relax before the dance."

"That's good. Did you tell him that if for some reason, he cannot come, you and I will fly there and bring her back here with us."

"Yes, I did. John said that there was no problem. He had promised her and he intend to be there for her no matter what. He prefers to come with her. I told him that they would be staying here and he said that he appreciated it."

"Good. They seem like good people. I know that she will always be special to me for what she is doing for our family."

"Yeah, like we said, we are going to celebrate afterwards." Tex looked at his watch to check the time. They still had a few minutes before the guests would arrive. Hopefully, they would all arrive about the same time and be in the yard when he brought Cody downstairs.

They both were halfway laying on the bed, but comfortable. Tex said, "Cody, we haven't had time to talk about Traci and me. Do you have an opinion about us, good or bad? ..Before you answer that, forget about our college days. O.K." They both laughed. "Just give me your opinion, remembering my better days." Then they laughed again.

"Tex, Old Boy, let me see. Should I give you my bad one first and the better one later or should I reverse it?"

331

"Forget the bad one. Just give me the good one."

They were laughing and enjoying themselves especially Cody. Cody was enjoying seeing the expression on Tex's face change from puzzlement to joy and to concern, especially when he said, "She had a crush on Rich and he really loves her and will take care of her. And I know that he would look after her, and by the way, she is the stronger of the two. So, I know that she will have her way and run over him like a steamroller. He is rich so he will be able to take care of her financially and she will be able to live on the hill. I know that she will be happy with him and they will have beautiful children because he is a very good-looking specimen and my sister is beautiful inside and outside. I, also, know that she has good blood in her.

Tex was really getting angry now and he had a scowl on his face that made Cody burst out laughing. Finally, Tex said angrily and very loud, "To Hell with him. I don't want to know about him. And stop your laughing. This is not a laughing matter. I want to know about me. You SHITASS. Don't make me say something that I will be sorry for later."

Then they heard footsteps on the stairway running up the stairs. Just as Steven burst into the room, Cody was bent over laughing. Tex was sitting up now and just looking at him with a frown on his face that would scare a mule.

"What in the world is going on in here. We could hear you all downstairs."

Tex said, "I asked your brother a question and he is trying to get my blood boiling and it is close to it now. I want you to know that it is not funny. Not funny at all." He glared at Cody. Then he added, "You stay with your brother, I am going downstairs to cool off. Let him tell you what he thinks is so funny." He got up and walked out the door.

Steven sat on the side of the bed and looked at Cody with a surprised expression on his face. "You know, brother, Tex is really angry with you. Will you stop laughing and tell me what is going on."

Finally, Cody calmed down enough to tell Steven and then they both started laughing again.

After a few minutes, Steven said, "He is really angry with you. Evidently, he was wanting to have a serious talk."

"Yes, he was very serious. I guess I will have to apologize to him, but I couldn't help myself. I could not pass up the opportunity. It just seemed right to tease him. When he calms down, he will know that I was teasing him."

They both laughed again.

Then Cody took this opportunity to tell Steven all that had happened that day and informed him of the meeting on Thursday night. ...Then Cody said, "Oh, I just thought of something. John and Casey will be coming in Thursday evening. We don't know the time yet, but we can work that out."

Steven knew that he had a few more minutes to keep Cody here, so he asked Cody, "How do you really and truly feel about Tex becoming our brother-in-law? Picturing him and Traci together is something else, so surprising to all of us." He knew that Cody could talk about Tex and what good times they had had all day. So that was a good subject.

"Brother, I already feel that he is my brother and my feelings for him is not taking anything away from you and I. You will always be my real brother. Him being my brother-in-law will only make it legal."

"That is how I am beginning to feel about him. I haven't been around him as much as you have, but you made a great choice in selecting him to be your best friend."

"We selected each other. We just hit it off right away. I remember the first time I went home with him, he wanted me to meet his sister. He wanted us to hit it off so much. As it turned out, his sister was dating someone that she thought she was madly in love with and never noticed me other than being her brother's friend. The next visit, she and her boyfriend had broken up so she and I were paired off with Tex and his girlfriend when we went out. It was enjoyable. We enjoyed each other's company, but we knew that we could only become friends. She is a very beautiful lady and, like Traci, she has a mind of her own. She is only interested in the oil business now. She is taking over the Tyler Oil business. Tex doesn't want to have anything to do with it. Which works out well for Pop Tyler and Kristen because she can be a shrewd business woman. They are a great family. One day you will meet them."

"I would like that very much."

About that time, Traci came running up the stairs and as she came in the door, "What's keeping you all? But, first, Cody, what did you say to Tex to put him in a bad mood. He came downstairs and started growling at everyone. Mom sent him to the store to get some ice. We seem to be running out. She told him that maybe that would cool him off for awhile." She grinned.

Steven and Cody looked at one another and laughed. Traci just stared at them.

Cody said, "Nothing, Sis. You say dinner is ready. We are late tonight, aren't we?"

"Yes, we are. We got a late start and it takes time setting up outside. It seems that everyone wanted to eat outside. You two, come on down. Tex should be back by now." Then she went back downstairs.

Steven said, "Bro, you want me to go first and see if Tex is in a better mood?"

He laughed. "No, he'll get over it."

So, Cody led the way down the stairs out through the kitchen. "Hey, everyone's already outside. We better go before they eat up everything." As he walked out the back door, he yelled, "Hey, you guys, wait for us." Then he stopped. He opened his eyes and blinked them again. There were balloons and ribbon strings hung around and decorations of flowers on the tables and people. "What is this? Oh, my God. It's my birthday. I had completely forgotten about it. No wonder everyone was acting strange today. And Corrie, this is why you had to take a nap this afternoon. Gosh, you really did surprise me." He bent over and kissed her. Then he went over to his Mom and kissed her. Then everyone began singing Happy Birthday and came over and shook his hand or gave him a kiss on the cheek.

When that was over, everyone filled their plate and sat down and enjoyed a great meal. Jake, Sara and the boys were there, along with Mrs. Carillo, Corrie and Nick.

After the meal, Nick came over and said, "Cody, what happened between you and Tex today. He told me that you really pissed him off this afternoon, but he wouldn't tell me what it was about."

Cody started to laugh but saw Tex staring at him, so he stopped. Then he said, "If he is taking it this hard, I better go over and apologize to him. .....But he asked me what was my opinion about him becoming my brother-in-law. I couldn't resist. I just started telling him what a great life Traci would have with Rich and he got angry and walked out on me before I could give him the great life that she would have with him. I was just teasing him. He should know that."

"It hit him the wrong way because he is really angry with you. I have never seen him this upset."

"Yeah, he keeps staring at me with that frown on his face. I better go over and get this over with now." So they walked over to where Tex, Traci and Steven were sitting and they sat down in a couple of the empty chairs close by. Cody waited a few minutes before he said anything, but he was watching Tex to see what his reaction would be. Tex just looked at him. Finally, Cody said, "Tex, I guess I owe you an apology for this afternoon. I didn't realize that you were so serious. I had an opportunity to tease you and I took it. And that is all it was. I was teasing you and I am sorry about it. I had no idea that you would take it this way, but I can understand it."

Traci said, "What are you talking about Cody? What did you say to Tex?"

Tex interjected, "Honey, it was nothing. Think nothing about it, Cody. I'll get you back, though. As far as I am concerned, it is over."

Cody said to himself, he doesn't want Traci to know about it. I apologized at the right time, otherwise, he would have given me a hard time with it.

"Sure. But I am sorry. I would not say anything to hurt you, seriously."

"I said that it was over. I don't want to hear anymore about it."

"Alright. It's over."

Then Cody stood up and faced the other people that were there and said with a smile on his face, "I want to thank you all for putting this together for me and joining me and my family for a meal. I had forgotten all about it being my birthday today, but I appreciate very much you all reminding me of it. This was very nice. Thank you again." They all started clapping their hands while laughing and talking. He took a bow and then sat down beside Corrie. He bent down and whispered in her ear, "I am so glad to see you up and around again. Are you sure this is not too much? Are you feeling alright?"

"Yes, I feel fine. I can get around slowly. I just have to make sure that nothing bumps me on my right shoulder where the incision is healing. I have it protected just in case someone bumps into me or I bump into someone else. It will take a long time to heal because of the depth of the surgery."

He bent down and kissed her and laid her head on his shoulder. "Baby, I am so glad you could come."

"I am, too."

Nick said, "Alright, you two, we will have none of that here. We have some young guys here and we don't want to lead them astray. This is a family affair." They laughed. The boys were nearby and they joined in the laughter, too. *Nick was looking at them and thinking of how different their lifes were here and hoped that it would make a difference to them in the future. They had never had it so good. The life that they led was in a different neighborhood where life was not so rosy. When this investigation is over, I am going to talk to Cody about starting a youth camp or something.I think Jake would like that, too.*

After the meal was finished and the cake and ice cream had been served, Mama C came over to Corrie and asked, "Honey, are you getting tired and want to go home so you can rest?"

"Mom, I'm fine, but if you and Nick are ready to go, we will go. But don't rush because of me."

"It is getting late and I don't want you to get too tired."

Although he didn't want her to move from his arm, Cody said, "Sweetheart, I don't want you to leave, but your Mom's right. You shouldn't stay up too long at a time." He helped her up and she said her goodnight to everyone. Then he proceeded to pick her up with both arms and carried her to the car while Nick went ahead and opened the car door. He then got her settled in the back seat on the pillows that they had for her to lay back on so that she could be comfortable.

After they left, the ones remaining pitched in and cleaned up the tables and put the food away. The boys carried the trash to the dumpster. Sara, Traci and Mama E had gone into the kitchen putting the food away.

When the boys came back from the dumpster, Cody called them over to where he, Steven and Tex were cleaning the grills. "Now, Boys, I want to let you know that the investigation is not over, but most of the criminals are behind bars right now. But that does not mean that you can leave here. Things will go as has been these past weeks. Some of them may get out on bail. We are going to try to keep them in jail until the trial. They should stay in jail, but you never know what will happen at the Bond Hearing. I am just letting you know that Wilson, for one, is behind bars and has been for a couple of days. The Bond Hearing is set for Wilson and Santino tomorrow morning. So the rules here will stay the same until we change them. O.K."

With happy smiles on their faces, they all agreed. Then the question that Chip asked was the one that Cody was dreading.

"Sergeant Edwards, have you heard anything from Casey? When will she be coming home?"

Tex spoke up, "Chip, I talked with my father today and he saw John and Casey yesterday. They are fine. She sends her love and hope that it won't be long now."

Cody said, "It won't be long now, Chip. You all keep up the good work. You have done a good job. We wanted to keep you informed as to how things are coming along. And thank you all for what you did tonight. I appreciate it very much. And I want to say how proud I am of you all and how you conducted yourselves." And Cody went over to them and put his arm around their shoulder, each and every one of them.

Tex and Steven said, "Boys, we say, 'Amen to what Cody just said'. We all are very proud of you and expect you to continue to do a good job. Remember, Wilson cannot hurt you now."

By that time, Jake and Sara came out of the house and the boys said that they had to go. So they went over to where Jake and Sara were and they all walked back down the lighted path to the barn.

Tex, Steven, and Cody stayed outside for a while longer just discussing things in general. Tex finally got into a good mood, but Cody knew that he had not forgotten the teasing that he had given him and knew that somehow Tex would get him back.

Steven asked, "What are you guys going to do from now until Thursday?"

Cody thought for a moment and then answered, "I don't want to spook Samuels any more than he is now. I want him to think that we know nothing about him until Friday night. We don't want to mess that up. Since Tanner, Collins and Wilson are still in jail until tomorrow's Bond Hearing, we need to make sure that they do not get a low bond. I am thinking that we should go talk to the District Attorney before the Bond Hearing and, then, again, he knows our position on that. The problem with Samuels, we should just let it ride until Friday night. Our main concern tomorrow is to keep Tanner, Collins and Wilson in jail as long as possible. Santino has been denied bond so we don't have to worry about him getting out."

"Bro, what judge is going to hear the Bond Hearing? I may just come to hear it."

"Sure, come if you can. Lieutenant Moss said that it would be before Judge Walton Robinson. He has only been on the bench for about five years, and I hear that he is a very fair judge. He is located on the third floor to the right when you get off the elevator."

Tex spoke up. "I think I will go with you. It will be interesting to see how your courts work." He laughed while watching Cody's facial expressions. He knew what Cody was thinking.

"Tex, don't compare our system here with yours in Texas because they don't compare." Then he grinned.

Then Cody continued with a grin on his face, "Sure, I was counting on you coming with me. You are a witness, too. You were the first one in the warehouse, remember, ...or do you?" Then Cody started laughing.

"Alright, don't you start on me again. Yes, I remember. I was only out for a few seconds.

Cody and Steven started laughing. Finally, Tex joined in with them. "O K., have your fun. My time is coming."

Steven said, laughingly, "You keep saying that, but nothing ever happens."

"It will. It will."

Then Cody said, "Nick, Kato and Marci will meet us at the courthouse."

After a few minutes, they decided to call it a night and they went inside the house. It had been a beautiful evening.

Chapter 13

The next morning they were all gathered on the courthouse steps. Even Lieutenant Moss and Sergeant Thompson were there. They were introduced to Tex and Steven. They talked for about ten minutes and then they moved on to the courtroom. Cody and Nick talked to the District Attorney and they felt that everything was set. That they would not have any problem in keeping Tanner, Collins and Wilson in jail until trial.

When they were all in the courtroom and Court was called to order, in walked Judge Turner. Cody and Nick could not believe their eyes. As soon as they could, they headed for the District Attorney. Cody said very angrily, "Hey, Allen, we can't go before Judge Turner. He is involved in these cases. He will let all three of them out on bond."

"I know, Sergeant. That was discussed in our last meeting. I am as surprised as you are. Judge Robinson was suppose to reside over these cases. He told me that he would be here. Also, the Clerk's office told me that Judge Robinson would be residing over these cases.

After everyone was settled back into their seats after rising when the judge walked in, District Attorney Allen Mason stood up and said, "Your Honor, Judge Robinson was suppose to hear these cases this morning. May I ask why the change."

Judge Turner stared at him with a frown on his face. "You may. ...I am the Senior Judge and it is my decision to have Judge Robinson in another courtroom where he will serve Little County in a better way than being in this courtroom." Then in a very gruff voice he added, "Is that agreeable with you District Attorney Allen Mason?"

"No Sir, Your Honor, it is not agreeable with me." Allen was trying to keep his voice on an even level without showing any anger or animosity. "I object on the grounds that you are friends with the defendants and should step down from the bench."

"Whether I am friends or not, it will not pose a problem in my decision. I will not step down. I will be the one to reside over these hearings. Now sit down District Attorney Mason and let's get started."

"Your Honor, may I ask for a recess for about ten minutes?"

"We are just getting started, Mason. Are you ready for these hearings? If not, then I will dismiss these cases right now."

Lieutenant Moss came over to Cody and Nick and asked, "Do you all have enough evidence to arrest him now? We have to do something."

Cody said, "We have statements from Wilson and Garcia and the boys, but their statements would be second-hand because Wilson told them what would happen if they were arrested."

"You can't arrest him now and he is determined to hear these hearings and will probably let them go."

Kato was standing there listening to what they were saying. Then he thought about a complaint against the judge from a woman that had exchanged sex for her husband's charges to be dropped. But that wasn't the end of it, she was forced to meet him again and again or the judge would have him put back in jail. Also, a friend of hers had been forced to do the same thing. They were investigating it, but had not finished with it. Marci got the idea at the same time that Kato did. She looked at Kato and said, "Sara Greene." Kato said, "Bingo."

The others looked at them wondering what was going on with them.

Kato then told Allen as best he could and as short as he could so that he and Marci could go and pick up Sara and her friend. They were planning to arrest him when Cody's investigation was complete, but now was as good of a time as any.

Judge Turner getting very impatient said, "Alright, Mason, are we having a hearing or do I dismiss these cases?"

"Allen stood up and said, "I request a thirty minute delay, Your Honor."

"I denied your recess before and I am denying it now. Call your first witness." So Cody went to the stand and he testified trying to prolong his testimony as long as possible."

In the meantime, Tanner, Collins and Wilson were all smiles. They knew that they would be free until the trial or the cases would be dismissed.

Then Nick was called to the stand and he tried to prolong his testimony as long as possible. He talked on and on about the drugs in the warehouse.

Finally, Judge Turner said, "Corporal, you are repeating yourself. I don't have all day to listen to repeats. Do you have anyone else?"

Thinking about Tex and Steven, Allen said, "Yes, Your Honor, we have two more witnesses......" Then he heard the door open and Kato walked in with the two women. The two women sat down in the back of the courtroom.

Judge Turner started staring at them and looked a little startled and upset. At first, he didn't know what to say, but then he asked nervously, "What are those two women doing in my courtroom? Do they have anything to do with these cases?"

Kato was walking down the aisle and spoke up very loud before Allen could say anything. "No, Your Honor, they do not have anything to do with these cases, but they do have something to do with you. They have lodged a complaint against you and I am here to arrest you for several counts of rape and using poor, poor judgment."

Everyone was looking from Kato to Judge Turner wondering what was going on here.

"This is my courtroom and I am ordering you to sit down in my courtroom. I want order in this court."

By that time Kato and Marci were standing beside the judge, one on each side of him, and read him his rights and put the handcuffs on him. And at the same time, the police officers led Tanner, Collins and Wilson back to their cells.

Judge Turner was still yelling, "I'll have your jobs for this. What do you mean handcuffing me. You can't do this to me."

Kato said, "Yes, we can because now, Judge Turner, you can join your friends as criminals. Take him away. He turns my stomach." Two other police officers came over and led him out of the courtroom to be processed as a criminal.

There were so much noise in the courtroom that you could not hear each other talking. Reporters were every where trying to get to Cody, Nick, Kato and Marci. But they did not say anything, 'Just No Comment.'

Cody said, "Kato, I don't know how you did that, and I don't know how we can ever thank you and Marci. I had no idea. We were caught where there was nothing we could do. Neither of you said a word about it. But I am very happy. You have made my day, otherwise, those criminals would have walked. I know that I am babbling, but I don't know what to say. This is the best break that we could ever ask for and get. I am so thankful to be working with you all."

Marci, laughingly, said, "Cody, I believe you when you say you are happy." She laughed. "It is an ongoing investigation and we could not talk about it. We had to arrest him today to get you all off the hook or wait another week or two when the investigation is complete. We have enough evidence so today was as good a time as ever to arrest him." She smiled.

Nick said, "I, for one, am going to kiss you." And as he bent over and kissed her on the cheek, a reporter snapped a picture. Then he said, "Kato"....... Kato started backing away, saying, "Oh, no, you don't." Then Nick said, "I was just going to shake your hand." Then he grabbed his hand and shook it.

Cody said, "I am going to do the same thing." And he did. Then Tex said, "I might as well kiss you, too, but I am going to do it differently. He put his arm around Marci's waist and kissed her on the cheek and whispered in her ear, "Thanks. You were great." A reporter got that picture, too.

She smiled and said, "You are welcome. Glad that we could do it."

They had forgotten about Allen being there. He had been gathering up his files and talking to the reporters after Kato had explained everything to him a little better than before. Kato brought the two women over and introduced them to the others. A reporter got their picture, too.

Allen said, "Kato, I was sweating it out. I just knew the judge was going to find some reason to dismiss these cases."

Kato said, "I am sure that he would have, but thanks to these two ladies, he didn't get the chance."

Sara said, "I thought you had forgotten about our complaints. I had not heard anything lately about it."

"I hadn't heard anything, either. Now we know why. Thank you two for everything that you have done for us. I will be glad to testify against him," Beth said. Then she added, "I thought I was going to have to meet that slime again. He did call me at work yesterday, but I wasn't there at the time."

Marci said, "No, no, Sara, Beth. We hadn't forgotten about it. We were trying to tie it in with these cases that Cody and Nick are working on now. Judge Turner is involved with their case, too, but because of the judges attitude this morning, we had to work faster than we had planned, but it will work out fine. Don't either of you worry. We are still working on your complaints and a few others. He won't bother you again."

Then Marci led them out of the courtroom out the back way so that the two ladies would not have to face the reporters again. She drove them back to their work place and then she met the others at the station in Cody and Nick's office where Lieutenant Moss, Sergeant Thompson and all, except Steven, were there going over the event in court. They were laughing so loud and were so noisy, everyone that was outside the office were wondering what was going on in there, but word was getting around. Nick had made a pot of coffee and someone had stopped at Krispy Creme and got some pastries and donuts. They were enjoying themselves. Even Roberts heard them and came in to find out what was going on. They told him and he laughed and said, "It couldn't happen to a better guy. Maybe, now we can keep some of the drug dealers locked up for a change."

It wasn't long before the others in the outside office came in and congratulated all in the office. They had heard some bits and pieces of what had happened to Garcia, Santino and Wilson and the others. Cody introduced Tex, Marci and Kato to all. Then Moss explained to the others about what had happened that morning in court.

Lieutenant Moss said, "The events sounds like a movie, not real life. Oh, Kato and Marci, how can we ever thank you. God must be on our side. I felt like it was a losing battle this morning, but it sure ended with a bang."

Marci said, "You need to thank the two women. They are the ones that complained and no one would take their complaint. Kato and I started investigating their complaint and found it to be true. We have him on tape. I am glad that we could do that today, but I feel bad that it had something to do with what those two women went through."

They all agreed. And eventually, everyone went back to their desk and Kato and Marci had some work to do and they left. But before they left, Marci wrote down the addresses of the two women and where they were working and gave it to Cody. He wanted to remember them when they had their celebration at the end of the investigation. After all, they were a part of it.

Lieutenant Moss said, "Sergeant Edwards, why don't you two take off the rest of the day and show Tex some of our city. Maybe you can talk him into moving here and joining our group. We sure could use some more good help here."

Cody and Nick looked at Tex and grinned without saying a word. Then Lieutenant Moss said, "Did I say anything wrong? Has he already decided to settle here?"

Tex said aggressively, looking at Cody and Nick, "Lieutenant Moss, what they are looking so smug about is that, well, to put it bluntly, "I have fallen madly in love with Cody's sister and they have been teasing me about it ever since I have been here. But I keep telling Cody that he is going to wake up one morning and find that he has another brother."

They laughed.

Lieutenant Moss said, "Tex, if you do decide to settle here, I hope that you will come and see me before you go anywhere else."

"I will, Sir."

Lieutenant Moss went back to his office and the three of them left the station and headed for Nick's place to relax for a while. On the way, Cody and Tex stopped and bought some beer and pizza for lunch to have a little later. They hung out there for about two hours drinking their beer and eating pizza. They decided that they would go to a Braves ball game tonight. Captain Edwards had bought six seasons tickets several years ago and the family kept them year after year. The extra ticket was for Traci to invite a friend to go with her.

347

When Cody and Tex got home around four o'clock that afternoon, they went upstairs and took a shower and put on some comfortable clothes. When Cody came back downstairs, he went into the kitchen.

"Hello, Mom," and he went over and kissed her on the cheek. "Nick, Tex and I thought we would go to a Braves game tonight. Would you like to come with us?"

"No, you kids go and have a good time."

"Mom, I wish you would go with us."

"No, I really don't feel up to going out tonight. But, I must admit, I did enjoy the other night. It felt good just to get out, but tonight, I would rather not."

"O K., Mom, I don't want to force you, but if you change your mind, we would like for you to go."

"I know, Son. I know. Dinner will be ready around six o'clock. Will that be early enough?"

"Sure, Mom. Tex and I have already had our shower. If Traci and Steven want to go, it won't take them long. That will be fine. We already have our tickets."

A few minutes later Traci walked in the back door. "Hello, everyone, today has been a rough one for me. Bro, I know you had a busy one. I heard about what happened in Judge Turner's court this morning. I had heard rumors that he was a rotten judge." She went over and kissed him on the cheek. "Thanks to you and Nick, he is not on the bench anymore. Everyone in our section think that you all are heroes. They were all excited about it. Of course, they haven't heard everything that you all have been doing."

"What is this all about? I haven't heard anything about that. But, I haven't been watching television today, either."

"Mom, we had a little excitement this morning in court. Judge Turner has been part of our investigation. You know about Tanner,

Santino and Wilson being arrested a few days ago. I am sure that you saw that on television."

"Yes, I did see that on television, but I did not know that you arrested them."

"Yes, Kato and Marci, two GBI agents, have been working with us on this investigation. Well, anyway, the three were up for a Bond Hearing this morning. The District Attorney had made sure that they did not go before Judge Turner, but when we got in court this morning, Judge Turner had taken over. He is the Senior Judge and makes the rules among the judges. He transferred Judge Robinson, who was suppose to preside over the hearing, to another court and Judge Turner was going to preside over the Bond Hearing. Judge Turner was protecting the drug dealers and sending them back on the street so they could continue to sell drugs. When we objected to him hearing the case, he refused to step down nor to continue the hearing to another day. His intentions were to let these three criminals be free until trial. He also threatened us if we didn't have the hearing this morning, he was going to dismiss the cases. Which he wanted to do in the first place. Anyway, we didn't have enough evidence on him to arrest him then and there."

Mama E and Traci were watching and listening to Cody with a proud expression and a half smile on their faces. Also, Tex had come into the kitchen and was listening and grinning.

Steven came in the back door and when he saw Cody, he started grinning. "Hey, Bro, good work this morning. Judge Turner won't be on the bench anymore."

"Yes, I was just telling Mom and Traci about it. ......Anyway, we thought we had lost. We did not know what we were going to do. We had no other choice but to go on with the hearing. Then Kato said, 'start with the witnesses and keep them on the stand until I get back.' That was what we did. We were running out of time, when Kato appeared in the courtroom with two women." Cody started laughing. Then Steven and Tex joined in laughing, and Tex said,

"You should have seen the Judge's face when he saw the two women. He didn't know what to say."

The three were laughing so hard that Mama E and Traci joined in with them. They could imagine what was coming next.

Then Cody continued, "As it turned out, the two women had tried filing complaints against the judge, but no one would investigate him. Finally, Kato talked to the two women and he and Marci started investigating their complaints. The judge had forced them to have sex with him in order to get their husbands out of jail. They agreed that they would have sex with him one time, but the judge had different ideas. He forced them to have sex with him several times. Kato and Marci has this on tape. So, they had enough evidence to arrest him on the spot and Kato did. So Kato and Marci saved our day. Judge Turner was arrested and the other three criminals didn't look so happy. They were led back to jail until another hearing date can be set. So we owe Kato and Marci a hell of a lot. You will meet them, Mom. They will be at our celebration when this investigation is over."

Mama E had a confused look on her face. "I can't believe Judge Turner did those things. When I was on the charity board, his wife was on it, too. She seems like such a nice person. I really feel sorry for her."

"I'm sure she is, Mom, but her husband is a rotten, arrogant bastard. She would be better off without him." They were silent a moment. Then Cody said, "Nick, Tex and I are going to a Braves game tonight. Do either of you want to go with us?"

Tex spoke up, "Yes, Traci, would you like to go with us?"

She smiled at him, "Yes, I would. That would be very refreshing after the day that I had. A couple of kids gave me a hard time today, but I set them straight. They are now in the Youth Detention Center."

"Good for you, Sis. You and Steven go get ready for the game and Tex and I will help Mom finish dinner. That is if Steven wants to go."

"Yes, sure. Sounds good to me." He then headed upstairs and Traci went to her room.

"Mom, are you sure you don't want to go with us? We have another ticket."

"No, Son, I don't feel up to going tonight. Maybe another time."

"Then I'll call Nick and tell him that we have an extra ticket in case he wants to invite Angie." So he called and Nick said that he and Angie would meet them at the stadium entrance.

At the dinner table that night, they were laughing and talking about Judge Turner and the two women. Then Cody said, "You have to give the two women credit. If it wasn't for them, we most likely would have lost our case. By the way, I have their name and address. They don't know it yet, but they will be at our celebration, too. I never did find out if their husbands are still in jail or not. Of course, if they are out, they will be invited, too. Of course, depending on the charges."

Steven said, "Good, the more the merrier."

Traci looked at the clock and said, as she got up to carry her plate and glass to the counter, "We better get a move on if we are going to get there in time to see the program before the game starts."

"You all go and finish getting ready. I will clean up the kitchen."

"Oh, no, you won't, Mama E. We all are ready to go. We have time to clean this up before we go." So, they all pitched in and cleaned the kitchen.

After they left, she sat down in her favorite chair and picked up her knitting basket and started knitting Traci a sweater and watching her favorite programs.

At the ball game, some of the sports reporters and fans recognized Cody and Tex from the T.V. news and came over to them to congratulate them and some of them had some bad things to say about Judge Turner. And some said that they had no idea that he was a corrupt judge. It made them feel good, but after a while, it was getting to be annoying. Other people were going by looking trying to figure out if they were ball players or who they were. Finally, Nick and Angie came up and they went to their seats. Things were better there. No one was thinking about television. They were thinking about the game and their team and that was all that they were talking about.

The Braves played good that night. They beat the Mets eight to three. The Mets were not happy, but you win some and you lose some. The Mets had not lost by that large of a margin and because it was the Braves that beat them this time, the fans were really angry and booing. Of course, that made the Braves fans use their voices and clapping their hands to drown out the Mets' fans. It worked.

After the game, they all stopped by Johnnie Lee's for a while for a drink and relaxation. Nick and Angie danced a few dances and so did Tex and Traci. The brothers did not cut in this time. They let Tex dance the whole time with Traci.

When Tex and Cody came down for breakfast the next morning, Traci and Steven had already left for work. Mama E was getting ready to go shopping with Sara.

"I didn't know if I should have awaken you or not, so I let you sleep. Sara and I are going shopping. Your breakfast is on the warmer next to the stove."

"That's alright, Mom. You go with Sara. We can get our own breakfast. No, Mom, things are slow at work for this week. We are just taking it a day at a time unless something comes up that need attending to."

"That's good, Son. You all need a rest. We will see you later." And Mama E met Sara out by the car and they took off toward the shopping mall.

After Cody and Tex had fixed their plate and poured their coffee, they sat down to the table. After a while Tex said, "Cody, yesterday, I noticed the farm down the road from here was up for sale. Do you know what they want for it?"

Cody looked at Tex in astonishment. 'Tex, I didn't know you were interested in buying a farm here. What brought this on?"

"You didn't answer my question. ... Damn it. .... Don't start with me this morning. I am talking serious business with you."

"Well, Tex, I think I have a right to be startled with what you just said, but to answer your question, no, I don't know what they are asking for it. I didn't even know there was a farm on this road for sale. Which one are you talking about?"

"The one next to this one. The sign over the iron gate said 'Graves Farm' and there was a sign next to the gate that said 'For Sale' and then under that it had 'See Owner'. Do you know them?"

"Yes, I know Mr. and Mrs. Graves and their son, Rusty, we called him. I am not sure what his real name is. He went off to college and then got a job up north somewhere. Haven't heard anything about him since. Mr. Graves is in bad health and has been for about a year. Mom probably knows. She and Sara visits Mrs. Graves once in a while and take them cakes and different foods. You know how women are. Are you really serious about buying a farm?"

"Yes, I mentioned it to Traci last night. She was confused about it. She wants to live here, but she said that she would think about it. Her words were, 'We are moving too fast. I'll have to think about it.' But I would like to invest in it, anyway."

"Are you seriously thinking about relocating here?"

"I'm thinking about it. I would like to, but I am not sure how my father will feel about it."

"We could go over and see Mr. Graves and you can talk with him. Then decide what you want to do. It is adjoining our place. I think after Traci thinks about it, she would like that. At least, if she is going to move from here, that would be the place she would want to go. By the time we finish breakfast and clean up here, it would be late enough to go over and talk with them. We don't want to go too early."

Cody was so startled, but yet happy about what Tex had said. He only hoped that he was not speaking too soon, and maybe, change his mind later.

As Cody and Tex rode up the driveway, Tex said, "This is a pretty driveway. It curves near the house. It has trees along the driveway, but not the oaks like you have. These look like Crepe Myrtles. They are beautiful when in bloom, though. Needs cleaning around them."

As they neared the house, Cody said, "The house could use some work. It use to be a beautiful place, but since Rusty left, there hasn't been anyone to oversee the place the last couple of years."

"Could I count on you to help me out here, the work, I mean. I may have to do some of the work myself if I buy it."

"Sure, we all will help you out. No problem on that. But let's take one step at a time. I am wondering why they are selling it and where they will move if they do. Mr. Graves is an invalid and Mrs. Graves is up in the years. Rusty was born after they had been married ten or eleven years."

They stood in the yard looking around for a moment before going to the front door. By the time they had gotten to the steps to the front porch, Mrs. Graves' housekeeper opened the door.

"Mr. Cody. I thought that was you. We haven't seen you in a long time. Sure glad to see you. I see your mama quite often. Who is this you have with you? It sure don't look like Mr. Steven."

"No, Ma'am, this is a friend of mine from Texas. He is visiting here for awhile. We would like to talk to Mr. and Mrs. Graves about the property if this is a convenient time. We noticed that they have a 'For Sale' sign down by the gate."

"Sure, come on in and have a seat. I'll tell them that you are here." So they went inside and sat down in the living room, looking around at what they could see while waiting. Cody could tell that Tex was pleased at what he was seeing. He had that certain smile.

A couple of minutes later, Mrs. Graves came into the room and she came over and shook Cody's hand. "I am so glad to see you again, Cody. And who is this gentleman with you?"

Mrs. Graves, it is nice to see you again, too. This is Tex Tyler, a friend of mine from Houston, Texas. He is visiting with me for awhile. How is Mr. Graves? I haven't seen either of you for some time, but my work keeps me pretty busy."

"Yes, I expect so. I saw you on the news yesterday morning. That was surprising news, but if he is crooked then he should be removed from the bench. You all come around and set down. Mr. Graves is sleeping now. He wakes up so early and by the time we eat breakfast, he is ready for a nap afterwards. Claire and Sara came by a couple of days ago. They brought me one of Sara's cakes. She sure can bake. I always enjoy their visit. I don't see too many people now adays."

"Yes, Mom enjoys getting out once in a while. I am so thankful that she has Sara to do things with her now. ....Mrs. Graves, we noticed that you all have a sign at the gate about selling your farm. We came by to inquire about it. When would be a good time to come by and see Mr. Graves. We would like to talk with both of you about it."

"Rusty was here over the weekend and we discussed everything between us as to what we need to do with this place. Rusty has a good position with some company in Pennsylvania and it would not be right to ask him to give that up. He never was interested in farming, anyway. You know, he got married last year and he and his wife bought a house and it has a little cottage there in the back yard. They want us to move there and that is what we all decided to do this weekend. Rusty put the sign up Sunday before he left. As you can see, we can not do everything around here that should be done. Once this farm was a beautiful place. Now, look at it."

Then Tex spoke, "Mrs. Graves, it can be again. I see a lot of potential for it. I am very much interested in buying this farm if you are planning to sell it. How many acres go with the farm?"

"I think about one hundred and seventy-five acres. Russell can tell you exactly how many, but it is somewhere in the vicinity of what I said. We sold all of the cows we had last year since we couldn't take care of them. The couple we had living in that little house out back left when we sold the cows. Of course, there was no reason for them to stay. They got a good offer from a farm in the next county and they felt they should take it. We encouraged them to because you don't get offers like that often around here."

"Mrs. Graves, do you know approximately how much you all are asking for the place?"

"Rusty said something about $200,000, but I'll let Russell talk to you about that. I don't get into things like that. He will be up in about an hour. If you would like to stay, I'll have Mary Bell make some coffee or tea for you."

"No, no, Mrs. Graves. We'll come back later. Oh, one more thing. Have you had anyone else asking about the farm? If not, I wish you would consider giving my friend, Tex, here first choice."

"No, we haven't. You are the first one to inquire about it. If you are interested in it, Cody, we would rather sell it to you since it is adjoining your property. You have first choice. I promise that if you are willing to meet our price."

"I do not want any misunderstanding here, Mrs. Graves, I am interested in buying it. You see, I plan to marry Traci, Cody's sister. We haven't gotten that

far yet in planning a wedding, but that is my intentions."

"I see. I must say that you and Traci would make a charming couple. You are getting a very beautiful girl, Tex, and, I might add, a very sweet girl. She comes over to visit with us once in a while with Claire. It would be nice if you could live here close by."

"What time should we come back?" asked Tex. He was getting anxious. He liked what he saw of the house. His mind was already remodeling it inside.

"About eleven-thirty. That will give him an extra thirty minutes just in case he sleeps a little later. Most of the time, he is up by eleven o'clock."

They both stood and shook hands with her. Then Cody said, "We will be back around eleven-thirty, Mrs. Graves. And thank you for your time."

Tex said, "Thank you very much, Mrs. Graves I really like this house. I hope we can come to an agreement on it."

"Me, too. See you all later."

They left, looking around as they went. As they turned on the road, Cody was explaining where their property stopped and the Graves' property started. "It doesn't have a lot of frontage, but it goes way back. The frontage is plenty, though. It use to be a trail that goes way back to the river. It has a stream on it, also. A couple of wells. One for the farm and one for the house."

"Sounds like you are trying to sell it to me."

"No, I am happy for you if this is what you want. I'll help you any way that I can. You know that. But I am wondering if this is a spontaneous idea or if you are thinking it through. I just want you to be sure of what you want. Like Traci said, everything is happening so fast. The whole thing between you and Traci seems more like a dream. It is hard to believe."

Tex was watching Cody's expression on his face. "Are you having second thoughts about me becoming your brother-in-law?"

Cody grinned, "No, you know better than that. It makes me very happy. It just seems too good to be true. Nothing would make me happier than to see Traci married to you. Well, other than Corrie married to me." He laughed. Then they both laughed.

Just as they were going up the driveway toward home, Tex said very seriously, "Cody, don't say anything about this to Traci. I don't want her to know about this now. Maybe, I will surprise her later when we talk some more."

"Sure, but I thought you said something to her about it last night."

"I mentioned that it was for sale and asked her if she would like to live there. She said she would have to think about it. So, she doesn't know that I was going to pursue it. I want to buy it whether we live there or not. O.K."

"No, I won't say anything to anyone. It will be up to you to tell them. O.K."

They both laughed.

"Cody, do you think the farm is worth $200,000?"

"I think Mrs. Graves is going to be a hard nut to crack about the price. She said, 'If you will meet our price." It doesn't sound like she will come down any. You may be better off talking to Rusty. But to answer your question, that sounds about right, but it depends on how much work that needs to be done on the barn, small house and the big house. Also, the land, if it has been fertilized and taken care of. An Inspector will come in and go over the houses and barn and give you a better idea as to the worth. If you are not satisfied with his report, we can always get one ourselves. If all goes well this morning, we can go over and ride over the land later. Also, Jake can be available to go with us. He can tell you more about the land than I can."

"Good, I didn't know how they did things here. In Texas, everything is higher than here."

By that time, they were parked in the back yard. The shade trees looked so inviting that they walked over there and sat down. It was a few minutes before either one said anything. Finally, Tex asked, "When do you plan to tell Chip that Casey will be here Thursday?"

"I think maybe Thursday when she gets here. If we tell him too soon, he will get all excited and if anything happens that we have to call it off, it will be worst for him."

"I agree. I will talk to my father tonight to find out what time they will be here. I wish he could come. I would like for him to see that property."

"Maybe he can come later. You never said how much leave time you have or how long you plan to stay."

"Are you trying to get rid of me, Friend? Or are you worried about your sister. Don't worry, I have never gotten a girl pregnant and I have no intention of getting Traci pregnant until after we are married."

"As far as you know, you have not gotten any girl pregnant. That does not mean that you didn't."

They both laughed.

"I know that I am not a daddy anywhere. No one can pin that on me. Can you say that?" Tex grinned.

"Yes, I can. But I am not admitting to anything else."

"Neither am I. Do you remember Chuck Hall when we were in college? This girl tried to pin her pregnancy on him. She swore that the baby was his. He took a DNA test and it turned out that he was right."

They both laughed again. It was nice just the two of them. Like old times. Cody got up from his hammock and said, "I'll be right back. Do you want a glass of lemonade or ice tea?"

"I'll take ice tea and some of Sara's cookies. She makes the best cookies that I have ever eaten. Does she come with Traci?"

"No, she does not. She stays with Mom. That means that she stays with me. You'll have to eat Traci's rock hard chocolate chip cookies."

"What do you mean? Does Traci know how to cook?"

"Yes, she does. She is a good cook when she wants to be. One day she was in a hurry and made some chocolate chip cookies. She forgot about them in the oven and they cooked too long. They were hard as a rock. She ended up throwing them out. Ever since then, we have teased her about her chocolate chip cookies."

He laughed. "I'll have to ask her to make me some cookies and see what she says."

Then Cody went into the house to get the ice tea and some of Sara's cookies. He was back in a few minutes. They sat there drinking their ice tea and eating the cookies and discussing the farm.

"I really want that farm, Cody. I want to be close to you all and I know Traci does, too. If we can't get the farm, I don't know what we will do. It is so ideal for us."

"That would be great if you can get it, but you know you are always welcome to stay here. Even after you are married. I realize that it could be a little crowded for you, sometimes, but I want to make the offer anyway."

"I appreciate it, but I want a place of our own. That doesn't mean that we won't be over here putting our feet under your table."

"I know what you mean. You don't have to explain anything to me. I am not sure what Corrie and I will do when we get married. If Traci leaves here, and then Steven decides to leave, I don't want to leave Mom in this big house by herself. One thing that I am happy about is that Corrie doesn't mind living here. We have talked about it. She says that wherever I am, that is where she wants to be. Whether it is a small apartment or one upstairs bedroom with your mom. Now that I know what you want, I need to find out what Steven's plans are. Of course, that is in the future."

"I know one thing. If I get that farm next door, I am going to have a hammock under the trees. This is so relaxing. In Texas, we don't have enough room in our yard for big trees and a place to sit out under them. If I lived here, I would eat outside all the time."

"It is nice, isn't it?"

Then Cody got a little more serious, "What do you think your father will say about you living here?"

Tex was hesitant at first. He wasn't sure how his father would feel, but he hoped for the best. "I don't know. He always said that if we left home, he was going to sell the house and move into an apartment. I don't want to see him doing that. He has lived in that house ever since he and Mom married. I am in the same boat as you. I need to talk to Kristen. But I still want the farm. Who knows, Dad may come here and live with us and leave the house to Kristen. That is a thought. I would like that very much."

Cody, thinking back to other times, laughed. "I remember when I first met you. All you talked about was Texas. You would never leave Texas. You were so proud to be from Texas. Now listen to what you are saying. If only some of the guys could hear you now. They would flip out laughing."

They both laughed. "I did, didn't I. That was because I had not met your family nor had I been to a nice warm, hospitable place like Georgia. It reminds me of Texas, not as big, but just as potent."

They both laughed again. *Cody knew what he was talking about. He and Tex liked the same things in life. It will be so nice to have Tex as a brother-in-law. I am looking forward to it.*

Tex was thinking about preparing for the wedding and all that goes with it. "Cody, why don't we have a double wedding? I haven't talked to Traci about it, but why not?"

"First of all, it would not be fair to the girls. They each want their own wedding. That is something that will have to be decided later. Corrie and I have not set a date yet, but I want to as soon as possible. Right now, the important thing is for her to get well, completely well before we decide anything."

"I see what you mean. I am not thinking straight now. My mind is wandering today. It is almost time to go see Mr. Graves. I can hardly wait until I know that it is a done deal."

They both laughed. It was funny how impatient Tex could be when he wanted something and had to wait for it. They laid back and closed their eyes waiting for the time to go see Mr. Graves. Cody went sound asleep, but Tex was too excited to sleep.

Finally, it was close to eleven-thirty. Tex got up and went into the house to the bathroom. When he came back outside, it was eleven-forty.

"Hey, Cody, wake up. It's eleven-forty. Let's get ready to go."

Cody trying to wake up, said, "Hey, Man, wait a minute. Let me wake up first. You don't want to seem too anxious, do you?" Then Cody said, grinning, "Mrs. Graves may go up on the price if she sense that you want the farm regardless of the price."

Tex laughed. "I am being overly anxious, but I am excited. Other than my car, this will be the first big thing that I will own."

"Hey, I share your anxiety, but let's cool it until we are sure that you will own it."

"You sound like you have doubts that the Graves will sell it to me."

"No, I don't have doubts. If they sell it, they will sell it to you. I trust the Graves completely. Now, as for Russ, when we were growing up, he was very trustworthy. Now that he is out in the business world, that may be a different story. I have a feeling that he will be the one that will have the last say in this deal."

"I see what you mean."

"Well, I see that I will not have any peace until I get up from here and we are on our way. Let me go to the bathroom. That tea is going straight through me." Cody got up and went into the house. He stayed a little longer than he had to so that they would get there a little late. He wanted Mr. and Mrs. Graves to have time to discuss it before they get there.

When Cody came out of the house, Tex was standing near the car. "It took you long enough."

Cody laughed to himself. "Keep your cool, Tex. We will get there." Cody got into the passenger side of Tex's vehicle. They were on their way and very quiet until they got there.

Mary Bell met them at the door just as it was before. They were seated in the living room when Mr. and Mrs Graves came into the room. They shook hands with Mr. Graves. He was in a wheel chair. And they had a few minutes of pleasantries and general conversation.

Finally, Mr. Graves says, "Grace tells me that you are interested in this farm. I understand that you are marrying Traci and want to buy this farm. I tell you one thing, Tex. You are getting a wonderful girl. All of the Edwards are wonderful people. They have been very good neighbors and still are. Claire and Sara comes over all the time with one of Sara's cakes or pies and all kinds of food. We appreciate them very much."

"Yes, Sir. I saw your sign by the gate yesterday and I am very interested in this farm. As I told Mrs. Graves, it has great potential. I understand that no one else has inquired about it."

"You are the first to talk to me about it. Grace give Tex and Cody that paper that Russ left here. It has all the information on it. You can look it over and if you are still interested, you and Cody may look around the house and the farm. I talked to Rusty a few minutes earlier before you all came. He was thrilled that a friend of Cody's was interested in the farm. He said that if you were really interested and wanted to buy it, he would come down this weekend and handle the paperwork."

"I appreciate that Mr. Graves." Grace handed Tex the paper and he and Cody took about five minutes to read over the paper. After a moment, Tex said, "Mr. Graves, it says that the price of $200,000 is a firm price. Just what little I saw on the way here, there is a lot of work to be done. Is that negotiable?"

"You boys look around all you want. The house is open to you if you would like to look now. The roads around the farm are good. You can use my pickup if you want to ride out in the pastures. As for any changes in that paper, you will have to talk to Rusty about it. He is handling that. Grace will give you his number and you can call him after you have decided."

"Yes Sir. I would like to look at the houses and around here, and if we have time, we will ride out in the pastures."

"You help yourselves. We'll be here if you need to ask any questions."

"Thank you, Sir."

So Cody and Tex followed Grace upstairs and they looked at the rooms upstairs. There was one bathroom and three small rooms and a large closet. Everything looked good and Tex had a plan in his mind as to how he wanted to fix that. Then they went downstairs and there was one complete bathroom and one-half bath similar to the Edwards house. Tex liked the house and knew at first sight how he wanted it remodeled. After about thirty minutes, Tex told Mr. Graves that they were going to ride out to the pasture, but he would take his four-wheel vehicle. Grace showed them the best way to go and they went down that road and then another and another. They were taking their time looking around because they had all day. Then they came back and looked over the barn and the small house.

They left with the understanding that Tex would talk to Rusty and then he would get back in touch with them.

On the way home, Tex was looking over the notes that he had made during the tour. The first thing that he wanted to do was talk to Jake and see what his idea was on the Graves farm. He wasn't too interested in the house other than he wanted it inspected for termites and rotten wood. He and Traci would remodel it like they wanted. The farm is what he wanted to know about. So, when they pulled up into the back yard, Tex said, "Let's go to the barn. I want to talk to Jake and see what his thoughts are."

When they pulled up to the barn, one of the boys came over to see if anything was wrong. After Cody told him 'No', that they wanted to talk to Jake. Tim left and a few moments later, Jake came out and got in the vehicle with them. Tex talked to him about the farm. A couple of times, Jake laughed. "I can't believe what I am hearing here."

Tex said, sternly, "Believe it. I plan to marry Traci and I want to buy that farm." He handed the notes to Jake. Jake looked over the notes and finally said, "Tex, it has been awhile since I have been over there, but I would say that the farm is in pretty good shape. It may need some fertilizer to build the land up, but it is a beautiful piece of land. I would say go for it. I would try to get the price down, though. That seems to be a little high. I would go along the fence line and see if it needs a new fence or if that one is alright. A lot of things to take into consideration on a farm. Look at the equipment and see if it is in good running condition. If you want, I can ride over with you after about thirty minutes here."

"O.K., Jake, I would appreciate it. I would like for you to see it before I talk to Rusty tonight. We'll be at the house when you get ready."

"O.K."

So Tex and Cody went back to the house and sat at the table in the kitchen. Cody got some cold cuts and lettuce, mayonnaise, bread and put on the table while Tex made a couple glasses of ice tea. They were just finishing their sandwich when Jake came in. He sat down and made a sandwich while Cody talked to Mrs. Graves to let her know that they would be back with Jake to look at the pastures again, but would not disturb them. She said that would be fine. She appreciated him letting her know.

When Jake had finished his sandwich and they had cleaned off the table, they left for the Graves farm. After riding over it a couple of times, riding along the fence line and looking at the barn, a couple of hours had passed. Jake looked over Tex's notes and then he gave Tex his thoughts on the matter. "Tex, the fence looks good. A few places that it could be repaired, but nothing important now until you get some cows or horses or whatever. The pastures could use some fertilizer to get it back ready for cattle. The equipment seems to be in good shape, not as old as I thought it would be. A couple of pieces is rusted and could use some cleaning and painting. The barn and the small house could use some repairs. I would add up approximately how much this would cost to do, so that when I talk to Rusty, I would try to negotiate with him. He use to be a fair person. He will probably treat you right." Tex was writing all of this down.

When they got back home, Mama E and Sara had gotten home and were in the kitchen. So they sat out under the trees. Tex showed Jake what he had written down. "Now, I want you to fill in approximately how much you think it would cost to repair the barn and small house. And how much it would cost to paint the big house outside. And, another thing, Jake, don't say anything about this to anyone, not even Sara right now. I don't want anyone to know about it until it is a done deal. O.K."

"O.K., Tex." Jake took the note pad and started writing in figures and then he added them up to a total of approximately $25,000. "Now, Tex, this is approximately. It is a number you can bargain with. The fertilizer is the most expensive because of the large coverage and the cost of fertilizer. If he comes down that much, you will get a pretty good deal. But it depends on how much you are willing to pay and how bad you want it."

"I want it pretty bad, mostly because of the location of the farm. And I can see a great potential for the house and surrounding area. It could be made into a beautiful place."

Cody and Jake agreed with him. They each were picturing what it could look like in each of their own minds.

"Have you thought this thing through, Tex? That farm is a lot of responsibility. In fact, any farm is a lot of responsibility. If you are planning to do police work and keep the farm going, you are going to need some help. Farm living alone is not a good living. Some years it might be good and some years it is not so good. Most folks around here have other income coming in year round."

Cody laughed. "And, Brother, you can't live on love alone."

They all laughed. Then Jake said, "That's right. I tried it one time. It don't work that way, Tex. You may end up starving to death. Take my advice. Get a real job with money coming in every week or month."

"Have your laugh, you two. To answer your question I have thought it through. This is what I want, and, yes, I do plan to stay in law enforcement. I will have to look for someone to run the farm for me. That is something that you two can do for me."

Cody laughed and said, "What? Run the farm for you or look for someone to run the farm for you."

"You know darn well what I mean," Tex said angrily and staring at Cody. "Jake, he's just trying to be funny and give me a hard time."

They all laughed.

Just then Mama E and Sara came out where they were. "What is so funny out here? Sara and I had to come out and see what is going on?"

Sara looked puzzled, "Jake, what are you doing out here? Aren't you suppose to be looking over those boys in the barn? What have gotten into you?"

"Yes, the boys are fine. I just decided to take a break, that's all."

The radio had been on low and a song that Tex liked started playing. He did not want the conversation to get into his buying the farm, so he jumped up and turned the radio up and grabbed Mama E. "Let's you and me show these folks how to dance. He put his arms around her and whirled her around a time or two. "Hey, Tex, I am not as young as you are."

"That's alright. You love to dance. I love to dance, so we both dance."

Everyone was laughing. Jake said, "Sara, we use to cut a rug once in a while. Want to try it?"

Before she could answer. Jake had gotten up and was twirling her around the yard. Cody sat on the sidelines laughing. Then he got up and started dancing by himself. About that time Traci drove up and came out with an expression of wonderment on her face. "What the world are you guys doing? Jake and Sara. I can't believe it. You all have gone crazy." Then Cody came around and grabbed her and was twirling her around. They were still dancing, switching partners every couple of minutes, when Steven drove up.

When he got out of the car, he walked over, "What in the hell is going on around here? Did something big happen today that I don't know about." No one could say anything. They were laughing so. "Well, I might as well jump in, too." He then grabbed Traci from Tex and started dancing. Tex just fell over into one of the hammocks nearby, laughing at the expression on Traci and Steven's face.

When that song and a couple more had finished playing, they all just fell in a hammock or chair. Jake said, "I don't know when I have danced like that and enjoyed it as much."

Steven looked at Traci, "What's going on, Sis? No one else can talk around here." She stared back at him as she said, "I don't know. When I came over to see what was going on, Cody grabbed me and started dancing."

Then she looked over at the group and said, "Alright, you guys, what brought this on."

By that time, they had caught their breath and was tired out from laughing. Mama E said, "Sara and I came out to see what these three guys were laughing at and to tell them to get ready for dinner. The next thing I knew Tex turned up the radio and grabbed me and we were dancing. Then Jake and Sara joined us, and finally, Cody was dancing by himself until Traci came. Then we all danced for two or three songs. Tex, you are a joy to have around. You are always up to something. I am glad to see you all having a good time. All work and no play is not healthy."

They laughed again.

As they got up to go into the house, they noticed that the boys were sitting on the sideline laughing. They got up and ran over. "One of the boys said, "you grownups are something else." Another one said, "This is a fun place. Could I live here permanently?" And then he laughed.

They all laughed. Cody said, "Don't mind us, we just go crazy once in a while."

Steven said, "Don't be coy with me. I saw you all dancing over there."

"Yeah, but we didn't have a girl to dance with."

They laughed and they walked into the house, except Jake, Sara and the boys. They walked down the path to their home.

At the dinner table that evening, Steven asked, "What did you two do today? I saw Nick and he said he hadn't seen you two."

"Cody and I rode around looking at the scenery in this area. Other than that we hung out under the trees drinking ice tea and eating Sara's cookies."

Cody looked puzzled, "Where did you see Nick? He wasn't working, was he?"

"No, he was at that supermarket in their area. He was getting some things for Mrs. Carillo. She had two wedding cakes to bake by tomorrow. He was coming out of the store when I saw him and pulled over."

"Does she have any help with those cakes? She works so hard, that woman. I know Corrie did help her some, but she is not able now."

Cody said, "A next door neighbor helps her when she has a big order. I am sure they can handle it or Mama C would not have taken the order. Besides, Nick is handy in the kitchen, also. He is a big help to her."

After dinner and cleaning the kitchen, Cody, Tex and Steven went upstairs. Tex explained everything to Steven. Steven was exasperated and excited at the same time. "I don't know what to say, except that would be great. What does Traci say about it?" Then he laughed. *I can't believe this. It would be wonderful if he could do what he says he wants to do. Tex living in Georgia. That's great.*

"She doesn't know about it yet. At least, about today. I did ask her last night if she would like to live on a farm next to this one. She said that things were moving too fast. She would have to think about it. That was all that was said. I don't plan to tell her about the farm until we start making wedding plans. So don't say anything to anyone. Only the three of us and Jake know about it. If Traci decides that she doesn't want to live there, I want it for investments, anyway. I want to own my own place."

"I understand, Tex. I think Traci will come around when she finds out what you have done. Now, if it was moving to Texas or anywhere else, I would have to say 'No'. But, this, I think she would love that."

"Thank you, Steven. I think she will, too. ..... Well, you two, wish me luck. I am going to talk to the one in charge. Cody, you talk to him first so that you can get him in a good mood."

"Sure, it has been awhile since I have seen Rusty. It will be nice talking to him again. After Cody got Rusty on the phone, they talked for a few minutes and then Cody put Tex on the phone. They talked and talked back and forth about what needed to be done. The cost of everything. Finally, they negotiated to $180,000, but Tex was to pay the closing cost. Which Tex expected to pay anyway. The Graves were only to take their personal items and furniture. They would pick what they wanted to take and sell the rest. Tex would have first choice on what furniture was left. Also, the Graves would have a month to move out and two, if needed. Tex agreed that it was no hurry on that point, but, if possible two months the most. Rusty would be down that Saturday and they would sign the papers.

When Tex hung up the phone, they laughed with joy. Cody said, "This calls for a celebration." He went over to his mini-bar and fixed three drinks. They drank to Tex's success. They fixed another drink and then went outside and sat under the trees. Traci came out to be with them.

"I want to know what this celebration is. You all have been celebrating all afternoon. And I might add with a sheepish grin on your faces."

"Come over here and set by me, Beautiful. Then I will feel complete. We accomplished a lot today, and yet we haven't accomplished anything. It was a day for just being together, Cody and I. And now, Steven and you."

They stayed out under the trees until after dark just relaxing and listening to the music from the radio.

Traci, looking from one to the other, asked, "Does anyone want to go anywhere or have anything special they want to do?"

"No, Sweetheart, as for me, I am happy to just sit here and enjoy you all and the music. We can always go somewhere. Just being together is good for me."

Steven said, "Amen to that. I have been riding all day. It feels good just to sit and relax. Oh, Cody, the guys are still talking about Judge Turner. They can not believe that it turned out like it did. They are happy about it, of course."

"That was something. My buddies back in Houston would never believe it. I have not heard of anything like that happening in Houston. They would say that things like that only happen in the movies, but I can tell them that I saw it in person. Even involved somewhat in it."

"Yes, you will have some tall stories to tell them when you see them again. Also, you can take them the front page of the paper with your picture on it kissing Marci." They laughed. Then Cody continued, "Everyone laughs at the Georgia Boys, but that is because they don't want to think that they are smarter and better than they are. It is better to make fun of someone else than to admit their own faults."

"Cody, I was thinking about taking Thursday and Friday off. I thought I could be of some help Thursday and Friday, and I wanted to be with Tex as much as possible while he is here. What do you think?"

Tex spoke up, "That would be great, Steven. I am going to have to get some more time off, or I will have to leave to go back to Houston by Saturday morning. I will probably get a couple more days off and leave early Monday or Tuesday morning. There are some things that I have to straighten out there and I want to talk to Dad in person. He won't be able to come this weekend so I will have to go there unless something changes."

"I wish he could. Would like to meet him. Maybe sometime soon."

"Yeah, sure."

"Well, you guys can stay out here, but I have to go inside. Some of us work, you know. Cody, I put in to take off Thursday and Friday. I would like to be here with Casey while she is here. That way, we can get to know one another."

"That's great, Sis. Thank you. I know she will appreciate it. She will be quite nervous, I'm sure."

"O.K. goodnight, you all." And Traci left to go inside. Soon Steven followed. Cody and Tex stayed outside a little longer.

Chapter 14

The following day Tex and Cody stayed around the house waiting for his father to call. Mr. Tyler was to call as soon as he heard from John Branson as to when they were to leave for the airport and when they would arrive in Littleton on Thursday.

In the meantime, Tex called his Lieutenant at work and asked to extend his time until Wednesday of the following week. The Lieutenant approved it.

"What did the Lieutenant say about extending your leave time?"

"He said that he would extend it through Tuesday, but they needed me there today. They have seven new cases to investigate. I wonder what he is going to say when I tell him that I am relocating to Georgia."

Cody laughed, "If they are that busy, he is not going to be happy about it. Just when are you planning to tell him?"

"I am not sure right now. I am just playing it a day at a time. My plans are that if everything goes as we think it will Friday night, I will leave Monday morning so that I will be there in plenty of time to go into work on Wednesday morning. After that will depend on what plans Traci and I make and when the Graves move out of the house."

"It seems to me that you have your mind made up on what you want. I'm very happy you chose to make a life here. I only hope that you won't live to regret it."

"I won't."

"You seem to be sure about that."

"I am. Traci is worth every change that I make. I only want her to be as happy as I am."

"I'm sure she will be. She is as happy as I have ever seen her now. You know that she want to become a deputy on the department. What is your feelings about that?"

"If that is what she wants, we can work it out. I know that we will have some inconveniences, but as long as we can talk about it, we can work it out."

"That is a very good outlook. Of course, I am not the one to be talking to you about it. That is between you and Traci."

About that time the phone started ringing. Tex answered it. It was his father.

"Yes, Dad. That will be fine. We will meet them and they will be set up here in the Edwards home. ... .Great. Oh, Dad, I have extended my leave until Wednesday. I will leave here Monday morning. I will see you sometime Tuesday....O. K., Dad. See you. Bye."

"Dad said that the Bransons will arrive here about three o'clock Thursday afternoon and their return time is eleven o'clock Sunday morning. They set that time in case you all had things to talk about or needed to take her statement or whatever. The time to leave can always be changed."

"No, that will be fine. She will need some time to get herself together and relax before she leaves. And we will have to get a statement from her along with the recording that you will be wearing. It would be best for you to wear it rather than she. You will just have to make sure that you are with her at all times."

"Sure, no problem."

"Do you want to take a ride over to Nick's place and see what he is up to these days since we don't have anything to do."

"Sure. We could hang out with him for awhile." So they got into Cody's car and took off over to Nick's place. Nick was home reading a book. He was an avid reader, especially police stories.

They sat down and talked for awhile and then they decided to go see Casey's mom and tell her about Casey coming in Thursday.

When they arrived at the office where Mrs. Branson worked, Cody went in to talk with her. They did not want to scare her with all three of them walking into her work area.

Cody knocked on her door. She looked up with a somewhat puzzled look on her face. Then she smiled as she recognized him and saw that he had a smile on his face. She knew then that nothing was wrong.

They had agreed before just to use his first name. "Come in, Cody. How are you today?"

"I'm fine, Mrs. Branson," he said as he closed the door. Then he came in and sat in the chair across from her desk. How have you been getting along?"

"I'm fine. I saw on television what you all did with Judge Turner and I understand most of the criminals have been put behind bars. I know that you all don't get many thanks for what you do, but I want to thank you for everything that you all have done and what you are doing for my little girl."

"You're welcome, Mrs. Branson. I only wish more people were as cooperative as you, Casey and John are. I came by to tell you that John and Casey will be arriving in town around three o'clock Thursday afternoon. If everything goes like we think it will, they will be leaving around eleven o'clock Sunday morning. I would like to invite you to spend some time with her at our place over the weekend. If you like, I will pick you up Thursday afternoon to have dinner with us. Then, you may be able to spend some time with her Saturday. I will have to let you know about that."

She got up and came around the desk just as he got up. She put her arm around his shoulder. "Cody, I would love to. I want to see my daughter so much, but I don't want to interfere with what she has to do."

"You won't. That is why I said I would have to let you know about Saturday. That is depending on what we have to do then. Either Steven or I will pick you up when you get off work Thursday if that is alright with you?"

"Sure, that will be fine. You have made me so happy."

Then as he neared the door, he said, "We'll see you Thursday." He grinned, "By the way, we haven't told Chip that Casey is coming in Thursday. We don't want him to get too excited until Thursday." She laughed.

"Good day, Mrs. Branson."

"Good day to you, Cody." Then she went back to her desk smiling.

Then they went by to speak with Mrs. Stevens and Jeanne. Jeanne had gone to see her mother for a few minutes. They had heard that Wilson was in jail, but did not know if he was still there. Nick assured her that he was still there and that they were doing their best to make sure that he stayed for a long time. Between the three of them, they told Mrs. Stevens what had happened as they sat down and had a cup of coffee. Just before they left, they assured her that it was almost over.

Then they went to a restaurant to have lunch and then to Nick's place. After about an hour of just bumming around, Tex and Cody went home and sat amongst the trees. They just seem to end up there when they were at home. The smell of the gardenias, honeysuckles, lilacs and shade trees gave the area a very welcoming congregating place. They were there when Mama E and Sara came back from visiting with Mrs. Carillo. But Mama E and Sara went inside and started preparing dinner for both houses. They did that when they prepared beef stew or vegetable soup, or roasting some type of meat. Today, they were preparing beef stew and corn muffins. Mama E prepared the beef stew, while Sara made two big peach cobblers.

Steven came home a little early and joined the two under the trees. About forty-five minutes later Traci came home and joined the others outside under the trees. She sat down by Tex in a hammock. Then she said, "Tex, you know the other night you asked me something about living at the farm next to ours. I told you I had to think about it. Well, I have been thinking about it, so on the way home from work, I drove by it to get a good look at it. The sign was gone. ...I'm sorry. I guess they have sold it. I should have given you an answer then. Now we don't have a choice. If I lived anywhere else, I would want it to be close by and that would have been perfect. I'm so sorry."

Tex winked at the others as he put his arm around her shoulder and laid her head on his shoulder. "Honey, are you sure the sign was not there."

"No, I drove by twice to make sure. I'm sorry."

"Sweetheart, you've said that about three times already. It's O.K. We will look around the area and look for something else. Don't worry about it?"

"But that would have been perfect. I guess someone else thought so, too. Maybe we can find out who bought it and try to buy it from them.

Tex laughed. "It's alright. Don't worry about it. I'll check into it if that is what you want to do."

"Yes, it would have been perfect."

"I think you have said that about three times, too. We'll talk about it later. O.K. Now, I talked to Dad this morning and Casey and John will be arriving about three o'clock tomorrow afternoon and they will be here until Sunday morning."

"Oh, great. I am looking forward to meeting her. Oh, and by the way, Rich has called me three or four times the last two days to make sure that I will go to the dance with him."

Tex frowned at her. That wasn't what he really wanted to hear. *He may dance with her but that is all that he is going to do with her. And this will be the last time that he will be around her. I guarantee that.*

Then the subject of conversation was changed to her and Stevens' day at work and then what Tex and Cody had done that day.

After a while, they all were quiet and before long they had fallen asleep in the cool breeze. That is the way Sara found them when she came out to tell them that dinner was ready.

As they sat down to the table, Mama E said, "Sara and I decided that we would clean out the refrigerater tonight so that there would be room for the groceries that we will be getting tomorrow morning."

Cody said, "Now, Mom, don't go to any trouble. We will have what we usually have. We will just have four more people than usual."

Traci said, "Four. I thought only Casey and her cousin were coming."

"Yes, they are, but I invited Casey's mother to eat with us tomorrow night. She hasn't seen Casey in four or five months. Casey can't go there, so I invited her here."

"Why, Cody, that was real nice of you. I know she will want to see her daughter while she is here. But who is the other person?"

Cody grinned. "I thought we would surprise Chip and let him eat with us, too."

Steven and Tex started laughing. Then Steven said, "Bro, you think of everything, don't you. I guess that is why you are the oldest."

Mama E laughed. "No, he is the oldest because he was born before you."

Everyone laughed. "Bro, are you going to give them some time alone?"

They all were still grinning. "I haven't decided yet. Maybe a little while, but not enough to complicate things."

They all laughed. Then they all started calling Cody, "Bad Boy With No Heart. Bad Boy. Bad Boy."

It was a lively dinner. Everyone was feeling good and enjoyed being together. After dinner and the table had been cleaned off, they all went outside under the trees, except Mama E. She stayed in to watch her television programs.

The next morning was exciting for everyone. Steven and Traci did not have to go to work. After a late breakfast, Traci went into her room and made sure that it was set for Casey, clean sheets, etc. Then she went upstairs and put clean sheets on that bed for John. If a bed was not being used for any length of time, they normally just put the covering on it until someone would be sleeping in it. When she was satisfied that the bedroom was clean, she came back downstairs. Sara had made sure that the downstairs was clean. She then went into her bedroom and started selecting what she would wear to the dance and making sure that it was pressed and ready. She did not want to do any work at all while Casey was here. She was looking forward to this weekend, but a little nervous about the dance. Rich was not the one that she wanted to go with, but none of them would be going unless Rich invited them. So he was important to Cody's investigation and she would do anything to help her brother. This identification was very important to Cody and what was important to him or her family was important to her.

Then about one-fifteen, Traci went into the kitchen to help her mother make some sandwiches and ice tea. It had not been long since breakfast, but Mama E wanted everyone to eat something for lunch because dinner would be a little later than usual. Then they called the men in for lunch.

They had decided that Cody and Tex would meet the plane. They would leave about two o'clock to make sure that they were there on time. Sometimes the traffic was terrible in and around the airport. Traci and Steven would help Mama E prepare what they could ahead of time for dinner. Sara was helping, too. If Cody and Tex were not back by four-thirty, Steven was to go and pick up Mrs. Branson. Jake was to tell Chip that Cody wanted him to help serve at a dinner party they were having and he was to be cleaned up and at the house by four-thirty. That way Chip and Casey could have some time to be together before Mrs. Branson arrived. Everything had been planned as to how they wanted it.

As it turned out, Cody, Tex, John and Casey came in around four o'clock. Cody had cautioned John and Casey about mentioning the case at all. He explained that his mother and sister did not know anything about Casey's testimony. Traci only knew that Casey is going to identify the murderer of one of the murders that they are investigating. John and Casey, both, said they understood. Cody also told Casey that Chip was still at the farm, but he had not told him that she was coming. He thinks that he is coming to the house to help serve for a dinner party. John and Casey laughed. .....So they planned a joke on Chip. They all would be outside under the trees when Chip came and they wanted to see if he would recognize Casey. The dinner was to be outside under the trees.

When they drove up in the back yard. John said, "Wow, this is beautiful." Then he looked at Casey, who was a little nervous, and said, "Honey, think of this weekend as being on vacation. Don't think about why you are here. The dance tomorrow night is just a night out. O.K."

She smiled, "O.K. John. I'll be alright. It is beautiful. isn't it?"

Cody said, "Yes, we think so. This farm has been in our family for years. My grandfather did some things to what his father had done when he owned it. Then my father has added to it. Each time, we have tried to make it more comfortable and added things to make us relax and not want to leave it."

John laughed, "I thought I might come back and go into law enforcement if they pay this good."

"No, I'm afraid not. Jake and Sara are the ones we have to thank for making the farm into what it is today. They have really worked to make it show a profit. But, as the old saying goes, you can't make it alone on a farm you have to have money coming in from somewhere else. That is very true."

"I was kidding, Cody. I know that officers are not paid what they are worth. I, for one, appreciate what they do."

"I believe you, John. I sure wish most of the citizens would think like you do. Our job would be a lot easier. Casey, you do what John told you. Don't think of this as a job you have do. Just relax and try to enjoy it. ....You don't know how much we appreciate what you are doing."

Then Cody continued, "We treat all our visitors like homefolks around here. We use the back door all the time, very seldom the front door. Then they all got out of the car and went into the back door. Steven and Tex had gotten their luggage out of the car and brought it into the house with them. After all the introductions were concluded. Traci said, "Casey, come and I will show you to your room. I am going to love having you here." Then Cody took John upstairs and showed him his room. "John, you will have to share the bathroom with Tex. If he primps too long, just kick him out." They laughed.

Then he showed him his room and Stevens. "If you want to freshen up, take a nap or come on downstairs with us. We stay out under the trees most of the time. In fact that is where we will have dinner tonight."

"I am fine. The flight was comfortable. I am not one for taking a nap during the day. If you don't mind, I'll come out and set under the trees. They look so inviting."

"Sure, that will be fine. Sara was making some tea and lemonade to take out there for now and I know she has been baking cookies and snacks. So we will go back downstairs and see what's cooking. Maybe we can grab a snack before dinner."

When they got downstairs, everyone, except Sara and Mama E were outside. So they joined the others amongst the trees where the tea, lemonade, cookies and chips were set up.

Cody asked, "Where's Steven?"

"He went to get the beer. We can't have a party without beer." Then he looked at Traci and Casey. "The tea and lemonade are for you two." They laughed. Then Steven called out from the back door. "Hey, Tex, come help me with this."

Tex went to help Steven bring out the beer. When they got closer to the others. Tex said, "I think there are going to be a lot of drunks here tonight."

Steven said grinning, "It's light beer. You don't get drunk with light beer."

John said, "Says, who." And they laughed again. John joined in with the group. Traci and Casey were talking and joining in with the others when they could.

Then Steven looked at his watch. He said, "I'll be back in a few minutes." Then he looked at John. "John, would you like to take a ride with me. I'll show you some of God's country."

"Yes, I'll go with you. It has been a long time since I have been back here." So he got up and went with Steven.

When they got in the car, Steven said, "I didn't want to say anything in front of Casey, but we are going to pick her mother up. She will be having dinner with us, too. I thought maybe you might want to talk with her without Casey being around. It was just a thought."

"Oh, thanks, Steven, that's great. I have talked to her on the phone some, but Elaine, my wife, talks and writes to her most of the times. Yes, I am sure she has some questions about Casey."

"We didn't want to take the chance of taking Casey to see her mom into her neighborhood. Someone may see her and recognize her."

"I see what you mean. You folks do think of everything. I really appreciate what you all are doing."

"I don't know if Cody told you or not, but everyone that is involved in their investigation is in jail, except for the one Casey saw. We think that he is the one that killed one other person other than my father. At least, they were shot with the same gun."

"I sure hope that Casey can clear those two murders up for you, especially your dad."

"Yes, me too."

"They even got the judge that was involved in the drug operation in court the other day. That only happens in a movie. I'll have to get Tex to tell you. He can tell it with such drama that you will laugh yourself to death. Not that any of this is funny, but the look on the judges face said it all. That was thanks to Kato and Marci, two of our GBI agents working with Cody, Tex and Nick."

"I bet you all could write a book on diffent situations that you all run across in your line of work."

"Yeah, we probably could. We hear all kinds of excuses and see people where they shouldn't be. This one meeting that one and that one meeting this one. It is not a dull job at all."

"I'm sure it isn't. I have a few friends that are cops in the little town we live in which is located outside of Houston. They tell me some stories, but nothing like what you all could tell, I'm sure."

Meanwhile, back at the farm, Mama E and Sara are in the kitchen preparing the meal to be taken outside.

Cody looked up and saw Chip coming up the path. He said, "Don't look now but Chip is coming up the path toward the back door. He is looking over here like he is trying to see who all is here. Evidently, he doesn't recognize you, yet, Casey. He is going for in the back door. ....Casey, we need to go help Mom with the food. ....We will send Chip out here so you two can be alone for a little while." He laughed and then added, "Don't worry. No one will peep, I promise."

She laughed and said, "I don't care if you did. I want to see him so bad. I have missed him."

"He has missed you, too. Everytime he saw us, he was asking if we had heard from you. We'll go in before he comes out here. We'll see you in a little while." And with that he, Traci and Tex got up and went inside.

Cody picked up a tray of plates, napkins and things and said, "Here, Chip, take this outside. Just put them on the table with the other utensils." Chip grabbed the tray and went out the door. They all grinned at each other.

A few moments later, they heard him let out a war hoop. "YA HOO. CA-SEY, CA-SEY, I don't believe it." Everyone in the kitchen laughed. Cody said, "Don't look anyone. I promised Casey that no one would be watching." Cody did look out the window toward the barn and he could see the other kids behind the barn looking. Cody pointed out, "Evidently, Jake has told the other kids because they are peeping out from behind the side of the barn." They were waiting for Steven to get back before they carried any of the food outside.

After waiting several minutes, they heard Steven pull up in the back yard. They waited until Steven came in, and he told them that John and Mrs. Branson had gone under the trees with Casey and Chip.

Cody said, "We'll give them a few moments to be alone and then we will carry the food out."

Steven asked Cody, "Is Nick coming over?"

"Yes, there is plenty of food for them," chimed in Mama E. "I didn't mention it today when we were there because I didn't know exactly what you all had planned."

"To answer your question, Steven, I mentioned it to Nick earlier but he said that he and Angie were going to see some play that she wanted to see. It was the last time it would be performed in this area. Angie has been so helpful to his mother and to Corrie that he didn't want to disappoint her. He said that he will see us tomorrow."

Mama E said, "As long as you all invited him. I don't want him to feel slighted, after all, he is involved in this case, too."

"Mom, he knows that he is always invited here at any time," Cody said as he walked over to her and hugged her. Then he whispered in her ear, "Mom, you are always thinking of other people and their feelings. That is one of many reasons that we love you." She smiled. "I know, Son, I know."

John walked in as Cody was talking to his mom. He said, "They are having a joyous reunion out there. The three of them. Casey and her mom, Mary Ann, and Chip. I came in to give them a little more privacy."

They laughed. Mama E said, "That is why we are waiting in here so that they can have more time together now that they can. The food is ready whenever you all want to take it out. It is on the warmer now and will stay warm for awhile."

Tex said, "Have a seat, John. We will give them a few more minutes and then we will take the food out. It is always nice to see people unite like that. I sure hope everything works for them."

"Yes, me too. I'm glad that Casey got to see her mom ...and Chip. She has been worrying me to death, as well as Elaine about finding out how Chip is or how Mom is. I understand how she feels so we do what we can."

Mama E smiled at John, "That's what we parents do for our children." They all smiled at her.

After a few minutes, Tex stood up and said, "I think those young people have had enough time for kissing. we don't want them to get worked up into something else now, do we? My stomach is telling me it is time to eat." They all laughed.

John said laughing, "I agree totally on all of what you said, Tex. I don't want to take an addition to our family back with me if I can help it. Not at this time, anyway."

They laughed. Cody said, "O.K., everyone get a tray so we don't have to make but one trip. John, you go first and warn them that we are coming right behind you."

Mama E called Sara to tell them that they were ready to eat. She had gone home to change clothes and they were waiting for the call. Jake, Sara and the other boys came up right after the food was spread out. Introductions were made for the ones that didn't know each other and then Jake said 'Grace'. Then they all filled their plates. There were enough chairs for everyone to sit at a table.

Of course, Chip, Casey and all the other boys sat at one table. Mama E, Sara and Mrs Branson sat at the small table, and Tex, Traci, Cody, Jake, Steven and John sat at the large table. It worked out right. You could tell they were enjoying their conversations because each table was getting very loud at times. Just about the time they finished with the meal and before they were to eat the cakes and pies, Tex got up and turned the radio up to a song that he liked. He walked over to Mama E and pulled her up and started dancing with her. Everyone started laughing. They were having fun.

Tim said real loud and pointing his finger, "Look, they are doing it again. These people are crazy."

Everyone laughed. Steven went over to Mrs Branson and pulled her up and they started dancing. Chip and Casey got up. Then John asked Traci to dance. Before long they were switching partners and all were dancing.

After about thirty minutes of dancing, they sat back down and started on the deserts. It was very late when they decided to break up the party. Mama E talked Mrs. Branson into staying the night so she could spend more time with Casey while she was here. Everyone was told that there was no certain time to get up, but breakfast would be set up at approximately eight-thirty and kept on the warming plate.

The next morning being Friday, the important thing was to make sure each one would be ready for the dance by eight-thirty that night. That meant that they had all day and that it would be a relaxing day. Mama E was up and in the kitchen around eight o'clock. That was the time that Sara was coming to help with breakfast. By the time that breakfast was ready, all the men from upstairs were down and sitting at the table with mama E and Sara. Then Mary Ann came in and joined them at the table. So, by the time that Traci and Casey came in, all had eaten except them. The men went outside to set amongst the trees and share their experiences with one another. Mama E, Sara and Mary Ann cleared the table so that Traci and Casey could eat.

Mary Ann said, looking from one to the other, "It is so nice to be among a big family. I was raised as an only child and I had only a couple of good friends. My parents were very strict with whom I hung around with at all times. I have often seen big families and most of the time, they seem so happy."

"We wanted a big family, but we only had the three children. Thomas and I really enjoyed their growing up years and we both are very proud of them. I say are because Thomas was killed almost seven months ago and he often said how proud he was of the children. I feel that he sees them now."

Traci spoke up, "Mom, I'm glad that you enjoyed our growing up years, but the least you could have done was have another girl. Then I would not have had to fight my brothers to let me tag along."

They all laughed.

"That's not funny. I was a tomboy and wanted to do what they did, but I was a girl and they didn't want to be seen with me."

Mary Ann said, "That is the way it usually is. I wish Casey had a sister or brother, but it didn't work out that way."

"Mom, I think you and I are closer because of it. We have always had a good life together. You are my best friend and my mother."

"Thank you, Honey. That makes me feel good."

They all smiled at Casey.

When the women finished putting the dishes in the dishwasher, they sat down for a second cup of coffee and they all talked for a while longer. Then Traci said, "Casey, let's go lay out our clothes for the dance tonight so that we won't have to do it later."

"Sure." So they got up and went into the bedrooms.

Casey laid out her dress. It was a beautiful blue-green dress with a jacket with it. As she was spreading it out on the bed, she asked, "Traci, do you think this will be alright for the dance. Elaine helped me pick it out. I would appreciate it if you would help me fix my hair. I have never been to this type of dance before."

Traci said, smiling, "It's a very pretty dress, Casey. You will look beautiful in it. It matches your eyes perfectly. It looks as though it was made for you. ....Only because of you needing to look older, leave off the jacket. What about any accessaries? Did you bring any with you?"

389

"The only thing that I have is a gold locket that my mother gave me when I was sixteen. I thought maybe I could borrow something from her."

Traci looked in her jewelry box and came out with a choker. "This would look perfect with it. I have ear rings to match."

"Oh, Traci, those are beautiful. ....I can't wear these, I may lose them. But they are so beautiful. You are right. They are perfect with this dress."

"Casey, I will not take 'no' for an answer. You will wear these and I will fix your hair up and in curls with a few strands hanging down. Oh, you will be the prettiest girl at the dance. You want to look a little older because you are going to be Tex's date. He is twenty-four, almost twenty-five."

"I understand. He is such a handsome hunk. I feel like something special to be going as his date.'

"You are something special, Casey, and you are so right, he is a hunk. I didn't realize how much he meant to me until this visit and now we are planning to get married. We haven't had time to do much planning. The feelings between us just seems to be moving too fast. After this investigation is over, then we can settle down and take our time and plan things out."

"Traci, you are a wonderful person. I am so glad that I can do something for you all. Cody told me not to talk about it to anyone so I won't say anymore, except I am glad that I can help."

"I'm glad, too. Casey. I am sure Cody and Nick appreciate everything that you can do. They want to get the murderer and put him behind bars......Now, let me get my dress and accessaries out."

So, Traci put her dress on the bed, too, along with her accessaries.

"That is beautiful, Traci. You will be the most beautiful girl there."

She laughed, "No, Casey, we both will be the most beautiful girls there. All the others will be envious of us."

They both laughed.

Mary Ann came in to see Casey's dress. "Oh, Elaine did a good job in picking this out for you, Honey. You will look great in it. Mrs. Edwards has offered for me to stay until Sunday. That is very gracious of her, but I don't want to impose."

"Mrs. Branson, if Mom asked you to stay, she meant it. You will hurt her feelings and ours if you don't stay. I know you would like to be with Casey while she is here. Please reconsider."

Casey begged, "Mama, please stay. I want you to see me dressed up tonight. I need your support."

"Well, if you put it that way. I'll need to go home and get some clothes and personal items."

Traci spoke up, "I'll take you home if you like. We'll set our hair later, Casey." So the three of them went down the hall to the kitchen. Traci said, "Mom, I am going to take Mary Ann home to get some things. We will be back as soon as we can. Casey sat down with Mrs. Edwards and Sara. Traci and Mary Ann went out the back door toward her car.

When Chip finished his chores for that morning, Jake let him come over to be with Casey. He came into the kitchen and talked to the women for awhile. Then he and Casey walked outside and down the driveway for a stroll and then came back and sat outside with the guys.

Traci and Mary Ann were back in about an hour and a half and they joined all the others outside.

It was a slow morning because everyone was feeling drowsy from going to bed late the night before. They did not feel like doing anything strenuous. Just setting around and getting to know one another. It was just a lazy morning. Soup and sandwiches were served for lunch outside.

After lunch, Cody called John aside, "John, I'm sorry, but Tex, Steven and I have a meeting this afternoon. We were suppose to have it last night, but we decided to postpone it until this afternoon because some of the people had other engagements. It should not last more than an hour or an hour and a half. We want to make sure that each person knows what they are suppose to do tonight."

"I understand. I suppose it would be useless to ask if I can go and stay on the outside tonight."

"John, I know that you want to be with Casey all the way through this, but for safety reasons, I would prefer that you didn't. Remember that Casey's safety is our first priority. Second is getting the killer."

"Sure, I understand. I know that you all will take care of her. I am not worried about that."

"We'll see you later. I'll think about the other."

So, the three left for Kato's place. Nick and Andy Thompson were to meet them there. After they all were assembled around the table drinking some coffee, they discussed where each one would be. Tex, Traci and Casey would get there about nine-fifteen after the dance had started. They did not want to be standing around waiting, nor talking to too many people. All the others would be assembled outside around nine-thirty. By that time most everyone that was going to the dance would be inside the club. When Tex says 'Gotch Ya" and then give the vicinity where they were, Cody and Nick would go in after him whichever door Tex told them. Kato and Marci would be at the front, Steven at the door on one side and Thompson at the door on the other side in case the suspect ran.

Then Cody asked Kato, "John, Casey's cousin, wants to come with us and stay in the background. I told him I prefer that he didn't for safety reasons and I assured him that Casey's safety was our first priority. He said that he understood. But I told him that I would bring it up at the meeting today. What do you all think?"

Kato said, "We all have a position to take and there won't be anyone in the background to make sure he is safe. I would vote 'no'. If there were some others in the background, then I would say 'possibly.'"

The others agreed with Kato.

After everything was settled, Cody, Steven and Tex left to go back home.

Later that afternoon Traci and Casey went inside to set their hair. They had some nice chats. Traci was feeling good because she felt as though they were best of friends. It felt good to have another female around to talk to that was about her age. She hoped that they could stay friends. Casey felt the same way. She had grown up alone and it felt good to have someone other than her mother fussing over her.

Jake came out of the kitchen about the time Cody, Tex and Steven got home. Jake went over and told them that Mama E and Sara had decided that the men were going to barbecue some chickens. They needed to go to the store and get some fresh chickens that wasn't frozen. So, Steven and Jake took off to the store to get the chickens and whatever else they would need. The three older women were busy in the kitchen making baked beans, potato salad, fruit salad and other things to go with the chickens. Mama E always kept a couple of Sara's cakes in the freezer to have for emergencies. So she took them out to defrost.

The dinner was a repetition of the night before except for the dancing. They were enjoying each others company trying not to mention the dance or think about it. Cody was keeping his eyes on Casey to see what her state of mind was. She seem to be nervous, but trying not to show it. Once in a while she would laugh and smile at something that someone said. Chip seemed to be more nervous than she was. Cody made a mental note to talk to Chip before he left and have a talk with Casey, too. He wanted to make sure that he did not worry and that she would be calm and act natural at a dance, or at least that she was having a good time.

After everyone had finished dinner, Mama E said, "Trac, you and Casey go and get dressed. You have an hour and a half to get dressed before you all leave. We will clean up the dishes. The men, except for Tex, will clean off the tables." And they started working. It didn't take long with everyone working. The boys got all the paper trash together that was to be burned and carried it to the pit. They would burn it the following day.

While the men were cleaning the yard, the women went into the kitchen and finished washing the dishes. After a little over an hour, Mary Ann said, "I can't stand it any longer. I have to go and see my baby in that beautiful dress. I know Traci told me not to come in, but I am going to take a peak. But, as she stood up and looked toward the door, there stood Casey ready for the dance. "Oh, Honey, you look beautiful. Traci did a great job on your hair. I wish I had a picture of you now." She went over and hugged her daughter.

Traci stood behind them with a camera. "Mrs. Branson, you and Casey come in the living room and let me take some pictures. You don't think we could let this chance go by without something for a keepsake, do you?"

"Oh, Traci, thank you so much for thinking about the camera," said Mary Ann almost breathless. She was so excited.

Traci, laughingly, said, "Mrs. Branson, wipe those tears from your eyes."

They all laughed. Traci took a couple more shots and then Traci spoke up, "I want to take one with my new adopted sister." And she walked over in front of the mantel and stood by Casey with their arms around each others waist."

Then Casey said, "Could I have one with Chip?"

"Yes, sure, Mom, call the men in. We want to get a picture of all of them. Sara, you, Jake and the boys, too."

By the time the group came in from the yard, Tex was coming downstairs. Mary Ann took a couple shots of Traci and Tex. Then Tex, Traci and Casey. Tex, Traci and Mama E. And then they took shots of everyone, even Chip and the other boys alone. By the time they had finished, they had taken three rolls of film.

Jake, Sara and the boys were getting ready to leave when Cody called Chip to the side. "Chip, I know you are nervous about tonight. But, Casey's safety is our first priority, O.K. As soon as she identifies the voice, Steven will bring her straight here. I'll tell her to call you when she gets back. O.K."

"O.K., Sergeant Edwards. I trust you. I know she will be safe."

Cody patted him on the shoulder and then he was on his way down the path with the others. Cody motioned for Casey to come over and she did. Cody put his arm around her shoulder and said, "Casey, I know that you are nervous, but try not to be. Your safety is our first concern. You will be watched at all times. You stay with Tex at all times. Listen to him and do what he tells you. Alright."

"I'll be alright. I know I will be safe. I will just be glad when it is over.

"I will too, Casey. We all will be."

Then she went over and hugged her mother and John before she got in the car beside Tex. He reached over and squeezed her hand. "Everything will be alright."

"I know. I know."

Chapter 15

After they left for the dance, Cody and Steven went upstairs and got their police paraphernelia and Steven left in his personal car and Cody in his county car. Steven was to drive into the parking lot as close to the building as he could. He was to bring Casey home. Cody met the other guys a block away.

Tex, Traci and Casey walked into the building and went over to the side of the bar where Rich had told her that he would be. His eyes lit up when he saw Traci.

She was so beautiful. He loved her so. Of course, Tex was seeing all of this and he could hardly keep his composure when Rich bent over and kissed her on the cheek and said, "Darling, you are so beautiful. I am so glad that you could come."

"So am I, Rich. And I would like for you to meet my cousin and her date. Rich, this is Casey and her date, Tex. They are staying with us for the weekend."

Casey said, "Hello, Rich. Thank you for inviting us to the dance tonight."

Tex said, trying to keep his dislike out of his voice, "Yes, thank you, ...Rich. I am sure that we will enjoy it very much and be overwhelmed by the time it is over."

Rich was amused at what Tex had said, but only smiled at him as he was thinking ' What's with this guy?' Then he looked at the girls and said, "Would you ladies like a drink?"

"Rich, you know I am not old enough to drink and neither is my cousin, but I would like a ginger ale for myself and my cousin."

"Tex, how about you?"

"No, thanks. Maybe something later. I don't want to start too early."

"I know what you mean." And Rich walked over to the bartender and got the drinks. Then he asked Traci to dance and she did. As she walked away with Rich, Tex had a frown on his face. Casey looked up at him, "You better get that frown off your face before someone sees it and figure out that you are in love with her instead of me. Would you like to dance?" She smiled.

He looked down at her and smiled. "Yes, sure. You are beautiful tonight. I can see why Chip is in love with you." She smiled.

Tex was looking around the room for Samuels, but he could not see him. They circled around the dance floor as much as the crowd would let him, but still could not see him. Casey was a good dancer and they did well together. Tex noticed that a few people on the side was commenting on what a charming couple they made. The dance ended and they went over to the side where they were before. Tex kept his arm around her waist and kept smiling at her. Rich walked Traci around and introduced her to several of his friends and then they walked over to where Tex and Casey were standing.

Rich and Traci danced the next dance, but Tex and Casey sat it out. They wanted to take it slow. They portrayed a couple madly in love. That way no one else would ask her to dance, and even if they did she would refuse. Also, Tex was trying to watch for Samuels without it being obvious. He couldn't do that as well while dancing with the girl of his dreams.

While they were dancing, Rich asked, "Sweetheart, how well do you know Tex?"

"I have known him for about a year and a half. Why do you ask?"

"He keeps taking little sneak looks at us, or at you. I was just wondering if he was in love with you instead of Casey."

"Oh, no, we are just friends. He and Casey are planning to get married. He is more like a protective brother to me."

"I am just over reacting. I love you and hope that we can work out our problem with my parents."

"You mean your mother's problem with me. Let's don't get into that here, Rich. You know how they feel and how I feel. Let's forget about that and just enjoy the dance. But I do see your mother here because she is giving me the eye, but I don't see your father."

"You're right. I should not have brought that up here. We can discuss that later. Dad will be here a little later. He had a meeting." He pulled her close and they finished the dance. Of course, Tex was watching out of the corner of his eye and not liking it one bit. But there was not a thing he could do about it but grin and bear it. Casey kept grinning and smiling at him and his expressions. He would see her grinning and then smile and change his expressions. He knew what she was trying to do. She was doing a better job at acting than he was doing.

The next dance Tex and Casey danced around the floor and then went out on the deck over to where it was empty. They talked low and he kissed her on the cheek lightly. After the couple, which was close by, left, Tex said so that Cody and the others could hear him in the microphone, "Nothing yet? Will report back later."

Cody said, "He'll be there. Just play it cool."

"Sure thing."

Tex led Casey back inside to where Rich and Traci were. Tex was getting very impatient, especially seeing Traci with Rich. It was getting to be close to eleven o'clock now and no sign of Samuels. When the four of them were standing by the wall again. Tex, with his mouth pointed toward the microphone, asked, "Rich, I understand that your father has a lot to do with this club. He is the President or Chairman of the Board or something like that, isn't he?"

"Yes, he is. He and a group of men in this area started this club several years ago. He has been Chairman of the Board since that time. When he comes in, I will introduce you to him. He should be here anytime now. He is in a meeting now in the back room. My mom is over on the other side of the floor in that blue long dress."

"Oh, yes, I see her. She is a very beautiful lady. She seems to be enjoying herself."

"Yes, she is. She loves to dance."

A few minutes later, a couple of men came from the back of the club house. They were walking together and whispering to each other. They were about fifteen feet away when someone said, "Hello, Mr. Samuels, it is a lovely dance. Of course, all of the dances that you are in charge of are lovely dances."

"Good evening, Mrs. Evans. Glad that you are enjoying yourself. Save a dance for me."

"I will."

Tex noticed that Casey stiffened and flinched when she heard his voice. At about that time, the music started up again. Tex looked over the dance floor and saw Mr. and Mrs. Samuels starting to dance. Tex watched Casey's face as he led her on the dance floor. He made sure that he kept her back to Samuels at all times. Every time she heard his voice, she stiffened, but said nothing.

Finally, Tex pulled her close and asked her in a low voice what was wrong. With her head laying on the side of his neck, she whispered, "That voice that I keep hearing is not the main one, but he was the other voice that I heard. The one that was not as strong as the other voice." Tex shushed her and led her over to the side where they were alone. Then she continued whispering, "The one that said 'you promised there would be no killing'. He was there with the other one."

Then Tex guided her out on the deck again at the end of the deck. He looked all around and made sure no one was close by. Then he turned his mouth toward the microphone and asked, "Did you hear that?"

Cody said, "We only heard part of it because she wasn't speaking into the mike."

Then Tex said, "He is not the one, but he was there with the main one. He is the other one. We will stay till the dance ends if we have too. If the other one does not show up, we can get this one."

"Right."

Then he guided her back on the dance floor and toward Rich and Traci. He wanted to keep an eye on Traci as well. They finished that dance and went back by the wall and then Tex and Casey went over and got a couple more ginger ales.

Rich had already had about three drinks, and as he looked at the glass of ginger ale in Tex's hand, he said, "Tex, you can't dance the night away without a couple of drinks in you. Why don't I get you one while I get me another?"

"No thanks, Rich. I am not much of a drinker." Rich then got himself another drink and then the music started again. They all were out in the middle of the dance floor when Rich said, "Good evening, Senator. This is a wonderful dance you and Dad put together. I would like to introduce you to my special girl."

Senator Charles Lawson walked a little closer and stared at Traci as he recognized her and felt the old anger rising up in his throat, and he could not control it, as he said with anger, "Rich, I know who she is." Traci looked up and she was flabbergasted. ...She was staring at a man who looked almost like her father. She was almost in shock because he looked so much like him. But before she could get her composure, the Senator said, as he grabbed her, "May I have this dance?" And before Traci knew it she was being practically dragged in his arms and he swirled her around and as they were halfway dancing, he started talking to her about her father. "I know who you are. You are my niece. You know you favor your old man. You know, he and I were brothers, but he wouldn't claim me." Traci was trying to get Tex's attention. Tex was trying to watch Casey's expressions and Traci at the same time. He was trying to get closer to Traci. He could see the fear on her face now. As they became closer, Casey stiffened and she started frowning with a look of fear on her face. Then she laid her head on Tex's shoulder and whispered, "That is him, that's him with Traci. I would know that voice anywhere."

Tex said into the microphone, "Gotch Ya. Left door. Be careful he is dancing with Traci." Then he led Casey to the front door where Marci grabbed Casey and led her to Steven. Then Tex went back onto the dance floor and started looking for Traci. He found them making there way toward the deck, but Tex got to them just as Cody and Nick came in the left door. As they saw Tex and Traci and a man to Cody's amazement look exactly like his father, they raised a hand with their badge in it and said, "Police Officers. Stay calm folks. This will be over in a few minutes." They grabbed the Senator and pushed Traci toward Tex. While they were handcuffing the Senator, Tex grabbed Traci and made it to the front door. He pushed Traci toward Marci and he and Kato went for Samuels. They found him making his way toward the back way. Finally, they had them both handcuffed and on their way to jail.

Everyone at the dance was in shock. The announcer said, "O.K. folks. We have another hour and a half to go here." The band started up again with a very loud tune. A few couples started dancing, but most of them stayed on the sidelines whispering and wondering what was going on. The police must be mistaken. How could they arrest these two men? What could they be charged with? No one could figure out what was going on.

Meantime, Steven was taking Casey home. Casey put her face in her hands and started to cry. Steven then reached over and put his arm around her shoulder and pulled her head on his shoulder, "Casey, it's over now. Everything will be fine. You have just done a very good deed. Always remember that, and feel good about it. I know the Edwards family will always be in your debt. If it had not been for you hearing that conversation, that man back there would have gotten away with two murders."

"I know. I understand how important it is. I am crying because I am so relieved that it is over. I also understand that I will probably have to testify in court and I don't mind that. ...I was just so afraid that I would not be able to identify his voice and disappoint you all, but when I heard it, I knew then that I could never forget it."

Steven got on the phone and called home and asked for John. "John, everything went good. Casey and I are on our way home. We should be there in about thirty minutes. Tell Mom that Tex is bringing Traci home. We had no problems, but I think we all are going to be in shock as to who the killer actually is. And, John, I want you to know that Casey did great. See ya."

On the rest of the way home, Casey kept her head on Steven's shoulder and closed her eyes. She was almost sleep when they pulled into the back yard. Steven did not want to wake her up, but he leaned over and said, "Casey, we're home." She opened her eyes and he leaned over and kissed her on the cheek and said, "Thanks, Casey......Let's go inside." She smiled and then they got out of the car and walked into the kitchen where everyone was waiting including Chip and the boys. Chip came over and put his arms around her. "You're shaking. Are you alright?"

"Yes, I'm fine. I am just so glad that it is over. I was so afraid that I wouldn't be able to identify his voice, but it was so clear. I did not have a problem with it at all." She smiled as John and Mary Ann came over and gave her a hug.

Steven said, "Tex and Traci should be here shortly. Cody will be later. They had to go to the jail and help process the two men, but they will be here as soon as they can." He did not want to reveal anymore than he had to until Cody was there. He wanted Cody to be the one to tell his mother that her husband was murdered and not killed in the line of duty.

Mama E was looking at Steven with a puzzled look on her face and asking, "What happened? Did anything go wrong?"

"No, Mom. Everything went as planned, except that there were two men instead of one. There was no problem at all. In fact, Casey and Traci did a fantastic job."

He grinned. "I wouldn't mind working with them anytime. They would make very good undercover cops."

They all laughed.

"Well, Son. I am glad it is over and that no one was hurt. Who are the killers? Do we know them?"

"Yes, Mom. It is finally over. I would rather you wait for Cody and let him explain. I wasn't inside. I stayed on the outside with Marci and Kato. When it was over Tex brought Casey to the door and Marci brought her to me and we came here. She and Traci were in good hands during the whole time."

"I know that, Son. I don't doubt that."

About that time, Tex and Traci came in. Traci was all excited. She went over to her mother and said excitedly, "Mom, the killer is a senator, and, oh, Mom, he looked just like Dad. I thought I was seeing a ghost." She was trying to get her breath back on a level scale. "He grabbed me and started to force me to dance with him. He kept saying that he knew me. He said that I was his niece. That he and Dad were brothers. Mom, he looked so much like Dad that they could pass for twins."

Steven came over and said, "What are you saying, Traci? Are you saying that the killer is Dad's brother. How could that be?"

"That is what he was saying, but, Steven, he looked just like him. Wait until Cody comes and he will tell you."

Steven said, "I think that is a good idea. We will just wait for Cody and let him explain everything." He looked at Tex and John.

He was trying to figure out what was what here. Did Dad really have
a brother and his brother is the one that killed him?

Tex said, "I think that is a good idea. What do you say that we
older folks have a drink while we are waiting. Rich was trying all
night to get me to have a drink and I had to keep saying, 'no, I am not
a drinker' or 'not now'."

They all laughed as John, Steven and Tex got up to get a drink.
Steven said, "You guys want some ginger ale or tonic water to drink.
I don't want to be contributing to the delinquency of a minor here."

Then Casey said, grinning at Tex, "You should have seen Tex. I
had to calm him down a couple of times when Rich kissed Traci on
the cheek and when he was dancing with her and pulled her close to
him. ..He really shows his emotions. ...I had to reach up and kiss him
on the cheek to soften the frown on his face. Traci, that was why I
was kissing him so much. I hope you don't hold that against me."

They all laughed again.

"You damn right. You don't know how hard it was trying to
compose myself when he was saying how beautiful she was. I know
how beautiful she is. She's mine." He reached around her waist and
kissed her lightly on the lips.

They laughed again. Then Tex said, "Honey, would you like a
glass of wine? How about you, Casey? You both deserve a glass to
calm your nerves. ....What do you think, Mom?" as he looked toward
Mary Ann.

"I think if Casey wants a glass of wine, she may have ONE. Like
you said, she deserves it and it may relax her some. She is still
uptight a little. Just don't get use to the idea."

"You know me, Mom. I don't really like alcohol, but tonight I
will drink a glass."

So Tex poured five glasses. "Mama E, Mary Ann, and Sara, you three deserve a glass, too." And he handed a glass to each of them.

One of the guys said, "Don't we deserve one, too?"

Jake laughed. "You guys, I would vote that you could have a mild drink or light beer. One only, but I am not the law here."

Tex said, "I'm with Jake, but we are in Georgia and I would prefer that the Georgia Boys make the decisions. I don't see no harm in it here, but I would not want to see either one of you on the road driving while drinking or be called to a rowdy bar because of you being drunk. ....I am going to say that I am proud of you guys for what I have seen while I have been here. I don't think that we will have to worry about you all abusing alcohol, will we?"

They each said, "No Sir."

Jake spoke up, "You're right. Tex, they are good boys. They have asked me to talk to Cody about them staying on here and working. Of course, that would be up to you all, and, of course, their parents. We will need the help during the summer months, anyway."

Tim said, "But we all, except Chip, are on probation. What will happen with us?"

Steven said, "Let me talk to Mom just a minute."

"What does Mrs. Edwards have to do with our probation?"

"Just wait a minute and I will answer you." He then walked over to Mama E. "Mom, we usually hire two or three men to help Jake during the summer taking care of the hay and feed and doing odd chores around here. Do you think that we could hire these boys instead just for this summer?"

"Well, Son, I don't see why not. ...,,,Of course, if Jake thinks that will work, it will be fine with me. You and Cody talk to Jake about it."

Then Steven walked over to where the boys were and said, "I tell you what. When Cody gets here and every thing has settled down, I will talk to him. To put your mind at ease, I think we can work something out on your probation time and working here. O.K. As for Chip, that will be up to him."

They grinned, "Yes Sir" was repeated about five times.

Sara stood up and looked around. Then she asked, "Are you all getting hungry? I know that it is late, but I have a suggestion. By the time that Cody gets here and we hear all the details and I know that we all do want to hear what he has to say, we can have breakfast prepared. And sleeping through breakfast time in the morning will be enjoyed by all. What do you think, Claire?"

"I think that is a good idea." So she, Sara and Mary Ann run all of them into the living room and they started preparing breakfast. While Casey and Traci went into their rooms and changed into something more comfortable.

By the time that Traci and Casey came back into the living room, Cody, Nick, Kato and Marci were there. Cody introduced them. Then Cody went straight to Casey and then looked at Chip and said, "Chip, I hope you won't mind, but I have to give Casey a big hug. She was fantastic tonight."

Mama E said, "Son, I hope that the family of the victim in this case can have some closure now. They should be proud of what you all have done."

He looked at her with tears in his eyes and said slowly, "I think they will, Mom. I think they will."

While he still had his arms around Casey, he said, "Mom, I have something to tell you and Traci, especially," and with that Tex went over to Traci and Steven went over and put his arms around his mother. And Cody waited a moment, and then continued, "Mom, we have been led to believe that Dad died in a shootout involving drugs. .....Well, part of that is true." Mama E and Traci looked at Cody as in disbelief. Mama E started to say something, but Steven shushed her and said, "Mom, just think about what Cody is telling you now. Let it sink in and when he has finished his story, you can ask questions. O.K."

She nodded her head up and down. Then tears began to come into her eyes. *She was beginning to realize that what Cody was telling her was that what happened tonight was about Thomas. ...Was he murdered? Was he mixed up with drugs? What is Cody trying to tell us. No, no, I will never believe that he was mixed up with drugs. Oh, Thomas, I wish you were here and this did not happen. I miss you so.*

Traci was watching her and tears began to form in her eyes, too. Everything was coming into place. Tex pulled her tighter to him and she put her head on his shoulder and started to cry.

Then Cody started again, "The drug part is true. Dad was investigating a drug operation that involved our sheriff's department, these boys' probation officer, Judge Turner, two prominent men that live on the hill which are Robert Tanner who lives across from Richard Samuels and tonight ...

Traci looked up as if in disbelief and said, "What? Richard Samuels, Rich's father. ....He was involved in selling drugs. I can't believe this."

"Yes, Tracy, he was one of the big men in the drug operation and he was also with Senator Charles Lawson from North Georgia when Senator Charles Lawson shot our father intentionally."

"Oh, God, he had his arms around me and trying to force me to dance with him." And then she started rubbing her arms as if to rub his touch off her. "And he kept telling me that I was his niece. Oh, God. He looked just like Dad. And Rich. Did he know? I have to talk to Rich. I have to talk to Rich."

Tex was trying to console her and quiet her so that Cody could go on and finish this up. Traci was just going on and on as if she couldn't stop.

Mama E was looking at Traci as if in disbelief. "This can't be true. ....Thomas didn't have a brother. Something is wrong here......"

Then Cody interrupted her with, "Yes, Mom and Traci, he is the one that shot your husband and our father in cold blood." He stopped because his mother and Traci were having a hard time taking it all in. Sara was crying, also. In fact, almost everyone in the room was crying.

When he started again, he said, "This girl right here" and he hugged her tight, "witnessed our father being shot. That is why tonight was so important and why Casey is so special to us." And he bent down and kissed her on the cheek and then said, "I think Chip would like for you to be with him now."

Then Cody went over to his mother and Steven and said, "Mom, I know that this is hard on you now, but after you have had time to think about it, you can have some closure with it. We all will have closure with it." He patted her on the shoulder. "When you feel like it we would like to ask you some questions about Dad's side of the family, but not now."

Everyone was quiet for a few minutes until Mama E and Traci got their composure back. Sara got up and went over and hugged all of them and said, "You all stay here for awhile, Mary Ann and I will put breakfast on the table and the ones that want to eat can sit down." So after giving their condolences to the Edwards family, she, Jake, John, Mary Ann and Marci went into the kitchen and started putting the plates, napkins and utensils out. It would be served cafeteria style as usual. Then came Kato, Nick and the boys. They left the Edwards alone so they could have their privacy.

The young boys had been startled by all of this, but they were feeling sad for the Edwards. They were just on the sidelines watching and being very quiet. But when Sara and the others went into the kitchen, they went also, including Chip and Casey. Jake and John set up two tables for the adults and a couple of card tables for the boys in the pantry which was adjoining the kitchen with a wide area in the center. With the folding doors open, it was an extension to the kitchen.

By the time the Edwards came into the kitchen, the boys had gone through the line and the men had started through the line. Sara was standing by the stove in case someone wanted fried or sunny-side-up eggs instead of scrambled. They had pancakes, bacon, sausages, biscuits, scrambled eggs, jelly, jam, syrup, whipped cream, and fresh fruit cut up to top the pancakes or to eat by itself, and, of course, orange juice and a large pot of coffee. After the men, Mama E and Traci went through the line. A few minutes later, all were setting down eating a good hearty breakfast. It was now three-thirty in the morning. It was somewhat quiet because everyone was going over what had happened tonight and it began to feel like a quiet peace going over the crowd. By the time that breakfast was over, Mama E and Traci had accepted the reality that Thomas Edwards was murdered by his supposedly half brother, the Senator.

Nick, Kato and Marci said their goodbyes and said that they would be in touch and then left. After the boys had gotten all the garbage together, they took it to the dumpster and then went to their rooms. It took them a long time before going to sleep. They were happy that Steven, Nick and Cody would help them with their probation. They were thankful that Chip had introduced them to Nick, Cody and Steven.

After the kitchen was cleaned and they had a second cup of coffee, Jake and Sara left knowing that Mama E and Traci would be alright.

Chip and Casey had gone outside when the boys left. They stayed out under the trees while Casey explained to Chip all that had happened at the dance. She came in when Jake and Sara left and Chip walked down the path with them.

When Casey came in, she and Mary Ann went to their room and John went upstairs to his room.

It wasn't long before each one was in their beds, but it was hard for them to fall asleep. Finally, sleep came for all of them and lasted a long time. It was very late in the day, when Cody, John and Tex came downstairs. No one else was up. So, Cody made a big pot of coffee. By the time the coffee was ready, Steven had come down. They sat there with a cloud over their heads and drinking a cup of coffee. You know, how you feel when you are sleeping at odd times and can't seem to wake up completely. Each one explaining what they knew and saw about last night. John was enjoying listening to them. He was happy that he and, especially Casey, could contribute to their sorrowful, but happy ending, if you can call it that. He had called Elaine early this morning and let her know that everything was fine and that Mary Ann was spending the weekend with them and that they would be home Sunday morning. He would go into detail when he got home.

After everyone had come into the kitchen, Mama E, Mary Ann, Casey and Traci started heating up leftovers. Traci asked, "Does anyone want anything other than leftovers for now. We had so much left over; it would be a shame to throw it out."

Mary Ann said, "No. Don't do that. We eat leftovers all the time. That is the pleasure of cooking a lot at one time. You don't have to cook for awhile. A lot of foods are better when they are left over."

Mama E said, "Yes, they are. But if anyone wants eggs, either way, just say so. They are better cooked fresh."

Traci said, "Tex, I am sorry, but I have to call Rich and see how he is. I know he must hate me now. I had no idea that his father was involved. He must know that. I can't live with myself if he thinks that I knew and did what I did to him. And his mother. She was so upset. She was screaming things at me."

"You're right, Sweetheart, but you need to give him the weekend to sort things out. You should talk with him, but not over the phone. You should do it in person and I will go with you to help explain the situation to him and to be there for your support. If he is angry with anyone, it should be his father, but that is his problem. Not yours.

You need to stay away from his mother right now. You understand what I am saying?"

"Yes, and I am glad that you will be with me, but I have to do the talking. O.K."

"Sure. That's fine, but not now." He knew how she must feel. It would only be right that she talk to him. After all, he was used in the worst way, but not by her. She did not know that his father was targeted in this investigation.

Then Traci turned to her mother, "Mom, I have to know about that man that says he is Dad's brother. Why haven't we heard of him before?"

'Traci, Honey, You know more about him than I do. This is the first time I have ever heard of there being a brother to Thomas."

Steven said, "You must have heard something in your earlier years when you and Dad married or sometime back then."

"Kids, the only thing that I heard back then was that your grandfather on your father's side was working in North Georgia with some construction company. He came home one winter when there was an ice storm and they couldn't work for several days. That was when he met your grandmother and fell madly in love with her and he never went back to North Georgia. They were married in three or four months. Of course, the families knew each other all their lives so no one thought anything about them getting married. It was not that they had to get married. You could look at them and see that they were madly in love with one another. Your father wasn't born until they had been married three years or so."

Cody said, "Our grandfather never said anything about having a son in North Georgia. This man looks to be three or four years older than Dad."

"No, Son. He didn't. Your grandfather was a good man. Evidently, he did not know about the boy if he was the father."

"Well, Mom, it would be hard for him to deny him. Like Traci said, he looks exactly like Dad. They could pass for twins, if it wasn't for the age difference."

"I'm sure your grandfather nor father knew about him. Your grandfather was not one to shuck responsibility. He would have supported him or brought him here to live with him. He loved children and would never deny a son or daughter. I am sure of that."

"Mom, he had a lot of hatred for Dad. ....He was very angry and adamant about anything that he said about Dad. He was a very angry man. ....I don't know how he could have become a senator."

"Yes, he had a lot of hatred in him for Dad and for us. When he grabbed me and was talking to me, he had a lot of venom coming out with his words." Traci shivered remembering last night.

"Evidently, he hated Thomas terribly in order to kill him."

Cody said, "Mom, I'm sure he hated him probably because he grew up with his father and he was without one. But, I think the real reason he killed Dad is because Dad was getting too close in his investigation of the drug operation. Mom, the Senator was the top man in that operation. The reason I say this is because he had one of the guys in our group destroy all the evidence that Dad had gathered. We looked everywhere for Dad's backup information that he always had for himself, but we could not find it. Nick, Tex and I had to start from scratch on this investigation. What started this investigation was Chip giving Nick information about Casey. That is why Nick and I went to see Tex that weekend. That is why Tex came here to help us in the investigation."

"Son, everything is making sense to me now. ...But you say all your father's information was destroyed."

"Yes, a guy by the name of Eduardo Garcia in our section destroyed all the paperwork."

Cody and the others were looking at Mama E because she had a frown on her face as though she was in deep thought. Steven asked, "Mom, what is it?"

"You know, before your father left that night, he gave me an envelope, very thin. I didn't think there was anything in it. He asked me to put it in the lock box. He said, 'This is something that the boys may need later.' He didn't act as though it was important, so I put it in the envelope with the copies of our marriage certificate and a few other papers."

Cody looked startled as he said, "Mom, we took out everything out of his lock box, even that envelope." ....Then he added talking slowly as he was thinking about that night they were going through his things. We went through ..everything,... but we didn't look ...in that envelope,...... did we? Because it was your personal things."

"I don't remember, Son. But the envelope is still in the lock box if you want to check. I know he did make copies sometimes of things at work and bring them here and put them in his box, but there weren't any when we went through it right after his death. But, he did say that 'this is something the boys may need later'. Do you suppose ...."

Before she could finish, Steven was up from his chair and was walking back to her bedroom to the lock box. He came back with the envelope and handed it to Cody. "Here, Bro, you look inside. It is thin, though. I don't know what could be in there that we may need later. It doesn't feel like a key. Maybe one sheet of paper. Maybe it's a code or something. ....Hurry up, Cody. It sure is taking you a long time to open that. Now, I am curious."

Cody finally got the envelope open and inside was one sheet of paper. Cody began to read the note, "Sons, in case something happens to me, all the information on my investigation is in a large brown envelope under the floor in my office. The file cabinet in the corner is on top of a loose board. Don't let anyone know about this, except Lieutenant Moss. Sergeant Roberts is a good man. I misjudged him at first, but he can be a big help to you."

"Also, Steve Sandberg, a jeweler at the shopping mall near the farm, made a watch for me. The one that I wore at all times while on duty. Cody, I left it to you since you are the oldest. On the back of the watch, there is a little tip of a knob. Raise the metal lip and press the tip. It is a recording device. I use it when I think it is necessary. You may find it useful."

They all looked at one another, not knowing what to expect. Finally, Steven said, "Bro, do you think there may be something on the recorder?"

Cody said with concern, "It may be. I put it in my lock box. I haven't worn it because I didn't want anything to happen to it. I will get it in a minute."

Then Cody continued to read, "Good Luck, Sons, in your investigations. I know that you will do a great job, especially if you follow in your old man's footsteps. Goodbye, Cody, Steven and Traci. I love you three, dearly. Continue with your good work and may Traci follow in our footsteps if that is what she wants to do. Goodbye Traci, my pride and joy. You three take care of your mother. She will need you. Signed, Your Dad forever."

Mama E and Traci started sobbing and in between sobs, Mama E said, "I'm sorry, Cody. I had no idea what was in that envelope. And with all that was going on, I completely forgot about it."

Cody walked over and patted her on the shoulder. He did not know whether to go get the watch and bring it downstairs and let everyone listen to it or to wait until he and Steven could listen to it first. "That's alright, Mom. It wasn't your fault. We were all there. ...It has turned out alright. What we will do is find his reports and compare them with what we have and then combine them before going to court." *If only we had seen this when we first started, but Mom didn't know and we didn't think to look there. We were looking for papers and folders and/or large envelopes. I'll call Nick and we will go to the office in the morning. I'll call Lieutenant Moss and let him know, too.*

About that time the phone began to ring and it was Nick. "Hey, did I wake you?"

"No, Nick, you didn't. We have even eaten breakfast again and were sitting here talking."

"Then I guess you haven't turned on your television today. You and I are heroes, except for a few others that are close to Lawson and Samuels. They are calling us publicity hounds and calling for an investigation on the Edwards. That is just a few of their friends. You know the news media, they want to sell, so they pick who they want to put on the air. Of course, that is the bias station and you are taking the blunt of it. That's the thanks we get, uh, Pardner. Overall, the ones that count think that we are heroes. The main stations are what counts."

"No, we haven't. No one has thought about turning on the television. Why? What's happening other than us getting blasted?"

"I guess the reporters got our pictures from the department. They are all over the television screen. Of course, the reporters are playing it up, and they are really praising our good work. I wanted to let you know that they want a statement from you on these arrest, and, especially about your father's murder. From what I can figure out, they are waiting at the station to talk to you, but Lieutenant Moss told the reporters that because of the circumstances, you were not available at this time. As soon as you were available, he would let them know."

"Thanks, we'll turn it on."

Steven got up and turned the television on and all you could see was Senator Charles Lawson and Richard Samuels picture plastered all over the screen.

Mama E looked up and she was flabbergasted. "He does look like Thomas. Oh, God. This is terrible."

Meantime, Cody was still on the phone with Nick. "Oh, Nick, we need to meet in the morning. I'll be there around eight. Is that alright with you?"

"Yeah, sure. What is this about?"

"You know we were looking for Dad's file a few weeks ago. Well, I think I know where it is. I'll tell you more about it in the morning. See you then."

"Sure, Cody. Bye."

Steven said, "Cody, you and Nick are heroes. Listen to this reporter. ...But, Cody, why are you waiting until in the morning?"

"Because that will be the best time to go into the office with less personnel there. Also, I have to contact Lieutenant Moss and have him meet us there. Plus, the reporters won't be expecting us then. Hopefully." Cody grinned. "It is the Lieutenant's office, after all, and I promised him that I would not go in it when he wasn't there, if he would not go in mine. Of course, that was when we weren't sure of him."

"Oh, I get it. You actually told him that."

"Yes, I did. We had a mutual understanding."

They laughed.

All of a sudden, Traci said, "Look, there is Rich and his mother, running from the reporters. Oh, I have got to talk to Rich. I know he hates me."

"Look, Sweetheart, I told you to give it a day or two and I will go with you. He is still angry now and will be the rest of today because of the way the reporters are after him and his mother. We'll see him later."

"O.K., but I have to talk with him."

They all watched television for a while longer and then decided that they had seen enough. Mama E went into her bedroom to lay down for a while. Mary Ann and Casey went to pack her clothes for tomorrow morning. John did the same. Traci decided to lay down for a few minutes to get her thoughts together and absorb everything that had happened. The three guys went out under the trees and laid in the hammocks, After going outside and settling down in a hammock, Cody said, "I didn't mention the watch on purpose. When it is convenient for us three, we will go upstairs and listen. I don't know if Mom and Traci should hear what is on it or not. That is why I want to wait. What do you two think?"

Steven and Tex both said that they thought they should wait and hear what was on it first before letting anyone else hear it.

About half an hour later, John joined them there. It was a lazy afternoon.

Later that evening they had dinner and just sat around and talked. Cody phoned Lieutenant Moss and he agreed to meet them around eight o'clock the next morning at his office. Cody did not tell him why he wanted to meet with him. The Lieutenant thought that Cody wanted to go over everything with him. He also informed Cody to have a press release written to the Public Relations guy to give to the press. If Cody wanted him to, he would help him write it in the morning. Cody agreed because he was not one to write up speeches.

Casey and John talked to Mary Ann about whether Casey should go back or stay with her Mom. After talking with Cody and Tex they decided that Casey should go back and just play it by ear. The Bond Hearing was coming up and they weren't sure what would happen with it. It would be safer for her there. They did not want to take any chances until after the trial. Tex assured her and John that he and/or his father would still check on her until the trial or as long as necessary. Since they would be leaving early the next morning for the office, they said their goodbyes that night and promised to keep in touch.

The next morning Cody, Tex and Steven left early to go to Nick's place so they all could listen to the recording on Cody's watch before going to the station. Steven wanted to be there, too. So he drove his car to Nick's place ,in case, for some reason, Traci could not take Casey, John and Mary Ann to the airport, he would come home in time to take them. Traci was to call him. ......As it turned out, Traci called Steven and said that she was feeling better and could take them to the airport and then take Mary Ann home.

While at Nick's place, Cody told Nick everything about the note that his father had left. Then he told him about the watch. They all were anxious to hear if anything was on the recorder. So, they sat at the table and Cody turned the watch over and hit the tip. There was a conversation in the beginning, but it didn't mean anything to them. Then they heard his father say, "Today is November 23rd, I just received a call from someone of which I did not recognize the voice. He stated that I should meet him near the Crafton warehouse if I want some information on the drug operation." ...Then there were a couple of clicks and then you could hear the car door open. "All right, you brought me down here, now show your face where I can see you." After a couple of seconds, "I'm right here, Edwards. Get away from your car." "I'll get away from my car, when you step out here." "All right, Edwards. I'll show my face. I think you will be surprised." "Who are you and what do you want?" "I want you to see me good. ..You see, I am your brother that no one wants to talk about." "I do not have a brother. Who are you?"

After a few moments of silence, "Like I said, "I am your lost brother. I am the one that you are after in this drug operation, but you will never catch me. I am smarter than you are. You are getting close, though. That is why I have to shoot you and I want to kill you myself." BOOM.....BOOM "Now, you Son-of-A-Bitch. You won't get in my way. I now have my revenge for being your half-brother." A little noise, then, "You killed him. He didn't know anything about us." ...."He was getting too close and too suspicious, that's why I called him and told him that a drug transaction was taking place here." "That's Edwards, you Son-Of-A-Bitch. You can't get away with that? The department will be all over you." "All we have to do is get his files and destroy the ones that point to us. He was getting too close. A friend of his told me Edwards knew that higher ups were involved in the drug deals, but he wasn't exactly sure who." ....Then the tape ran until the end with just street noise on it.

When Cody, Tex, Nick and Steven walked into the station, the outer office was empty. The Lieutenant was sitting in his office. After greeting each other and a few comments about the news media, Cody handed Lieutenant Moss the note. He read the note with disbelief. "You knew that he had copies somewhere, but no one knew where. Where did you find this?"

Cody answered, "Dad gave this note to Mom the night he left the house and told her to put that in his lock box because the boys may want to see this. She thought it was something personal and put it in the envelope with their marriage license and personal stuff. Then she forgot about it until we were talking about the investigation and something we said triggered her thinking cap and she remembered this piece of paper."

Lieutenant Moss smiled as he read the note. "You know that is one of the best compliments a person can give another." He actually had tears in his eyes. Then he added, "That man was a prince to me. ...Well, let's look and see what we have. It is a shame that we could not have had this information when you all started the investigation. What about the watch? Was there any information on it?"

Cody said, "Oh, yes, Lieutenant. I'll play it for you. We heard it a few minutes ago. We have the actual conversation when my father was killed." Tears were mounting in Cody and Steven's eyes, but Cody played it for the Lieutenant. When it was finished, they all had tears in their eyes. It took them a few minutes to compose themselves.

Lieutenant Moss said sadly, "You can't ask for more than that from a man who completed his investigation and solved his own murder."

"Let's get started and move this file cabinet. I am anxious to find out what he knew up to the time of his death," said Steven as he started to move toward the file cabinet and moving the tray off the top of it.

Then the others came over and they moved the file cabinet and sure enough there was a board that was not nailed down. They lifted it up and there was the box with files, video tapes and recording tapes in it. Each file was labeled and each tape was labeled as to what was on it. Everything was well organized. "That is my father's way," said Cody.

Lieutenant Moss said, "Yes, it is. He was a neat and organized man. I try to do things like him, but I come no where close to him."

Cody looked at Moss and said, "You do quite well, Lieutenant."

As they were looking through the files at the list of witnesses and what each witness said, Nick and Steven went into the conference room and brought the VCR back and hooked it up. They watched the videos first. One on Judge Turner threatening several women for sex. The two women that appeared in court were on the tape. One tape of the warehouse when the van drove up and Samuels, Santino, Tanner, Garcia and Wilson driving up to the warehouse and going inside with the van drivers. On one occasion the Senator was there with Samuels, but stayed away from the others. They did not know that he was there. Then it showed the men leaving with bags of cocaine and other drugs with them. Everything was well documented. Then they listened to the recording tapes of the witnesses.

Nick said, "Everything was here. We just duplicated what he had done. The main thing is that we did it. Cody, you are really following in your father's footsteps. The only thing is we have a witness to his killer. And we have the tape of the shooting that he had. That finishes his investigation."

Cody said, "Yes, another thing, I haven't seen any evidence that he knew that the Senator was his half-brother, but I am sure that when he saw the likeness, he knew then that somehow they were kin and the senator was telling the truth."

"Cody, it would not have made any difference to him because he would have arrested him anyway. You know how he felt about drugs and anyone selling it."

"That's true, Steven. It would not have made any difference."

Tex went over and stood between them and put one arm around each shoulder. "Brothers, he would be very proud of the three of you today. Don't either of you ever forget that."

They both just nodded their heads.

"Cody, I'll sign this out to you or we can keep it here where it was. I don't think we should put this in the evidence room. There are others that may not be involved, but would destroy evidence to keep the others from going to trial. Whichever you prefer."

"Lieutenant, I have our evidence locked up at home. I will leave the watch there. I will not let it get out of my hands, evidence or not. I think we should leave this where we found it and only the ones in this room will know where it is. We could use some of this with our evidence in court."

"That's a good idea, Sergeant. You know where it is if any of you need it." So they put it back and then talked for a few minutes. ...Then the Lieutenant said, "Oh, by the way, Cody, I wrote this statement for the news media. Read it and see what you think. I'll give it to our Public Relations person for the press if you approve it."

After reading it, Cody said, "You have done a good job on it, Lieutenant. It is a very good writeup. I would not change a thing."

"Good, then I'll take it there myself and make sure that it is not changed before being released to the press. Good work, you guys. Like Tex said, your father would be very proud of you. Somehow, I feel that he knows what you guys have done and that what he started you have finished."

421

Cody smiled at him and said, "Thank you, Lieutenant. I hope so. Well, Nick and I will see you in the morning at regular time unless something else comes up between now and then."

"O. K. Sergeant."

After they had put the box back, they walked out to the parking lot and decided that Tex would go back with Steven because Cody wanted to go by and see Corrie. He had talked to her a few times over the weekend, but had not seen her. He was really missing her now.

Cody dropped Nick off at his place and then went to the Carillo's house. Only Corrie and her mother were there. They were all excited about what they had done and praising him. Nick had told them all that he could about everything. Mrs. Carillo had called Claire and they talked for quite a while on Saturday evening. Cody spent about an hour there and then left to go home. His head was beginning to feel dopey. The weekend had been all messed up. Now, maybe, they could get back to normal. This was what he was thinking on the way back home. As he came up the driveway, he saw some reporters from different television stations in the front yard. He got out of the car and ordered all of them off the property. When he was asked a question, 'Did you know that the senator was your uncle? Or, 'When did you know he was head of this drug operation?' Or, what led you to believe that he killed your father?' He just said, "No Comment. The Public Relations person is getting ready to read a written statement for you at the station. You will miss it if you don't leave now." Then they all left.

He went into the house and Mama E and Sara were at the table drinking ice tea and eating a piece of cake. "Mom, how long have those reporters been outside? Have they bothered you?"

"No, Son, one came to the door and Sara told them that no one here was going to make a statement and then closed and locked the door. We have just ignored them outside. We figured that they would get tired of waiting and leave. Are they still there?"

"Not anymore. I sent them to the station. I told them that a Public Relations person was giving a statement at the station. He will be sometime. I am not sure when. They won't bother us again. If they do, let me know. I feel tired. I am going to lay down. Did Traci get John, Casey and Mary Ann off all right?"

"Yes, she called and said that John and Casey got off all right and that she was at Mary Ann's. She would be there for a little while. I think she, Casey and Mary Ann bonded while they were here. She likes them very much. Also, Tex and Steven are out just riding around. Steven called and said that they would be home later this afternoon. .....O.K., Son, you go get some rest. We will have an early dinner since we have just been nibbling all morning and haven't really had lunch."

"That's all right with me. See you later." And with that he went up the stairs pulling off his clothes as he walked into his bedroom. He put on his lounging pants laid across the bed. It wasn't long before he was snoring. It was like a load had been taken off his shoulders.

When Tex and Steven came home, Tex opened the door and saw how good he was sleeping, he closed the door again. *He wanted to let Cody know that he had not forgotten about the farm. That he talked to Rusty yesterday and they agreed to meet today. The deal on the farm is now complete. The Graves had one month to move out. In fact, Rusty had said that he was going to start moving them the following week. He and Steven had gone over that afternoon.* He went to his room and stripped off his clothes and laid across the bed. It wasn't long before he was sound asleep. Steven did the same thing. All three were exhausted mentally as well as physically.

A couple of hours later, Tex woke up with Cody standing over him. "Wake up, Tex. We forgot to go over and see Rusty yesterday."

Finally, Tex got his eyes open and looked up right into Cody's face. "Hey, man, give me a minute to get my head straight."

"I'm sorry I woke you up, but I just thought about we were suppose to go over to the Graves yesterday."

By that time Tex's head had cleared and he sat up. "Bro, I went into your room when Steven and I came in but you were sleep." Then he added very angrily, "I DIDN'T WAKE YOU." Then he smiled. "I came in to tell you that I had talked to Rusty and set everything up for today. That was where Steven and I went earlier. Now, I am the proud owner of a farm."

Cody put his arm around his shoulders and hugged him. "Congratulations, Bro, I am very happy for you. When do you plan to tell Traci?"

"I think I will wait until I come back and we start to make plans for our wedding. What do you think?"

"I think you should do what you want to do. We will not say anything. It will be up to you to tell her. But I think she will be very happy about it. .... Man, I can't believe this."

They grinned at each other. "I can't believe it either, but Cody, I know that this is right. It is so right."

"I'm happy for both of you."

Then Steven walked in and sat on the side of the bed on the other side. They talked for about thirty

minutes about the farm deal and Tex's plans. Then They heard a knock on the door. It was Traci.

"Dinner will be ready in ten minutes. Last call."

They laughed. "We'll be there."

When they came down for dinner, Mama E and Traci were sitting at the table. The three got their plates and filled it and sat down with them. "Well, boys, it feels good to just relax with the family. I enjoyed the company we had, but it feels good to be together with just us for awhile."

"You're right, Mom. It is so quiet around here now that it seems like someone is missing. I really enjoyed Mary Ann and Casey. I spent some time with Mary Ann today and we had a nice chat. I like them both very much and we plan to keep in touch."

Cody said, "I'm glad, Sis, because I liked them, too. Later on when the cases have been to trial and everything has been settled, we are planning a celebration and invite everyone that was involved in the case."

"Son, I think that will be real nice. Maybe a big down-home barbecue in the back yard."

Then the conversation was about Tex leaving and when he was planning to come back. Mostly, quiet and relaxing, nothing exciting or loud. They were enjoying it.

After dinner, Tex and Traci went outside and sat under the trees in one of the hammocks. Cody and Steven stayed inside and helped Mama E clean up the kitchen. They wanted to give Tex and Traci some time alone since Tex was leaving Tuesday morning. Traci would be working tomorrow.

"Tex, I sure wish you weren't leaving, but I know that you have to go back to your job and your family. You said before that we would have a serious talk after the investigation was over. ....Well, it's over."

He pulled her close to him, "Yes, Sweetheart, I say that and that is why we are out here right now. I dared your brothers to come out here tonight. So we have the night alone. First of all, I want to say that 'I love you'. This trip has made me realize more each day what you mean to me. You may not believe this, but I was thinking about you at home as I was packing and all the way here while driving down the road. When I got here and saw you and kissed you 'hello', I knew then why I had been thinking about you so much lately."

"I felt the same way when you kissed me when you came. I went straight upstairs to get Cody and I told him then that I knew who I wanted to be my first. I told him not to laugh and I am telling you now not to laugh at me. I know that I am an odd ball, but ...."

He didn't let her finish her sentence because he was kissing her right on the lips and a very passionate kiss. "Honey, you are not an odd ball and don't you dare feel that way. I told you before that you were exquisite and I meant every bit of it." He turned her to face him and he looked squarely into her eyes and said, "Sweetheart, I'm sorry, but I can't say the same. I did feel close to a couple of girls, but something always happened that I couldn't make a commitment. .... Now, I know why. I was waiting for you and I have no problem making a commitment to you. I am asking you to marry me. If you need to think about it, I'll wait for your answer."

"Oh, Tex, I love you, and I want to say 'Yes', but I am not sure I can live in Texas. I will if I have to, as a last resort, but what are your plans?"

"Then, you are saying 'Yes'. Sweetheart, I plan to go back to Texas Tuesday morning and give notice at my job and talk to my father and sister and see what we can work out. I don't want my father to be by himself, but I am sure that we can work things out. I want to live here with you. I don't want you to go to Texas if you don't want to."

"You don't mind living here. .....Are you sure?"

"Yes, I am sure. In fact, I was not going to tell you this until I came back, but I will so that you can

be thinking about it. I am the one that bought the farm next to you all." She started changing her expression from sad to happy and back to sad. She didn't know how she felt. But before she could say anything, he continued, "Listen, Sweetheart, I bought it in the hopes that you would live there. But, if you feel that you have to stay here, I'll stay here with you. I bought it for us to live in or for investment for us. I am telling you this so that you can talk it over with Mama E. Steven and Cody already know about it. All I am asking is that you

426

think about it and also, while I am gone, you start to think about what type of wedding you want and when you want to get married."

She put her head down on his chest. "This is all so fast. I do have a lot to think about, don't I?"

"Yes, you do. That will give you something to do until I get back. How long that will take, I don't know yet, but it will be as soon as possible."

They were quiet for a while. Each one thinking their own thoughts. Then he asked, "What are you thinking about?"

"I was just thinking how happy I am and how it would be living on the farm next to ours. Mom will be happy with me living there. Anywhere else, I don't know how she would feel, but there, she would be O.K. with it. My brothers, too. I think they would be O.K. with that."

"Yes, they would. They were very happy about it. In fact, Cody said, 'I am very happy for you two and don't feel bad about leaving Mom by herself. She will never be by herself. Corrie has said before that she had no problem living here if that was necessary. It didn't matter with her as long as she was with me.' So, he does not want you to feel that you have to live here. Of course, this will always be your home, too."

She reached up and kissed him, "Oh, Tex, I love you so. When do you think you will be coming back?"

"As soon as possible. Hopefully, no more than two to three weeks. I'll know more after I have a talk with my father. I'll call you every day or at least every other day."

"When will the Graves move out of the house and where will they go?"

"Rusty is moving them to their place up north. He doesn't want to leave them alone any longer. That is why they are selling the farm.

427

We signed the papers this afternoon. He is going to start moving them next week, but they have a month to get everything that they want out of the house. All the farm equipment and outside machinery will stay. They will not have room for all the furniture, so they are taking only what they want. The rest goes with the house or ours to do what we want with it. We will take a look at it and probably have a sale or something to get rid of it."

"Do you think they will mind if I go over and look at it? I am so excited about having a place of my own. Of course, I always thought I would be living here. I know that this will always be a part of me and my home, but having a farm of our own will be a part of both of us. Oh, Tex, I am so happy. It seems like a dream."

"It is, Sweetheart. It is our dream, and we will make everything that we possibly can come true. You haven't mentioned an engagement ring, but I plan to bring it when I come back. Then we will announce our engagement and set a wedding date. O.K."

"O.K." And then she snuggled in his arms and they were quiet for a while.

After a while she said, "Tex, I haven't talked to Rich yet. I wanted you to go with me when I talked to him. I have to set things right with him. He probably won't see me, but I have to try. Do you understand?"

"Yes, I understand. Tomorrow night we will make it

a point to go and see him. Remind me. O.K."

"O.K. I will. ....Oh, Tex, you are so understanding."

When they came into the house, everyone had gone to their own room to read, watch television, or whatever. Tex walked quietly upstairs to his room, as Traci went to hers. She had changed the sheets on the bed and made it back into her room again that afternoon. It felt good to be in a room by herself again. She was so excited that she could hardly go to sleep, but it finally came. She slept very good and woke up feeling great.

She dreaded going into work this morning because she knew that there would be talk everywhere about what had happened on the weekend, her brothers, her uncle.

And as she expected, everybody gathered around her asking her questions and she answered as best she could without being personal and getting too much into the police part of it. Steven did the same where he worked. He said as little as he could without being rude. Any reporters, they referred them to Public Relations personnel. Hopefully, it would be over soon.

Cody and Nick were having the same problem, so the Lieutenant told them to go out on the road and do whatever they could find to do away from the office. So they went into the neighborhood of Mrs. Stevens and Mrs. Harris and checked with them and talked to them and told them everything they could. They were very appreciative about it. No one had given them this much attention before. This experience began to renew their faith about the police department because of Cody and Nick. After spending some time there, they also went to see Chip's mother and told her how sorry they were that she was not able to come over part of the weekend that Casey was there, but they expected her to be at the celebration later. They only talked to her for a little while. She was at work so they did not want to take up too much of her time. They also went to speak with Tim's mother for a few minutes. They explained to her that they plan to speak up for Tim and that the boys wanted to work on at the farm the rest of the summer. If they did, it would take care of their probation. Of course, they would get paid, but only a little each week. At the end of the summer, they would get the rest of their earnings. They thought that would be best for them. She agreed and was very appreciative of what Cody and Nick were doing. She hoped that Tim had learned his lesson. Cody told her that he felt sure that he had. He was a good kid.

Then they left and went to the Edwards' place for lunch and to be with Tex since it was his last day. He was probably ready for someone to drag him away from Mama E and Sara. They were sure he had had enough of woman talk. But, actually, he had enjoyed himself. He had two women laughing at his jokes and innuendoes. He was entertaining them and they were enjoying it. A lot of it was about him being a farmer. They were just sitting down to lunch when Cody and Nick came in. So they sat down with them and ate lunch.

After cleaning up the kitchen, the three guys went out under the trees to pass the time of day. Tex had already packed his things and was ready to go first thing in the morning. He was dreading the trip, yet he was looking forward to it. He would like to see his father and talk to him. The sooner he made this trip, the sooner he would be back. They were talking about things in general and Tex told Nick about the farm. Then Tex asked, "Cody, when would be a good time to put in an application for the Sheriff's Department? I was thinking that maybe I should go see Lieutenant Moss and see what he has to say. He told me to see him if and when I decided to move here. What do you think?"

"I think that you should go talk to him now. It may be that he can request you to be in his section. With Garcia gone, we will have an opening. The sooner you get your name in the pot, the better chance you will have of working with the experts. Are you sure that is what you want to do?"

"Yes, damn it. How many times do I have to tell you that. I am serious about moving here. I bought the farm next door, didn't I?"

The others laughed along with Cody. "I was just kidding you, Man. Why don't we just take a trip to the station and then to personnel and have you fill out an application. Maybe we can find Kato and Marci. You could see them before you leave. How about that?"

"That would be great. I would like to see them before I leave. Although, I plan to be back in a few weeks. But let's go."

So Cody went inside to get his keys and to let Mama E know that they were going to ride off for awhile and would be back later.

When they arrived at the station, Lieutenant Moss was in his office with Roberts and Thompson. He was going over some new cases that came in that morning. He motioned for Cody, Nick and Tex to come in the office. Roberts congratulated all of them and said a job well done. He was glad that it was over. They talked for a few minutes and then Thompson and Roberts went out front to their desk and started the routine of organizing the new cases that they had received.

Lieutenant Moss looked from one and then the other and then said, "What can I do for you?"

"Lieutenant, you said before that if I decided to move here to come and see you. Well, I am here to see you. My plans are to relocate here and work for the Sheriff's Department." He laughed, and then continued, "Since we have made a vacancy in this section, I was wondering what I could do to fill that vacancy?"

Lieutenant Moss laughed. "I was hoping you would stay. You go to personnel and get an application and I will hand carry it to each section that it will have to go. Wait a minute, I may have an application here." He looked in his personnel file cabinet and came out with an application. "You take this home with you and Cody can bring it in tomorrow and I will take care of the rest. O.K."

"Yes, thanks, Lieutenant. I really appreciate it. Thanks again."

"Thank you for helping us out here. I'm sure you were a big help to Cody and Nick and the others. When are you planning to come back."

"I hope it will only be a couple of weeks before I can be back. I need to talk with my father and make sure that he won't be living by himself. Although he is healthy and capable of doing so, I want to talk with him first. But I will be back. Here is my card if you need to reach me, and, also, I will be in constant contact with Cody." Then Tex stuck his hand out to shake hands with the Lieutenant and they said their goodbyes. Then the three left to find Kato.

After they got in the car, Cody called Kato, but did not get him so he left a message on the answering machine. They started toward Nick's place and thought they would hang out there until they could reach Kato. Before they reached Nick's place, Kato returned the call. "Hey, Man, you caught me in the shower. I heard the phone ringing, but couldn't get to it."

That's O.K. We are just hanging out. Tex wanted to see you and Marci before he left in the morning."

"Sure, I am here by myself, though. Marci called me earlier and said that she would talk to this witness that we were to see today. There was no need for me to go with her. Come on over. I'll leave a message on her machine and tell her to come over when she gets in."

So they headed for Kato's place. He had a big pot of coffee ready and some pastry. After they talked for a while, Marci came in and joined the group. After she greeted everyone, she said, "You know, Judge Turner sure had a lot of sex. Since those two women came forward, there have been six more wanting to talk. Of course, you have to weed out the ones that just want publicity and the real ones. Out of the six, I would say five are telling the truth. The other one I'll have to talk to a little more before she convinces me that she is telling the truth."

Nick said, "That should put Judge Turner away for a while. He won't be on the bench anymore."

They all agreed with Nick and laughed because they felt good about getting him off the bench. In fact, they felt good that they had concluded the investigation and put as many as they had in jail.

Then Cody told Kato and Marci about finding his father's file and that he had a video tape of some women meeting Judge Turner. He would check it to see which women were on the tape. Also, he told them about all the information that his father had found out and about the watch.

They were very happy to hear that and they talked about that for awhile. Of course, Cody did not tell them where the file was hidden.

Then Cody and Nick started teasing Tex about being shot and Marci saving him. Then Kato joined in with them. Marci was quiet for a few minutes. Then she said with a half grin, "Leave Tex alone. He has had enough of that. Besides, his problem is that he is in love and can't get his mind on anything else."

Cody said, "Yes, he is in love, alright. Tex, did you tell Kato and Marci about the farm you bought?"

"No, I haven't. You all have not given me any time to say anything. Yes, I bought the farm next to the Edwards. Traci seems to be pleased with the idea. We were lucky in that respect because she said that she wasn't sure she could live anywhere else. But next door would be great. And, also, I have an application to fill out for the Sheriff's Department and Lieutenant Moss is going to use his influence to try to get me in his section since they now have a vacancy. I would be very pleased if I could work with you guys again. I have enjoyed this visit so much. It has been very fruitful for me. The Good Lord must be on my side. I have a lot to be thankful for right now."

"Yes, we all do. I have a lot to be thankful for, too. One is to have friends like you all and, especially, Marci. She has given me a new lease on life. I have finally come to terms with Lisa's death and feel that I can get on with my life now. Thanks again," said Kato as he reached over and squeezed Marci's hand.

"I guess this is confession time for all concerned. But, to set the record straight in case you think that Kato and I have something going. We don't. We are just good friends who look out for each other. He lost someone dear to him and so did I. So we console each other. I have a friend that I am trying to get Kato interested in and I think he is getting there. She would be good for him. As for me, I'll keep hanging in there until I meet someone who will fill my void."

Nick spoke up, "Marci, since I know that you are not interested in anyone and I am not matched with anyone right now, how about you and me getting together some time and go out for dinner and a movie or dance? Just friends going out with friends."

"Nick, that is real sweet of you. I would love to go out with you ....as friends, of course," she said laughing.

Cody said, "Nick, I thought you and Angie were beginning to get serious. What happened?"

"She and I had a long talk last night and we both realized that she and I could never be anything other than good friends. She has a friend at work that she is interested in and he is interested in her. I wished her the best and she did the same for me. Then we promised each other that we would always be friends and be there for each other, if need be. So, here I am alone again and I thought that since Marci is not connected with anyone either, we could keep each other company. Who knows. It may develop into something in the future, but right now we both could use some companionship. Right?"

"Right," Marci said as she smiled at Nick. She seemed happy at the new relationship that they may have.

Cody said, "Gosh, everything is ending so well for everyone. We must be doing something right. I have a feeling that with all of us working together, we can accomplish a hell of a lot in life. Let's have a toast to the last two or three weeks and to the future." So they did, and then the three guys got up to leave, and Tex said his goodbyes to Kato and Marci with the understanding that he would be back and hopefully working with them again. Each one wished the other the best of luck.

Then they dropped Nick off and Cody and Tex went back to the farm. Tex filled out the application and Cody put it in his brief case to take to the Lieutenant the next morning.

Traci came home a little early. She had caught up with her workload at the office so she took an hour off so that she could be with Tex a little longer. Sure enough, he was there when she arrived. It was such a beautiful day with a breeze blowing. She went out under the trees and greeted him with a kiss and asked, "Tex, do you think the Graves would mind if we went over and looked at the house. I have been thinking about it all day. Even though, I have been in the living room and like it very much, I would like to see the other part of the house so that I can have an idea of how it is set up and what type of furniture we can get so it will be us."

"Sure, I can understand that. I think that is an excellent idea. I'll call Mrs. Graves and see if it is convenient for them if we took a ride over now."

"O.K., I'll go in the house and see if Mom needs any help while you call. I'll be right back." So she walked into the kitchen and saw that Sara was there helping Mama E with dinner.

"Mom, if you don't need me to help you with dinner, Tex and I are going over to see the Graves house. Tex is calling now to see if we can. Anything you want me to do before we go?"

"No, Honey. You and Tex go on. I know how anxious you are about it. I don't blame you. I would be, too."

Traci went over and hugged her mom. She could see that she was grieving over the news of her husband being murdered instead of being shot in the line of duty. It was happening all over again. But she knew that in the long run, her mother would come to grips with it and the truth was best. "I love you, Mom." Then she went outside and she and Tex drove over to the farm next door. The Graves were glad to see her and Mrs. Graves showed her the rest of the house and they made comments to each other while Tex and Mr. Graves talked in the living room about farming and different things.

Afterwards, Traci thanked Mrs. Graves and Traci was told to come back whenever she wanted to. It would be fine. On the way home, Tex said, "By the way, I took it upon myself to call Rich this afternoon. I told him that we would be over there after dinner around eight o'clock. At first he was a little arrogant, but after a minute or so, he calmed down and said that he would like to hear what you had to say. I thought it best if I called him instead of you. I was right because at first he said he did not want to see you and almost slammed the phone down. ....Is that alright with you?"

"Yes, that's fine. As long as I get to explain my part in this weekend."

"I told him that I thought he should hear you out because you were in the dark, too. I think he will talk to you now. He said he did not want us in the house, so he will meet us out front and we can sit in the lawn chairs. His mother will not be home so we will not have to see her."

"That's good. I know how she feel about me, anyway. It is Rich that I have to make it right with. You do understand, don't you, Tex?"

"Yes, I do." He squeezed her hand and she laid her head on his shoulder the rest of the way home.

At the dinner table, Traci was excited and talking a mile a minute about the house and changes she could see that she wanted to make. In fact, that was all the conversation was about during the meal and Traci was the one doing all the talking. All the others just smiled at her. They were enjoying seeing her so happy after such an awful weekend.

Then at the end of the meal, she announced to the others that she and Tex were going over and talk to Rich. Mama E said she thought that would be nice for Rich to understand her position in this matter. After-all his father was there and did nothing to prevent the senator from killing Thomas.

Cody said, "Mom, from what Casey heard, Samuels did not know that the senator was going to kill him until after it was over. You can't blame Samuels for that, but we can blame him for organizing the drug operation and causing the deaths that are involved. In a way, he is to blame indirectly. The senator killed Dad and Mr. Harris.

Santino killed the two young boys. Now what we have to do is try to put as much of this behind us as possible. I realize that it is going to take time. It is like grieving for Dad all over again, but we can have some closure in it because we know the truth now."

"That's right, Mom. It will take time, but it will come sometime in the future for all of us." said Steven.

Traci got up from the table and took her plate to the counter to be put in the dishwasher. "Mom, I have to freshen myself up before going to see Rich. Cody, will you and Steven help Mom with the dishes tonight?"

They both agreed. So, Traci went to her room and the others got up and started cleaning up the kitchen. When Traci came back in the kitchen, she and Tex left to go see Rich. The others were hoping and making comments that everything would go all right for her.

On the way to Rich's house, Tex kept his hand on hers to help calm her and let her know that he supported her. And when they arrived, Rich was sitting out in the yard. He did not get up. He just sat there and told them to have a seat. "I'm sure this won't take long."

Traci could tell that he might be hard to deal with but she was going to give it a try. "Rich, I know you must hate me and I can understand that. I had to come and talk with you. You mean too much to me as a friend not to try to set things straight."

"Some friend you are......"

"No, wait a minute and let me explain. Then if you have any questions, I'll be glad to try to answer them."

He nodded his head that he would, but he still had that disgusted look on his face.

She began again. "Rich, I had no idea that your father was mixed up in this case that my brothers and Tex were investigating. Nor did I know that the reason for me coming to the dance was to find out who killed my father. The only thing that I knew was that this witness, who came as Tex's girlfriend, could identify the killer's voice of one of the murders that they were investigating. I had no idea who. The only thing that I deceived you with was about inviting Tex and his girlfriend to the dance. I'm sorry that your father was involved. I know that this hurt you very much. And I want you to know that if I had it to do over again, I would. I will do all I can to get drug dealers and murderers off the streets. I'm sorry that your family was involved with this case, but that is what we do."

At this point, Tex had set quiet and let Traci do all the talking. This was between Rich and her.

Rich was in deep thought, then he said, "You mean that you did not know anything about my father being involved in this mess?"

Tex spoke up, "I can vouch for that. Rich, she was not told that her father had been murdered until after we went home from the dance. She wanted to call you then, but I stopped her and told her to wait until you were more settled. She is telling you the truth. The only ones that knew the full story was Cody, Steven, Nick and I and then the others that were outside the dance Friday night. To be honest with you, we suspected your father of killing him, but after hearing his voice, the witness said he didn't and he did not know that the senator was going to shoot him. Your father was very upset when the senator shot Mr. Edwards. But, your father was there and he did not report it. I hope that is some comfort to you and your mother. I'm sorry it ended this way, but we were just doing our job. You will have to talk to your father and ask him 'Why'?"

Rich's face had softened a little as he said, "While we are being honest, I have to tell you that my mother is seeing a lawyer tonight about suing you all because she feels that my father is innocent. I just thought you should know that."

"Thanks for telling us, Rich, but there is too much evidence against him for him to be innocent. We have a tape of your father being at the scene. The sooner you and your mother face reality and put the blame where it should be, the better off you will be. I hope that you will not hold a grudge against Traci. She had no intention of hurting you."

After a moment, he said, "I understand your part in this, Trac, and I understand why you did that part. I know that things cannot be what it was before. I really and truly thought I loved you, but, now, I don't know. By looking at you two, I feel that you have feelings for one another other than friendship. I would like to be able to speak to you when I see you and I do wish you both the best of happiness." He put his hand out to shake Tex's hand. Then he went over to Traci and put his arm around her shoulder and kissed her on the cheek. "Thanks for being honest with me now and taking the time to come over and talk with me. After all, you always have been honest with me because that is the person that you are. See you around. O.K."

They both said, "Sure, Rich."

He then turned and walked into the house. Tex and Traci watched him walk away and then they went to the car and drove home silently for a while. Then, Tex looked at her and said, "I think he really loves you. I know that he really knows what a kind and honest person that you are. He will come around. Give him time."

"I know. I know. I feel better now. We can go on with our lives." She smiled at him.

When they got home, everyone was in the kitchen having coffee and cake. Jake and Sara had come to say goodbye to Tex. They could tell by the smile on Traci's face that she felt better. She told them about Rich and how he had accepted what she had said. Then the conversation turned to the farm next door and when Tex would be coming back. After a while, Jake and Sara wished him good luck and they left. Tex and Traci went outside under the trees and sat in the hammock while the others went to their room. They talked about the farm, the wedding and what his father would say as to Tex moving here and if he would come and live with them. They talked for another hour or so and then they went inside. Mama E was sitting up watching her favorite program, and Traci went to her room and Tex went to his. It took her a long time to go to sleep. She was so excited about everything. So much had happened to her this weekend that she had mixed emotions. Some sad, some happy and some very confusing. She was mentally tired as well as physically tired, and finally, she drifted off to sleep. The last thing that she remembered was 'Things will start to settle down after tomorrow. She will get back to normal then. Everything will be alright.'

The next morning everyone made it a point to eat breakfast together and then Tex would start out for Texas and the others would go to work. The conversation was quieter this morning. No one was saying very much. Finally, Mama E said, "It has been a long time since it was this quiet in this house. I guess everyone is worn out from everything that has happened over the last two or three weeks. It is winding down time now."

"Yes, Mama E., we all have been through a lot of different emotions. That can exhaust you in a hurry."

They all laughed. Steven said grinning in a slow drawl, "Tex, are you speaking for yourself or for all of us. Us Georgia Boys are use to this type of thing. I guess, we can train you when you get back. We don't want you to get shot again."

Traci cried out, "WHAT? Tex, When did you get shot or is Steven clowning?"

Cody said very slowly, "Sis, Steven isn't clowning. Tex really did get shot, and to make matters worse, a woman took the shooter out." He laughed, looking at Tex. ......"You thought you were going to get by with that, didn't you, Tex? Make sure you tell your buddies in Texas about that."

Tex's face turned red and he said, "You're right, Cody, I was hoping you all had forgotten about that."

In the meantime, Traci was asking, "Will someone tell me what happened? When did you get shot? Where did you get shot?"

"Take it easy, Sis. He wasn't hurt, just his ego. He had on a vest. ...Lucky for him. .....It was when he and Cody raided the warehouse. Tex and Marci were closer to the back door and when Tex knocked the door open, one of the bad guys shot right away. Tex went down. Marci was behind him, and in full view of the shooter, so she shot the guy before he could get off another shot. ..She bent down to see where Tex was shot and he was out cold laying on the floor. The bullet hit the vest and knocked him out. By the time we had all the guys together, he came too."

They all laughed. Then Tex joined in with them. "No, you guys, I am not going to tell anyone about that and if you all are smart, you won't say anymore about it. Do you understand?"

"No, Tex, we won't say anymore about it. I just wanted to rib you a little about it before you left."

Mama E put her head in her hands, "Oh, Lord, I am so glad I don't know about these things until after it is over. That was the way Thomas was. He never told me anything before it happened. It was always afterwards."

Cody said, "It's alright, Mom. We can take care of ourselves. We have good backups. That is why I work only with someone that I know."

Tex started to get up as he said, "Well, you good folks, I have to get on the road. I want to get home as soon as possible. You don't know how much I enjoyed this stay. I always felt that this was my second home and it sure was this time." He hugged Cody and Steven and then gave Mama E a big hug, "I'll be back before you know it and that will be to stay. Then he grabbed Traci by the hand and led her out to the car. He had put his clothes and things in the car earlier. Then he put his arms around her and kissed her long and passionately, and then said as he looked into her eyes, "I love you, sweetheart. I'll call when I get home."

"I love you, too. I'll be waiting for your call." And he kissed her again and then got into the car and drove down the driveway. She stood there and waited until he was out of sight and then went into the house. She went to her room and got her purse, said goodbye to her mother and brothers and left for work. Cody and Steven were on their way out at the same time. Sara waited a little later this morning before coming over to help Claire. She wanted to give them enough time to say their goodbyes.

That evening, it was so quiet in the house that no one could relax. It was the first time that everything that had happened over the weekend was being thought about and absorbed by the Edwards family, especially Mama E and Traci. With all the visitors in the house, they had not had time to really think about what this investigation was all about. Now, they were by themselves and they had time to think about everything. Cody had planned to go see Corrie, but Mama E and Traci were having a hard time of it. It was the beginning of the grieving process all over again and he knew that it was going to take time. It was hard on all of them, especially Traci and their Mom, because he and Steven had known about it and were involved in it. They all just sat around the table and drank coffee and eat some of Sara's cake and talked. It was the first time that the family had been alone and could say what was on their mind. They talked until late that night and Mama E and Traci were feeling better before they went to bed.

That night Tex stopped on the road to get a bite to eat and thought about calling Traci, but he knew in his heart that it was not a good time to call. He could picture the family either at the kitchen table or sitting around in the living room. He knew how his family felt when his mother passed away and so many people was there and the feeling after everyone left and they were alone. He decided to wait until the morning. He would be home then because he was driving straight through.

The next morning Traci decided not to go to work and stay home with her mother. She did receive a call from Tex and they talked a few minutes. He just wanted her to know that he made it home all right. He would call her tomorrow night. Cody and Steven had gone to work.

It was a slow process for the Edwards family, but over the next couple of weeks, they started back on the right track. Mama E never asked to hear the tape from the watch and Cody nor Steven said anything to her or Traci about it. They were beginning to get their lives back to normal or as near normal as they possibly could. Of course, Tex helped a lot by calling every other day and brightening things up for them. He was making progress there. His father was very happy for him and wanted to come back with him and help him remodel the farmhouse. He was itching to do some physical work. The only problem was he did not want to leave Kristen by herself, but she encouraged him to come back with Tex. Tex had given his notice at the Sheriff's Department, and, of course, his supervisor was upset with him, but he wished him good luck, anyway. They told him that his father retired from there and he should too. But his mind was made up and he was not about to change it.

Cody had called Tex and told him that all the men that they put in jail were still there. Judge Mason heard the hearings and was so disgusted with all the people that were involved, he did not want to take any chances of any of them leaving town so he denied bail on Lawson, Santino, Samuels, Tanner and Collins. On the others, he set it so high that he was sure they could not make it. Besides, they were the little guys.

Chapter 16

Three days later when Tex and his father were ready to leave for Georgia, Kristen reassured them that she would be fine. Mr. Tyler had talked to Kelly and he promised to look in on her once in a while. And she promised that if she needed anything, she would contact Kelly. Kelly lived down the street a couple of blocks. She would also call her father often and let him know what was going on with the oil business.

Because Tex wanted his father to enjoy his trip, they stopped in Mississippi just before going over the Alabama line. He found a nice motel with a swimming pool and there were good choices of restaurants nearby. So, they checked into the motel and put on their swimsuits and took a swim for about forty-five to fifty minutes. There were only a couple in the pool. After the swim and exercise, they laid down for about an hour and watched television to keep from going to sleep. Then they got dressed and went to one of the restaurants close by. They were really enjoying themselves because they were not in a hurry and did not have to be in a certain place at a specific time. Tex had told Traci that they would be there Friday evening or Saturday some time, not to prepare a special meal for them. He had explained to her before what he intended to do on the trip. Although, Tex and his father got along very well, he wanted special time with him, to bond and talk about things that father and son talk about even at their age.

In the back of his mind was the thought that Cody, Traci and Steven could not do that now. And he knew that they would very much like to talk to their father again. The grieving process is very slow and fragile.

They took their time eating and talking about the good times and the bad times they had had in the past and what they were looking for in the future. His father was looking forward to meeting Traci, her mom and Steven. He had talked to them on the phone, but had never been able to meet them. Then the conversation turned to the farm that Tex had bought. Mr. Tyler had made arrangements with his lawyers that if the farm met his approval, they were to rewrite the trust fund for Tex to get one-third of his now instead of next year. The rest would stay the same. He would get so much every five years after he turned twenty-five. The one-third would be plenty for Tex to remodel the farm and make it livable as to what he and Traci wanted. And also to hire a couple to take care of the farm until it was profitable. He knew that would take some time. They could live very comfortable on their salaries. Tex had it all figured out as to how he wanted to remodel the house, but he wanted his dad to see the whole farm before he explained that to him.

When they finished at the restaurant, they came back to the motel and both were exhausted so they went straight to bed. After a good night's sleep, they left the next morning after having a good breakfast. The drive was wonderful and Tex was able to show his father some beautiful scenery along the way. And as they drove up the driveway to the Edwards home, "Son, this place is beautiful. It looks like the southern plantation homes that you see in pictures and movies. No wonder you fell in love here." He grinned at his son.

"Wait until you meet Traci. Then you will see why I fell in love. They are such a loving family, like ours as we were growing up and even now without Mom, even though, I feel she is still with us in spirit."

"Yes, she is, Son. Don't you ever forget that. She is watching over you and Kristen. Who knows. She may have led you here to meet Traci and fall in love." He was smiling at his son because he was feeling very happy for him.

As they drove into the back yard, Cody, Steven and Nick were out under the trees. Tex and his father got out of the car. Mr. Tyler could not believe how beautiful everything was and all this space. He could not take his eyes away from looking around the yard. They walked over to where Cody and the others were. After the greetings had taken place, Cody introduced him to Steven. They talked for a while and then Cody said, "You all probably want something cold to drink or maybe something to eat. Come on inside."

Mr. Tyler said, "It is so beautiful out here, I could stay outside all the time. Even sleep out here. I was telling Tex as we were driving up the driveway that this looks like a southern plantation that we see in the movies. Gosh, the space that you all have. It must be wonderful to live out in the country."

Steven spoke, "We are proud of it, and yes, we do sleep out here sometimes. We fall asleep and no one will wake us up and we end up sleeping out here all night." They laughed.

"You see why I stay over here as much as possible," laughed Nick.

They each grabbed a bag from Tex's car, and as they walked into the kitchen, Traci let out a yell, "Oh, Tex, you're here." And she ran over to him and he put his bag down and hugged and kissed her. Then he said, "Dad, this is what I fell in love with."

Mr. Tyler went over and hugged her, "Yes, Son, I can see why you did. She is beautiful." Then he leaned down and kissed her on the cheek.

Then he went over to Mama E, "I am Chuck as you know by now, and I am glad to meet you, Claire, after talking with you over the past couple of years. And I can see where Traci got her good looks." He hugged her and kissed her on the cheek. "I know that the past few weeks haven't been easy for you and your family, but hopefully, time will heal some of the pain. I was very saddened, when the boys came back from talking with Casey and told me the story. Let's pray that the worst is over. .....I hope that this is not an inconvenient time for me to visit."

"No, I am glad you are here. It will be a big help to us having you here. And, yes, we are bouncing back now and am looking forward to the future. ...How about something cold to drink now? We will have dinner in about an hour."

"Mama E, I would like a beer and I think Dad could use one, too. How about it, Dad? We help ourselves around here."

"Yes, Son, that sounds good."

Tex went over to the small refrigerator in the pantry and brought out two beers. "Anyone else care for one?"

Cody nodded, so Tex brought out three others and they sat down at the table. In the meantime, Nick and Steven had taken the bags upstairs. When they came down, they sat down at the table with the others and drank their beer. Then Sara came in and ran them outside so she and Claire could finish preparing dinner. Traci stayed in the kitchen to help prepare dinner. "Oh, Mom, Tex is just like his father, isn't he? He seems like such a likable guy."

"Yes, he is, to both your questions. Now, let's get the table set and the tea made."

"Mom, let's eat outside tonight. It is such a beautiful evening. Sara, you and Jake eat with us, too."

"I would love too, but the boys will have to be fed, remember."

"Yes, I forgot about them, but we have plenty for them, don't we, Mom?"

"Sure, Traci, that is a good idea. That way Chuck will be able to meet everyone here."

So, Traci started getting the table cloths and everything needed for outside together. Then she took it outside and told the guys to set the table in a few minutes. She would let them know when. "We are going to eat out here tonight and Jake, Sara and the boys are going to eat with us."

"Great Sis. It's nice out here. Who's idea was that?"

"Steven, it was mine, so you can thank me for it."

Chuck spoke up, smiling, "Thank you, Traci. That was a wonderful idea. It is so nice here. I could stay here all the time."

"Mr. Tyler, you're welcome. We eat out here a lot and just relax after dinner most of the time. Besides, it is easier to clean up after the meal here than in the kitchen."

"I don't blame you, Traci. I would, too. We only have a small patio and small back yard at home. The front yard is on the street and no room there, either."

"Yes, we even dance out here once in a while. Ask Tex about that," said Steven, grinning.

They all laughed. Then Tex said, "Dad, one night we were all uptight and had just finished eating dinner out here. It was nice. The radio was playing one of my favorite songs, so I turned it up and grabbed Mama E and we danced all over the place. It wasn't long before everyone was dancing, even the boys."

"Son, sounds like you all had fun."

"We did. You see why I like it here so much."

"Yes, I can understand how anyone would like to live here. It is so beautiful."

Traci went back into the house and a few minutes later called back and told them to set up the tables. That they would be bringing out the food in about fifteen minutes.

By the time the food was ready to take out, Jake and the boys were there and willing to help with anything that needed to be done.

All during the evening meal, Chuck kept saying, "It is so beautiful. I would love to have some pictures of this evening."

Cody got up and went to his car and came out with a camera, "Yes Sir, we will have some pictures. Mr. Tyler look around here. You, too, Mom." So Cody took some pictures of everyone and then sat back down to finish his dinner.

After everyone had finished, Tex turned up the radio and grabbed Traci and they started dancing. Chuck said, "My, Son, he sure knows how to have a good time. Come on, Claire, let's show them how it's done." And he grabbed Claire's hand and they started dancing. Before long, everyone was dancing. The boys were dancing their way with no partners. But everyone was enjoying them selves and that was what counted. Mama E and Traci were laughing and having a good time and that was what Tex wanted to see.

Then they all sat down and had some of Sara's peach cobbler and ice tea or coffee. It was up into the night when they cleaned up the mess and went to bed. They all were tired, especially Chuck and Tex. It didn't take them long to go to sleep.

When Tex woke up, he went to his father's room but he was not in there. Then he noticed that the door that goes out on the balcony was not locked. He went out there and he saw his father sitting there just looking out over the grounds and farm with a pleasant smile on his face. "Dad, it's beautiful, isn't it? This is what I want. Something similar to this. The house that I bought can be made similar to this. I want you to see it today. Cody tells me that the Graves have moved out, except for a few pieces of furniture. They left the keys with Cody to give to me. This may or may not be the time to talk about it, but Traci and I would like very much for you to move here with us. I know that I am being selfish because Kristen wants you to stay in Houston with her."

"Son, I know you mentioned it before, and I did not really think about it because I felt that I could not leave Houston. I want you to know that last night and this morning sitting out here, the thought has been in my mind and I can't seem to get it out." Then he gave Tex a big smile. "Somehow, I know that the three of us can work things out. Kristen is doing very well, in fact, great with the oil business. I didn't say anything about it to you while you were home because I felt she should be the one to tell you, but she did not get a chance before we left. She was on a couple of trips for the oil company while you were home as you know. But she and Clay Moreland, the guy you met, are getting very serious. He is a very nice, friendly, guy, and comes from a good family. I have known his family for some time now. His family is in the oil business and likes Kristen very much. We all had dinner together a couple of nights before you came home and it was wonderful. Mrs. Moreland said that she had always wanted a daughter and now it seems that she will have one. She seemed happy about it. Kristen will tell you in her own way when she sees you again."

"Dad, I'm happy to hear that. I hope that they will be very happy. That's great."

"Well, Son, I hear someone else is up now, but I have enjoyed just sitting here and watching the sun rise and feel this cool morning breeze. It certainly has given me an appetite."

"I'm glad because they fix a large breakfast around here and it is served cafeteria style. Let's go and see what we can do to help. We all do for ourselves around here. Just make yourself at home."

"That's good. I do know how to do that. I'm glad you talked me into coming back with you, Son." So they went back inside and downstairs to the kitchen. Everyone was there preparing breakfast.

"Well, good morning, you folks. What can Tex and I do to help you."

"Good morning, just grab a plate and fill it and set down to the table. Cody will pour the coffee after everyone is seated," said Mama E. So that was what they did and everyone enjoyed another meal at the table with the Edwards family.

During breakfast, Tex announced that he was taking his father over to the farm and asked if anyone wanted to go with them. Cody said, "The Graves have moved out except for a few pieces of furniture. If you like we could go over with you and see what you want to remodel and make notes to that effect. We can help you start to clean out what you want." He grinned, then he continued, "I am not trying to rush you, but I just thought that you might want to start right away."

"I do, Brother. I do. And I appreciate any help that you might give me. How about you, Traci? Would you like to go?"

"No, I'll go next time. You guys go and decide what needs to be done. My work is after you all finish with the woodwork. I'll stay here and help Mom clean up the kitchen. You guys are off the hook this morning."

Chuck said, "Now, Claire, I know how to clean up a kitchen. Let us help you."

Then Mama E spoke up. "No, we'll clean the kitchen. Tonight, the men will cook. How about some steaks or chickens cooked on the grill. We'll even let you men decide."

"Sounds good, Mom. We'll stop at the supermarket on the way back from ....the other farm or should I say Tex's farm," grinned Steven.

So the four men took off for the farm. Mr. Tyler was very impressed with it. "Son, I see what you mean by having great potentials. This could be made into a beautiful place. Of course, it would take some time to get it to the fullest potential. You are making me want to stay here more and more. When I decided to come, it was just for a week or so. Now, you are making this into a long drawn out stay. You know how much I like to build things. This is right down my alley, but you knew that when you asked me to come here."

"Yes, I know, Pops. That is why I agreed with you when you said that you would come but could not stay over a week." He grinned. "I knew when you saw it, you would not be able to stay away from it."

They laughed as they walked through the house and making notes as to what was the first things to do and what they would need. Making note that the kitchen was the first thing to be remodelled because it had the most work and then the rest of the downstairs. They spent a couple of hours there and then they rode down to the barn and out in the pasture and down by the stream that was running through the farmland and onto the Edwards land. They got out and was walking around the area.

"Son, this is wonderful. Smell that fresh air and being out away from other people. This is great." He walked over to Tex and put his arm around his shoulders and hugged him and they stood looking out over the land. They stood there for quite a while, just looking. Then they got into the car and rode back to the Edwards' farm just in time for lunch.

After lunch, they sat under the trees at one of the tables and figured up approximately what lumber, nails and other things that they would need to get started. Tex said, "Dad, you and I will go Monday morning and make arrangements for this stuff to be delivered. Cody, you did say that you and Steven had to go downtown and give depositions Monday morning?"

"Yes, we do, Tex, but it shouldn't take long. The materials probably won't be delivered until the afternoon. We will be able to help you in the evenings. Also, I know Nick would help, too."

Mr. Tyler said, "Good, we will need all the help that we can get." Traci came out and sat for awhile as they were discussing the remodelling and the farm. Tex asked her to pick out the appliances that she wanted. The type, coloring, etc. And where she wanted to put them in the kitchen. Since they were going to tear out the old cabinets, she could place everything where she wanted it to be. She and Tex decided to take a ride over to the farm while the other three men started up the grill to get ready to prepare the steaks that they had gotten earlier.

When Tex and Traci came back, they had a drawing of what she wanted and where she wanted it. She went inside to prepare the vegetables that they were going to grill along with the steaks. It wasn't long before they were sitting outside enjoying their dinner.

Unbeknownst to Tex and Mr. Tyler, Kristen called that morning and talked with Traci. She and Clay had become engaged last night and she wanted to tell her father and brother in person. Clay had suggested that they fly to Georgia and surprise them, but she wanted to make sure that it would be convenient for them. Traci had invited them to stay there, but Kristen declined and said they did not want to disrupt the household. So, Traci gave her the name of the nearest hotel to their place and they were going to fly down the following Tuesday morning and go back on Wednesday morning. Traci agreed to keep it a secret.

Everything went as planned on Monday. Traci, Cody and Steven went to work and Tex and his father went into town to the nearest building place, ordered the material and whatever they would need. Cody and Mr. Tyler convinced Tex to at least have the cabinets built by an expert. Then they went to the cabinet builder that Cody had recommended and talked to him. When they had concluded their talk there, they headed toward the farm and started cleaning out the kitchen. It was late in the day when they arrived back at the Edwards' place. They were sitting outside under the trees when the others came from work.

When Cody walked up to where they were sitting, Mr. Tyler was saying to Tex, "Son, there will be a lot of work to do in remodelling that house like you want. Why not ask Cody about some carpenters around here to help you. It will take a long time with just us working on it. Of course, having the cabinets built by an expert is a big help. ...That is, if you are in a hurry." He laughed and then the others joined him.

"I know, Dad. But I want to do the work myself. I may call in some carpenters on some things, but right now I want to do what I can. You convinced me on the cabinets, but give me a chance to show you my handy work. I want to be able to say that I did it." He laughed. "That may sound corny or like I have an ego problem, but it is not. Can you understand what I am trying to say?"

"Yes, Son, I understand. We will do what we can, but I don't know how long I will be here. I will stay as long as I can, but I don't know when I may have to go back to Houston."

"That's alright, Dad. I understand. But I have friends here that will help me. They do their own work, too, if they possibly can."

Cody said, "That's right. We will get it done, Tex Old Boy. You appreciate a thing a lot more when you do it yourself. Around here, we do our own unless it is something that we can't handle. If it comes to that, I know someone good that will help out. Everything will work out."

"Good, I'm glad that is settled. Tex and I went to the builders supply place and ordered the material and things to get started with and then we found the cab net builder and talked to him before going to the farm. We cleaned out the pantry cabinets and shelves in there and then started on the kitchen. Surprisingly, we got a lot of work done, just the two of us."

"I think Mom and Sara has dinner almost prepared. After dinner, we all can go over and do some cleaning. The electricity is still on plus the fact that we will have a lot of daylight left."

A few minutes later, Steven came in and they all sat down to eat dinner in the kitchen. During the meal, Mama E and Sara assured them that they would clean the kitchen because they were going to bake a couple of pies and cakes to have in the freezer and they did not want them hanging around. So, right after finishing the meal, they all left for the other farm, including Traci with a big broom and dustpan.

They accomplished quite a lot of work that night. As the men tore the wood down, Traci was carrying it outside and putting it into a pile. The old wood and the cabinets in the kitchen were pretty much cleaned out by the time they were ready to leave. As they were getting out of the car at home, Traci said, "Tex, I took tomorrow off from work. You mentioned something about wanting me to go and pick out what type of cabinets we would want. I thought maybe you and I could go first thing in the morning. Maybe Mr. Tyler would like to go with us so that he can find his way around this area."

"No, you kids go. I'll stay home and keep Claire company. This will be your home and you should decide how you two want it."

Tex looked at his father with a surprised look on his face. Then he looked at Traci trying to figure out what was going on. *Could it be that my father has an eye for Mama E and Traci doesn't want him to be alone with her. That is not like Traci.*

Traci said, "I would prefer that you went with us so you can give us some pointers on picking out cabinets and which ones would be best."

Tex looked at her again with a blank stare. "You don't think that I know anything about cabinets."

"Yes, I am sure that you do, but I would like for your father to be a part of this adventure. Would you like that Mr. Tyler?"

"Well, if it means that much to you, I'll certainly go with you. I don't want to start off on the wrong foot with my daughter-in-law."

They all stared at Traci, wondering what was going on here, but they thought that she knew what she was doing so they did not interfere. Traci thought '*they will have a surprise when we come back.*'

They were home in a few minutes and they all went into the house and to their own bedrooms. After taking a shower and getting rid of the dust and grime, they were ready to fall into bed. It didn't take them long to fall asleep. They had worked hard the last couple of hours.

The next morning Steven and Cody went to work and Tex, Mr. Tyler and Traci went into town to look at the cabinets. Traci and Tex picked out the style of cabinets that they wanted and then drove to the cabinet builder's place and gave him the measurements of the kitchen and where each appliance would be.

"Mr. Tyler, I will have to look at this sketch a little longer and go out to the house and look at the kitchen and measure for myself. I am sure that these measurements are correct, but I like to do my own."

"Mr. Crane, I can understand that. When would you be able to start if your estimate meets my price?"

"I have two days work where I am now. I can start probably Friday morning and I will work through the weekend. I have a helper to work with me. He is good or I would not have him work with me."

"Sounds good, Mr. Crane. We would like for this work to be done as soon as possible. While you are

working with the kitchen, we will be working on the other part of the house."

"You do realize that I build the cabinets here and then take them to your place and mount them, don't you?"

"Yes, Sir. I do." And then Tex shook hands with him and they had an understanding that Mr. Crane would call him when he was ready to go to the house to get the measurements and Tex would meet him there and they would sign a contract if it met Tex's agreement. On the way home Traci looked at her watch and saw that they were a little earlier than they were suppose to be so she suggested that they go by the farm and take another look.

Mr. Tyler said, "Traci, I don't know why you wanted me to come along, but I am glad that I did. I think you all made a good choice."

"Yes, Mr. Tyler, I want you to be a part of this farm, also. This is your home away from home. Or, your home, period. Your expertise means a lot to us. I know Tex has knowledge about building, but I appreciate your input as well. Thanks for coming with us."

They went into the house and looked at the kitchen picturing and discussing the cabinets in there. They came away from the house with a better understanding of what the finished product would look like. They were feeling good about it. They were silent on the way home. Each one picturing in their mind how the kitchen would look.

When they pulled up into the back yard, Tex said, "There is a rental car. Traci, were you expecting anyone today?"

"Yes, I am. I can't wait to meet them. Come on in, you two." And she dashed out of the car and walked fast to the kitchen door. She wanted to be inside when Tex and Mr. Tyler came in.

Tex was startled. He didn't know what had gotten into Traci, but he was going to find out as soon as he got inside. He walked into the kitchen and there sat Kristen and Clay at the table having coffee and some coffee cake. Tex was so shocked he couldn't say a word. Then Mr. Tyler looked up and was so surprised that he couldn't say anything.

"Well, what's wrong Dad and Brother. Can't I come to Georgia, too?" And she and Clay got up and she met her Dad halfway and hugged him and then Tex while Clay hugged Mr. Tyler and then went over and introduced himself to Tex.

"Traci, you knew about this, didn't you? That is why you wanted Dad to go with us."

"Yes, Kristen called yesterday and said that they were coming. And I say, 'Welcome, Kristen and Clay. I am very glad to meet both of you."

Before Kristen and Clay sat back down at the table, Kristen said, "Dad, Tex, I have something that I would like to tell you. We came all the way to Georgia to tell you that Clay and I are engaged to be married." And they all stepped forward to congratulate them with hugs and kisses again. Then they all sat down at the table and the conversation was about Kristen and Clay getting married and then it turned to Tex and Traci and about the farm. Kristen wanted to see the farm before they left the next morning. She was surprised and well please with what she had seen of Georgia. She had a dreary picture of it in her mind, but it didn't take it long to disappear. *She thought it was beautiful, especially the Edwards' place. After a while, she could tell by the way her father was talking that he liked it here very much and she was happy for him if he wanted to stay for a while. She would let him know her thoughts as soon as they were alone.*

After about an hour of coffee, coffee cake and conversation, Tex decided to take Kristen and Clay to the farm so they could see it. He was very proud of his purchase and wanted to show it off. The five of them got into his Explorer and took off to the farm. Listening to Tex explain how he wanted to remodel the house, they all were excited about it. Kristen and Clay were very happy for Tex and she liked Traci and her mom very much and she let Traci know that.

When they left the farm, they rode around the area so they could get an idea of what was close by. Then they rode to the station where Cody worked. Tex wanted to show them where he expected to be working, but had not heard anything definite on it yet. Cody and Nick were out giving depositions and was also at the jail earlier. It seems that Wilson and Samuels wanted to talk. Cody had them write down whatever they wanted to say. He wanted it on paper and in their own handwriting. Tex walked them into the station and into Lieutenant Moss' office. The Lieutenant was by himself and waved them to come in. After Tex introduced them, he smiled at Tex and said, "Sergeant Tyler, I would like to be the first to welcome you to this office. The papers came through this morning and you will be working here and I have assigned you to work with Cody, Nick and Thompson. You four work good together, but you will be partners with Thompson. I think you all will be a good team. By the way, you will be hired as a Sergeant, but you will be on probation for six months. That is standard procedure for hiring someone with experience. When you begin is up to you, but I hope it will be soon. I understand that you have some things you probably need to do, so if you would like to put the starting date in two weeks, I will go that distance for you, but I can't go any longer. That is, unless an emergency comes up."

"Thank you very much, Lieutenant. Yes, I would like the two weeks, but if I see where I can come in earlier, I will. Thank you for what you have done for me." And he reached over and shook hands with him as Mr. Tyler, Kristen and Clay grinned at them. They were happy for Tex if this is what he wanted to do.

"Well, Son, looks like you are very serious about living in Georgia. So far, you have gotten yourself engaged, bought a farm and now you have a job with the Sheriff's Department." He laughed. "Not too many men can do all of that in about a month's time. I am very proud of you, Son." Everyone laughed.

"That is quite a lot to do in a month's time, isn't it?" said Tex grinning. "I guess I am an exception. When I see what I want, I go for it."

The whole time that they were in Lieutenant Moss' office, Tex kept his arm around Traci. She stayed in the background. This was for Tex and his family.

They all laughed.

Lieutenant Moss saw Thompson come in and motioned for him to come in the office. When he came in, the Lieutenant introduced him to the others and told him the news of Tex and him being partners, etc.

Thompson shook hands with Tex and said, "I can't think of anyone better to work with, Lieutenant. I am very pleased to be in this working group. And Tex, welcome aboard. I am looking forward to it."

Tex said, "Me too, Andy. I am very happy with this news."

They all talked and joked for a few minutes longer. Then Andy had to leave for a phone call and the others left at this time. Yes, Tex was very pleased at how everything was turning out for him. They went over to a barbecue place to eat lunch. Tex wanted them to taste the barbecue in Georgia. It was different than Texas barbecue.

Although, both were very good. During the meal, the conversation was about Tex and his life and then he turned it to Kristen and Clay as to what they had planned for the future.

"Bro, we haven't really planned anything, not even the wedding date. We just got engaged night before last and I wanted to tell you both in person. It was Clay's idea to fly here and see you all. Neither one of us has ever been to Georgia before. You know what you hear about it, but it is so different. I think these people are either jealous or don't know what they are talking about. It is beautiful here, especially the Edwards' place and your place, too. Tex, you can make it into something beautiful. I can picture it now."

"Yes, I saw it in a picture of my dreams when I first looked at the house and the setting. My problem now is trying to talk Dad into staying here for awhile and help me make my dream come true."

"Son, since you put it that way, a father would be a fool to say no. Yes, I do want to be a part of your plans. My concern is not being there when and if Kristen needs me."

"Dad, don't you worry about me. You know now that you have two places that you can stay and know that you will not wear out your welcome. Right now, Tex needs you. I am fine. I have Kelly to help me with the oil business and I have Clay to keep me company." She smiled at Clay and squeezed his hand on the table. Because you are here does not mean you can't fly home for a few days or weeks. I say you just play it by ear. Right now, help Tex as much as you can if that is your plans. If I need you, I will call you." She reached over and squeezed his hands that was crossed on the table and smiled, "I love you, Dad."

"You, kids, I love both of you so much," he said, smiling proudly.

Clay was smiling at them. "I am a very lucky man to be a part of this family. I am very grateful for you all giving me a chance to be one of you. ..And, another thing, Traci, this barbecue is very good, but Texas still has Georgia beat by a small margin. It's not the barbecue, but it's what you are use too."

They all laughed. Tex paid the bill and they left to go back to the Edwards' place so they could spend some time out under the trees enjoying some ice tea and some of Sara's cookies. *Traci was thinking of how grateful she was, too, to be a part of the Tyler family. I am so happy. I love Tex, so. And I like his father and sister very much. Clay seems real nice and I am sure that I will like him, too.*

That evening when Steven and Cody came home from work, they joined them under the trees. Cody told Tex and the others about the statements that they had from Wilson and Samuels. And Tex told them about their day with Kristen and Clay joining in telling them how much they enjoyed it and how beautiful everything was that they had seen. They both said that they were glad that they had decided to fly here and meet all of them.

It wasn't long before Mama E called out to say that dinner was ready. Clay had wanted to take everyone out to eat to keep Mama E from cooking, but she would not hear of it. "We can talk and enjoy each other here a lot better than at some restaurant. Besides, I like Sara's peach cobblers better than any a restaurant could serve."

After they finished their meal, they decided to take the desert outside and have it there with some coffee. It was pleasant. There was a little breeze blowing and it was a large shaded area where the tables were located.

Kristen said, "Mama E, I sure am glad that you talked us into staying here for dinner. I don't know when I have enjoyed any meal better than this one."

"Me, too, I agree with you wholeheartedly about Sara's peach cobblers. It is the best," Clay spoke up.

Chuck said grinning, "I have learned in the short time that I have been here that when Claire says something, everyone listens."

They all laughed.

461

Tex said proudly as he smiled at her, "Yes, Mama E is the voice and rightly so."

"Kristen, do you and Clay have to leave in the morning? Can't you stay another night or two?"

"No, Dad, I have to be at an important meeting at two o'clock tomorrow afternoon and Clay has to get back to his office. But, I promise that we will be back and stay longer next time. And don't you worry about me."

"I won't. I know you can take care of yourself most of the time. I am glad that you have Clay to lean on, too. I am grateful for that. ....I will stay here for a couple of weeks until Tex goes to work and help him. He has a lot of work to do at his farm." Then he smiled at his son. "It will give me some physical work to do. I have missed that the last couple of years. If you need me, you know where to find me."

Mama E, Cody, Traci and Steven went inside to give the Tylers and Clay more time to be by themselves. They stayed outside until it was late and Clay and Kristen finally said goodbye and promised that they would be back soon. Then Tex and Mr. Tyler went into the house as Clay and Kristen were driving down the driveway.

The next night Tex announced that he and Traci were going out to dinner and he made it perfectly clear that they wanted to go alone. He said, "This is a special occasion for us. Besides, I don't want anyone else to hear what I have to say." He laughed and then the others joined him. Everyone knew what his plans were, but they didn't say anything. Mama E had heard him earlier make reservations at a swanky nightclub in town. And sure enough, Traci came home with a big, beautiful diamond on her hand. She woke everyone up that had gone to bed to show them her ring. She felt like a princess as she had never had a diamond so beautiful. She had fine jewelry, but nothing like that. They were excited for her and wished them well. Mama E said, "Honey, it is official now. I am very happy for you." The others joined in with their sentiments. It took them awhile before going back to sleep, but it was worth it.

During the next two weeks, they all worked on Tex's house when they could. Even Nick came over in the evenings and helped. By the end of the two weeks, they had the kitchen ready for painting or wallpapering whichever Traci wanted to do. That was her job. She decided to do that before the cabinets were mounted. The carpenter agreed with her because he was not quite finished with the cabinets. Mr. Tyler decided to fly back to Texas and take care of some business, but promised to be back in a week or two. Tex was going to work the following Monday at the Sheriff's Department and he, Cody, Steven and Nick started getting ready for court on the murder cases that were coming up soon. Lieutenant Moss did not give them any new cases because he wanted their full attention on these cases. They were important. There was a lot of public opinion going on in the news media and he wanted to make sure that what they did was right and there would be no technical reason for the cases to be dismissed. That lasted for about two weeks and they felt that they were ready. In the meantime, Thompson had been given two murder cases to be working on until the others could help him. By then, Thompson had contacted all the witnesses on the two cases and set up appointments to talk with them. Cody and then Thompson were the leading investigators in the group, but they all were to work together.

They all worked on the house most evenings, but not all and on the weekends for the next three weeks. They had completed the kitchen and torn out the living room and put in a foyer and a coat closet there by the front door. The fireplace had been redone to a more modern one by someone Cody knew. Tex wanted a foyer and a big fireplace. By that time Mr. Tyler had come back and was working by himself during the day most days. He did the painting of the living room and the foyer during the day. In the evenings, the other three and sometimes four with Nick did the tearing out of the other rooms. They locked the kitchen door which was at the side of the house and the front door to keep anyone from going through there and messing it up. They used the back door of the house for the rest of the time that they were carrying out torn up stuff; such as, pieces of wood, old carpet, etc.

After about another three weeks, they had the downstairs remodelled except for the floor. That was to be the last thing done.

They decided it was time for rest and relaxation. Mr. Tyler took another trip back to Houston and stayed there with Kristen for the next two to three weeks. The trial was starting in Georgia and there was not much they could do until this was over. While the trial was going on and the guys were there, Traci and Mama E were planning the wedding. Traci wanted to get married at home out on the lawn and have the reception there, also. There was plenty of room for both.

And in Houston, Kristen was planning her wedding, also, but it would not be until the following year. She wanted to be married in June. It was now at the end of summer. Traci and Tex had decided to get married on April the 18th. April was Traci's favorite month. Tex finally agreed that was a good time. Although, he really wanted to get married right away.

By the time October rolled around, the trials of all the men that had been arrested had ended. Judge Mason and Judge Johnson heard all the cases and made sure that they got the maximum, especially the ones that were suppose to be serving the people. Of course, they would not serve all that time, but the judges and district attorneys felt that they had done their part. At least they would serve several years and the senator and Judge Turner would not be serving the people again.

Mama E was feeling much better. The trial did not upset her as much as they all thought it would. They all attended Senator Charles Lawson's trial. There was too much going on after that trial for her to think too much about it. Traci's wedding and, too, Kristen was calling her to get Mama E's advice and suggestions on planning her wedding. Mr. Tyler was prompting Kristen in doing that. He felt that he was a second father to the Edwards' children and he wanted Claire to be a second mother to Tex and Kristen. Kristen got the idea and thought it was a splendid one. She liked all the Edwards very much. They grew up with principles and values, same as her and Tex.

They decided on having their celebration on the second weekend of October. The trials were just over and it was the best weekend for the majority of the people. All the people that were involved in the case were there either on Saturday or Sunday. The Edwards had a big barbecue of pork and chicken. Most of the women brought dishes so it wasn't too much work for the Edwards. They had a band for Saturday night and games to be played on Sunday. Everyone was feeling excitement in the air because of the reason for the celebration. For many, it was a different type of life, but they felt just as welcome as the others. To them, the Edwards and their friends on the Sheriff's Department were their heroes. They all were celebrating for the same reason and had their hopes for a better tomorrow in the drug areas, but they knew that it would be a fight to keep it clean. For many, they knew that they had a chance at a better life now.

Tex and his father spent Thanksgiving with the Edwards and they spent Christmas with Kristen and Clay. Then the day before New Year's Eve, they all flew to Georgia to start a new year as a complete family made up of two families.

By the time Tex and Traci's wedding day rolled around, they had the downstairs completed and furnished and all of the upstairs ready for painting and carpeting. Tex and his father had moved to the farm a couple of months before the wedding and were working on it as much as possible. Of course, during the last three or four months, they were not working all the time. They went out occasionally and enjoyed themselves. Nick, Marci, Kato and Sandy were included on these occasions. Marci and Kato worked closely with "The Georgia Boys" as they were called by the people that knew them and appreciated what they had done for their county and was still working to improve it.

On one of the occasions, Tex made a toast to now being one of the "Georgia Boys" and I am very proud to be a part of the group.

There was too much going on during that winter and then spring, so Cody and Corrie decided to set their wedding date the following September.

And Steven, well, he is still playing the field, but he is taking Jan out more than any of the other girls. He was beginning to think more about settling down, but it would be a while yet.

As for Mama E and Mr. Tyler. Well, they are good friends and enjoy each others companionship. As they both wanted, they came together as a family and that was enough for them. For they each had no desire to marry again.

About the Author

Joanne Haynes Carani lives in Lincoln County, Lincolnton, Georgia, and a population of approximately 10,000 people. She has two sons and three grandchildren. She spends valuable, quality time with her, grandson and two granddaughters whenever possible making memories.

The first written novel, *Home Is Where The Heart Is* (Captain's, Hideaway), is still yet to be published. The second written novel, *Georgia Boys* (A Father's Legacy), was chosen to be published first because it is dedicated to her late husband, Frank Carani, who passed away suddenly in February 2001. He was in law enforcement in Miami, Dade County, Florida, until he was medically retired. She was employed with the State Attorney's Office during that time. Later, the family moved to her hometown of Lincolnton. Her two sons and a daughter-in-law are currently in law enforcement. She is currently working on her third novel, which is a sequel to *Georgia Boys*.

Printed in the United States
1172000002B/283-287